Marta's Ride

Ride Book Three

Gordon L. Rottman

HARTWOOD PUBLISHING
PHOENIX, AZ

Published By: The Hartwood Publishing Group, LLC,
Hartwood Publishing, Phoenix, Arizona
www.hartwoodpublishing.com

Marta's Ride

Digital Release: November 2017
Print Release: February 2018

Dedication

To my truly wonderful family.

Author Acknowledgement

I wish to thank all who helped give Marta a voice and develop her story. I am grateful to CEO and Editor-in-Chief Georgia Woods, who also designed the cover, Executive Editor Lisa Dugan for her enthusiasm and encouragement., and Jennifer Roques, my excellent line editor. I was fortunate to benefit from my excellent critique group: Stan Marshall (author of Half the Distance, Hartwood, 2017), Linda Bromley, Heather Walters Schudiske, and Linda Sherman. A special thanks goes to Steve Seale, a longtime friend, for war-gaming with me on plot and action scene ideas, and to Dr. Keith Souter, a Western author writing as Clay More, who provided details of vintage medical procedures, drugs, and treatments to include arrow and bullet removal. His book, The Doctor's Bag: Medicine and Surgery of Yesteryear, was extremely helpful and informative. My cousin Consuelo "Chely" Garcia was extremely helpful in checking and correcting the book's Spanish. Invaluable was my wife Enriqueta's patience with the long hours I spent on the computer.

Author Notes

A commentary on geographical directions

When one speaks of the Texas-Mexico border or la Frontera and the Rio Grande or Río Bravo del Norte—depending on which side of the border one resides—we tend to think of Mexico as "south of the border." In a broad sense, this is true. Mexico is indeed south of Texas and the United States. However, a look at a map of the south-central Texas border region shows the Rio Grande flows southeast from the upper end of the river's great loop known as the Big Bend in West Texas and snakes to the Gulf of Mexico. After the pursuit of El Xiuhcoatl (shee-oo-ko-ah-tl) and his bandidos begins at the DeWitt Ranch ("the Dew") south of Del Rio, Texas, the Texans cross the Rio Grande traveling due west, even though they are "south of the border." If they had kept heading west, they would have re-entered Texas enwrapped in the Big Bend from the east.

Glossary

Marta's unspoken Mexican-Spanish (español Mexicano) words are translated into common American English, which she thinks of as Americano rather than Inglés. She uses certain Spanish words, though, rather than the English equivalent because while they may be literally translated into English, in the Mexican context there is often a difference, sometimes subtle, sometimes patently dissimilar. For example: While vaquero may be translated as "cowboy," in Marta's mind a vaquero and a Texican cowpoke are two different things, the vaquero being so much more. The campo is not simply wide open rangeland, but to her, a land unconstrained by ownership, a peaceful yet dangerous land with almost mystic potentials. The Sun and the Moon (Sol y Luna) are capitalized in Marta's mind because of their spiritual importance. Spanish words are not italicized in the narrative unless of unique use.

Marta leaves a comment at the end of each chapter in Spanish. Its Americano meaning follows on the first line of the next chapter.

Marta has some familiarity with the Náhuatl language, what today is called Aztec. It is still spoken in parts of Central Mexico. She knows her parents came from Durango in southern Durango State, which still harbors the northernmost group of Náhuatl-speakers. That background explains some of the unusual given names in her familia, including her own real name.

abrazo greeting or farewell hug

abuela grandmother

arroyo gully, wash

bandido bandit, outlaw

bla, bla, bla blaw, blaw, blaw (What English—Inglés—sounds like to Marta. She can understand little English, a word here and there.)

bodega small grocery store (A business place, not only for food and goods but to hear the news.)

bruja witch (much different than Anglo-Saxon culture witches)

campo rangeland, wide open spaces

carne seca jerky—dried beef, goat, or venison

casa home

carnitas Generally "goat meat," but also a generic term for chopped or shredded meat, including beef and venison.

cuarta short riding crop

familia family (a close-knit family extending beyond the immediate family)

frijoles Okay, it's just beans, but they're Marta's beans.

frijoles

refritos refried beans (Actually "well-fried beans." Mashed beans, onion, and chilies fried with lard, a main source of protein.)

la Frontera The Frontier—the Mexico-Texas border

gerente manager, supervisor

granja farm

gringo American (not necessarily disparaging), also Americano or anglo (gringa, Americana, or angla is a female)

hacienda A large land holding—ranch, plantation, farms, and mines owned by a hacendado. Also referred to as the main house.

indio Indian

jacalito crude shack made from any available materials; also jacale

jefe chief, boss

liga Mexican unit of measurement, a league = 5,000 vara (see below). Approximately 2.6 miles. Texans thought of a league as 3 miles. Either way, it is defined as the average distance a person can walk in an hour, so in that context, its length actually depends on the difficulty imposed by the terrain and weather.

niños kids, boys and girls (It also refers to solely boys.)

niña or chica girl (niña) typically refers to a preteen girl and chica to a teenage or early twenties girl but can be used interchangeably

nómadas nomads, wanderers, migrant workers (which describes Marta's familia)

peón unskilled laborer, farmhand (also braceros—one who swings his arm, a worker)

potrero circular corral made of mesquite limbs stacked between paired posts

pulque fermented alcoholic drink made from

maguey (agave) plants

rancho ranch (a smaller holding than a hacienda)

remuda herd of spare saddle-broke horses from which cowboys choose their mounts

rebozo cape reaching to a girl's waist front and back with a square, centered head hole

Río river; The Río refers to the Rio Grande, or as Marta knows it, Río Bravo del Norte—Rough River of the North.

Rurales Guardia Rural (Rural Guard), federal mounted police

Tejano Mexican-Texan (Mexican born in Texas)

Tejas Mexican-Spanish for Texas

Texano Texican or Texan (a gringo)

Tía y Tío Aunt and Uncle

tientos saddle strings (rawhide cords for tying items to saddles)

tortilla thin, round, unleavened flatbread made from maize (corn)

vaquero cowboy (The vaquero tradition was heavily borrowed on by the American cowboy.)

vara Mexican unit of measurement = 32.999 inches. A Texas or Austin vara = 33 1/3 inches; thus three vara equal 100 inches.

Author Notes

To prevent confusion, the Mexican town referred to as Las Vacas, Coahuila, was across the Rio Grande from Del Rio, Texas. In 1887 its official name was Congregación las Vacas—meeting place of the cows. In 1912 it was renamed Villa Acuña, and in 1951, Ciudad Acuña, the name it bears today.

Bud carries a Winchester rifle while most cowboys

used a carbine with a shorter barrel. In Spanish, a rifle is a fusil, but the more common term for both a rifle and a carbine is simply carabina, which is what Marta refers to all shoulder-fired rifles and carbines. In Spanish, both pistola and revólver are used as in English, but pistola tends to be the all inclusive term for handguns.

Shotguns (escopeta) are identified in English as, for example, 12-gauge or 16-gauge. Gauge is determined by the number of equally sized balls cast from one pound of lead. A 12-gauge shotgun means its bore is the diameter of one of the 12 balls cast from a pound of lead, which is why a 12-gauge (.73-caliber /18.5mm) shotgun's bore is larger in diameter than a 16-gauge—16 balls (.66-caliber /16.8mm). However, in Spanish, a shotgun's bore is called, for example, 16-calibre rather than 16-gauge, which has nothing to do with American firearms' definition of caliber. An American caliber is 1/100th of an inch, so for example, 45/100th of an inch is a .45-caliber weapon.

Reference: The Big Book of Gun Trivia: Everything you want to know, don't want to know, and don't know you need to know by Gordon L. Rottman (e-book, Osprey Publishing, 2013).

BUD

CHAPTER ONE

The morning my *familia* was killed began as a very fine day.

Mamá nudged me awake. I was always the first up, at least in the winter. My job was to entice the fire back to life. No one would crawl from the blankets and serapes until they saw its glow.

We slept warm, almost, bundled up with Tlayolot, my brother, between myself and Mamá with Malinalli, my little sister, between Mamá and Papá. We huddled under a piece of old canvas wagon cover in a clump of trees. We camped away from the road so no one would trouble us. Mamá always made a crucifix from two sticks and placed it at our feet to keep brujas from stealing her children. She would put nothing past the witches.

Cold. Frost covered my serape, the ground, the mesquite leaves, the dead weeds, and my hair where the wool shawl slipped.

My fog-breath and the ash dust mingled as I blew embers back to life. I enjoyed sharing with the fire my breath as it shared its warmth. I liked to watch it spring to dancing life. I liked to feel its generous warmth. I liked to watch it burn itself to sleep as my eyes closed for my own dreams. Did fire dream in its sleep? Did it remember me when I awakened it?

Mockingbirds teased other awakening birds and scolded each other.

Splinters and dry leaves. I slept with the tinder to keep it dry. The awakened embers ignited the tinder. The tiny flame grew. Twigs and sticks. There was enough flame then to add bigger sticks. I added the sticks Mamá had made the crucifix from to the fire. I once asked her if this was blasphemous. No logs for this fire.

"No, *mija*, it is for our salvation. It was provided by God first to protect us and then warm and nourish us."

No logs for the fire. There was nothing for coals to cook that morning. When my familia emerged, I would add cow chips and boil the coffee. Mamá would toast tortillas and warm the *frijoles refritos*—refried beans. I placed the iron skillet on the fire to heat.

The fire, awake and growing, would let me leave to squat in the weeds to pee and brush my hair. The brush pulled and hurt. I hoped when we reached Uvalde I could wash my tangled hair. It had gone too long without a soaping.

I always watched the Father Sun rise, a yellow or orange disc, the giver of life. It was the Sun of the Fifth Cycle, the Sun of Movement. It passed over the One World, *Cem-á-nahuac*, which had existed for millenniums. The Suns of the previous four cycles were controlled by Water, Earth, Fire, and Wind. Their cycles ended in catastrophes. The Fifth Sun watched over us, and it was not expected to end in devastation. Mamá told us these legends were passed from the Aztecs a long time ago before even Papá's own papá was born.

I kneeled beside Mamá, and we said the rosary, touching our beads.

The wet-looking clouds were low, and the rising sun soon passed into them.

How far to Uvalde? I have not seen the place for so long. Papá said there was work there. The cotton had been harvested. Next, the men would chop up the stalks with machetes. Then they would grub-hoe the stalks and roots into the ground for the February plowing and planting. It was now November. It took many men to work all the farms. He said there were never enough *braceros*—laborers—for such work in South *Tejas*. He would work ten hours a day, chopping and hacking the muddy ground in the chilling wind and rain for pennies. He never complained.

I would work as well, keeping a fire going under the thatched-roof lean-to for the men to warm themselves. It was always hard to find enough dry wood. I ground coffee beans, boiled coffee, and heated their dinner frijoles. There was no pay for those chores except they let me eat a little. Being able to stay beside a fire sheltered from the rain was payment enough.

And the church. I wanted to sit in the quiet calm of a church to pray and think and listen. I had listened to priests and brothers read from the Bible and say their prayers and listened to other readings. It helped me learn many words. There were no schools for us nómadas. I only wished I could speak them to others.

We had left Leakey three days before. It had no church.

We had good work in Leakey. Papá sawed down cypress and cedar trees growing right on the edge of the rocky *Rio Frio*. He and other men sawed the big logs into pieces as long as my arm from elbow to fingertips. They squared the short logs and split them into shingles. The scraps became firewood. When the men driving the ox carts returned, they loaded the shingles. The carts left for the Rio Grande Valley where there were no trees useful for shingles.

When I showed I wanted to split shingles, there was much argument about allowing me to work.

"A girl does not do that kind of man's work, Jaimenacho," the *gerente* told Papá. "She is so small. She will exhaust herself and hurt herself, even her delicate womanly parts." He said that with great embarrassment.

Papá convinced him to let me try. I would work for a week without pay. "She will show you. She has more heart than any other girl."

"But she cannot speak," said the gerente. "How can she learn?"

"She is mute, not stupid," said Papá.

I laughed in my peculiar way, which upsets some people.

Papá did not always stand up to gerentes and jefes, but he did that day, for me.

I did not do well the first two days. I used a cutter called a *froe*—a blade on a handle and looked like an "L"—and a heavy log club. My hands were not guided by skill or God.

Papá said, "We are in need of thick and thin shingles too."

I said the Prayer to Saint Joseph for Success in Work, *"Glorious Saint Joseph, model of all those who are devoted to labor, obtain for me the grace to work conscientiously, putting the call of duty above my many sins; to work with thankfulness and joy…"*

By the end of the week, I was making shingles as good as any man, straight and all the same thickness. Maybe not as many. In the second week, no one complained about my work. I would start splitting shingles while the men were still sawing down logs. We passed our quota for shingles this way. I was blessed. They even paid me half of a man's wages!

Every night my hands, arms, and shoulders hurt. I would not complain, even to Mamá. She plucked splinters from my fingers and massaged them, whispering that I should not work so hard. But the pennies I made helped feed the familia.

It was so much better than sitting cross-legged beside saloon doors with my eating bowl—*my eating bowl*—for gringos to toss pennies into and ask me how much I charged for my body—"*¿Cuánto, chica?*" or "How much for a bang, *niña*?" I understood those *Americano* words.

I looked up at them and nodded like a simpleton. I laughed abnormally, showing my grinning white teeth and empty black eyes. They left me alone. It was degrading, but we ate.

Now my feet and legs hurt. So much walking from dawn to dusk. So slow with the little ones. Most of the time Papá carried little Malinalli. Tlayolot was too proud to ask to be carried ever since he was five. He stayed right beside Papá, no matter how muddy or rocky the road. Sometimes the little ones rode on a wagon or cart driven by Mexicans going our way. But not today.

No one built houses in the winter, so there was no need for shingles. We were turned out of the cedar plank *jacalito*—shack—we had built. "Come back in March," the gerente told Papá. Nodding at me, he said, "Bring your shingle cutter."

It did not take long to eat, pack up what little we had, and roll up the wagon cover, blankets, and serapes. Everyone except Malinalli carried something. My big gray wool shoulder bag held my one set of extra clothes, two blankets and a serape, the full frijoles pot, little bags of cooking spices, tortillas wrapped in newspaper, water gourd, my clay drinking and eating bowls, wooden spoon, boning knife, and my bag of menstrual rags.

We walked.

We lived on the road. We were *nómadas*. We worked as hard as we could. We lived as best we could. Papá said it was a better life than slaving for a dominating, cheating *hacendado. El poder de los poderoms*—the power of the powerful—Papá called it.

Our home was where Papá chose to camp, always away from the road. When we worked on a *rancho* or *granja*—farm—we built a jacalito with our wagon cover and whatever we could find: old boards, hay thickets borrowed from haystacks, tree limbs, cornstalks, or *carrizo* cane cut from riverbanks.

We walked up the road. It began to drizzle.

When we crossed streams and rivers, we filled the water gourds. We camped near streams when we could for water and washing. Papá always said to cross a stream before camping in case the water rose during the night. It also kept us from suffering wet feet all morning.

When we started off, I ran ahead with my bag bouncing on my hip. For the last two years, since I was fourteen, my job was to walk ahead of the familia. I watched and listened. When I heard the snort of a horse, the jingle of wagon chains, a cough, or any sound made by men, it was the sound of danger. I would run back to my familia waving my arm, and they hid in the bush. I usually could not reach them and had to hide alone. I was good at hiding. I was quiet and still. And small. I was an *espabilada*, a road-wise girl.

We would watch in silence as they passed—cowboys, drifters, freight wagons, ox carts, stagecoaches, soldiers, *indios*, tradesmen in their wagons, whomever. Sometimes it might be Mexicans—*vaqueros*, *peóns*, nómadas like ourselves—and we would greet them. We would talk about the road behind, any dangers, and news and maybe trade for food.

One time I heard someone coming and warned the familia. We hid for the longest time. Papá became impatient and asked if I was sure I had heard someone. I nodded hard. Papá sent me to investigate, and I found a nómada familia hiding because they had heard us. We all laughed and traded food and clothes. I traded a rope I had braided from horse tail hair for a beautiful brown *rebozo*, a cape reaching to my waist front and back with a square, centered head hole and embroidered with red, orange, and tan.

It was dangerous to meet *gringos*. Papá had been beaten once. We had been robbed, or they only took a few things just because they could. Fortunately, nothing bad had happened to Mamá and me, something I feared. Papá now carried a short 12-caliber shotgun under his serape. If gringos found him with that, they would take it.

I walked on the road's edge, always looking at the hoof prints and wheel ruts. I could tell which way a wagon was going by how mud splatter and dirt grains were thrown from the ruts. I mostly listened, though.

And then I heard it.

The shrill war whoop behind me.

I will never forget it. I have never stopped hearing it.

It went on and on.

Gunshots! Papá's shotgun banged. It fired four times.

I heard the screams. That was Mamá! That was Malinalli!

Many gunshots.

I ran to my familia.

The screaming, the screaming. It would not stop.

I could see them, the indios, through the mesquite.

Two were holding someone on the ground. Another

was on hands and knees hatchet-hacking.

Gunshots. Screams. Blood-tinged whoops. Sounds I could not believe.

My thin boning knife was in my hand, shaking. There were at least six indios. My soul, my heart, told me to go at them. My mind, my wisdom—did I have any?—held me back. My hands shook until I dropped the knife and pressed them over my ears.

I hid, shaking. I cried. What was happening to my familia? I hid until the screams stopped. Then I crawled, shamefully, deeper into the mesquite, where I huddled in a ball.

I waited, cried, prayed, and cried even more. Even though the screams and other terrible noises had stopped, I held my hands over my ears, because for me the sounds did not stop. They never have, and I think they never will. Ever.

I laid in the mesquite for what seemed like hours, or was it days? I heard the wind flowing across the campo, rustling in the mesquite. I heard birds undertaking everyday bird doings as if nothing terrible had happened. Over the screaming I still heard in my head, I said the rosary, finding my beads in my deep skirt pocket. Rosary beads in one hand, my knife in the other. One for life, one for death. For a time, I wanted death, but the Virgin told me that I should live to remember and honor my familia. I finally, after so long, rose to my feet. At first, I pushed through the mesquite, but my mind told me to slow down. To move silently and listen with each step. Were the indios gone? I crouched for a long time only listening. My mind was numb. There was a pain I knew I should have felt, but instead, I was numb. I feared what I would find. I knew what I would find. I did not want to, but I had to. I walked forward, slowly, listening.

They all died in the worst ways.

They were destroyed, gutted, scalped. Their faces caved in. Blood, blood, blood. Things I could not even imagine. The smell…

I vomited until my insides, even my mind, were empty.

I would not cry. They did not want to see me cry.

I dragged each of them to lie in a line, as we did when we slept. Except I did not lie beside Tlayolot. "*Heart of the earth*" was what his name meant. Ten years old. Mamá—Asalia—the name I thought so beautiful and she so strong, and Papá—Jaimenacho—our guide in life. Malinalli—"*little plant*"—four years…what they did to her…

I had no way to bury them. No shovel for the hard ground, no rocks to pile.

I prayed over them, every prayer I knew. It rained, my tears spilling over the whole world.

Leaving them there tore my heart in two. It was hard to do, but I cut a lock of black hair off of each of my loved ones. Cutting a square of brown cloth from the hem of Mamá's dress, I tied the hair locks in it.

The indios had headed southwest. Blood drippings followed one set of moccasin tracks. Another left bloody footprints and splotches of bubbly blood. I followed to make sure they were gone. More blood spilled in one place. I found one. Smelly in greasy buckskins. His friends had taken his moccasins. Dead, hit by Papá's shotgun in the side. He had bled out. Good.

They left nothing except clothing they did not want, which they tore up and peed on. The indios had stolen everything, including stealing my familia from me. I had only what was in my bag and my skirt pockets. I had no money, not a penny or a *centavo*.

Where could I go? There was no one to go to. There were relatives in Durango, far away, whom I had never met.

Uvalde. I would go to Uvalde. I would work in the

cotton fields. I would show them I could do the work, even when they said I could not. I had no other choices.

I walked to the road. I stood. I stood for a long time. I turned and walked south in the direction of Uvalde. My familia would stay behind to rest. Maybe a Mexican familia would take me in. Why should they? Another mouth to feed. I would have to be careful. I could not weaken. I could not feel sorry for myself. I did not have time to mourn my familia. Later. For the moment, I had to look and listen. There was still danger on the road. From any indio, gringo, or Mexican. Especially if they were alone as I was alone. Mamá had told me many times what happens to girls alone on the road. Men only wanted to use my body to feel themselves. I used to think she said that to keep me from running away when I was angry. She always said I was too warm blooded for my own good. I knew I was in danger alone.

I had to stay alive.

I was alone, had nothing, and I wanted only one thing. I prayed for that one thing.

Yo quería un protector.

CHAPTER TWO

I wanted a protector.

Crossing a small arroyo washing over the road, I heard a horse nicker ahead. The indios did not have horses unless they had hobbled them some way off. My first thought was to run back as I always did to warn my familia. The pain was sharp when I remembered they were no longer following.

I ran into the mesquite to the right. My heart pounded, my hands shook, and fear tore through me.

I was too scared to look but made myself. I had never been quieter or stiller. I wanted to be smaller. I was not the *bruja* I liked to pretend I was, an invisible witch. Not all brujas were evil. There were *Brujas Blanca*—white witches—and *Brujas Negra*—black witches. The white witches performed good deeds, and black witches cast spells, created mischief, and made people's lives miserable. Mean and envious people paid them for these spells.

Most brujas also practiced as *curanderas*—healers—using herbal medicines and home remedies.

It was only an old gringo cowboy. He was talking to his horse, a roan. I wondered what they were talking about. He rode on north. What would he think, what would he do when he found my resting familia? Would he and the horse talk about what they saw, what they thought had happened? I wished they would not see them. A gringo, he may not even notice them.

I waited, longer than I would have before for only a passing gringo. I tried to pretend my familia was still behind me, but only resting. Finally, I found the courage to move on…without them. I stayed off the road for a time, but the brush was too wet. My foot wraps were soaked. I made for the road. It was not too muddy except for a few short stretches.

Two times I had to sit on the wet grass and scrape clay mud off my sandals. The rain had stopped. The Sun made the clouds glow. It was still cold. I had been walking for over an hour since seeing the cowboy, but I did not care about the time. I never knew what time it was anyway. Clock-time was no matter to us. Up at sunrise, work all morning, maybe eat dinner, work until almost dark even on long summer days, eat supper, talk around the fire, and sleep.

Behind me, a horse snorted quietly, and a voice muttered. Someone was close behind me. The road curved a little, and they could not see me. I ran to the right. There was a small clump of trees and brush not too far away. The indios, were they looking for me? Had the cowboy come back? Why would he?

Whoever it was was very quiet. I would not have heard them except for a horse's snort.

Water dripped from the bushes as I peeked out. I was scared, breathing hard. I should not have been breathing so hard for such a short run.

It was a cowboy. I was relieved to see it was not the same one. He was on a bay with a mangy burro strung behind him. Strange. Not something one often sees, a cowboy with a burro. There were a big bedroll and bags on the burro. Strange, gringos.

But he had stopped and was looking at the ground. What was he doing? He raised his head. He looked straight at me!

It was like he knew I was there, that he could see my trail through the brush and weeds leading to the trees. I was no bruja now. In no hurry, he looped the burro's lead rope around a limb. He was trotting toward me, still looking at the ground. Yes, he could see my tracks on the wet ground and where I had brushed water off the bushes. He knew that made leaves look different. The clump of trees I was in had limbs high enough for him to ride beneath.

He was coming for me.

Not far away was another bigger clump of trees, lots of thick brush. He could not ride into it. If he dismounted, I was sure I could scramble through the bushes faster than he. I was so small, barely five feet. And fast.

I ran.

My bag bounced hard on my side, throwing me off balance. The ground was slick clay under a layer of gooey mud.

I heard the pounding horse behind me coming fast. I did not dare look back. I ran and ran. It was a mistake. The bouncing bag, the slick, muddy clay, the tangling weeds and vines. I slipped and stumbled into the ground, sliding face down.

I desperately rolled over sitting up, and the big horse was sliding with its hind legs hard in the mud, the gringo pulling back on the reins. I got to my feet as fast as I could. I needed to be on my feet if he came at me, which I was certain he would. The horse stopped, and the cowboy swung off his saddle. His boots shot out from under him, a clumsy, silly sight, and he slid into me and knocked me back down. I kicked, expecting him to grab me. No gringo would have his way with me! I would fight! Seeing him rise to his feet, his anger, I felt so small and weak.

I did not pull my boning knife out. Not yet. Papá, who had knife scars, said to wait and surprise them at the last moment. I was breathing hard and getting more frightened.

He grabbed my arm, and I tried to pull away and then kicked him again, missing. I even growled. He shouted something, and all I understood was "*Niña!*" and "*Alto!*" He dragged me to his horse, which looked at me like I was a distraction. Instead of kicking again, which he managed to sidestep both times, I swung at him. He ducked that too and held me with a firm grip. He pulled his canteen off the saddle, handed it to me, and said, "*Niña. Lavate.*"

The way he said it, him just using some Spanish, made it feel like he was not a danger. Not yet anyway. I let him know I was angry and did not take my eyes off him. I took the canteen and washed my face and hands. I had let go of the knife I gripped with my hand inside my bag. He was looking me over, probably wondering why a Mexican girl was out there alone. Had he seen my familia resting? I hoped not. He did not do anything else, only stood there looking at me. He did not look menacing, just curious. Well, he was going to have to stay curious because I could not tell him anything even if I wanted to, even if I could speak, even if we could understand each other.

I handed the canteen back and nodded thanks. He said something like he was asking a question. The longer he looked at me, the more it seemed he did not want to be bothered by a Mexican girl. Maybe he would simply get on his half-asleep horse and ride away. I could take care of myself. I sure did not need some cowboy trying to figure me out. Nobody else ever had.

And that was what he did. He hung his canteen and climbed onto his horse. He said, "*Adiós, niña.*" He rode back to the road after picking up his burro, muttering to himself, or maybe to his horse, and was on his way in no hurry.

I tried to clean some of the mud off my skirt with handfuls of dead grass. It did not do much good. I would have to wait until I came to a wet arroyo. Giving up on the mud, I walked to the road and started down it. It was a long straight piece. Far up ahead I could see the cowboy. One time he looked back. That made me nervous again. I hoped he was not having second thoughts. Mamá's warnings of what could happen to a girl by herself came back to me. I truly wanted a protector now. But I knew that without my familia, that would be impossible. I would be alone for the rest of my days. It came to me that the rest of my days could be short in number. I thought again of what happened to my familia.

I also remembered the story about Maria Sanchez. She was fourteen and had gone by herself to visit another familia's camp only a few minutes' walk away. Her parents had let her go in the dark. The campfires of the two camps could be seen from the other. After two hours, Maria's father and brother went to the other camp to bring her home. She had never reached it. In the morning, they found her half a *liga* away on a muddy stream bank, stripped, beaten, raped, and strangled by more than one man. Many of the nómadas thought the killers were gringo bullwhackers who had come through during the day and camped near the river. They had left very, very early. The gringo sheriff said he had questioned them and they knew nothing of it. He said we should talk to other

Mexican workers and the Negros who worked the cotton press. Mamá reminded me of the story many times. It was serving its purpose now, scaring me.

I came out of my day-nightmare and the memory of Maria's body, bruised, face bloodied, and bites on her…I tried to think of something else.

But I could not. The cowboy ahead had stopped. That scared me, and I started to run into the bush. But then I felt steel. I told myself I was not afraid. I would ignore him and go on my way. Something too told me he was not dangerous. Was I only fooling myself? Telling myself I was hard and fearless?

I knew I was not.

I came upon him and walked past like he was not there.

I was so proud. I had shown no fear, even if I was fearful.

I sensed he was surprised or at least baffled.

He said "*¿Niña, burro?*"

Was he offering me a ride on his burro? I kept walking.

His horse was moving, and he passed me, riding ahead a short way, and stopped. The fear built again, but I would keep walking as though he and his horse and burro were not there. He dismounted, and I was feeling genuine dread. I would not show my rising fear. I could run faster than he could on foot.

I felt for the knife in my bag, found it, and slipped it into my loose right sleeve. He suddenly grabbed my shoulder strap. I have never moved faster. Fear could do much. I twisted out of the shoulder strap and jumped away. I was terrified, even with the hidden knife. At least I had not cut myself when this happened. I backed away a few steps. *Show strength*, I told myself. *Do not show fear!* I crossed my arms and gave him the meanest glare I could summon.

I stretched out my arm for the bag. He did not move. I stamped my foot and pointed with my finger. It looked like he was waiting for me to say something. Little did he know.

Instead of giving me the bag or throwing it at me and then jumping on me, he smiled, turned, and hung it on the burro of all things! "*Adiós, niña*," he said as he patted the burro's behind.

He was offering me a ride. I stared at him a long time, watching his eyes. He stared into mine, but he was a gringo, not like a Mexican who could just about read your mind through your eyes. What could he tell of me? What could I tell of him? But I saw something in his eyes, like an amusement or curiosity. I did not see danger.

I nodded, stepped over to the burro, tucked my skirt's hem into the right side of its waist band, bent over, cupped my hands so he could see I needed a boost up, and then stood up.

He looked really surprised. I almost laughed, but I did not even allow a smile to show. He bla, bla'ed something, looking a little put out. I guess he was not in the habit of boosting Mexican girls onto burros. I could have gotten on by myself, but demanding his help might show me if he really was trustworthy.

He bent over and boosted me onto a big bedroll. I had to move around to get comfortable. The burro did not seem happy with the extra weight. Without looking at him, I made a show of slipping the knife out of my sleeve and dropping it in my bag.

I looked the cowboy in the eye. There was a certain kindness in there. His eyes were blue like the sky. His hair was the color of sand or winter-dried grass. Then I recognized the shade, the light tan of a coyote. I would think of him as *Güero*—Blondie. I nodded to him…we could go now.

We rode on south with me trailing behind him.

¿Qué pasará después?

CHAPTER THREE

I had no idea what would happen next.

Where was he going and what for? Uvalde, I guessed, but what would happen there? Did he live there? Was he passing through? A thought came to me. Was he married or maybe had a girl waiting for him? I thought not. He did not know much about girls. What would he do with me once we got there? I needed to be on guard and ready to run if things were not right. I could vanish in Uvalde. There were many people, many Mexicans. I remembered Papá saying he had heard the town had grown.

I passed the day praying the rosary for my familia and praying for strength, wisdom, and guidance. I prayed too for this man to be trustworthy and honorable. I prayed he would make good choices. And I prayed this burro would walk without bouncing me so much.

The ride was boring and not much faster than walking. When walking, there was much to do. One always looked and listened for dangers, picked where each footstep was made to avoid mud, horse shit, puddles, and ankle-turning ruts and rocks. No rocks there, only clay and mud. I did not like winter, and this one had been colder than any I could remember, which was not very far back.

In a way, riding was good because I did not have to be on the lookout for danger and ready to run and warn my following familia. I had a protector, I thought. I was sure he was on the lookout for danger. I did not have to trouble myself. But I would look behind me often since he did not give that much thought. He had a carbine, a long Winchester, and a pistol. I wondered what he would think of me calling him Güero. Maybe he was a Matthew, Mark, Luke, or John.

My mind ambled like the burro. I wondered what this gringo would have done if he had come upon my familia when the indios attacked them. I imagined him hearing the screams and shouts and gunshots. I saw him on his horse charging in, pistol in his hand, shooting the indios as they scattered like quail. Then I saw in my mind him charging in with the frantic burro trying to keep up, and I laughed.

Güero turned to look at me. I did not want him to see me laughing, so I gave a serious look and crossed my eyes.

He shook his head.

Would he have done that, one gringo, charging six murdering indios alone to save Mexicans he had never seen? Probably not. He would have heard the war cries, screams, and shots. He would have waited, hiding in the mesquite, waiting for it to end and then gone on his way uncaring.

I would not have blamed him.

The sun was very low and the clouds dark. It could rain. Then I remembered there was no longer a wagon cover. I had no shelter from the rain. Soon Güero was looking for a campsite. I could tell because he would look in the direction of the setting sun and back to the east where it was darker. And he looked at clumps of trees, sizing them up as a hidden campsite…just like Papá.

I wanted to camp with my familia as I had all my life. That was not to be. I knew that. I accepted it. It did not make it any easier. And I was going to camp, to spend the night with this stranger, with this gringo. I would keep my knife close.

He slowed, and we turned off the road to a stand of trees. He had picked a campsite a good way off the road. I slid off the burro, happy to set foot on the ground. Güero dismounted and led the horse and burro into the trees. Unsaddling and unloading the burro, he laid out his bedroll and set his saddle there. He only did that after checking the trees for dead limbs that could fall. This was a good place for a camp, a little clearing surrounded by brush. We could hear anyone coming at us. This gringo knew what he was doing…so far. While he hobbled the horse and burro nearby, I started gathering firewood. It would be cold, so I picked up much. As I had done for my familia, I built my little kindling pile and flint and iron-started the fire, gradually building it up. The cowboy seemed satisfied to let me do this and watched with interest.

With the fire going, I scraped and kicked leaves into a pile and spread them out for my two blankets and serape. *Please do not let it rain*, I prayed. My threadbare and holey blankets were embarrassing. Sitting down, I pulled out my crockpot of frijoles and opened the wire clamp. I poked a twig through the little hole in the lid to make sure it wasn't plugged.

Fortunately, the pot was almost full. I did not know where or when I would find more food. That was nothing new. We had always found some kind of food, even if we had to wait a day or two. On those days we at least had a little something to chew on, although it might only be stale tortillas or a few kernels of parched corn. Mamá had always held back something. She said farmers' fields were our market. There were times we feasted on raw cob corn and cabbage. Other times we followed farm wagons hauling sweet potatoes. Some might fall off. Farmers broke open sweet potatoes and held them to the horse's muzzle to eat out the insides. They threw the husks on the ground, and there was enough pulp left for us to eat.

One time we were so hungry. Papá kept urging us on because he knew a particular farm ahead was generous. I kept asking how much farther. "Not far now," he would say. After the third time, I knew we still had a long way to go. A produce wagon turned onto the road and rumbled past. The gringo farmer driving it ignored us as was customary. A boy riding on the tailgate, maybe my age, looked straight at me with kindly eyes. He gave a little smiling wave, and a bundle of turnips somehow fell off the wagon. Not all gringos were uncaring.

There were also many wild growing things we could eat, and I have eaten everything with four legs…everything. And birds and most things caught in the water. I only had to catch it and kill it. Oh, and snakes too, but they were harder to catch.

I thought about the campo. What I would not give to be out on my own on the campo. I could live there. Others often feared the campo, looking upon it as a hiding place of death. It was an unknown thing to be feared.

With the frijole pot open, I stirred in dried tomato, tomatillo, cilantro, onion, green pepper, garlic, and jalapeño peppers from my little bags. They were almost empty. I set it to heat beside the coals. There was already dried goat meat and a little venison in it.

Güero sorted through his gear, pulling out an iron skillet and something wrapped in newspaper. This was good because Mamá's skillet had been stolen by the indios. It was a chunk of white bacon. I got up, and in my excitement, took it and the skillet from him. I was embarrassed for not asking and almost gave it back. He did not say anything, so with my boning knife, I cut up the bacon after setting the skillet on the fire. Once it was sizzling, I dumped the bacon and grease into the frijoles. He made a pot of coffee, and its smell made me hungrier. We had been low on coffee, and Mamá had to make it weak. While it was heating, I made a little frame of green sticks beside the orange coals and hung tortillas on them. I sprinkled water drops to make them soft.

Güero unwrapped a bandanna holding some white squares, what gringo soldiers called hardtack. Mexican soldiers call it pan galleta. Once a gringo soldier had offered me a handful of hardtack to borrow my body. I must have looked very hungry. I had shaken my head and drooled. Acting not right in the head always scared them off. He had dropped a hardtack brick. Wiping off the mud, I tried to chew on it. I really was hungry. Throwing it away, even coyotes and raccoons overlooked it. Instead of taking Güero's hardtack, I offered tortillas, and he thanked me in Spanish. Maybe he was a good man. I gave him a smile.

"*Mi nombre es Güero*," he said pointing at his hair.

It completely surprised me that he went by the same name I had given him, Güero. Maybe he worked with vaqueros, and they had nicknamed him. Every Mexican had at least one nickname. Vaqueros only nicknamed gringos they liked. I wondered what his gringo name was. Maybe he would tell me sometime. It was a strange thought—that I would be with him more than another day. I would disappear like a bruja in Uvalde tomorrow. I might find a

Mexican familia to work for or some other kind of work.

He asked my name, I think, and there I realized he did not know I could not speak. People did not expect someone to be mute, so they usually thought I was the quiet kind, awkwardly silent. I did what I always did. I frowned, pointed to my lips, shook my head, and pointed to my lips again.

He said something else with a sad look, and I knew he was probably saying what everyone said, that they were sorry and it was sad.

It was not as sad as most might think. I had been mute since I was nine, for seven years. I was used to it, and people did not expect much from me. In some ways, it made my life easier…but not always. It could be annoying. Some things were difficult to be made known. It was hard to ask questions, and I often had many questions, or to warn someone. One thing I always laughed at was when they spoke loud like I could not hear either. Some women told Mamá she should have listened to music while she was pregnant because she had not and I was deaf. Mamá could not make some understand that I was mute, not deaf or both.

Sometimes I did not care that I could not speak. Other times it made me angry or unhappy or wretched—especially when they thought that it made me stupid and tried to take advantage of me. It did give me an advantage because I was always on guard and had become crafty and devious when I needed to. When I was sad, I told myself not to feel sorry for myself. There was some spiritually mysterious reason why God took my voice, letting a mule kick me in the head—the only thing making a mule respectable is the great accuracy of its kick. That would lead me to a whole different sadness. What did I do to make God so angry, what did I do to offend or disappoint Him? At other times, I understood. There was a sacred reason, but I would never know.

It might bother Güero that I could not speak. I paid it no mind. The frijoles were ready. They smelled good along with the coffee. With the air growing colder, I was becoming hungrier. He poured coffee into his cup and my pottery drinking bowl while I filled his tin plate and my eating bowl. I wrapped my serape around me and said a prayer, adding my thanks for Güero and hoped he would remain a gentleman.

I watched Güero take his first taste and laughed when his eyes went wide. He most certainly liked my frijoles and ate them like a starved man. He kept talking about the frijoles, and I gave him a second plate. He even folded tortillas and dipped out the frijoles as I did. Satisfied, he poured another cup of coffee for us both and rolled a cigarette. I watched how he did it. I had often rolled Papá's cigarettes, the rare times he could afford such a luxury. Leaning against his saddle, Güero gave the loudest burp I have ever heard, and that set me to laughing, and I burped, but not nearly as loud. We were both laughing, and my mind was telling me I should not.

Once we stopped, he told me in half English and half Spanish that my frijoles were real good and called me "*señorita*."

I gave him my "thank you" smile. While we finished the coffee, I watched him from across the fire. For a moment though, he gave me a strange look, staring into my eyes. Maybe he could read eyes like a Mexican. Güero was not tall. He had a thin chin beard and needed a shave. He parted his hair down the center like many vaqueros. His face, when he relaxed like now, was kind looking. At least that was what I told myself.

Had he given me a name yet since I could not tell him mine? Probably not as he only called me "niña." There was no way I could tell him my name. Strangers used to try and guess it. They called out every girl's name they could think of. None ever guessed my name was Chicahua Josefa Hinojosa Francisca. Papá said it as "Chi-cahua." *Chicahua* meant "strong" in the ancient language. Hinojosa was Papá's familia name, and Francisca was Mamá's familia. Mamá told me I was named Chicahua moments after I was born because I fought so hard to breathe and scream my lungs out. Both men and women were given this name. I tried to live up to it, although I could not scream very well or make much noise at all.

I scrubbed our dishes with sand and water. It was cold, and we both picked up more firewood. I stoked up the fire while Güero checked the horse and burro. It was so cold that gathering wood did not warm me up. I lay under my two blankets and serape, pulling them over my scarf-covered head. I said my prayers with extra special ones for each of my familia. I prayed for Güero too. Entering the foggy land of dreams, I heard Güero's quiet footsteps near me and tensed. I gripped the knife. I felt something and jerked my head from beneath the blankets. He was only laying a couple of his blankets on me. One was black rubber in case it rained. He was a kind man. I was confused and did not know what to do.

"*Buenas noches, niña*," he said.

I could only grunt.

He put more wood on the fire and got into his bedroll.

Later, I awoke again. Güero was making a quiet snore. I pulled down my blankets enough to peek at the misty clouds drifting over, lit by the moon. Mother Moon, the world of the dead to the ancient ones. This always confused me because the Mother should be the giver of life. The Father Sun as the giver of life made no sense to me. Those were the ancient beliefs. The sun was a ball of fire burning all. It was men who soldiered, who protected, who hunted. They took life because it was necessary. But some men did evil to others and murdered. The church the Spanish brought here made no such distinction about the sun and moon as the givers of life and death. It was always the woman who gave life. There were none who gave more to life than the Virgin.

Then I remembered Mamá's treasure, the beautiful silver and turquoise rosary she carried around her neck, hidden by the folds of her clothing. A rosary was not normally worn around the neck but kept in a leather pouch in a pocket. It was precious, she told me. I had no idea how it came to our poor familia. It was to be mine someday when it was my turn to care for my brother and sister. I did not find the fine-looking rosary on Mamá's body.

In the moon's glow, all I could see was my familia. Their faces gazed down upon me from the soft clouds. I could even feel them, but they were not with me. They would never again be with me. Wherever they were, at least they were together. I was alone. Was I being punished again? Was taking my voice not enough? I cried for a very long time, and no matter how much I told myself I should not feel sorry for myself, I could not stop. The pain was in my chest, in my mind, and in my heart. I had no one, not one person in this hard world who would ever take care of me.

Alguien que me consuele.

Chapter Four

Comfort me, someone.

I did not know who that might be. I had to face that I was on my own. I had to harden my spirit. The only person I could rely on was myself. Was I strong enough? I did not know if I could make it on my own.

Those were my first thoughts when I woke up. My next thought was that I was so cold I could not stop shaking. Crawling out from under the covers, I was grateful for the extra blankets Güero had given me. I wrapped my serape around myself and brought the fire back to life. Güero got up, shivering and slapping his arms. He said, "*Buenos días.*" I tried to smile back, but it was no good. I wondered if he could see the nightmares in my eyes.

I had not seen my familia murdered. It was worse. I had heard them.

He started the coffee pot while I opened the frijoles, put what was left in his skillet, and set it on the fire even though there were no good cooking coals yet. Walking away from the campsite, I sat in the weeds and peed. I noticed Güero turned away embarrassed. He was still acting the gentleman. I picked up firewood, and he was clomping around the camp trying to get warm. I almost laughed at him.

After filling my bowl with frijoles, he ate the rest from the skillet, as pleased as last night. He was dipping those hardtack squares into his coffee before cracking off pieces. He must have had teeth of iron. I cleaned our dishes while he rolled up our blankets and readied the horses. We were working together without saying a word. Me, a mute Mexican girl working with a *Texican* cowboy. Strange-this.

I showed him the empty frijoles pot. He said, "*Alimentos. Uvalde. ¿Comprende?*"

I nodded and smiled. That was good, going for food. What would happen to me in Uvalde? Would he leave me there? I had not thought about what he would do with me. There was no reason for me to stay with him, and he had little use for me.

I had seen *mexicanitos*, boys, and even girls, living alone on the road. They looked like a dog I had once seen. Its gringo owner kicked and beat it for no reason, even when he fed it, which was seldom, I thought. It looked haunted and afraid of any person coming near. Those roaming *niños* looked the same. One time we saw a band of eight niños, six girls and two boys, maybe five to twelve years old. They were like a pack of wild dogs and as dangerous, but I guess the girls survived because they were in a pack. Did the girls have to do things the boys wanted so they would protect them? Papá said they stole food, looted farmhouses, fed off goats and calves they killed, and even robbed lone travelers, mobbing them with clubs and stick spears. Later we heard Mexican and gringo farmers had hunted the band down, like the old wolf hunts, and killed them all except one girl a gringo farmer kept.

Mamá said such niños were abandoned, simply left behind or orphaned as I now was. She said the reason there were so few lone girls on the road was that they were mostly taken in by families and made to cook and wash and any other work. The girls also pleasured the husbands so the wives would not fear for having more babies. Some men were that way, she said. Mamá had kept me away from gringos ever since I was ten. She kept me away from most Mexican men too. I was twelve when Mamá told me the reason. It terrified me, and I slept little for a couple of nights. She told me sternly, "The reason we see so few girls alone is that they are caught by men to do what they will to them, and when finished, they kill them." That scared me half to death, as it was meant to.

I watched Güero closer, and he did not seem that way. Anyone could be like that, no matter how they looked. I made up my mind that it would be better if I went away on my own.

We rode into Uvalde after passing many farms. If I left on my own, maybe I could find work heating water in a bathhouse, washing clothes, cleaning spittoons in the many saloons, or cleaning outhouses. Looking around and sniffing the rank air, it did not look or smell like there was much cleaning of outhouses underway. The *chinos* ran all the laundries. The strange shaved-head pigtail men—*coletas*—would never hire a Mexican girl.

Papá had been right. Uvalde looked much different than when we were there over a year past. Now there were many more houses and buildings. Many more people. Too many. They were everywhere. Rough men. It looked dangerous.

Two mean looking saddle tramps in shoddy homespun stopped an older Mexican man who was leading a goat. It was tied to his leg. They began shouting at him, and one man shoved him, sending him tripping over the goat. They both started kicking the man, and the goat was *loco* with fear, tugging to escape. They even kicked the goat. I tapped my sandals into the burro's sides and moved closer to Güero. His hand slid to his pistol, but he only held it there. I guess he did not consider it his business, and he would not jump into trouble. I saw he was vigilant to danger, and his slitted eyes told me he could deal with whatever happened. Other people only watched. No one moved to stop it. I did not like this wild place. In the mud in the front of a saloon lay a man in a fancy frock coat. His white hair hung in the mud and horseshit. I did not know if he was dead or alive. No passerby seemed to care. I prayed there was someone for him.

We rode through the town's muddy streets. Too many people. Freight wagons everywhere. Gray and brown coal smoke hung over the evil place like a divine cloud trying to smother the wicked life here. The brown smoke meant they were using cheap coal. We rode into one of the town's four squares, and Güero headed for two gringos wearing black suits. Did he know them? One had a white clerical collar and black shirt. They were some kind of religious men. Neither was a Catholic priest, so I paid no attention. The gringos had brought so many different religions to Tejas. They were split off from the Catholic Church and even split from one another. I did not know what Güero was talking to them about, and I did not feel he was a religious man. Few men were. I thought for a moment they were talking about me, but probably not. One of them made a speech, and I recognized some spiritual words. Then I heard "harlot." I knew that word. Did he just call me a *putana*, a whore? It was not the first time men supposed that. I held my anger because I did not know what they were speaking of. Both men were very aloof. It sounded like they were talking down to Güero. He looked disgusted with whatever was said.

Güero left them with a hand wave. He asked an Anglo-speaking Mexican where the Catholic Church was. I recognized those two words. Was he looking for the church for me? I was excited. I had been there before, celebrated mass there last year, and the Day of the Dead two years ago. This past Day of the Dead had only been a few days before, but we had started our trek to Uvalde. We had not celebrated. I had also attended a funeral there for Juana Mendoza. Also a nómada, she was twelve when she died of break bone fever along with her seven-year-old brother. The familia was so poor that they could not afford to give up blankets to bury them, much less buy caskets. Their funeral shrouds were only feed sacks pulled over their heads and shoulders. I did not expect any better for myself when I died. I'd be laid in a hole shrouded in my shirt and skirt, a rag tied around my head under the jaw or my lips stitched shut, a feed sack or my rebozo pulled over my head, and dirt kicked onto me. My familia left back on the road did not even have that. I cried within myself. I could not show weakness, ever.

I knew where the Sacred Heart Catholic Church was on another plaza. We tied up outside and entered the darkened narthex. I immediately felt comfort. Quiet, calm, the thick adobe walls shielded us from the noises and dangers of the outside world. Upon entering the nave, the candles gave just enough light to make our way up the aisle. I kneeled and crossed myself before the altar and began my rosary. Güero stood to the side, turning his hat in hand, not sure what to do. I paid no attention to the padre who entered and began to speak quietly in Inglés to Güero. They went into a side room, leaving me in peace to pray and mourn my familia.

Time passed slowly, and Güero and the padre returned quietly. Güero looked unhappy. They spoke softly, and I think they were talking about me. It suddenly came to me that maybe Güero was going to leave me here. I was surprised I did not like that thought. Yes, I had thought about disappearing here, of getting away from this gringo. Now, I did not want to. Why? It was not that I wanted to stay with him. But why did I not want to stay here, either? To be in a church was a wonderful, consoling thing. To live in a church, that would be wonderful, so safe and spiritual. What was it? Why did I not want to stay here? It came to me. I wanted to be on the move. I was a nómada. I did not like this town or most any town, even if I was safe within this church.

I would go wherever my fate took me. That was my lot.

The padre came over to me, and Güero left. Was he leaving me here?

The padre sat beside me. He introduced himself as Padre Bernardo.

He told me Güero had asked if the church would take me in. That disappointed me. I felt the edge of anger. I was only a simple greaser girl who could not speak, no better than a street beggar. What good was I to him other than for what men do to women or use me to cook and wash?

Padre Bernardo told me the gringo was going to Eagle Pass and had work there. Then he asked, "Has this man molested you or done anything to you that you did not like?"

I shook my head firmly. *No.*

He nodded with approval. "I think he is a good man and can be trusted. The gringo told me he could have left you on the road, but he could not bear to do that. He knows how dangerous it is."

That surprised me. He had taken responsibility for

me.

Father Bernardo asked me about my muteness, and I went through, for me, the dull routine of making him understand what had happened. He asked for my name, and of course, I could not tell him. At least he did not waste time asking me the same everyday names of Mexican girls—Are you Maria, Juana, Carmen, Rosa?

The padre reminded me of the Bible story of Marta and Maria, two orphaned sisters offering hospitality to Jesus and his disciples. Maria would spend all her time listening to Jesus, leaving Marta to do the household work. Marta complained to Jesus, and the Christ told her not to mind the small things and to concentrate on what was important. Father Bernardo said he had told the story to Güero. He asked if I was good with Marta as a temporary name.

I nodded. I knew the story. I liked the name.

We walked through the narthex, and Güero was arranging the bags on the burro.

Father Bernardo blessed Güero and me and bid us a safe journey. He told me that I might have a hard ride ahead of me, but in the end, all would be well.

I was not happy, though. I guess it was because of all the confusion I felt. I did not know what was to become of me, why Güero was taking me along, and why at the same time he wanted to be rid of me. It made no sense. It made me angry. I came out of the church angry. That should not be. I should be tranquil and joyful. The padre followed. Güero looked confused too. I only glared at him.

I tucked my skirt's hem into the waist band to make it easier to mount. He boosted me onto the burro after looking around to see if anyone would see, and to my surprise, he said in Spanish, "*Tu nombre es Marta. ¿Está bien?*"

I gave him a sharp nod.

The padre spoke some more to Güero. He looked more uncomfortable. I think the padre said he had told me he was trying to leave me here. I glared at him more. He said, "*Lo siento.*"

Why should he apologize? Then I knew. He was only trying to do the right thing. He thought I should be with my own kind, with those who spoke my language. But if no one would take me in, he was not going to simply abandon me on the road or give me away to just anyone. Maybe he was a good man. I was still confused and angry, but that was because of losing my familia, my life completely changed, and not knowing what would happen next.

I heard Papá one night telling Mamá he could not give their children anything better in this life, that it would never be better. He could give them nothing more than our life then. His voice was so filled with pain and the embarrassment of his failure. He said someday that the two of them would be gone, and all they could give us was how to stay alive on the road. Mamá put her arms around him and said, "You gave them your love, Jaimenacho, and I love you for that."

I understood then what love was. I thought I could do more, and when I got older, I would do something for my familia. And now that had been taken from me too.

As we rode away, I felt suddenly foolish. Why had I not asked the padre Güero's true name? If Marta was good enough, then so was Güero for now.

¿A dónde voy ahora?

CHAPTER FIVE

Where am I going now?

Güero said something about food, and we rode down the crowded street and found a store. It had Bodeguita on the sign, telling me they tolerated Mexicans, even if they only wanted our few coins.

I loved the gringo general stores. They had so much more to look at and dream about than little Mexican *bodegas* and *misceláneas*. I liked those too. They may not have held as many wonderful things, but they were the best place to hear news and gossip.

I slid off the burro to save Güero the embarrassment of anyone seeing him help a Mexican girl. God forbid.

There were gringo women coming out of the store. Suddenly, I was angry again, as quickly as a flock of birds taking wing. Maybe it was the way they looked at me. They saw a too-young dirty Mexican girl on a burro following meekly behind a scruffy cowboy. I was just more of his baggage. Frowning and nodding to each other, they thought they knew what I was, and I hated that feeling.

I did not hear the ringing in my left ear meaning someone was talking bad about me. If the ringing was in my right ear, it was something good being said. I bit my tongue anyway. Mamá said that would make the person talking bad about me bite their own tongue for punishment.

I lifted my chin, ran up the steps, and barged into the store as if I owned it. I was so angry I thought I would burst open. It was not only the women who set off my anger. Things had changed so much and kept changing. It confused me.

"*Buenos días, señorita,*" said the shopkeeper.

I could only nod and tried to smile. There were so many wonderful things to look at. The shelves were filled with cans and jars, pots and pans, cups and coffee pots. I walked around looking at all the delightful things. Kettles, lanterns, and buckets. There were things I always wanted—like a washboard, a little grill, and more. My anger slowly crept away…some.

Maybe Güero knew what he wanted, but I knew better since I would be doing the cooking. I did not know how much money he had. He would stop me if I bought too much. The first thing I pointed to was a five-pound sack of frijoles. I cut a small hole with my boning knife and smelled them. Fresh enough. Three cans of tomatoes. A quarter-pound of salt. The shopkeeper's wife wrapped handfuls of dried cilantro, tomatillo, and garlic in paper packets. A pound of tortilla flour, two pounds of rice, four sweet onions, and a half-dozen jalapeños wrapped in newspaper.

I looked at Güero with a question in my eyes. He nodded.

This was a good store. They sold meat. I got a half-pound each of salt pork, ham, and white bacon wrapped in wax paper and newspaper. They even had chorizo. I got four of the spicy sausages.

Güero bought a pound of coffee, good. He also got a box of square crackers, soft ones, not hardtack. He picked up a lot of boxes of matches and cigarette fixings.

The last things I bought, which surprised me that Güero did not have, was a half-gallon can of coal oil and a bar of soap. He seemed surprised. The shopkeeper knew we called it *queroseno*.

Güero counted out the money. I moved to where I could see how much he had. I could not tell, but it was more than I had ever seen at one time. No, I would not rob him in his sleep. That was not me.

Leaving the store, we went to a public stables, and Güero bought a bucket of oats and fed his horse and the burro. Strange that. I had never seen anyone buy a burro feed. We reached the stables just in time to shelter from a hard rain. When the rain slowed to only a few drops, we headed south out of Uvalde. I was glad to see it disappear behind us and to be back on the road, wherever it might lead. I prayed to Saint Menas, the patron saint of travelers.

We were not far out of town when we came across two freight wagons bound for Uvalde. One was buried to its hubs in a mud-filled stream crossing the road. Both of the six-mule teams were hitched to the stuck wagon and unable to dislodge it. Güero offered to help the two discouraged mud-splattered teamsters. They decided it was impossible to unload the barrels and kegs to lighten the burden because of the deep mud. The wagon would have to be dug out. Güero pulled his boots and socks off and waded into the mud. This was going to take time, and I wanted to be on the road. I do not know why I was in such a hurry to go someplace I did not know with someone I did not know if I could trust. Behind our horses, I rolled my skirt and petticoat up over my knees and tied them up with a cord. The men were shocked to see my bare legs, but not for long as I waded into the mud with a shovel in my hands. Güero looked both surprised and pleased I was willing to help.

The four of us shoveled the thick mud from in front of the huge wheels, and as the mud oozed back in, one of the teamsters whipped the mules forward, sometimes only a foot or two. My anger oozed away like mud. I was working, doing something useful.

The German teamsters were coarse and profane men with thick black beards, a feature that discomforted me. They were kind, or at least tolerant of me, probably not because I was a girl but because I was helping them. That did not temper their swearing, most of which I understood. Behind the wagon seat was a crate of cooking gear and canned goods. One can pictured a corncob. Güero noticed me eyeing it. Catching my eye, he firmly shook his head. I did not like to, but in my life, I would steal if I had to. I always prayed for forgiveness and tried to find a way to make it up by helping someone else. It embarrassed me that Güero caught me thinking about it, and he seemed to know what wickedness I was scheming.

We finally brought the wagon out of the mud with much lashing and mule squalling. Obnoxious animals they were. The men found a better passage beside the road and used both teams to drag the second wagon past. The mud may have only been mid-calf deep for Güero, but it was above my knees. I found a place upstream with clear water to wash off and soak some of the mud from my skirt. I was shivering from the two hours of wallowing in cold mud and water.

For all our trouble, the teamsters gave us cold bean sandwiches on stale and bitter black bread. They had been kind enough to scrape off most of the mold. I was ready to start up a cook fire then and there for an early supper, something hot and good tasting. But I wanted to get back on the road. I wanted to see where we were going.

We had not been on the road long when the rain came again with no place to hide from it. With it again came my anger. What was wrong with me? The cold and rain and mud. I was tired of it.

Güero pulled on a yellow rubber coat. He tried to help me cover with his black rubber blanket. I waved him away. I did not want him near me. I do not know why. I made do with my thick wool serape as always. After a time, I wished I was not so angry. The rubber blanket would have been better, I thought.

After a couple of freezing hours, Güero picked a campsite. The rain had passed. It was an early stop, for which I was happy. He was teeth-chattering cold too. I was so chilled I had trouble concentrating, but the faces of my familia kept passing through my mind.

Güero was looking around at the deadwood. There was a lot, but it was soaked wet. I picked up armloads while he unsaddled and took the gear off the horses and hobbled them. They looked as cold and sad as us.

I stacked the wood and built a smaller pile for our fire. Unscrewing the kerosene can, I spilled some on the mesquite sticks and bent over to protect the match. I struck it on the flat piece of sandstone I used for knife sharpening. I kept tossing on sticks, the smaller pieces drying out and catching faster than bigger logs. Once the fire was going good, I laid on larger pieces for the flames to dry.

I had no heart to do anything. I should have been cooking for my familia, but I could not. We needed hot food, and no matter what I felt like, I had to cook. Setting the skillet on the fire, I poured in a little water and rice to brown, and then a cube of white bacon. When it was sizzling good, in went cut-up ham, onion, and jalapeños. Güero made the coffee. It was not very good. After he opened the bag of coffee, he pulled out a red and white striped peppermint candy cane and gave it to me. I had seen gringo niños sucking on them in towns, but I had never tasted one. I ate a little piece and wrapped up the rest. I liked it, but I would not let Güero know.

With everything in the skillet bubbling, I poured in a can of tomatoes. Güero filled my drinking bowl with coffee, and I spooned out his share of tomato rice. He offered me some of the white crackers, and I tried them. They were good. I laughed to myself because gringos were sometimes called *galletas*—crackers. Crackers were white too. I laughed to myself.

I cleaned the dishes. Güero tended the horses and gathered more wood. I had to laugh, or tried to, when I realized his horse's name was Crackers.

As I was putting my things back in my bag, he came over to me, went to a knee, and handed me a small mirror with a handle. I was surprised like never before. He gave me a gift. No one but my Mamá and Papá had ever given me a gift, and nothing like this. I looked at him quickly, too quickly. I was so embarrassed because I did not know what to do. I could not say anything. What would I say if I could? I did not know. He went to the other side of the fire and spread his bedroll.

By firelight, I looked at myself for a moment and set the mirror down. Something made me pick it up and stare into it. Who was this person? Why was she alive and all those she loved were dead and gone forever? Why?

I saw an angry, sad face, full lips over a straight and kind of wide nose. My coffee brown eyes peered out from under the shawl made darker by my thick eyebrows. My face blended into the shawl's shadows to hide my hair.

Mamá said I should always hide it, my thick black hair. She said men would have bad thoughts and desires if they saw my hair. I did not understand. How could that be?

Güero whispered across the fire to me, "*Niña, lo siento por tu familia.*" He did not say it exactly right, but he said it. His face was sincerely sad.

I nodded and turned back to the mirror and studied my face for a long time. I learned nothing I did not already know. I was unwanted, alone, and my days were likely numbered. I dozed off praying for guidance and salvation.

I woke up, cold. The air was still. I could not hear the horses. Güero was a lump across the almost burned-down coals. I crawled out and set on more wood and blew the embers to glowing orange. Crouching by the fire, I drew its warmth and then slipped under my blankets.

Again awakened, the eastern horizon beyond the mesquite was a thin yellow line. I laid there shivering under my blankets. What was I to do? My mind was fuzzy and confused. Thoughts crept through me like scorpions seeking the spiders they fed on. What did this man intend for me? He had been kind, but what did he really want? Everyone wanted something from you. I was completely in his hands. He could do anything he wanted to me, even murder me or worse, and no one except God would ever know. Was he the kind of man who would care if God knew what he did? Trying to explain things to myself, I asked why he would do that? I was so confused and should not be thinking that way.

I knew I could take care of myself. I did not need anyone. I thought of those abandoned niños and what had happened to them. It would be safer alone than with a pack like that. I would be like an invisible bruja.

I kept everything packed in my bag. I rolled up my blankets. I thought about taking a share of food. No,

Güero had paid for it. I left the wool and rubber blankets he had given me, and I placed the mirror atop them. I put more wood on the fire and slipped out of the camp. It is better to be alone and not trust or depend on anyone.

I made for the road. I heard a faint noise behind me and turned expecting to see Güero coming at me. It was the burro. He had slipped his hobble and was following me. I tried to shoo him off and threw sticks, but he followed like a pup. Stupid burro, why was it following me? All I did was ride on it. It cannot like me for that.

At the road, shivering all the more, I turned left for Uvalde. I knew it was dangerous, but there were no other towns nearer. Eagle Pass was still far away. Besides, Güero would not turn back in the opposite direction and return to Uvalde for the likes of me or the burro. He wanted only to be rid of me, which was obvious at the church.

After walking for an hour, the sun was above the trees and threw long shadows across the mesquite. The stupid burro was still following, its head bobbing. I heard the quiet jingle of trace chains behind me. For a moment, I thought of my familia following after me, but they were not there. *Run*, I thought. *No! I will demand a ride no matter who it is.* I gripped my knife and was ready to run if needed.

The freight wagon rolled out of the shadows. Six prodding mules, a half-asleep teamster. He must have gotten an early start, could not sleep, like me, or was just one of those who rose before daylight.

I stood to the side of the road fighting the need to run and hide like always. I looked closely as the teamster's white bearded face. He looked to be a kind-hearted old man. I waved, and he pulled the reins hard to stop the mules.

I motioned with my hand and pointed to the wagon, myself, and then up the road.

He said something, and I understood "ride" and "Uvalde." He said something about the "donkey" too. I knew that was what gringos called burros.

Pitching my bag in, I climbed onto the tailgate and sat where I could watch the gringo.

Looking back down the road, I did not see Güero.

The teamster started singing some song. About the only words I recognized were "fools, whiskey, and women."

The burro was following me close and still would not leave. I could see he was blind in his right eye. The burro and I were both crippled.

Soon there were farmhouses and people on the road on foot and on horses and more wagons of all kinds. I was almost back to Uvalde.

¿Que voy a hacer ahora?

CHAPTER SIX

What am I going to do now?

The dreary sky brightened with the wet clouds glowing blue and gray and black and dirty white. What were clouds made of? Where did they come from, and where did they go? The Earth was supposed to be a big ball. Did clouds fly all the way around the Earth? Had I seen these same clouds passing before?

The air smelled dirty. More rain was coming.

Off to the southeast, a streaked gray wall hung under a vast cloud, a thunderstorm. How did the water get into the clouds? They must have slid over the ocean like bats skimming across a river for a drink. Maybe they soaked up water like a rag mopping up sweat. I still was not convinced there was really an ocean, the water said to cover most of the Earth.

The Earth, the big ball, was covered by land and water, more water than land, they said. They called all that water the ocean. I had never seen the ocean. While at places my familia had been, Papá told us the ocean was only a few *ligas* away. One time, only a liga away, I wanted to walk there and see if the ocean really existed. I could do it in a day, but Papá would not let me. It was just as well. I used to think the story of the ocean was only another myth of the ancient ones, but Papá said it was so.

The teamster shouted something, probably asking me where I was going or where I wanted off. I looked around. The Catholic church was a couple of blocks off the road. I jumped off with my bag almost knocking me from my feet. I gave the teamster a little bow and waved.

He waved back and surprised me with, "*Adiós, niña.*"

There were some good gringos. The burro stood blinking his good eye at me and then followed the wagon. Maybe he liked the wagon because he was not made to carry anything.

I stood on a corner. Now what? The church did not want me. I had no money. I had little food—some tortillas and a few dried frijoles. It was late in the day, and it might take days to find a job. I needed to eat. There was one way to get a little food money.

I did not worry about a place to sleep. I would find a place to hide, maybe even a dry place. I once asked a lone boy on the road where he slept in towns. He told me he could always stay in a livery stable. Before closing time, he would walk into the stable and shovel shit out of the stalls. He asked not for pay, but only a place to sleep. After the usual warning not to smoke or make a fire, he slept in a hay pile. If the owner was married, his wife often gave him leftovers. I feared that a man knowing a girl was sleeping in the stable might have dangerous, unpleasant thoughts. Find and keep a pitchfork with you, he suggested. The boy told me not to stay in a stable if there was gambling or cock or dog fights. Meant to increase the stable's income, it also attracted the town marshal. The marshal might chase off the men, and you too, or they might place bets with the others.

Standing on the muddy plaza, I saw three saloons and a bathhouse. Maybe I would be blessed and could get a job at the bathhouse. As I walked in that direction, I watched the saloons. By the time I reached the bathhouse, it looked like the saloon in the plaza's far corner had the most men going in and out.

The bathhouse was nearly empty this time of day. A man came out with a fresh shave and gave me a passing glance. The small front room had a couple of rickety plank tables and benches. On one wall were pasted pictures torn from magazines and newspapers of different haircuts, mustaches, and beards. A big picture on another wall showed the back of a naked woman washing herself beside a metal tub. A woman in blue kneeled beside her, wringing out a washcloth. From a building across the way, a man watched her from a balcony's shadows. The scene looked familiar. And then I knew. It was from the Bible story of King David seeing the beautiful Besheba for the first time. David sent the woman's husband off to war to be killed so he could have Besheba for himself. Men are like that.

A squat man wiping his hands on a towel came out of the back. He looked at me with disapproval. I made out that he was saying he had no food, but he pointed to wooden bowls on the tables holding pretzels like in saloons.

I shook my head, kneeled, and made like I was stoking a fire and lifting on a bucket of water. I had gotten good at acting out what I wanted to say.

He understood, I thought, that I could not speak. That alone usually made sure I would not get a job. Mute people are obviously dumb. He told me to leave. Many disliked me for not being normal.

Gazing at him with my "helpless" look, I pointed to a bowl. He nodded for me to take it. I tipped the pretzels into my bag, smiled, bowed, and darted out the door. I headed for the busy saloon, and looking back, saw the bathhouse man in the door with a sad stare. I waved goodbye without a grudge for him turning me away. There was a reason for that wave. Some people really did feel sorry for me, and on occasion, they waved for me to come back. Not this time.

Saloons were the best to beg at. They were better than churches or stores, but not as safe. People leaving churches had given money up for the offering, and few wanted to part with more. Besides, if it was not a Catholic church, they did not allow Mexican beggars since Mexicans are Catholic. Catholic churches allowed beggars and were more serious as alms for the poor was one of our obligations, given out of love and not out of duty. The Three Pillars of Lent are alms giving, prayer, and fasting. Fasting was never a problem, and I had much time to pray during my endless wandering. Alms giving was a problem for me. Sitting in front of a Catholic church was more lucrative during Lent. That was months away. Stores were the same. People had spent their money inside.

I never asked permission to sit in front of a saloon. They would always say no. They wanted customers to spend their money inside. Drunks were sometimes more generous with their coin. If the bar owner found me there, he would only chase me off, mostly. One time I was kicked three times before I could get off the porch. Passing people laughed at me. That was a bitter day. Sometimes I was only smacked with a broom. Another time a saloon owner set two boys about my age to beat me up. One left with a black eye and split lip and the other a broken finger. I had two black eyes, and it took a long time for my nosebleed to stop, but no one laughed that day. They did make our familia leave town. Papá said it was a bad day for me to have fought back. He lost work there. Mamá licked a penny and stuck it on my forehead. When it dried and fell off, the nosebleed would stop. So she said, but since we were walking, it kept falling off.

I peeked through the saloon doors. It was no better and no worse for such places. No fight was underway, and only a few men were having an afternoon beer. I sat to the right of the door. Most men are right handed, making it easier to drop a coin in my bowl as they entered. I set my bag on my right side to protect from kicks and made sure my knife was at hand. Using my eating bowl as a begging cup was what I hated most. I said a prayer to Saint Martin of Tours, the protector of beggars. He was also the patron saint of winemakers, which seemed fitting in my circumstance. I hated begging among all things. Shoveling shit was nobler.

I looked around the plaza. It was wise to watch what was happening and who was coming in my direction. Two men were walking toward another saloon. A fat man came out of the far saloon and was trying to decide where to go. An old uncle-looking Mexican was looking for cigarette butts at the same saloon's hitching rail. A woman and a little blonde girl went into a millinery. A well-dressed man came from one shop and went into the saloon. He paid me no mind. Soon a young man with a thin mustache rode up and tied his sorrel to the rail. Seeing me, he smiled, reached into a pocket, and dropped two pennies in my bowl. Three or four more blessings like that and I would have enough for a meal of sorts. It was so cold with the wind blowing across the plaza that I shivered. I wanted to eat some of the pretzels, but I could not let patrons see that I had food.

I looked around again. Four boys, maybe ten and

twelve years old, chased a scrawny dog across the plaza, throwing rocks. I hoped they would not see me. They were dangerous. A large woman came out of an apothecary and violently swept the porch, I think to keep an eye on the boys. She shouted something at them. Two old women in black went into the church, crossing themselves. A man was dismounting his horse at the church… and had a burro. *No! No! All that is Holy, no! Why is he here? He is looking straight at me!* Leading his horse, he walked across the plaza. The burro followed. I started to stand. *No, I will not budge.*

There was no reason for him to be here. He wanted to be rid of me. He walked up, staring at me with a disappointed or disgusted look, I could not tell. A man came down the sidewalk, dropped a penny in my bowl, and kept going. I was suddenly overcome with shame like I had never felt. Why should I care? Güero was just another cowboy. At that moment two greasy and dirty men came out the door. Seeing me, they said something nasty to each other. One made a disgusting throat noise and spat a thick glob of chewing tobacco toward my eating bowl. It hit my shoulder and splattered on my shawl. Güero's face turned ugly. He was disgusted with me. They laughed mean and said more nasty things of me. I could tell by the tone of their voices. Güero gripped his pistol and gave those two awful men a look that would scare a bruja. He did not say a word, and they left, almost running around the saloon's corner. This was a man who did not need words to make known what he would do.

I struggled not to cry. Relief poured through me, and at the same time I was embarrassed to show weakness and for him to see me begging. Why did he come back?

He said something about "damn Yankees," gave a glare in the direction they fled, and pulled off his gloves. He kneeled, and the most extraordinary thing I had ever seen happened. With his bandana, he wiped the sticky spit from my shawl. A gringo cowboy did that for me!

He stood, and with the kindest of faces, reached out his hand. I looked into his blue eyes. I almost did not take his hand, but I did. The warmth of his calloused hand sucked the cold out of mine. I gripped his hand and arm as hard as I could. My mind folded into itself. I do not remember any clear thoughts. I thanked God for sending him. He wrapped my serape around me after I tucked my skirt, and not caring if anyone saw us, he lifted me onto the burro.

I was as weak as a newborn sparrow. I could barely hang onto him and stared at the ground. Some kind of feeling overcame me. Relief? Why should I feel that way? Because of a cowboy? Should I even be grateful for a cowboy? But I was. Unwanted tears ran, and I shook all over.

He said something about Eagle Pass and a job. From his saddlebags, he pulled a pair of gray socks and slid them onto my hands like gloves. I had never had gloves. Why was he doing this?

He said something about "fire" and frijoles. He likes my frijoles. He put the small mirror into my bag. At a public well, I motioned for him to draw water, and I set frijoles to soak in my pot.

We left that town behind us. I did not like the things that happened there, except for one thing, or maybe two. I had a new name I liked, and Güero came back for me. I do not know why or if that was important or even if I should be happy for it, but I was, for now.

We passed drunken damn Yankees, chuck-line cowboys, and Mexican nómada familias, all desperately seeking work or just a place to sit out the winter. There were farmers running errands, freight wagons, and a stagecoach. Güero picked a camp well before dark and far from the road. It was an early stop because neither of us had eaten all day. I worked up the fire, starting it with the kerosene as usual, and he took care of the mounts and gathered wood as usual.

I started on the frijoles, dicing up ham and two chorizo sausages. I added cilantro, tomatillo, jalapeños, onion, and garlic and set it to cook as I made fresh tortillas. They were much better than gringo crackers. I wanted to warn Güero that if he dropped a tortilla, it would bring unwanted visitors.

Güero laid out his bedroll and set a canvas cover over it. I piled leaves for my bedroll. He took his rubber blanket and the yellow rain jacket and made a cover for my bedroll. I had not expected him to do that. Sniffing the air, it was hard to decide if it would rain or not because it was already so wet. He gave me back the blankets he had given me before.

Supper was good. After a long emotional day without food, it was even better. Güero liked it, nodding his head and giving me a pleased grin.

He did not say much during the meal or after. He was not one to speak if not necessary. I think people would know what he was thinking when they needed to. Those terrible damn Yankees at the saloon did. While I washed our dishes, he picked up more wood and built up the fire. We both knew what we had to do and did our chores without the need for words. I liked that.

I liked to be able to sit with my arms wrapped around my legs and pray and remember my familia. I missed them. I thought about the hard and bad and good times we had.

And I was alone. What would become of me? I knew this cowboy would go in another direction someday, any day. That was their way. Why should he be any different? I stared into the mirror. I watched him as he smoked and gazed into the fire. With the passing away of the day's light, it became colder. I crawled into my blankets and serape. Even with the hot frijoles and coffee, I was already cold. Before long a small rain came over and came down harder. The fire died fast.

I awoke shivering like a dog shaking off rainwater. I expected Tlayolot to be huddled between me and Mamá. He was not there. Mamá was not there. No one was. There was no sound from the horse. I peeked from under the blankets over the dead fire. It was so dark I could not see if Güero was there. My damp blankets were frozen stiff. I was cold, as cold as I had ever been. I huddled in a ball, wrapped my arms around myself, and shoved my numb sock-covered fists into my armpits. My breath trapped underneath my shawl and head-covering blankets held no warmth. I could not stop shivering.

I huddled and prayed for warmth, for forgiveness, and for daylight. I knew it would still be ice cold even as the sun climbed up, which was hours away. The firewood and any banked embers were dead and soaked through. I thought of the kerosene. It might dry out the frozen logs, but trying to spark an ember and grow it kneeling on the ice-covered ground sounded like a poor notion.

The way my familia huddled together in the cold, I missed them so much. Güero, he too had to be as cold, even though he had more blankets and even quilts. Would he share his warmth? Could I trust him? Would he misunderstand that I only wanted to be warm? I thought back to the past nights with him. He could have done to me anything he wanted. He had been a gentleman and appeared to be an honorable man. I did have my boning knife.

Three times I almost went to him. Praying that I was

making a good choice and not a terrible blunder, I finally crawled out into the bitter cold. With my blankets wrapped around me, I ran across to his bedroll and almost tripped over the fire logs. As carefully as I could, I lifted his blankets with ice crinkling. I had to feel around to make sure I was crawling under the right ones of the many layers. For a moment, I waited to see if he would do anything. I eased in and pulled my blankets the best I could to cover my front. They tangled, and I could not sort them out without a lot of moving around. Güero moved, muttered something. He was lying on his left side. I spooned up to him with my back against his chest. He did not move or say anything. I was now shivering so violently that it had to have woken him. I hoped I was not making a mistake. I had gotten even colder just running a few steps. After a time, he laid his arm over my shoulder. I clutched his hand with both of mine. Eventually, my shivering faded. I realized I had not brought my knife. I did not need it. I felt protected. I was warm. I slept.

A caballo dado no se le mira el colmillo.

Chapter Seven

Do not look at the teeth of a horse given to you.

Gray dawn. Warmth. For such a bitterly cold night, I never slept warmer. Mother of God, I was in the bedroll with a gringo! I suddenly felt so out of place, as if I had done something sinful. He moved his arm hanging over my shoulder. I flung open the covers and scrambled out, dragging my blankets with me. What had I done?

I calmed down. After all, nothing had happened. He did not burst out of his bedroll after me. I remembered I had forgotten to take my knife into his bedroll.

He sat up, scratched his fingers through his shaggy hair, and put his hat on.

I kicked the frozen logs of the dead fire and smiled at Güero.

"*Buenos días, Marta.*"

I gave a sharp nod as I splashed on kerosene and

sparked it into a fire. As I put my bedroll back together, I thought no matter how cold I was, I had better not do that again. Sooner or later he would get those urges Mamá tried to explain and I was only starting to understand.

Güero made the coffee, as usual, rolled his bedroll, and cared for the horse and burro as usual. I heated up the frijoles as usual.

We ate fast, wanting something hot inside and to get on the road and get warm. He set his saddle a *vara* from the fire to warm it. Soon we were headed southwest.

We had traveled a little over a legua. The rising sun had barely started to warm the air. Güero even took off his coat. At least it was not raining, and the wind was barely felt. Bouncing on the burro, I watched Güero's back. He paid little attention to me and very seldom looked back. He usually nodded when he did. Everything told me I could trust this man. I still had to be careful. Men were so unpredictable, Mamá said.

A sudden whoop sent a chill up my back. Fear slashed through me. An indio war cry.

Güero pulled out his carbine and charged into the mesquite without a moment's hesitation, just like I imagined if he had been there to save my familia. He left me behind on the road. I dismounted and led the burro into the mesquite on the other side of the road where I could hide. I wanted to run away from those remembered noises, but I could not on the burro. I could hide in the brush and wait it out. I pulled out my knife.

A shot cracked. There was another indio whoop and two more fast shots. It was quiet for a short time, and then a carbine shot, a running horse, a shotgun boom sounding like Papá's, and another carbine shot.

A horse burst out of the mesquite all excited, ears up, eyes wide. The small sorrel saw me and came my way like it wanted my company, to be reassured. It was not an indio's horse. It had a saddle, saddlebags, and bedroll; a gringo's.

I moved so he would look at me. Horses could only think about one thing at a time. Seeing me, the horse had to decide if I was to be feared or not. He stopped, eyed me and the burro. I tied the unimpressed burro to a bush. I walked toward but not straight at the horse, as though I would pass him. Clicking my tongue, he looked at me closer and forgot what scared him. The noises from the other side of the road were scaring me, but I forced myself to stay steady. The horse's reins were dangling past his head. Those were worrying him. I held out my hand and made a fist so he could not bite my fingers. He sniffed curiously and let me take the reins. Clicking more, I moved close and patted his neck. His withers quivered. Arranging his reins, I put a sandal in a stirrup, barely reaching it, and lifted myself onto the saddle. I tugged lightly on the reins. I was now the *jefe*. After turning him in a couple of trotting circles, I rode over to fetch the burro.

There had been no more shots or whoops. If there were, I would have left. On a horse, I could flee like the wind. Instead, I thought about what to do. I carefully rode in the direction Güero had charged off to. Coming through the mesquite, I found a terrible and bloody sight.

A dead cowboy was lying on his back in a muddy pool of blood with a bandana laid on his head. All bloody, it looked like he had been scalped. Then I saw a scalp clutched in the hand of a dead indio. Another indio lay dead with half his head blown open and his brains a lump in the mud. *God protect me!* A third indio writhed in the mud and cactus, groaning while clutching his belly.

"*Burna, chica*," said Güero, seemingly unconcerned with the mayhem around him.

Why did he say that? Oh, because I had caught the

horse. It was an easy thing.

I dismounted and went to the dead gringo. He was no older than Güero. The live indio went from groaning to screaming and rolled around even more.

Güero ignored the indio and took things out of the cowboy's pockets; a tobacco pouch, some coins, and a pocketknife. He took the man's pistol belt too. I prayed for the poor man as I had for my familia. Like my familia, he could not be buried. Güero laid the man's blue and white bandana, now blood red, over his face. There was nothing with his name. Güero picked up three indio knives and a tomahawk. Then he picked up a very fine shotgun lying on the ground. He wiped it clean with his bandana and put it in the leather and canvas case on the sorrel's saddle. There were no other guns.

The dead gringo's gray hat was on the ground, and I picked it up. Mamá would never let me wear such a hat. It was something women never wore. Behind the horse, I lowered my shawl but kept it around my neck and shoulders to cover my long hair. I put on the flat-brimmed hat. It would protect me better from sun and rain than a knitted shawl.

Güero started to mount. The live indio was in such raging pain that his death song was only his screaming. I had always heard a belly shot was terribly painful and death was certain. I was angry. These were not the indios who murdered my familia, but God forgive me, I hated all of them. These were no better. They had ambushed a cowboy the same way they had killed my familia, to take what little they had. I grabbed Güero's arm and pointed at the indio.

"*¿Qué?*" he said. He could not believe I wanted him to kill the indio rolling in agony. He argued with me. I do not know what he said, but I understood the tone. I stamped by foot and jabbed my finger. I think he was too cheap to shoot more bullets. Glaring at me, he finally shot the indio through the chest like shooting a deathly sick calf. He was still complaining when we mounted, saying something about "eight." Maybe that is how many shots he fired. I did not care.

Güero tied the burro's lead rope to my saddle. I realized something. It was my saddle and my horse. I caught it. It would have run away if I had not. Güero might think differently, but I thought I could convince him. He had put the shotgun in the case on my horse's saddle. He may have argued about that, but I knew how to use it, and I could probably change his mind.

I knew about horses. I used to fear them because they were so big and I was so small. And often bad men, or at least selfish men, rode them, gringos and Mexicans. When I was thirteen on a rancho we worked at, two vaqueros thought it would be amusing to teach so small a girl to ride. They did it for their own pleasure, but I took to the horses. They taught me that they were to be respected, not feared. They were powerful animals but would do your bidding if you tried to understand their ways. It did not take me long to become friends with the horses. I only needed help mounting them, but I found ways to do that on my own. The big heavy saddles were also difficult, but by using a corral fence, I could manage. If riding only a short distance, bareback was easier. Dismounting was not difficult. I had only to slide or fall off.

A Mexican girl with a horse and saddle and a shotgun. That is something. And a gringo hat too. A big one.

I tried not to think about what had happened and what I had seen back there. I had to be strong. I wanted to be sick.

I thought of the three dead indios, all killed by Güero.

He must hate indios too. He seemed not to have a bit of regret, being more concerned about how many bullets he fired. At least he was frugal.

On Güero's left arm I noticed some blood spots. Was he hurt? Maybe it was only spatter. I would check when we stopped.

I prayed for the dead cowboy. It was seldom that I ever prayed for a gringo.

It was two hours before sunset when Güero turned off the road after crossing a stream. We went upstream until he picked a place to camp. There was a good windbreak of small oaks and guajillo. The thick mesquite would hide our fire from the road. He looked to be in pain, and he pulled off all the gear, saddlebags, and saddles, letting it fall into a pile under a willow. I loved willows. They were like a woman bent over a stream washing her hair. He hobbled the horses, and I gathered firewood. While the two horses argued about who was the jefe, I built up the fire. Güero laid his saddle blanket beside the fire and took off his wool shirt and long johns' top.

I was surprised to see that his left arm had been hit by many small pellets. It was not serious, but it was more than I expected. I got the coffee pot of water boiling, and he gave me the cowboy's pocketknife. How did he get shot by the cowboy's shotgun? Maybe one of the indios had taken it from the cowboy and turned it on Güero. I washed out his bandana with the hot water and washed his arm using the yellow soap we bought in Uvalde. He complained, and I thumped him on his head with my knuckles. He should not have been so touchy. I heated the knife blade in the fire and let it cool before I picked out the little pellets. I knew it hurt, and he tried to show how tough he was. Let us see how tough, I thought. I pretended one of the pellets was very deep, and unfortunately, I had to dig the blade in to work out the pellet—

not really. He took it pretty well, as expected, as men do not like to show weakness before a woman. There were thirteen pellets. I tossed them into the weeds. I cleaned the wounds again with hot water and soap. I think he complimented and thanked me for doing it. It was something that any nómada woman could do.

I started on supper while Güero went through all the cowboy's belongings. He had little food, only four tins and some jerky and corn dodgers. Working on farms, we sometimes were given corn dodgers. They were not as good as tortillas.

The horse had sores on his back from being poorly cleaned, and its saddle blanket was crusted with dirt and dried sweat, which had helped cause them. I made a sage paste to put on the raw areas, and I washed the blanket in the stream using soap. I needed to take care of my new horse. I would wait for a sign before naming it.

The cowboy's bedroll was only four old wool blankets and a rubber blanket. He had a very good brown corduroy coat, blanket-lined with a high canvas collar.

While I was mixing the tortilla dough, Güero took two of the cowboy's best blankets, the rubber blanket, canteen, and the coat and said, "*Por usted.*" He gave me the pocket knife too. I was very surprised. He was giving me all this? It made my eyes tear. That embarrassed me. I had stuck him with a knife to see how tough he was. Now I was the weak one. I had no way to thank him other than nodding.

For supper, I made my frijoles and fresh tortillas. He truly liked the frijoles.

We bundled up good for the night. It was not as cold as last night. Regardless of me thinking I should not do this, I crawled under the blankets with him. Güero had to lay on his right side because of his arm, so I spooned against his back and put my arm over him. He must feel my breasts against him. That embarrassed me, but I did not bother keeping a knife with me.

It took us two more days to reach Eagle Pass. In Spanish, it was *Paso del Águila*, but even Mexicans call it Eagle Pass. It was said that if you went to Eagle Pass, you had a purpose for going because there was nothing worth much there unless you were going into Mexico. There was not much there, either.

Güero never said anything, but I had the idea that the horse and saddle were mine now and the big hat. The shotgun too, but I do not think Güero thought so…yet. I would probably have to show him I knew how to use it. A Mexican girl with a shotgun. The few people we met on the road looked at me peculiar, but no one said anything. Güero was like that. If anyone asked questions, he gave short answers and made it clear he did not wish conversation. Maybe that it is why Güero tolerated me. He did not talk any more than me. Well, there were the frijoles. When he did speak, it seemed he was complimenting my cooking or for doing some chore.

We sat our horses on a ridge overlooking what there was of Eagle Pass. I rolled Güero a cigarette and one for myself. That is another chore I had taken up. I used to roll Papá's when he had tobacco, which was seldom. I had started smoking too.

Papá enjoyed it when I shared a cigarette with him. Mamá hated it and complained until Papá told her to quiet her mouth and rest her mind. We would sit on a riverbank, smoking, sometimes with bowls of coffee when we had it. It was seldom we had both coffee and tobacco. We would watch the water, the clouds, the stars, Mother Moon. It made no matter that I could not speak. Papá enjoyed it and said it helped ease him after a hard day of many hours.

I clicked my tongue, tapped my foot into the side of Güero's horse to set it moving, and then heeled mine. We rode into town side by side. I had no idea where we were going or what we were going to do. *We*. I said we a lot.

¿Ahora qué?

CHAPTER EIGHT

Now what?

We followed the railroad tracks, but instead of going into the town of brick and adobe buildings, we headed for the army fort on the east side, crossing a bridge over an arroyo.

At the gate, Güero talked to a soldier, and others came out one at a time wearing yellow stripes on their sleeves. I did not like soldiers. They always thought I was a whore if I was anywhere near a saloon or bathhouse or alone on the street. They wore thunderstorm-blue jackets and pants the color of a clear sky. I did not think any two had hats alike.

A lot of soldiers gathered around Güero. I squatted beside the horses and rolled a cigarette. Güero took out two of the indios' knives, and the soldiers started bidding on them. He made a little over a dollar each. That is a lot of money! The third one, though, was different. There was some serious bidding, and he got three and a quarter dollars! I do not know what was so special about it except for the dried blood. It must be the one that scalped the gringo. Why would anyone want a knife like that? Pointing at his blood-stained sleeve and the shotgun on my horse, my shotgun, he must have been telling of his battle with the indios. I hoped he was not planning on selling my shotgun. I would have something to say…well, I would throw a fit. He sold the tomahawk for almost as much as the knife. It was not even a real tomahawk like the ones I had seen. It was a trade hatchet with some feathers. I had watched Güero tie on the vulture feathers he found on the road.

An officer, I guessed, came out and talked to Güero. He brought out the cowboy's pistol, and the officer looked it over, took it out of the worn holster, unloaded it, and snapped it a couple of times. He bought it for sixteen dollars! I had never ever thought about how much a pistol would cost. A shotgun or carbine must cost a great deal. I was grateful that he did not try to sell my shotgun.

We rode down to the Río. There were more Mexicans than gringos in this town. I drew many looks riding a horse. Mexican woman seldom sit a horse, nor gringo women, unless they were ranch women. I guess it was the way I was dressed too, the coat, the big gringo hat, and the shotgun. Mexican women followed their men. Seldom did I follow Güero. I rode beside him. I realized I had been doing that since the battle with the indios. And he let me. Why was that?

There was a Mexican barter market on the low río bank, but not all that many people yet. A steel rope was stretched across the river from the top of the bluff on the Mexican side and down to the Tejas shore on the river's edge. There was a big wooden box hanging from the rope on little wheels. People were in it, and it slid slowly down the rope to the Tejas side. That was amazing.

What is this thing? I asked a man by pointing and giving a questioning look. It was a *tranvía*, a "tramway" he said the gringos called it. Oxen would lower and pull the box back up. Farther down the river was a great iron bridge for the railroad. I had never seen such a big bridge. I wondered what it would be like to ride across it in a train. Maybe I would see one cross.

Güero strung his lariat between little trees and hung the blankets and spare clothes from the dead cowboy's bags and his cooking gear too. Most everything was sold, but it only brought in a little money. Thirty cents for the two blankets. I bartered with a Mexican dealer for the clothes no one wanted and sold all for twenty cents. I gave the shaving brush to a boy who helped chase away beggar children trying to steal from us. It was more money than Papá made in three or four days sometimes. With everything in our shop window sold, we rode up the steep bluff.

We tied up in front of a shop. I could see through the window that it was a gun shop. Güero told me to "*Quédte*"—stay—and went in. I guessed he wanted me to watch our things and the guns, his carbine and my shotgun.

He was inside for only a short time, and when he came out, he had a package. I guessed he bought some ammunition. I hoped he bought some for the shotgun as there were only three shells left. They were smaller than Papá's 12-caliber shotgun and had a "16" on them.

We turned the corner onto a side street, and he dismounted, unslung my shotgun from my saddle, and hung it on his own. He looked up at me when he took it off with a sad look. I started to stop him, but I think he had a reason for taking it. He was not going to sell it. We had left the gun shop.

We rode up the muddy, potholed street. Güero asked

a gringo for directions. A two-floor hotel was our next stop. Again, I waited outside while Güero went in. I looked at the top floor and wondered what it might be like up there. I had never been on a building's second floor. People who stay in hotels must be wealthy. It might be a good place to beg, but they would probably run beggars off. He soon came out with a letter envelope in hand and shoved it into his vest. A letter? Maybe he was more important than I thought.

Getting on his horse, he said, "*¿Quieres una buena comida, niña?*"—Do you want a good meal, girl?

I nodded. I did not know what he had in mind, and I wondered where we would spend the night. Outside of town, pay a quarter to stay in a livery stable?

Güero asked a teamster for directions to some place. We rode to another hotel. It also had two floors. Instead of going to the front door, we rode around to the back where the stables were. The stalls smelled like they were in need of a good mucking out. Now what?

He dismounted, again telling me to "quédte" again. He walked up the back stairs, stomping mud off his boots, and tried to slick down his blond hair. With hat in hand, he knocked on the door and glanced back at me. I grinned.

A woman opened the door. I could not see her well except that she wore a green dress. They were speaking, and she peered over Güero's shoulder to look me over. She had kindly eyes below her gray and yellow hair.

The door closed and Güero came down the stairs with a pleased look. "*Comemos.*"—We eat. We put the horses in stalls and unloaded our gear and saddles. Güero gave them some green hay. Taking up his carbine, he nodded at the shotgun, and I picked it up. We walked around to the front and went in. We went in the front door! I had never gone through the front door of a place like this.

I had never been in a place like this. I had been in few gringo businesses, except general stores and mercantiles, if they let Mexicans come in. Never a hotel or eating place like this. So much more than a cantina. It was the most beautiful place I had ever seen other than churches.

We carried our guns inside. I think Güero had asked if we could. The lady wore a beautiful, shiny green dress, very fancy with white ruffles. She was a handsome lady, maybe in her forties. I followed Güero down a hallway to washing rooms. It had a washbowl and a big pitcher of clear water. The pitcher showed flying birds and flowers of all colors. I was afraid to pick it up. There was also creamy soap that smelled like flowers, but I do not know what kind.

There was a mirror. I peered into it and pulled my hat and shawl off. I did not like what I saw. A dirty, tired face smudged with charcoal and grime. My hair was filthy, greasy, and unbrushed. I looked older. I scrubbed my face with the soap and a little towel. There was a hairbrush. I tried to fluff my hair out and brush it, but it was too tangled and dirty. I washed myself the best I could under my shirt.

Pulling my shawl over my head, I hung my hat on a rack thing with Güero's. He had tried to clean up too, but we looked used up. I was embarrassed to look this way.

The lady led us into a big room full of round tables covered by clean white sheets and four chairs at each one. I had never seen furniture this fancy. We sat at a corner table by a window. There was no one else in the room. It was too early for supper, I guess.

Sitting, I could not stop looking around. The floor was covered by a great blue and green rug. Everything looked so clean and made me feel dirtier. I wondered what the lady thought of us. She seemed kind and had invited us in, after all.

She poured water into the most beautiful glasses I had ever seen. A silver spoon, a knife, and two forks—two, I guessed in case you dropped one—were lying on the table with white towels.

The lady asked Güero his name. "Bud, ma'am, Bud Eugen."

Bud Eugen? He had never told me. Bud? What kind of name was that? The only Spanish word like it was *buding.* That meant "pudding."

The lady said her name was Mrs. Moran. Bud told her I was Marta, and I guessed he told her I could not speak.

She asked me, "*¿Como estás, Marta? ¿Bien?*"—How are you, Marta? Good?

All I could do was nod and smile.

She told us to have a good dinner, "*Buen provecho.*"

A pretty young Mexican girl, older than me, wearing a black dress and white apron, brought a big platter with our food. We got thick slices of beef, gringo beans, little skinned potatoes, some kind of green leafy stuff, and big white soft rolls. There was creamy butter, something I seldom ever saw. I could not get over how much food there was and how good it tasted. I had trouble cutting up the meat. I watched Bud—I still thought that an odd name—to see how he did it. Using the fork to hold the meat still, he cut it up in little squares. I would have only cut it up in strips and eaten it with my fingers. He switched plates with me so I could easily eat. That was very kind.

The girl brought fancy cups and kept them filled with the best tasting coffee I ever had. Much better than… Bud's. There was a bowl of sugar, and I put three spoonfuls in my coffee cup. Bud only put a little. The cups looked as fragile as egg shells and even whiter.

I was not used to potatoes and the green stuff, but I ate them, even if the potatoes were bland and greens bitter. I was hungry. The soft rolls were good with butter, but I would rather have tortillas.

The young woman brought us apple pie. I had eaten pie one or two times, but it never tasted this good, and this was hot too. I ate it fast, and Bud gave me his after eating only a few bites. I did not know why he would not like it.

Mrs. Moran asked if we liked the food, and Bud said we did. I thought they talked about how much it all cost.

Bud brought out the letter and asked Mrs. Moran to read it. She had him open it, and he handed her the letter. She read it, and I could tell by her voice and how Bud looked that it was not good news.

Mrs. Moran sat at the table talking to Bud, and he told her about how he found me, I guessed. I could not understand what was going on. They talked for a long time, and I heard my name often. Was he trying to leave me here? If he did, I thought they would put me to work. This would not be a bad place to work, but I did not like the idea. I do not know why. For some reason, Bud was protecting me, even if he did want to leave me someplace. What did that mean? With all that had happened to me and knowing how dangerous life on the road was, having a protector was something I wanted above all things. It felt strange that it was a gringo, a simple cowboy, who made me feel safer and more protected than I ever had.

They kept talking. I became bored and lit a cigarette. The girl brought me another piece of pie. I certainly liked that. It was boring watching people pass on the street. Finally, something seemed to have been decided, and Bud was pleased.

We moved our gear into a small room at the end of the stables. It could have smelled better. There were two small beds. I pushed one against the other and laid out our bedrolls. To make sure death would not visit us, I made certain the foot of the beds pointed toward the door. Bud looked at me strangely but shrugged his shoulders. It looked like we were staying here for now. I hung Bud's saddlebag and canvas bag on pegs. Bud put the saddles in the tack room. I cleaned out the dead cowboy's saddlebags, making them mine. While I swept out our room and dusted, Bud cared for our horses and looked over Mrs. Moran's two carriage horses. He went to work mucking out the eight two-horse stalls. He dug out the wet spots in the stalls where piss had settled and sprinkled lime dust. By the time Bud was through, it smelled better.

I was washing our saddle blankets and hanging them on a fence when the Mexican girl beckoned me from the back door. I went to her, and she said her name was Yolanda Ruiz Barros. She was eighteen and taller than me by a head. She came from *piedras negra,* across the Río.

"I speak good Americano if you need to talk to Mrs. Moran. I can help you."

I nodded and smiled. I wondered what she thought of me, being mute, all dirty with worn-out clothes and following a gringo cowboy. She probably thought I was a whore or at best a beggar. I was I guess, the second one, not the first.

"We can go inside and talk. Will you?"

I followed her in. At the bottom of the stairs, I looked up. I was going to get my wish to go to a second floor. It was not hard to do but seemed strange. There was a bar on the wall, and I held onto it. There were sixteen steps. We went into one of the eight upstairs rooms. Four more were downstairs. It was a very nice room. I went to a window and could see across the Río into Mexico.

"Do you understand any Americano?"

I squinched my face and held my thumb and forefinger a nail head's width apart.

"Only a little," she said, smiling.

Yolanda pointed to a chair for me to sit on, and she sat on the bed. She told me about the hotel and Mrs. Moran and what a kind woman she was. She had taken us in because we looked like we were in need. I did not like that. We could take care of ourselves. That surprised me thinking that. "We can take care of ourselves," as if we were together. Yolanda said Mrs. Moran told Bud we could stay here a week or so and work for room and board.

Bud's letter. He had been laid off from a ranch near Austin for the winter. The rancher thought highly of Bud and had recommended him to a friend with a ranch near Laredo. Bud was supposed to meet him at that other hotel when the rancher visited for business. Things had turned bad for the rancher, and he could not hire Bud and had to leave early. So here I was throwing in with an out-of-work cowboy with no prospects, much like me.

I thought about this as Yolanda said Mrs. Moran had talked to Bud and said he was a good, honest man.

I knew that. So Bud had no job. If I had to, I could take care of myself, in a way, with God's grace and the Virgin's intercession. Maybe he would find work. With the two of us together, we were better off, I thought. Bud might not understand that. I was not sure if I did.

Yolanda asked many yes and no questions, and it took much time for her to understand me. To say Bud, I would hook a finger over my lip like his mustache. She learned I was a nómada and that I was from Las Vacas, across from Del Rio upriver.

She wanted to know why I could not speak. I tried to show how I was kicked in the head, my left forehead where there is a scar under my hair, by an animal. Her third guess was a mule. I did not understand it. How would a kick to the head do that? I could understand if I had been kicked in the throat. I was unconscious for three days and came to surrounded by candles. That frightened me, and my familia had thought I would never return to them. I had a gash on my forehead, and I simply could not speak or even make sounds anything like words. Laughing, crying, screaming, I could only make strange, embarrassing noises. I was nine and did not want to ever be seen by anyone. I was totally silent, making no noise of any kind. I did not want Mamá and Papá to tell people I could not talk. I was only a very quiet girl. Mamá told others it was in my nature to be shy and hide from sight. It made some people uncomfortable when I gave out my strange laugh. When they found out that I was mute, they usually thought I was stupid too and even deaf. I let them believe that, and I could learn a great deal by listening. Over time, I grew out of my shyness. Later, I did not care if they knew, and I did not even miss not talking, usually. I wished I could talk to Bud, though. We had much to learn and understand about each other.

"I saw that you pushed the two beds together." She was embarrassed, but she finally asked if we were intimate.

I shook my head no and tried to laugh.

"I am only asking because I want you to be safe. I have never heard of that. I mean you sleep with him, and he has not made advances toward you?"

Head shake. I wrapped my arms around myself and shivered.

"You do it to stay warm?"

I nodded and smiled.

"Is there anything he has done that you do not like?"

Strong head shake. I did not like that he was trying to give me away. I was unable to explain that to Yolanda. It looked like he was letting me stay, for now anyway.

"Mrs. Moran says he likes you, as a sort of friend."

That surprised me. I had not thought about anything

like that. Why would a gringo like a mute Mexican girl who was…troublesome, that others thought was a whore or stupid?

With much explanation, I managed to ask Yolanda what Bud meant.

She looked thoughtful and said, "I think it means like a friend. They have a word for that. Buddy. Bud is like the nicknames many of us Mexicans have."

So, Bud meant friend. That was good, I guessed. If that was a nickname, then what was his real name? I did not know how to ask that. Another mystery.

Yolanda looked at the floor and then asked, "What does he mean to you?"

I could not answer. I only smiled and nodded my head. There was a word I wanted to answer with.

Esperanza.

Chapter Nine

Hope.

That was what Bud meant to me.

Bud took me bird and rabbit hunting with him. He did not want me to go at first, but I found that if I ignored him, I could usually do what I wanted. He did not understand anything about women. He was easy.

To make a point, I did not ask him to saddle or boost me onto my horse. I rolled a nail keg over, saddled the horse, and climbed on. Bud had me carry a feed sack for dead game.

Outside of town we dismounted and walked through the grass to flush out rabbits and quail. Bud was a pretty good shot, but I knew that. He only missed a rabbit once and was a little angry with himself. I think he judged himself too hard.

I grew bored picking up bloody rabbits and birds and finally got his attention, letting him know I wanted the shotgun. He said something, and I was sure he questioned if I could shoot it. He probably thought it would knock me on my butt. With a smile, he handed it to me unloaded—I guess to see if I would check and know how to load it. I thumbed the lever to the right to break open the barrels and held out my hand. He gave me two shells. They were smaller than Papá's 12-caliber. The bottom of the shell had a "16" on it instead of a "12." I pushed in the shells and closed the barrels. Bud moved behind me, the safest place, I guess. I cocked the right hammer, and keeping the shotgun pointed up, I turned to Bud. I pointed to the front trigger and then the right barrel to let him know that I knew which barrel it fired. He started telling me how to shoot it, but I paid him no mind.

Standing still, I waited for the surroundings to return to its natural calm. Only the wind. Bud knew enough not to move, not to speak.

I brought the butt stock up to my shoulder, the barrel down a little, and I stepped forward slow and easy, feeling with my toes before setting my heels down. A quail lifted out of the flourensia bushes twenty *vara* before me. I snapped the barrel up, pulled the butt harder into my shoulder, and squeezed the trigger. The bird dropped in a puff of feathers. I ran to the bird and held it high with feathers dropping off.

Bud's mouth fell open. I shot two more and wasted not a cartridge. Heading back to the hotel, he let me carry the shotgun. On the street, Bud stopped an ugly cowboy. His beard was mangy and as filthy as could be. His lip was cut through up to his nose and unhealed. Bud asked him something, and the man snarled as ugly as he looked. I would not have asked this man anything, even if I could speak his language and could speak, for that matter. He sounded rude and crude. Bud shook his head and rode on. Most Texicans would have gotten into a fight. Bud did not bother.

I realized how grubby and dirty I appeared one morning when I was mopping the upstairs hallway. I swept and mopped all the hallways and public rooms every day.

A pinched face Texican woman with a little girl, maybe ten, I thought, came out of a room. She glared down her nose at me and pulled the girl to the side. She said something to her and pointed at me. I understood two or three words. She probably told her to stay away from the dirty Mexican.

I was used to such, and it did not bother me. I was dirty most of the time. I did not want to be, but on the road, one had little choice. Then I thought how embarrassed I would be if someone said that when Bud was with me. I resolved to clean up, for Bud.

Friday, I washed clothes and bed sheets with Yolanda and an older Mexican woman who came every Friday to help. It took most of the day and was hard, hot work. Washing my two dresses, petticoats, and shirts, the water turned muddy. I did not know I was so filthy, but we never washed in the winter. When I dunked myself in the hot water tub set in the laundry room, the water muddied almost as much. It had been almost two months since the streams were warm enough to bathe. I had never bathed in a galvanized tub with hot water. There was all the soap one needed, and it smelled of flowers. Yolanda washed my hair with castile soap, and then the lye soap used for clothes. The water in the washbowl was river brown. She rinsed my hair with a little apple cider vinegar in water. It smelled so good. After drying it, she brushed my hair for the longest time. I felt clean for once. Yolanda loaned me a traditional white, flower-embroidered dress. It was far too big for me but would do until my clothes dried.

I had never worn a dress like this and certainly never a white one. The few skirts and shirts I had were all black, brown, or gray. I ran out the back door into the cold wind to fetch my shawl that was hanging to dry. Bud had already bathed and was in our room stitching on some of his gear. Running into the room, I dropped the towel from over my combed hair. It hung in waves past my waist. I never let men see all my hair for fear of lustful thoughts.

Bud's mouth dropped open. We both stopped, and I gazed into his eyes. In some way, I felt he liked what he saw, and then this turned into embarrassment. I threw my towel over my head, grabbed my shawl, and ran back into the hotel kitchen. Bud just about ran into the stable. I could see out the window that it was suddenly necessary to feed the horses.

I felt uncomfortable about going to bed that night. Bud had held a strange look in his eyes. I feared what Mamá had told me it could lead to. I stayed up late that night learning to knit from Yolanda. Bud was asleep when I quietly crawled into bed. With clean bedding and clothes, he smelled good. I only wanted to be close to him.

Saturday night, Bud disappeared. I guessed he might have gone drinking as most men did. I worried because he knew no one that I knew of, and there were rough men in the saloons. Yolanda told me that Mrs. Moran said she was worried because Saturday nights seemed to be the worst with fights and even shootings. I thought about going to look for him, but wandering the streets alone and visiting saloons was not a good idea. Anyway, most men did not like for their woman to watch over them.

Did I think that—that I was his woman? That was a

sudden and unexpected thought. I would have to think about this.

Everyone usually turned in at eight thirty or nine o'clock. Ten came and went, and I was worried. So was Mrs. Moran.

I showed that I wanted to look for him and put on my coat. Mrs. Moran told Yolanda I could not go. The streets were not safe for a lone girl. I did not think she could stop me.

A knock on the door, and a boy came in, glancing about the foyer. "*¿Señoría Moran? Del mariscal.*" He handed her a note.

She paid him a penny and looked up with a serious face. "*¡Bud está en la cárcel!*"—Bud is in jail!

A great fear plunged through me. In jail? I headed for the door without my coat. I did not know where the jail was. Mrs. Moran stopped me. She would go with me. The three of us hitched the horses to the wagon. Mrs. Moran had Yolanda bring two blankets for him. It was very cold, and Yolanda said the jail had no blankets or a stove.

At the jail, we found Bud had gotten drunk, was thrown out of the saloon, and was beaten up by several men. One of the men attacked him with a knife, but a deputy marshal knocked the man out. Bud and the man were thrown in jail. We could pay his fine in the morning.

I was let into the room with the cells. The jailer, a horrid nasty man, banged a ladle on the bars to wake up Bud. He was lying on the dirt floor in his vomit and blood. He was a mess, covered with mud and horseshit from being dragged through the street. Lying in the next cell was the terrible man with the split lip we had seen the other day. Bud looked horrible, peering up at me like he didn't know who I was, but he was embarrassed too. I felt sorry for him, but I was angry. I stuck the blankets through the bars. I was so disappointed in him that I ran out of the jail.

Mrs. Moran would not let me stay in the stable alone and especially on such a cold night. I stayed in an empty hotel room. Alone, worrying, I barely slept. I was angry. Why did he let himself get into this? I had expected better of him.

In the morning once the guests were taken care of, Mrs. Moran and I took the wagon to the jail to fetch Bud. It was so cold on the wagon seat. The horrid jailer, who looked like he should be locked in a cell on principle, brought Bud out. For a moment, my heart skipped, but I looked at Mrs. Moran's hardened face and put that look on my own.

Bud looked terrible leaning against the door. Mrs. Moran riled at him for the longest time. She was not at all pleased with his conduct. Bud was shamefaced to no end. Mrs. Morgan paid his fine. I was grateful for that. She made Bud drive the wagon. Mrs. Moran continued to give him her mind, even pounding her hand on her leg. I was going to wrap up in his blankets, but they were too filthy.

Bud had to take another bath, and I again washed his clothes and blankets with Yolanda's help.

That night Bud was very sad and quiet. He had a long talk with Mrs. Moran. He barely ate. Bud avoided even looking at me and just hung his head. He was surprised when I crawled into bed that night, as if he expected me to sleep someplace else.

In the morning, he picked at his breakfast and went to his chores without saying a word. At supper, he gave me a hairbrush he had bought. It had a Texas star carved into its black walnut handle. I knew he was asking for forgiveness. I gave him a smile and patted his hand. I could forgive him. He made a mistake. He was only a man, after all, but a good one.

Something else happened that day, something not so good. I had gone upstairs for towels when Bud was bathing. I got two out of the hallway linen closet and went to the stairs. A guest came out of number eight and motioned to me. He was a horse trader. He motioned to me saying, "Señorita bla, bla, bla…" He went back into his room and picked a used towel off the bed and held it out to me. I started into his room to give him one I had. I stopped. That look. I cannot describe it, but I knew what it was. Mrs. Moran and Yolanda had told me never to go alone into a guest's room, ever. I shook my head and crossed my arms. Then he held up a silver dollar. I saw now what he wanted. I motioned for him to follow me. He waved for me again, but I turned and went down the hall. I unlocked a door, opened it, and smiled to him. He walked right into the room, I guess thinking it was empty and I was taking him up on his offer. I was only a working Mexican girl, so I must have been a whore. I shut the linen closet door and locked it. Going downstairs, I thought he would think about his transgressions in the dark for a while and I would send Bud to let him out.

Later, Mrs. Moran wanted to know what had happened to the linen closet door. It appeared to have been kicked open from the inside. Strange. I knew nothing. The next day number eight was very courteous, trusting I would say nothing of his indiscretions to anyone. I did not think he knew I could not tell anyone anyway.

Yolanda told me the next day that Bud had asked around if there was a place in Piedras Negras for me. I became angry. He was still trying to give me away! She also said he had looked into placing me in the St. Josepha's Academy, a fine girl's school. That would be wonderful! Like me, Bud was illiterate, but he had actually thought of putting me in a school. I was surprised he cared for me that much. But they told him they could not take me because I could not speak, and it cost twenty dollars a month, more money than Bud had expected. Now I was sad.

The next day we saddled our horses, and I thought we were going hunting. When I picked up my shotgun, he shook his head. Instead, we rode down to Our Lady of Refuge Catholic Church. I knew right away what he was doing. He was going to see if they would take me. By the time we got there, I was scared. It was a bigger church than in Uvalde. They probably had more money. They might take me in. Why was he so set on giving me away? I tried to take care of him. I liked him. I knew he was a good man. Was it because I could not speak? When we tied our horses to the rail, I grabbed his arms and looked into his eyes. I shook my head, trying to show my great sadness. *Keep me!* I wanted to scream. *I am only safe with you!* He looked as miserable as me. Why was he doing this if it made him unhappy?

A Mexican monk appeared behind Bud. Brother Miguel spoke Americano, and I could tell Bud was asking him if they could take me in. I thought he said I was a good worker or good cook.

To me, the brother said, "I have told him I have no place for you. I do, but I can tell that you do not wish to be left here." Looking at me with an arched eyebrow, he said, "You would rather stay with him?"

I nodded fervently.

"So I thought. Does he treat you well?"

Nod.

"Has he forced you to fornicate out of wedlock?"

I shook my head hard and gave him a glare, but not too hard of a glare. He was religious.

He was surprised. "Are you telling the truth, my child? You would say this in confession?"

I nodded. Not that I could do confession in the normal manner.

He gave us a blessing and said he hoped he would see me at mass. After talking more with Bud, he said, "Go with God."

Mrs. Moran and Yolanda were happy to see us when we returned. Yolanda worked out what had happened.

I was still angry with Bud. I tried not to show it. Somehow, he thought he was doing what was best for me, and maybe he thought he could not provide for me, being out of work. He was better for me than me being alone. He was better for me than anyone I knew. Why was I feeling this way?

Perhaps to make up to me, he gave me two sets of long johns and three pairs of black socks. These were warmer than my shirt and skirt. I would wear them under my regular clothes. The socks were better than my foot wraps. In the icy cold of morning, we would run into the kitchen in our long johns with our clothes in our arms. I wore my shawl. Yolanda always laughed at the sight as we rushed to dress by the stove. Once Bud toppled over trying to get a leg in his pants, and we all laughed. He just sat on the floor and asked for a cup of coffee.

We stayed at the hotel beyond a "week or so." Yolanda said that Mrs. Moran appreciated our work, and we did not cost much to feed since we hunted up quail and rabbit stew. Her guests paid well for quail.

I was peeling potatoes on the back porch one day. It came to me that I now had a horse, saddle, shotgun, and some warm clothes. Those were things that no girl like me could have. I was very fortunate, and I took time to pray to God for his generosity and thank Him again for Bud.

I went to Yolanda, and with much effort, I used my hands to show a flying bird and then a hopping rabbit. Then I acted like I was shooting my shotgun and played like I put the shot bird in a cooking pot. The birds and rabbits we shot were free for the hotel but cost Bud for the shells. Maybe we should be paid for our trouble? I held up five fingers and rubbed my other two together—the money I wanted.

"*¿Cinco dólares?*"—Five dollars? she asked, laughing.

No, I shook my head.

"*¿Cinco centavos?*"

I nodded.

Laughing, she called Mrs. Moran into the kitchen and told her I wanted to hunt birds and rabbits for her to cook and how much I wanted for them.

Mrs. Moran looked at me with a half-smile. "*Se hace*"—it is done—and shook my hand.

I put on my coat and socks and pulled on my sandals. I cut finger holes in a pair of old socks to use for gloves. Bud was mucking out the stables as I saddled my horse while standing on the nail keg. With my shotgun and feed sack, I rode out. Bud looked back and watched me trot down the street. At least he did not try and stop me. Maybe he was learning that I was hard to stop.

When I reached a secluded place, I tied the horse to an acacia sapling and looked out over the campo, so full of life even in the winter. It was a much colder winter than what I recalled from the past. As much as I disliked the wind and cold, it enlivened me. It felt like I drew from its strength facing it head-on. I prayed to Saint Hubert, the patron saint of hunters, for a sure eye and steady hand.

I was blessed. I filled the bag with rabbit, squirrel, and quail in three hours and only wasted a couple of shots. I brought back the empty shells because Bud could sell them to the gun store. Mrs. Moran paid me sixty-five cents. I could find time to hunt two or three times a week. That was good money.

I had to gut and clean them, which did not take long, but I was not very good in picking out all the birdshot.

Bud was proud of me. I could tell by looking into his eyes the color of the sky. But he was still sad. Yolanda told me that cowboys did not like doing other work, especially in a hotel or shops. The only other thing he could do was ride the chuck line. She told me what that was. Out of work cowboys rode from ranch to ranch asking for handouts. It was like the begging I have had to do. I could not see Bud doing that. He was too proud. He would consider that dishonorable. I think too he would not want me to see him doing that. I knew in my heart that he would not let me beg.

We were blessed with good fortune as we were in a safe place for now, but we could not count on staying here. Bud especially. This was not the place for him. Where was his place? Where was my place? Were our places with each other? No! That could not be. I was only a poor mute Mexican girl. Undeserving of...anything really.

Bud, he was different.

Creo que me gusta.

Chapter Ten

I think I like him.

Yolanda hurried up the stairs all excited. "There is a man here, a friend of Mrs. Moran. He is a rancher with a big spread up near Del Rio, the DeWitt Ranch. They call it the Dew. He is talking to Bud!"

My eyes went wide. That could mean a job. Yolanda laughed at my expression. We crept down the stairs and listened. Yolanda whispered what she could hear, which was little.

"He is *Señor* Clay DeWitt. He is a good man. He is asking Bud about what work he has done.

"He says there are troubles with bandidos from across the Río. He needs guards to stop the rustling. He also needs a good tracker. Is Bud a tracker?"

Yes, he is, I thought grimly. At least he could track lone girls. I nodded.

Yolanda grew excited. "Señor DeWitt asked if he

wants a job! Twenty dollars a month and twenty-five after the first month!"

That was a great deal of money. I gripped Yolanda's arm.

"They are going to have supper together," she said. "I think Señor DeWitt likes your man."

My man? I did not expect her to say that, even if we slept in the same bed.

Then she turned to me. "Bud will leave for the ranch in the morning."

That surprised me. I had not thought about that. With him gone, what would become of me? We were only to work here for a short time.

Bud left on foot before supper, but he came back soon. He had a package and put it on his bunk. I peeked, and it held cartons of pistol and shotgun cartridges.

During supper, there was a lot of laughing with Bud and Señor DeWitt telling ranch stories. Mrs. Moran called Yolanda and me into the kitchen. She told me that Bud asked her to take care of me, that he would send her money.

He was leaving me here? Just like that? He had bought shotgun shells. Was he leaving those for me to hunt, or was he taking my shotgun? Where would I sleep? I could not stay in the stable alone. Why was he doing this? Did I do something wrong?

"He says he will come back and take you to the ranch later."

Why not take me now? Would he really come back and when? He probably would forget me. I had no way to ask those questions.

"You are to share my room," said Yolanda.

So be it. My face burned with anger. I went to our room and took my bedroll, saddlebags, and tote bag to Yolanda's room. I left my saddle in the tack room. I did not see Bud. I would let him know what it is like to sleep alone on a cold night.

I cried during the night. Yolanda held me, saying that he would come back. I did not think so.

I awoke angry. Bud and Señor DeWitt had an early breakfast. Had they left already? I found out Bud was going to the ranch while Señor DeWitt would stay longer for business. It was two days and a morning's ride to the Dew Ranch. While they ate, Yolanda and I moved my bed into her room. I could not find my shotgun. That bothered me. I did not leave the kitchen.

Mrs. Moran through Yolanda told me that Bud was saddling the horses and loading the burro.

Saddling the horses? He was taking my horse?

Mrs. Moran told me that I should take all my gear to the front porch and be ready to ride.

What did she mean? Yolanda urged me to hurry, and she helped carry everything. I put on my coat and hat. What was going on? Yolanda and Mrs. Moran were acting like they were plotting something.

Bud rode from around back with both horses and the burro. My saddle was on my horse, and my shotgun hung from his saddle. He was surprised to see me.

Yolanda said he was going to sell my horse and my saddle.

Bud was looking at me all sad. Yolanda translated for him, "Marta, I cannot do this. I cannot take you. Where I am going is not safe. There are bad people."

"He says he will be back for you sometime."

Sometime? There were bad people here too, everywhere.

He turned his horse, and with the others, trotted up the street and turned up another. Snapping his *cuarta*, they picked up speed. He did not look back.

I would not give up. I would shamelessly run after him. I could see what was going to happen or what I wanted to happen. If I could catch up with him, I did not think he would run me off.

There was God and destiny and accepting whatever came to you.

I would not accept this. I knew I could catch him.

I picked up everything with Yolanda's help, the bedroll, saddlebags, tote bag with the bean pot, and the canteen. It was almost impossible to carry.

Yolanda yelled, "*¡Corre como el viento, Marta!*"—Run like the wind!

I tried to run but could not, and the mud made it worse. I trudged up the road as fast as I could. My knees hurt, and I dropped things. I knew I could reach him late tonight after he made camp. How far would I have walk?

Up the street he had turned onto, I could see him at the livery stable. That was where he was going to sell my horse and saddle! If he was going to come back for me, what was I supposed to ride? Walk behind him like a *peón's* woman? I went faster.

The owner, his name was Juan, and Bud were going to unsaddle my horse when I ran through the gate and slipped in the mud. I scrambled to my feet.

Bud turned. Now he looked angry. He came stomping over. I thought he would start yelling at me to go back. Instead, he yanked away my saddlebags and tied them behind the sorrel's saddle. I tried to pull them back but let go and fell against the corral.

Bud and Juan were talking, and I realized they were talking about Juan buying my horse. Then I realized he was telling Juan that he was keeping the horse. He changed his mind. Why? Because I would not quit and came after him? He was taking me.

Tears filled my eyes, and I could not think straight I was so happy. I flung my bedroll and tote bag onto the burro and tied them on with diamond hitches like Bud had taught me. *He is taking me!*

I hung my canteen on the sorrel, and I took my shotgun from Bud's horse and hung it on mine. Bud and Juan were still talking about me, I thought. I was trying to wipe the mud off after breaking the ice in the water trough.

Bud did not say anything. He turned his horse and headed out. I tucked my skirt, dragged a sawhorse to the sorrel, and scrambled onto it. I waved to Juan, and he waved back grinning. I followed, wearing the biggest smile in the world.

I breathed a prayer of thankfulness and felt deep inside that my world was going to change further, more than it had already.

Yolanda had told me the ranch, the Dew, was about fifteen ligas. At first, Bud talked to himself, and I am sure he was talking about me. Maybe he did not know why he had taken me or what our future was. Mostly we traveled in silence. We did not have to talk.

I did not think about what would become of us together. I just knew I had a protector, one I could trust without question. He had a job, and I was sure I could find some kind of work at the ranch. Maybe that was one fear of his. He had been hired by Señor DeWitt, and I was not. Maybe he feared they would not like him to show up with a mute Mexican girl. I tried not to think that they might tell me to go elsewhere. Maybe they would let me stay. I could be very useful, and I worked hard.

It felt good to be on the trail again. I liked to be on the move. I would miss Yolanda and the generous hotel food, but we were going someplace new to work. It grew a little warmer, and the clouds cleared up. It was a nice day for a new beginning.

Every liga or two, we crossed a deep arroyo with gravel-bottomed streams running to the río. After crossing one, we stopped for dinner. Bud unsaddled the horses and relieved the burro of its load. We ate fried chicken, frijoles, and biscuits Mrs. Moran had given Bud. We ate them cold sitting on a saddle blanket. Mrs. Moran had also given Bud a jar of molasses. Bud called it "lick." It made the anglo biscuits taste better. I put it on any kind of bready stuff. It was good on tortillas too. I think other Mexicans would disapprove. We packed up. Even the horses seemed happy to be on the move after over two weeks in a stable.

I mostly rode beside Bud, but coming up out of the arroyo, I was behind him. The road turned to the left at the top of the bank. I saw a flash of white just ahead of Bud. A skinny peón stepped from behind a creosote-covered mound. I could not fully see him because he was blocking the trail standing in front of Bud. What was this? Was he looking for a handout?

Oh no! Bud raised his hands. I looked around. I saw no one else. The peón could not see much of me, and I could see little of him. I heard him order Bud off the horse. I slid the shotgun out as Bud slung a leg over his saddle, his hands still up. He slid onto the ground, revealing me to the bandit, an old worn-out peón holding a huge pistol, a kind I had never before seen.

I cocked both hammers. His already wide eyes went wider. He was so scared doing this holdup that he had no wits left. He pleased me by dropping the pistol and reached as high as he could.

Bud glanced at me with a little grin. He walked up to him and kicked the big pistol away before bothering to pull his own. He stuck his pistol between the peón's eyes.

For a moment, I thought he was going to shoot the man, and I prayed he would not. Instead, he holstered his pistol and told the old man off. He turned to his saddlebag and took out the leftover chicken and biscuits and handed them to the man. I thought that was amazingly kind of Bud, but this man had threatened us. It was obvious the man was desperate to have done this.

Bud told the would-be bandit to vamos. That is when I thought this foolish man was getting off too easy. He needed to be taught a lesson.

The horses and Bud jumped when I squeezed the shotgun's trigger, and the man flipped over.

"Marta, no!" Bud shouted followed by, "bla, bla, bla!" His face was shocked.

I laughed my strange laugh. I pointed, and Bud turned to see the unwounded peón scramble up, grab the dropped food, and run like a chicken.

Bud bla, bla, bla'ed about something, all angry with me, but I could tell he was trying to keep from laughing.

I reloaded my shotgun. I do not think there would be any question that it was my shotgun now. I do not think the peón would attempt any more holdups.

Shaking his head, he called me "treacherous," which must have been the same as *traicionero*. I laughed, sort of. Bud pulled his carbine and laid it across his lap. We kept our eyes open now.

We met only some freight wagons on the road and a few lone drifters. Bud always talked to them, seeking news about the road ahead. He always told them about the would-be bandit and showed them the pistol. I learned it was only a single shot, an old army pistol. They would peer at me and my shotgun.

One bearded teamster would not speak to him when he saw me. I guess he did not like the idea of a Texican taking up with a Mexican. That must be what he thought.

No matter. I was used to being disliked by gringos.

Bud was talking to a Mexican teamster with a load of brown coal, and he asked about a name for my horse. The teamster said *Rojizo* was good because of his reddish color. I liked that, Rojizo would be his name. It was the sign I was looking for because we had not spilled red blood, and maybe an otherwise good man had learned a lesson.

That night we cooked and ate far off the road, only simple trail food, and moved to a no-fire campsite. Bud was cautious because the Río was no more than a liga away, sometimes closer.

Late the next morning, we came upon a shaved post with "DeW" branded on it. A side trail ran up a low ridge.

"*La mitad liga,*" Bud said. "*El rancho.*" Half a league.

I could not wait to see this new place. It might be our…my new home. It might be for only for a short time. If Bud stayed, I hoped to stay. I did not know why this was so important. Protection, I felt safe with him. That was all there was to it. I was safe.

We stopped side by side atop the ridge. We were looking down on the rancho. It looked so small from here. There were whitewashed adobe buildings. This made the place look comfortable and wealthy. It was unusual to see painted ranch buildings. The windmill turned, standing tall among the mesquite trees. There were many corrals, some with horses.

We looked at each other and shrugged. Tapping our heels into the horses, we followed the road down the side of the ridge and were soon on the ranch grounds.

Mi esperanza era que este fuera un buen lugar.

THE DEW

CHAPTER ELEVEN

My hope was that this would be a good place.

I heard the rider come up behind us before Bud did. He had his carbine out and spoke to Bud while riding around us and giving us a good look-over. He was suspicious, and I could tell things were on edge here. The cowboy was maybe a little older than Bud. He was asking Bud questions about himself and then me. I was used to being talked about and not knowing what was said, as if I wasn't there. That did not mean I liked it. The cowboy relaxed, and then they were talking about his carbine, just like men. For the first time, I noticed Bud's had a longer barrel than most others.

The cowboy rode with us to a *potrero* where we put the horses and burro and unsaddled them. Bud piled out gear while I led the horses to the water trough. Three Mexican kids were making mud and stick dolls and showed them to me, saying the names they had given them. I fed the horses some stale tortillas, and Rojizo rubbed his muzzle against my face. I think he was starting to like me. He had forgotten by now the cowboy who owned him.

A Mexican lady walked up to the potrero. She was tall and handsome, her long hair done up in a bun. Her dress was tan with just enough green leaf embroidery to add color. She looked sure of herself, and I knew that somehow she was in charge.

"*Buenos dias,*" she said. "*Soy Gabriella Guerrera.*"

Bud told her he had been hired by Señor DeWitt. He introduced me and told her I could not speak and why. He also told her that I could cook, clean, and wash in hopes I might be given a job. She was the majordomo, the jefa overseeing the ranch house and the workers. She could be called Doña Gabriella, but everyone called her Gabi.

"*Marta, ven conmigo.*" I went with her to the house where I could clean up and she wanted to talk to me. Taking my saddlebags, I looked back at Bud and gave him a little wave. I had good feelings about this.

Sitting in chairs on the front porch were a lady and two girls, both blondes and very pretty. I was surprised that Gabi introduced me in Spanish. Señor DeWitt spoke a little Spanish, but the two girls, Doris and Agnes, spoke very good Spanish. They were sixteen and fourteen and green-eyed like their mother. Agnes was shy, but Doris was very outgoing and shook my hand. They were all tall. Even Agnes was half a head taller than me. Gabi told them why I could not speak. Everyone shook their heads and said they were sorry. That embarrassed me. It was just the way I was.

Carmela Flores was the *jefa* of cooks, and her daughter Inés was with her. I liked her looks, a big smile. She was seventeen and also taller than me. Everyone was taller than me.

The house was very nice with shiny plank floors and furniture like the hotel. There were many rooms and inside and outside kitchens. Gabi took me to a washroom outside and said I could clean up. It had a water pipe from a windmill. She stayed and talked asking yes and no questions much like Yolanda. I took off my shawl, rebozo, shirt, and long johns top. I tried to keep my back turned to Gabi, but I had to turn to show expression, shake and nod my head, and wave my hands. It was the only way I could talk. She asked about Bud too, if he was a good and honest man, if he worked hard, and if I had no problems with him. I nodded yes to all of her questions.

She asked if I was his woman.

No, I shook my head. I could not explain that we slept together but were not intimate. Maybe Bud could explain. Maybe she would understand. Maybe she would believe it, maybe not. But I knew that men did not like to speak of these things to women.

She told me much about the Dew, the nickname for the DeWitt Ranch. It was 48,000 acres, and while times were hard because of the harsh winter, they were doing well enough. Señor DeWitt was a good man and treated everyone well. He was a good businessman too. He had spent a great deal on a fine huge bull called Quicksilver to improve his stock.

Cleaned up and feeling very good now, Gabi said that night I could take a real hot water tub bath. "A good woman is a clean woman." She took me to the kitchens. They had everything needed to cook good meals. Like the washroom, a water pipe ran to both kitchens. There was a beautiful Glenwood double-oven and stove in the inside kitchen like at the hotel—its brass polished bright. The outside kitchen had an old style single-oven and stove. Huge pots of frijoles and goat stew bubbled on the stove. Also, outside was a big brick oven and grill.

The coal bin was full of black coal, not cheap brown coal making a lot of smoke and poor heat. The inside kitchen had a linseed-polished oxblood floor. Very fine indeed.

I thought it strange that at the stove Gabi asked me to fry her an egg. "I do not like burned eggs or runny yolks."

I melted a dab of lard in a skillet and gently cracked the egg so the yolk did not break. I slid the egg onto a plate. Not even the edges were brown, and the yolk was firm.

Gabi took a bite and said, "I cannot pay you, Marta, but if you cook and work hard, you will eat and have a place to sleep."

I nodded my head, smiling, and bowed.

"None of that here," she said. "Then let us start. We can use the help. Most of the crew will be in for dinner."

She found me a too big white shirt and a red and white checkered apron. I would not have been able to fry such a fair egg if not for Yolanda at the Fitch Hotel. Gabi gave me the egg to finish.

I met the two cook's helpers, daughters of ranch workers. Gabi said there were ten or twelve Mexican workers with their families here, and Señor DeWitt gave them odd jobs. They were not vaqueros, but some helped the cowboys when needed. There were also two vaqueros. One was a guard like Bud would be, a monitor they called it.

I did not understand why guards were needed on a ranch. On most ranches, the vaqueros and cowboys protected the herds from rustlers and predators. Here they needed full-time guards, like vigilantes. It must have been because we were close to the Río. That made me worry about Bud.

They put me to mashing frijoles to make frijoles refritos. It all happened very fast, and the place was unknown to me. I was a little confused, and I wanted Bud near me.

Maybe like me, he had already been put to work.

As I stacked tortillas on a platter, I thought, *Where am I going to sleep? Where will Bud stay? In the bunkhouse with the rest of the cowboys?* I had not thought about that. The bunkhouse was a place that no woman entered, ever. Inés said I would be dismayed at its state of cleanliness. They threw cigarette butts and matches on the floor, sweeping them out with the accumulated dirt only when they too often stuck to boots.

Agnes called. The cowboys were coming in. We all rushed to the front of the house. Inés said this was fun to watch.

There were nine of them. Inés pointed out Lee Cleland, the foreman, and Chico Munoz, a vaquero. She liked him, but he was the silent kind—cold and calm. Bud was like that, but he was warm, not cold, I thought.

They came in hard, whooping and yelling, and thundered into a potrero, putting on a show. Some leaped off their horses with flamboyant style, a couple of them landing on their faces and acting like they had meant to do that for fun. They were all what we called *camoiso duro*—range tough. As they unsaddled, we girls carried the food to a pole barn where plank tables stood. We set the pots of goat stew, frijoles refritos, coffee, and a platter of tortillas on a long table.

Some of the men were looking me over. That did not feel good, even if I was used to it. I saw Bud with Lee, the foreman, and he gave me a wave and smile. I felt much better. Bud and Lee ate together, and I guessed Lee was telling Bud about the ranch and what his job was.

The girls told me about the ranch. They all liked it here, and none of the men gave them trouble, too much. By the questions they asked, I could tell that Gabi had told the other girls my family was murdered, that I was a nómada, and I rode in with Bud.

We started to clean up and took the pots back to the kitchen. As the cowboys finished eating, they scraped their plates into a big can. They also washed their dishes in a tub of soapy water. They did not do it very well, and Inés and I finished washing them. She did not complain. At least most of the grease and crud had been scraped off. We carried the can of scrapings and tortilla bits to the pig pen. At the kitchen, everything was washed, the floor mopped, and tables cleaned. Carmela would not tolerate a messy kitchen.

Three meals a day. This would be a lot of work. The family's meals were made separate from the cowboys' and other paid workers. The unpaid Mexicans did their own cooking. They were nómadas like my familia and had found a place with some work. They would not have to spend the winter on the road, a very bad life that my familia had sometimes endured.

I would show them how good a cook I was. I looked over the food supplies and found everything I needed to make my frijoles. It took convincing on my part for Carmela to let me cook supper, especially because she did not really understand what I would make. They would have a treat tonight, even if I had not made my meal for such a large number.

We had enough frijoles going, but much needed to be added. That had to simmer in the frijoles so the flavors would merge into the frijoles. There were no tomatoes this time of year, so I put in three cans of stewed tomatoes. Not the best, but better than none. I chopped up onions, green peppers, tomatillos, and jalapeños. Next were garlic cloves and cilantro. There was some bacon and chorizo sausage left over from breakfast. I chopped them up. Once all this was stirred in, I dropped in some ham hocks and diced smoked ham that I first browned.

There was a knock on the back door, and I found Bud

there. I was happy to see him. I took him by the hand and showed him tonight's frijoles. He took in a deep, exaggerated breath to show how much it pleased him. He wanted to see Gabi, and I took him into the dining room where she was setting the family's table.

He seemed sad talking to Gabi, and I heard my name. Gabi told me that Bud was going out to guard on the Río for three or four days. He was to pick up the food he needed. He could come in once a day for a meal. That was good; I could see him then. Gabi had Inés give him canned food, jerky, hard biscuits, and tortillas.

He gave me a goodbye hug, and I hugged him back. I did not care if others saw us. He was sad when he left, giving me a last look over his shoulder.

Gabi told me he was sad because he was going to sleep in the feed shed tonight. There was no room in the bunkhouse. They had a tent for new hires, but I do not think Bud liked that, either. I would sleep with Carmela and Inés in the adobe used by the house staff. They had their own room there. Gabi and Lee had rooms there too. She said Roberto would make both Bud and I cots.

I would miss Bud when he was out. I accepted that. Work was important, but when he was there, I did not like that we could not sleep together as we had for so long. I would miss his comfort and warmth. And that night I was to sleep in the adobe.

The crew came in just before dark and were much quieter than at noon. Such was their work day. They were hungry, though, and my frijoles caused much comment and praise. We also made biscuits and apricots and pears boiled with sugar for dessert. Carmela called me out and introduced me to the crew. They actually applauded.

Bud sat with Lee during supper and talked more.

After supper, the men sat around a fire talking like men did and not about anything important. On the trail, Bud and I would sit together at our fire and drink coffee and smoke the cigarettes I rolled. We did not have to talk to feel comfortable. I missed that.

We cleaned the dishes and pots, mopped the floor, and washed down the tables and benches. At least we did not have to clean up what the men dropped on the ground under the tables. The ranch dogs took care of that chore.

My thoughts turned sour. Did Bud want it this way? Here among all these men, did he not want to be associated with a simple mute Mexican girl? A nómada no better than a peón?

The men were walking off to the bunkhouse and new-hire tent. They had to be up before dawn. We had to be up even earlier to make their breakfast.

I walked toward Bud, who was kicking dirt onto the fire. The air was chilly. I stood looking at him, trying to understand why he wanted to be alone. I was angry too because his job took him away from me. It was all so confusing.

He said, "*Lo siento*"—I am sorry.

Was he telling me goodbye? That he did not want to be with me there? I wished I could speak, even if only in Spanish. So I could say something. It was so hard to understand all this.

I walked off to the courtyard and the adobe where I would sleep. It took a great deal for me not to slam the door to Carmela's and Inés' room—they were already in their cots. A candle was burning on the windowsill. I unrolled my bedroll in the corner, took off my shirt and skirt, and crawled into the blankets. My anger refused to let me sleep.

I woke up. I thought I heard Bud's breathing as I was used to, but it was only Carmela. It was too lonely and too cold there. I would not let that man do this to me. My place was with him when I could. The candle was almost burned down. I crawled out and rolled up my bedroll as quietly as I could. I bundled my clothes under my arm. Lifting it over my shoulder, Inés whispered, "Where are you going?"

I kneeled beside her cot and jerked my head to the side, toward the feed shed.

"Go to him," she said.

Yes, I thought. *I will.* I stalked out of the adobe wearing only long johns.

Bud had spread sweet-smelling alfalfa in a thick comfortable pile. His feet were toward the door. He was learning.

I laid out my bedroll beside him, and I did not try and get in his. I did not want to wake him. It would not be as warm, but it was not too cold. There was more to being next to him than only keeping warm. My anger for him was gone. He brought me here even if he was going to leave me behind on some days. That must mean something.

Inés hissed from the door, barely heard. It was time to start breakfast. I realized Bud was already awake. I got up and rolled my bedroll. He had slept dressed and pulled on his boots. It looked as if he wanted an early start. My anger clouded again, and I stood staring at him. He was sure in a hurry to leave. I snorted and went to the kitchen to start coffee. Some of the cowboys saw me leaving the shed. They would be talking about that, I was sure.

No matter. I knew Bud was an honorable man.

The sky was dim and hazy. I ran outside and watched

Bud and Lee disappear over the ridge.

Es mi lugar.

CHAPTER TWELVE

It is my place.

I had doubts. Why would I want to take up with this gringo? We were so different. We could barely speak to each other, even in only the simplest ways. But I could understand him sometimes. Sometimes he might have even understood my arm waving, stomping, and expressions. Maybe he would learn more Spanish. Would he do that for me? Maybe I could learn more Americano. Did I really want to? For him, yes.

He was protecting me. Even then, when he was out on the campo guarding the cattle and the ranch, he was protecting me. Bud was gone for four days, but since he came in each day to eat, I could see him.

Gabi told me that with Bud, now there were three monitors or guards. They rode alone along the Río and Sycamore Creek. The other two were a gringo named Gent and a Mexican they called Flaco. I did not know his real name. Flaco was a nickname for a skinny man. There were stories about him—that he had been a rustler himself and had also been a Rurale, the federal mounted police. They were often just as bad as bandits.

If one of the monitors needed help, he would fire three shots, and the others would ride to him. I found myself listening and fearing to hear three shots, but they were usually too far from the ranch house to hear.

Today four men rode into the ranch. The Mexican workers disappeared with mothers running out and grabbing their children's hands. I saw no reason to be frightened, but I stayed out of sight and watched. One of our cowboys, the one guarding the ranch house that day, followed them. I had not learned his name yet.

They wore gray and brown vaquero's outfits, tight trousers buttoned up the sides of the legs, short jackets, vests, sombreros, and guns. I thought they were Rurales. They had that hard look.

Their leader was an older man, aloof and distant. He wore a black jacket and vest. He had the look of a *hacendado*, with a huge mustache and sideburns down to his jaws. He was not to be trusted. They were not Rurales.

Señor DeWitt and Lee were not there. Gabi was. They spoke, and the hacendado pointed toward the distant little huts where the few nómadas stayed.

What is this? I asked myself.

Inés was hurried into the kitchen by her mamá. They were both very frightened.

I looked at Carmela with a question in my eyes.

"The man is Don Alejandro of Hacienda San Nicolas. There is nothing saintly about the hacienda or that man."

Roberto came out and talked to the man with Gabi. Roberto did most of the blacksmithing and carpentry work. Inés said he was also a kind of jefe for any nómadas here. I at first did not even know any were here.

When I found out, I visited them, but I did not know any of them from past wanderings.

One of the hacendado's men rode over to the nómadas' crude little camp.

Carmela came back to the kitchen. More frightened than before. Why? "That scorpion Don Alejandro wants to buy a nómada family who can cook and work in his kitchen."

Buy? He wants to buy a family? That happened. My own familia, God protect their souls, had been bought several times. It was only temporary. Families were not kept. But I have never heard of them being bought outright from an Americano ranch. It was not slavery. That had been outlawed in Mexico long before it was in America. It was a gratuity paid to the ranch or farm on which the nómadas worked.

It was not long before the family was hurried to the hacendado for inspection. Besides the mamá and papá, there were three boys and a girl, the oldest.

Carmela said, "The girl, Lucrecia, is fifteen. If she is still a virgin, she will not be for long. Don Alejandro will see to that."

I could not believe Gabi was giving them over. They were not chattel. What was he paying her? I knew it would not be much. It never was for our familia. I could not stand this. I ran out the back door. Carmela tried to stop me, but I was fast and agile. I ran to Gabi, jammed my fists on my hips, and gave her my most severe, "*What is the meaning of this?*" glare.

Gabi was obviously angry that I came out.

I looked at the girl. She was pretty. She was scared.

Don Alejandro dismounted and made a show of looking over the family and asking the papá questions. It was obvious he was more interested in the girl.

I did not like the man's look.

He turned his attention to me, like a coyote taking notice of a plumper chicken, not that I was plump. I suddenly felt naked with his piercing stare.

Looking at Gabi, he asked, "Is this one a good cook?" He said it like he was buying a horse.

Gabi put on an angry look and said. "No, she is not. She is only good for house cleaning."

"Then why is she wearing an apron with bean juice splattered on it?"

He was a hard man to fool.

"She helps with cooking, and as you can see, she is very sloppy and not very good at it," Gabi said back to him.

I am not! I thought angrily. But I knew what she was trying to do.

He nodded slowly, not believing her at all. "We will see." Looking at me with what he probably thought was a sincere and honest look, he said, "Would you like to cook for me? I will pay you fifteen dollars a month."

That was a huge amount. No cook was paid that. I knew he would not pay that even if he promised. He had something else in mind, and I had no doubt what that was.

Gabi gave me a very slight head shake. She did not have to warn me.

I looked him in the eye and firmly shook my head *no.*

"You are passing up a wonderful opportunity. I would like to hear you say that you do not want this."

Gabi said, "She is mute and a great deal of trouble."

I turned and walked away.

"No one turns their back on me," shouted the hacendado. "I will pay twenty dollars for her, the same as for this family."

I kept walking.

Gabi shouted, "She said no."

I went into the kitchen and slammed the door. Carmela whispered bitterly, "You should not have gone out there. You put us all in danger."

Danger? What was this?

Gabi came into the kitchen. "They are gone."

"Did they take the nómadas?" asked Carmela.

"Yes," Gabi said unhappily.

I gave her the hardest glare I could.

Gabi looked painfully at me. "Marta, Don Alejandro came because he is looking for Inés."

I was confused, and it showed in my eyes.

"Inés was caught by Don Alejandro when she ran off two weeks ago because she wanted to be on her own." Carmela glared at Inés like Mamá used to glare at me when I became rebellious. "He took her to his hacienda on the other side of the Río near San Carlos. He would have his way with her, but she escaped before he could. It took three days to find her way home."

I never thought anyone could be so brave, to be lost like that and make her way home on her own.

Still, I did not understand why Gabi had let the hacendado take the family for twenty dollars. Gabi tried to explain it to me. She needed to make him leave to protect Inés. She knew there was no justification for endangering the familia and one girl for another. It was the way it was. Sometimes we had to make impossible choices.

It was unfair and painful, but I understood. It was the way of the land.

One afternoon I made Gabi and Carmela understand that I wanted to go hunting. That took much explanation and waving my shotgun around—I assured them it was unloaded. I would bring back many rabbits. They let me go alone because they knew Bud and Flaco and Gent were out there on the range. I think too they did not want to confront my will. Bud had been out for three days.

I had split my skirt and petticoat front and back and sewed them up by candlelight. It made it easier to sit a saddle, and when on my feet, few noticed that the skirt was slit.

Filling my skirt pockets with shells, I took my shotgun and canteen and walked to the potrero. Rojizo was as excited to ride as I. I flung up the saddle and bridled him. He knew to stand with his left side far enough from the fence's mesquite limbs to let me climb up them and swing onto the saddle. I shoved the shotgun into its scabbard, strapped on the canteen, and tied on an empty feed sack. The air was cool with a promise of colder to come. The sky was free of clouds. "Only in Texas," I heard anglos say—freezing air and a clear sunny sky. I had on my heavy jacket. As a last thought, I started to set my sombrero on the gatepost, but kept it and later put it on because of the sun.

I pulled my hair out from under my shawl and let the breeze catch it. I wanted to be free like that wind. I realized the wind could go in only one direction. I could change direction whenever I wanted. Who had the most freedom?

Gabi pointed to the north-northeast and said if I went over the ridge, half a liga farther was where Quicksand Creek ran into Sycamore Creek. The Sycamore was the north side of the ranch next to our neighbors, the Vermejo-Maxwell Ranch, the V-Bar-M. Nobody trusted old man Maxwell.

I guessed that along the streams would be a good place to find rabbits and maybe squirrels in the trees. Squirrels did not offer much meat, so I always tried to get two with one shot. I never had too much luck at that.

There were rabbits all over the place. They were taking advantage of the cool sunny day to forage for food. Tying Rojizo to an oak sapling, I crept low through the brush, feeling as free as a deer. Creeping slowly, I was easily killing rabbits. I only missed once. The sun was in my eyes…really.

Searching for more rabbits, I saw a rider on the low ridge on the other side of Quicksand Creek. I recognized Bud in moments. I had seen him enough on a horse. I had seven rabbits when I mounted Rojizo and waved to Bud. He waved back with his hat, and my heart felt lifted as high as the sun. We splashed across the shallow quicksand. They had told me there was no quicksand in the creek. The sand bottom was hard. Galloping up to Bud, I circled around him, happy to see him. I held up a rabbit, and he understood I was asking if he wanted dinner.

Bud quickly built a small fire while I skinned and gutted the rabbit. I sharpened a spit and started the rabbit roasting. Bud cut open a tin of Americano frijoles and set them on the fire's edge. He had tortillas, and we tore off strips of meat, wrapping them in frijoles. We spread a blanket and sat side by side.

It was the simplest of hurried meals, but it was a grand one. Rolling cigarettes, I lit them with a burning stick. We watched the beginnings of the sunset over Mexico. The sky was like merging rivers of pinks, blues, purples, and pale reds.

I slid an arm around Bud's shoulder. After a spell, he wrapped me with his arm. This suddenly felt right. We could not speak to each other, but we could in a way. We could understand each other if we tried. I had to be patient with him. He could be patient with me. It only meant that he had to work a little harder.

I felt good for once. I felt safe. I pulled away from Bud and kneeled before him. Staring into his eyes, he did not look away but held my stare.

¿A dónde vamos?

CHAPTER THIRTEEN

Where are we going?

Bud and I, where were we off to? Not where we were actually going, but where were our lives going?

I slept on the floor in Carmela's and Inés' room when Bud was out. He spent the night at the ranch only once or twice a week. I missed him. I liked the feed shed, even with scampering mice. I liked the smell of the molasses oats and alfalfa. It was comfortable with the straw mattresses and pillows filled with *alforfón*—buckwheat husks.

There was no stove, and we had to be careful with the oil lamp. No candles. We had a bucket of sand in case of an accident. I had nailed a piece of canvas tarp to the inside of the plank door to keep out the wind. Our cots stood side by side, so I was always warm when Bud was there. I knew I could trust him. I started thinking of him now being my familia.

Why was that? He protected me. We worked together on our chores. It was not much, but he shared everything he had with me. He kept me warm. I knew he would be there if I needed his help. Yes, he was my familia.

I always gave him especially good beefsteaks or an extra ladleful of my frijoles at supper and a cup of buttermilk when I could get it.

I did what I could for him and our home. Was this our *casa*, our home? I washed the bedrolls, made them up like a real bed, swept the floor, and cleaned cobwebs from ceiling corners. I always had a smile for him and took his boots off when he turned in.

I wanted to show Bud I trusted him. Yes, I shared a bed with him, but there was something more I wanted to do. So one night I stepped into our little casa. Bud was stitching a repair in his saddlebags. He was always repairing something when I came in from finishing kitchen chores. I turned up the oil lamp on a crate.

I turned my back to Bud as customary and took off my shirt, skirt, and petticoat. I slept in long johns with my scarf over my head. I have been told that gringo women sleep in special clothes called nightgowns.

Bud always looked away out of respect. I looked at him over my shoulder and dropped my black scarf. I knew it would fall almost to my behind, my thick black hair. It glistened in light like this. I fluffed it out and swung around, spreading it like a flag.

I knew one thing. Bud's eyes said he liked what he saw. I smiled and cut my eyes to the side. I felt naughty, then embarrassed, but I did not let him know that.

He held me very close that night.

Gabi said barely a day passed that something unexpected happened on a ranch. She should try living on the road, I thought.

One morning a vaquero galloped in asking for Doña Gabriella. They were bringing in a man who was arrow-shot. Gabi told him to bring the man to the outside kitchen. She rushed inside and brought out the medicine chest.

Three vaqueros from Rancho Mariposa across the Río came in at a slow pace, one with an arrow fast in his right thigh. Gabi called for Carmela and Inés. I went too. I knew something about arrows. Indios sometimes enjoyed practicing on Mexicans they found on the road. I had helped take arrows out several times. Sometimes there were three to five arrows. When an indio arrow hit a person, it stopped them and made them an easy target. I remember a man arrow-shot four times in the legs so he could not run. Mamá and I got the arrows out. One we had to cut off the feather end of the shaft and push it through. He screamed terribly. One arrow we pulled out, but the arrowhead had stuck in a bone and came off the shaft. We could not get it out. He died horribly of gangrene infection in just a week.

Another time an eleven-year-old boy, then barely older than me, was shot in the belly. Mamá said there was little hope since it was in the upper belly. There would be more bleeding up there and more intestines to be pierced than in the lower belly. She said the shit from the opened intestines would burn like fire and was certain death. We got the arrow out, but the boy died a screaming death as the women prayed, asking forgiveness of his sins. Sometimes when a person was dying that way, the men cut his throat to spare him the unbearable and he could die with dignity. Dignity? Sometimes the women would not allow that. God gave life, and only God could take it away. But then sometimes mothers begged them to release their child or husband from their agony.

I sat beside that boy for a long time. I wondered what it was like to die that way. He knew he had no chance. He was only a year older than me. Would I have a short life like him? I should have already been dead from the mule's kick. And from another time when I almost drowned. Three times I suffered high fevers, but because of Mamá's care, I made it. There had to be more to life than this. I have heard priests say so. But then they promised eternal life with God if we did not sin and repented what sins we had committed.

I wanted there to be more to life than forever walking up a road hoping to find work and food and not be misused too often.

Gabi turned my attention back to the vaquero lying on the table. "Marta, take off his boot." She had already given him a draught of laudanum, with him making a face to its bitterness.

I worked it off and tried to move his leg as little as possible. The shaft had been cut off to a hand's length. Carmela very carefully cut the pants leg from cuff to waist band, which was tight as vaqueros favored. Gabi peeled the blood-soaked cloth open and slid it off. He was embarrassed with his loincloth showing.

"What is your name?" asked Inés.

"Antonio." He took a swallow of tequila from the bottle she held for him.

"This will hurt," said Gabi. She pressed down on the arrow, just a little.

"*¡Aye yai yai!*"

"See. I am always right."

Next, she tried to carefully turn the shaft. It did not move and got a groan from Antonio. "The arrowhead is lodged in the thigh bone. We must be very careful, or it may part from the shaft. They do that more often than not."

She took a leather belt with a buckle and turn screw from the medicine chest. She looked him in the eye and said, "We must remove your loincloth. I am going to put a tourniquet around your leg at the hip joint."

He shook his head no.

"Antonio, the arrow is very close to your main thigh artery. If the arrowhead cuts it, you could bleed to death before I could do anything. I am always right," she reminded him.

He covered himself with his sombrero, which Gabi pushed out of the way, calling him foolish. She took off the loincloth.

"Do not be embarrassed," she said. "I have seen real men before."

We all laughed. Me with my peculiar cackle. Antonio's *amigos* laughed with us. He held the loincloth over his privates.

The other vaqueros told us they were coming back from Del Rio to cross back to their ranch at the Sheep's Head, a good crossing place. They met two indios on horseback. Lipan Apaches, the others said. They wanted the vaqueros to trade two rabbits they had shot with arrows. They wanted a big knife one of the vaqueros carried, which he held up for us to see. They told the indios no, and as they galloped away, one turned and shot an arrow. They brought the wounded man to the Dew because of Gabi's medical reputation.

Gabi said, "That is good to know. Since they were rabbit hunting, this is probably a very small arrowhead." As she strapped on the tourniquet, she added, "If all goes well, we will not need this." She tightened it.

She had one vaquero hold Antonio's legs along with Carmela, and the other gripped his arms. Inés placed a short leather strap from the medical chest between his teeth. He did not look happy.

Gabi held a thin metal rod. "This is a bullet probe," she told me. "It will help me feel for the arrowhead and work it out." She gave me a bandage of cotton and gauze she had prepared. "As soon as I pull out the shaft, arrowhead or not, put this over the wound and press hard. This will hurt," she again warned Antonio. Crossing herself, she nodded to us all to hold the bold vaquero down. I crossed myself too, asking the Virgin to protect this man and guide me to do the right thing.

She carefully slid the probe down the shaft's side. Antonio sucked in his breath and clamped the leather between his teeth. "I can feel the arrowhead," she breathed. "Maybe three inches deep."

I did not know what an inch was. I questioned with my eyebrows.

"*Tres pulgadas*."

I nodded.

She had Inés place her fingers on the edge of the puncture and spread it open. Blood trickled out. Antonio bit even harder, inhaling with a gasp. Gripping the shaft with one hand, Gabi used the probe to work the arrowhead out. The shaft moved slowly. She shifted the probe. More blood flowed. Antonio's eyes were clamped shut as tight as his teeth.

Out came the arrowhead and a flow of blood. I slapped on the bandage and pressed as hard as I could. Gabi set aside the bloody shaft and took over from me. Satisfied the blood flow was light, she had Inés again spread the wound open, and Gabi dribbled in mercurochrome, setting Antonio to gasp.

Inés held the tequila bottle to his lips, and he took two greedy gulps. His head dropped back on the table. He muttered something malicious about indios and revenge.

Gabi pressed on the bandage, and I helped wrap it tightly. Holding up the arrow shaft, she wiped the blood off and looked closely at the tip. "It does not look like any of the point broke off."

Antonio's amigos carried him to a chair to rest. Gabi said they could stay the night, but they wanted to return to Rancho Mariposa for more men and go after the indios. She warned them to clean the wound. "Arrows are more likely to become infected than a bullet."

"Marta," said Gabi as I cleaned the bloody table to prepare dinner, "you did very well. You have treated wounds before."

I nodded and spread my arms to show I had many times.

"You are a very useful girl. We are fortunate to have you here."

That made me feel good.

Señor DeWitt returned from Eagle Pass the day Bud came in for a night off. I had already taken my bedroll to the feed shed and swept out the dust and mouse shit. I was excited. I would not feel alone tonight.

I could not finish my after-supper chores fast enough. Carmela let me go early. She is such a blessing.

Most of the cowboys sat around a fire, something they did every night no matter how cold unless it was raining or sleeting.

I wrapped up in my serape and took my place beside Bud on a log. I lit a cigarette and passed it to him, and then lit my own. I was the only woman. I wondered what the other cowboys thought of that. From what I saw, they were good men, hardworking, and got along with one another. I was treated with courtesy, if not the full respect that Gabi had earned.

There was one I did not like. On Bud's first day out with Lee, the foreman showing him around, they had caught two hungry drifters who had butchered a cow on the Del Rio-Eagle Pass Road. Gent, another monitor, had been with them. Lee had Bud and Gent throw ropes over a limb to hang the two cattle murderers, but it was only to scare them. Lee ended up hiring them. We had beefsteaks that night. Sessuns seemed a good man, but Weyland was bitter and mean spirited.

Weyland sat across the fire from us and was giving me a mean stare. He was trouble, I could tell. Some of the cowboys were telling stories, and I think a couple were making fun of Weyland. He did not like it.

After a time, the boys left to turn in. I lit the oil lamp I had brought. Weyland walked past us. Bud was still sitting on the log. With a mean look, Weyland started saying something about me. Mean things I could tell were making Bud angry.

Bud turned to look at me, and Weyland scooped up a burning log and threw it at Bud with sparks flying. Bud stepped back, and the log missed, but he tripped over a crate and fell hard on his butt. Weyland made a run at him, knocking Bud down again. I had never seen two men fight so. They were all over the place swinging, punching, and kicking. Everyone was yelling, and those who had gone in were outside again. I could not tell who was winning. They were giving it to one another pretty hard. Weyland picked up the burning log again, and Bud dove into him, knocking him down and sending the log flying. They were still swinging and kicking when Lee shouted something for them to quit the brawl. Both looked like they were about to fall over. Bud staggered back and turned away. Weyland again picked up the burning log.

I had to do something. Weyland was going to throw the log. Bud was barely staying on his feet. I did the only reasonable thing I could. With all my strength, I threw the oil lamp at Weyland's back and hit him solid. Sparks and flames burst, and his jacket caught fire. I clapped with joy.

Everyone was beating on the screaming Weyland with their coats and jackets, even Bud. Why was he doing that? I clung to my serape. I did not want it used to put Weyland out. Lee was still yelling. They rolled Weyland onto his back to finally smother the flames. Bud was on his knees, holding his smoking jacket after beating out the fire.

Lee and the cowboys were all making comments, I thought mostly about me. I did not know if I was in trouble. Probably so. I was breathing hard like I had run to the Río and back. I flipped my cigarette butt at Weyland. Then I was hoping Weyland was not too badly hurt.

Things settled down as Lee fussed at Weyland. His jacket was a little burned, but he was not actually hurt except a few little scorches. Lee told everyone to turn in and talked to Bud. He wasn't angry with Bud, and it did not sound like I was in trouble. Lee nodded at me and winked. Some of the men were looking at me a little fearfully, or maybe it was with respect.

I got a wet towel and caught up with Bud as he limped to the feed shed. I touched his face, gave him a worried look, and he smiled back. I think he was pleased I had watched his back. He nodded, and I took his arm as we walked. He talked to me some as we lay in bed. I do not know what he said, but I liked to hear him. It was not often that he said much. He said a lot that night holding me very close and tight.

That was our first week at the Dew.

Me gusta aquí.

CHAPTER FOURTEEN

I like it here.

Carmela treated me like another daughter, and Inés became a good friend. She could speak a little English taught by Gabi and Doris. We played tricks on one another, hiding kitchen utensils from the other. Sometimes we got in trouble because Carmela could not find something we had hidden.

Inés very much liked Héctor Vega—Flaco. They were together when he came in once a day. When Flaco came in for a night, Carmela kept Inés close at hand. I liked Flaco too. He was rugged and handsome. I knew that he and Bud had become friends; they trusted one another. I learned that the trust between two men is special. It is important that they be able to count on each other. There were stories about Flaco—that he had once been a bandido, but also a Rurale, who were scarier than bandidos. He had vaqueroed on different ranches in Mexico and

Tejas. It was also said he had been a scalp hunter and known by name to Apaches who sought him for revenge. They called him the *ch'ishoogi*—the Vulture—an eater of the dead. Scary, but he was very nice to me.

Bud would ride in once a day, usually for dinner. I was always glad to see him, but sad that he would not be here during the night. He would camp out in some hidden place near the Río as alone as me.

Inés liked beads. She bought and traded for them from indios and notions peddlers visiting the Dew. She made some of her own, finding unusual stones along the Río and streams, polishing them smooth, and drilling holes through them using Roberto's brace and bit.

I had an idea for a necklace for Bud. Inés helped me pick rocks, and I drew a picture of how I wanted it to look. On a rawhide cord, I threaded the big beads with knots separating them. I used blue and brown like the sky and earth, and orange too of different shades, like the sun. In the front, I put a white and a tan bead. White for Bud and tan for me. I felt silly using white for Bud. He was sun-browned almost as dark as me, but that was what gringos were called, white, even if they were pale rose to leather brown.

I wanted this to be special. It was a simple thing, but I made it, and it meant much to me just as Bud meant much to me. I could understand that now. He was a good man, he could be trusted, he protected me, he wanted a better life, and he was warm. Maybe I could be part of that better life. But I was only a mute Mexican girl with nothing of value beyond a horse and a shotgun. That was my dowry, and the only reason I had it was because of Bud.

When it was time for bed, I went into our sweet-smelling room. Bud was cleaning his cartridges as he did every time he came in. I took off my shirt and skirt, and then facing him in my long johns, I pulled off my shawl and let my hair fall in waves. He was surprised I had revealed my hair so suddenly. With the necklace in my hands, I stepped close and tied it around his neck. I held up my little mirror for him to see. The white and tan beads were tied in front, and with a finger, I pointed to each and then each of us so he would know what they meant, him and me.

He placed his hand over his heart and touched my lips. He understood. We had given one another our hearts. I threw my arms around him, and we hugged each other as hard as we could. Maybe not him. He could have hurt me with his squeeze. I laughed, or tried to, and after blowing out the lamp, crawled into bed to be protected in warmth. He could finish cleaning the cartridges in the morning before he left again.

I woke and Bud was making ready to leave. I hugged him, dressed as fast as I could, and made for the kitchen. I wanted him to at least have some hot tortillas, bacon, and frijoles before setting off into the cold fog.

I hated seeing him leave. He said he would try to come in that night for supper. If not then, for breakfast. I wished he did not have to leave, ever.

There was a strange occurrence at dinnertime, although at the time it seemed routine enough. With dogs nipping at his horse's fetlocks, a young vaquero was brought in by Musty.

Gabi and Carmela were suspicious as always, as they should have been of strangers on the *Frontera.*

He was seventeen or eighteen, I thought, and very confident and handsome. A thin mustache edged his full lips with eyebrows as thin. His teeth were white and smiling. His tight pants were buttoned their full length. Silver buttons dressed his short jacket and pants. His big sombrero and shirt were fawn tan. He was confident and at least one time had money. Being so young, I wondered if he was as good of a vaquero as he tried to look.

Gabi asked, "From where do you come and to where do you go?"

Still smiling, he said, "I come from the Winan Ranch up at Rocksprings. I was let go for the winter as so many."

"Where is that?" she asked. I could tell she knew. She was testing him.

"Edward County. Eighteen to twenty ligas northeast."

Gabi nodded in agreement. "Where are you going?"

"Home to San Miguel."

"That is not a good place to be," she said, a hint of suspicion on her face.

"It is home, and I have no other place to go." I knew how he felt. His smile turned into a grim expression for a moment. "Maybe I can make it a better place."

"Someone should." She looked doubtful.

I looked questioningly at Inés.

"A very bad village about six ligas across the Río," she said. "Bandidos have taken it over."

"Where is your carbine?" she asked. His carbine scabbard was empty. He had no gun belt, either.

"Road bandidos took my guns," he said and frowned. "Except one I hid." He patted a small pistol tucked in his sash. "They took my saddlebags too."

"Do you want something to eat before you go on your way?" Gabi was not very subtle that he should be moving on and soon. "There is no work here."

"I would be indebted for a simple meal."

Gabi sent him down to the nómadas' camp. Roberto's son went with him. I knew he was to stay with him and make sure he left when finished. His horse was a good one, a rojo—red. The horse was not the usual red-brown, but noticeably reddish. He had a good saddle and new boots. I wondered why the bandidos had left him with anything. They would leave a person naked on the road if it suited them, maybe alive, but more likely dead. His bedroll was next to nothing. He suffered very cold nights, although he could probably find a Mexican family who would feed and put him up for a night in their jacalito.

Passing Inés and me, he slowed and swept his sombrero in a wide fanfare arc. "I am humbled to be in the presence of such beautiful ladies." His eyes and white teeth flashed.

Inés giggled. I frowned. She should know better than to be tempted by such a boy. Still, he was handsome and seemed to be genuinely kind.

"Little one," he said with his eyes on me. I crossed my arms and glared. "You are so serious. I only compliment both of you for your beauty because it is true. Your beauty astounds me." He placed his sombrero on his head. "Perhaps fate will allow me to see you again." He bowed and waved and spurred his horse away with Roberto's son following, who was looking back at us with a silly grin.

"Both of you!" shouted Carmela. "Neither one of you have anything to do with that boy. Do not even speak to him. His golden words will only lure you into trouble."

We both started laughing. "Mamá, Marta will never speak to him!"

"You know what I mean. Stay away from him!"

"He is not a boy, Mamá. He is a real vaquero!" Inés was all smiles, her eyes flashing.

"He is real trouble. Now get back to work, you two! We have real men to feed." She swiped her ladle at Inés' backside.

I watched him ride off. There was something about him. I had met many people on the road, and I had learned to tell who was troublesome or deceitful. Him,

I could not tell.

I had expected him to visit with the cowboys when they came in for dinner, hoping to catch interest if they needed another man. No one saw him leave. He was there and then gone. He even slipped past Roberto's son.

Bud did not come in that night. I was looking forward to seeing him in the morning.

When I slept in Carmela's and Inés' room, I spread my bedroll in a corner. I did not want to be troubled by having to move my cot back and forth. Keeping it in the feed shed made it seem permanent. Carmela was concerned about how uncomfortable it was to sleep on the floor. It did not bother me. I had slept on the road all my life and seldom under a roof, much less on a bed. A pad of straw was a luxury.

"Marta!" Someone called me, but I was annoyed by popping noises and only wanted to be left alone. "Marta!" I rolled over, making an aggravated grunting sound. "Marta, get your shotgun!" More pops. I was awake and scrambling from my bedroll. The candle had burned out, and I ran into Inés in the pitch blackness.

A lucifer flared. "Put that out!" warned Carmela.

My shotgun was in the corner. Grabbing it and kicking my feet into sandals, I burst out the door. Jefe Lee and Gabi were running toward the big house. They both had carbines. Cowboys were running out of the bunkhouse and tent over to the right. Some ran toward the potrero and the horses. Lee ran there too. They were trying to saddle overly excited horses.

The only shots I heard were far off, beyond the ridge. Bud! He was out there somewhere.

There were sudden pops from the ridge. I saw some flashes and heard thumps as bullets hit the ground and the adobe behind me. One bullet splashed in the water tank beside the windmill. I ran harder and bounced into the big house's wall. I made out Gabi waving at me from the outside kitchen. I ran to her.

"Marta, go to the gate, and do not let anyone in you do not recognize." I took that to mean to shoot any strangers.

There were two walls running from the big house's back to the adobe where we lived, making a big courtyard. There was a plank gate in both walls. The wall was a little higher than me.

I got to the gate and realized I had left my bag of shells in the room. I only had the two shells loaded in the gun. I made sure it was loaded. I heard running footsteps and turned to find Doris with a huge pistol gripped in both hands and a gun belt with cartridges over her shoulder that made her look like a bandido.

Her mother shouted angrily from the kitchen door. Doris smiled and said, "*Tengo que irme*"—I have to go.

Even with the *El Nortada* blowing from the north, we could hear faint pops from the east, the Río. It went quiet. No shots, no shouts. Everyone was waiting to see what happened. Then a few more pops from the direction of the Río. *Bud*, my heart cried. Quiet again. More waiting.

Carmela came out and told me to come in and make coffee. There was a yellow line on the eastern horizon. Shadows were blue. Dawn was near. Lee came into the kitchen with Doris still carrying that big holstered pistol.

He said it was over, whatever it was. When it was light enough, they would ride out, find the monitors, and see what happened. Most likely a cattle-rustling raid. It had happened before. They would have breakfast when they returned.

I would worry about Bud all morning.

Señor DeWitt and Lee took most of the boys out to look for the monitors and to see how many cattle were stolen. They came in before dinner with Bud. Gent and Flaco stayed out. About twenty head were stolen. Bud, though, had a bandido's horse. It turned out to be Jerry Twining's horse the bandidos had taken from him a month before. It still carried his good saddle. The big news was that Bud had killed a bandido and wounded another who got away. They thought there were at least five or six bandidos. Flaco had visited his vaquero friends across the Río, and they too had lost a few head.

When Bud came in, I was so happy I ran out to the potrero and threw myself onto him. I could not hug him hard enough. He was surprised I missed him so much.

I recognized enough words that Doris said to understand she was telling Bud that I was frightened for him. He gave me a squeeze saying, "*Estoy bien*"—I am fine.

He looked tired and unhappy as he ate a late breakfast. I heard others say this is the first time a bandido was killed in these raids. Some were concerned there may be retaliation. I think Bud was troubled by that. Lee told him not to worry about it and that he could stay in tonight. Bud felt he should go back out in case the bandidos came again. That disappointed me, but I understood. I could endure another lonely night in Carmela's and Inés' room.

I gave Bud a jar of tomato-rice and extra fresh tortillas for supper. He liked that, and it is easy to heat up on a small fire. I tried to show in my eyes that I was worried about him, that I wanted him with me. I could tell he understood and that he longed to stay in our feed shed. He could not say it, but I knew he wanted to be with me.

A cat and a mouse could fall in love; it was possible. But would either family allow them to live with them? Would it even be wise to live with either family?

No me importa.

Chapter Fifteen

I do not care.

There was no retaliation, but we were always on guard. Another cowboy was sent to monitor, Dodger Lampe. Gent was shot at one time from across the river, and the monitors found hoof prints on the río bank. Nothing else happened.

Carmela told me about the bandidos. Their leader was a loco man called *El Xiuhcoatl*—shee-oo-ko-ah-tl. I knew what that meant—Fire Serpent in Mamá's and Papá's Náhuatl language. "They say he is a devil and does loco savage things to his victims. He is a master bandido and always outsmarts his enemies." She and Inés told me stories that frightened me. The band of up to one hundred men had a stronghold in San Miguel six ligas across the Río. They often wore gaudy colored shirts and jackets and yellow bandanas.

Carmela said they took over San Miguel a year ago

and had murdered the hacendado some months earlier. His hacienda was failing, and he had fallen from the governor's favor, so no one went after the bandidos. Saltillo, the capital of Coahuila, was far away. It was said the hacendado's son disappeared on his way from Monclova to take possession of the estate. His bones were found a month later in an arroyo outside of Sabinas. He had been dismembered and decapitated, his clothes gone. They knew it was him because he had twice broken his left ankle.

El Xiuhcoatl's band soon took over the hacienda, claiming the family had hired them to guard the estate. They expected the villagers to provide them food, but they themselves were so deprived the bandits had to raid ranchos for food and regularly stole cattle and anything on four legs. Two legs also as they have an appetite for chickens and women.

Carmela whispered, "When the devil El Xiuhcoatl took over the hacienda, he declared he was the law and would protect the villagers. Yes, he did keep away outsiders, but there was no one to protect the people from El Xiuhcoatl.

"Some foolish villagers protested and wanted to complain to the governor and the Rurales. El Xiuhcoatl picked a man and a woman, the loudest of the protesters, stripped them in public, and for hours slowly horse-dragged them through cactus and rocks until shredded and dead. He personally cut off their heads and stuck them on stakes. Their mutilated bodies were thrown in the hog pens."

She told another story. "A young Rancho Mariposa vaquero discovered two bandidos stealing a cow, and he shot at them to chase them away. They shot back and wounded him, knocking him off his horse. El Xiuhcoatl rode up like a black prince, and he ordered the boy stripped. The snake himself shot the boy through both hands, feet, and knees before throwing him in the río, never to be seen again."

I had heard brutal stories before of maiming and torture by bandidos, indios, and scalp-hunters hired by state governors to hunt Apaches. I had never heard of something as horrifying as this. I thought at first they were old wives' tales, but they were too horrible not to be true. Mexico was like that.

"They take the young girls to the hacienda and keep them for weeks at a time to cook, wash, clean, and to have their pleasure. If a girl runs off, they catch her, and after beating her, they drag her before the other girls…"

I waved my arm. I could not listen to anymore.

Most of the cowboys shaved about every three or four days. Most had shaggy hair. Inés and I laughed, watching Musty try and cut Jerry Twining's hair. The chopped hair looked terrible, worse than a mangy goat. Jerry said some bitter words, and all Musty did was laugh more and tell Jerry he did not need for him to cut his hair.

That gave me an idea. Gabi would not let me hunt anymore except near the ranch buildings, so I wasn't able to earn money like before.

Mamá had taught me how to shave and cut Papá's hair. I cut Mamá's, Tlayolot's, and Malinalli's hair too. I missed doing that. I found a wooden tray we did not use. With the nickels I had saved from hunting at the Fitch Hotel and here at the ranch, I bought a pretty good shaving brush and straight razor from some of the cowboys. I used a coffee mug as a shaving soap mug. Gabi gave me a bar of fancy Cody Carpenter soap. She also loaned me the mercurochrome bottle from the medicine chest, "Just in case." She told me that professional barbers hang a towel over their arm to wipe soap off the razor. I used to wipe Papá's on my skirt, but I wanted to be professional. In the barn I found a harness strap to strop my razor. Roberto had a rocking chair with a broken rocker he did not want to repair. He knocked the rockers off and gave me a board for a sign. With Inés' and Doris's help, I painted on the board with bootblack, "*Afeitado y corte de pelo*"—shave & haircut.

Some of the cowboys had to be talked into a shave and haircut. Weyland did not like the idea of me holding a razor to his throat, so he still shaved himself. I charged a nickel for a shave and another for a haircut. I would go down to the nómadas camp. I did not charge them or the other Mexican workers. They always wanted to share food with me. That was unnecessary as I worked in the kitchen.

When Bud came in, he was surprised at my new business. I sat him in the chair. Giggling kids gathered to watch. I trimmed his blond hair, clipped on his mustache and short beard, and shaved him. He went to sleep as I tried to hum a tune. The sun shared a little warmth for once. It felt good taking care of my man.

A few days before Christmas, Lee took Bud, Flaco, Musty, Dodger, Snorter, Slick, and Weyland to Del Rio. The other boys would go in on the New Year. I drew a picture of what I wanted to buy Bud. I saw it in a catalog. I gave Flaco the drawing and twenty nickels. They were buying supplies and going to act like cowboys in town. That meant they would probably get drunk and into trouble. I knew enough about men. They would enjoy the company of women. I did not understand that. Would Bud do the same? I hoped not. I had no claim on him. We were together—we lived together in a way. Would he come back with a pretty blonde gringa and throw me out? I did not know. Carmela and Inés told me not to worry.

He was my man. They could tell.

Still, I worried. I remembered the trouble Bud had gotten into in Eagle Pass.

They came back on Christmas Eve with stories to tell. No one was put in jail. Slick Sealeger, a new hire who had worked before on the Dew, was robbed, but they found the cowboys from the Wormwood Ranch who had done it and got his money and watch back. Weyland was fired by Lee. He was said to have pointed a pistol at Bud. That scared me. No one would say what had happened, but I suspected that it may have had something to do with me. Was Bud defending my honor? I might never know. In his place, Lee hired Ewart Rosecrans.

On Christmas morning we were all invited into the big house. A cedar tree was decorated by Señora DeWitt, Doris, Agnes, Inés, and me. I do not know why they asked us to help. I think Doris wanted us there. They did not see many girls their age. They showed me how to cut colored paper strips, and Inés glued them together, making rings and forming them into chains. We popped popping corn, and with a needle, threaded them together. The paper and popcorn strings were hung on the tree with little painted wooden animals. We set candles all about the great room and stoked up the fireplace. Hot apple cider bubbled in a pot. There were cookies and pies we had all worked hard to bake the day before.

I have never been to a fiesta like this. We all sang songs led by Doris and Agnes. They had beautiful voices, but then all voices were beautiful to me, except for crude men. Most of the songs I had never heard, but we sang a couple of Mexican ones. I say we all sang—I just made some quiet noise, setting Bud to laughing. Not because he was making fun of me but because I was happy. The cowboys did not make much better singing noises. Señor DeWitt gave all the cowboys gifts of tobacco, cigarette papers, and little devices that lit cigarettes. Señora DeWitt and the girls gave everyone wool socks and scarves they had knitted over the year. Bud and I were given gray wool gloves. They were wonderful.

The cowboys had given up money and bought Señor DeWitt an alligator carrying bag. I had seen an alligator once in the Río San Jacinto, like a giant lizard. Señora DeWitt was given a big silver spoon, and the girls got small porcelain angels. They were white and pink with yellow hair. To Lee, they gave a very fine hunting knife, and Gabi was given a beautiful comb. Standing in front of a mirror, she placed the comb in her hair and smiled. We cooked pancakes, eggs, and bacon for breakfast. Señora DeWitt passed a bottle of bourbon around the plank tables for the cowboys' coffee.

It was a wonderful day. I could not think of a place I would rather be.

Bud took me to our feed shed. He pulled a package from under his saddle. I was so excited that I tore the paper apart opening it. I should have saved it for another use. It held a deep blue wool flannel shirt and brown whipcord wool pants. They would be so warm! I hugged Bud and cried. Maybe for too long. Bud was embarrassed. I took off my split skirt and pulled on the pants. They were so high at the waist that they went up almost to my breasts. I put the skirt back on and tucked the pants' bottoms into my socks. Yes, very warm! They also cut the wind. I pulled the split skirt over them. Women did not wear pants openly.

I gave him the green paper package Flaco had brought back from Del Rio. It was a set of nickel-plated spurs like vaqueros wear—twelve-point star rowles. He was surprised and put them on, fastening the leather straps. Bud was acting emotional. I had not expected that. He was very quiet as I put the new blue shirt on over my old black one. My feelings for Bud had never been stronger. I could not tell anyone, even if I could talk, how I felt about him. I did not understand it myself. Would I ever?

We went back to the big house. All the cowboys had to say something about Bud's spurs. Gabi, Señora DeWitt, Doris, Agnes, Carmela, Inés, and I walked down to the camp of the nómadas and the other workers. Flaco and Chico drove a farm cart full of crates. We passed out sacks of rice, frijoles, and masa harina tortilla flour and cans of cooking oil.

Standing in front of their shabby jacalitos, they were grateful and showed much respect to Señora DeWitt, to all of us, really. They were thin and worn looking; that was the way of nómadas. The Dew made sure they were fed enough, and I knew no mistreatment was tolerated. It was embarrassing when they looked at me. I had lived like them. Were they jealous that I had a better life? I was so fortunate and all because of Bud. It came to me that without him I would probably be a rotting pile of bones and rags in the mesquite along some road.

The cowboys spent the afternoon and into the night around their fire. Señor DeWitt was with them much of the time. Bud too, of course. I sat beside him sometimes, but Inés or Doris would call me, and we would serve more food to the men. They must have eaten two hundred goat tacos, a thousand hush puppies dipped in honey, and a great deal of beer and later coffee.

Sitting beside Bud, the sun was long down. It was colder as the fire died. I had my new warm clothes on, and I leaned against Bud with our arms around each other.

"*Hora de dormir*"—Time to sleep, he whispered.

I nodded, and we walked to our shed, me hanging on

his arm. Sometime during the day, he had packed. In the morning he was going out for three days. I missed him already.

I wanted to talk to him so badly, but God proclaimed it not to be. It seemed not to matter. We could understand each other, the important things.

I had heard Papá one night telling Mamá that he could not give their children anything better in this life, that nothing would ever be better. He could give them nothing more than our life now. His voice was so filled with pain and the embarrassment of his failure. He said someday they would be gone, and all they could give us was how to stay alive on thc road. Mamá put her arms around him and said, "You gave them your love, Jaimenacho, and I love you for that." I understood then what love was. I thought I could do more, and when I got older, I would do something for my familia. That had been taken from me too. Maybe I could still make a better life.

I fell asleep nuzzled close to Bud, warm, safe.

In the early hours, I awoke. Bud's hand had slipped over my breast. Was that on purpose? I could tell he was awake, but he tried to make breathing sounds like he was still asleep. I did not mind. I liked it. It made me feel like a woman, not just a lost girl. Taking his hand, I slowly slid it down to the bottom of my long johns shirt. I should not do this. I hesitated, but I slid his hand back over my breast, under my shirt. His breathing never changed.

When I woke in the quiet, dark morning hours, his hand was still there. I had a moment's panic. What would he do if he woke like that? I yanked his arm down and started to roll out of bed. But I stayed, sitting up. Bud's eyes opened, and I could not help smiling. I leaned over and kissed him. It was something I had to do. I scrambled out of bed, dressed as fast as I could, and ran to the kitchen to start the day. The stove's flames were beautiful as was the dawn sky's colors. Even the bubbling oatmeal looked special somehow.

"Are you all right?" asked Inés.

I only smiled.

"Oh, I think I know," she laughed.

Bud rode off. He waved his hat from the ridge. I waved back, but I doubt he could see me so small and from so far. I was glad he waved anyway. It would be a very long three days before he spent another night in.

Bud, regresa pronto a mi lado.

THE TEN DAYS

CHAPTER SIXTEEN

Bud, hurry back to me.

It was so late that the candle in Carmela's and Inés' room has burned out. I hated this. I had to pee. It was cold, very cold and windy. I could not go back to sleep with this bloated feeling. I did not want to run through the cold and squat in the drafty outhouse. At least when it was this cold and windy, it did not smell too bad.

Sliding out of my blankets, I slipped on my sandals and blue flannel shirt and wrapped a blanket over my long johns. Unlatching the plank door, I eased it open. I had greased the hinges with lard so our early morning risings would not disturb Gabi and Lee. I ran to the outhouse and was glad to find it empty, not that I expected it to be in use at this hour. At least it was out of the wind, mostly.

I squatted over the hole, making sure my blanket's edge was away from the opening, and crumpled up a page torn from a catalog. In daylight I liked to look at the pictures of the many things that could be bought, some I expected never to see. Gabi told me that anything in the catalog could be asked for in a letter sent with a check giving the amount of money. Four or five weeks later it would arrive at the post office in Del Rio. That was amazing. I crumpled the ball of paper three times so it would not be so scratchy.

Wrapping the blanket tight, I started across the courtyard. With my eyes used to the dark and the faint light coming from the lanterns on the big house and bunkhouse that always burned, I could see how foggy it was.

Two pops, far off, beyond the ridge, I thought. Then three shots evenly spaced. The monitors' signal for trouble! Another raid, so soon after the last? Bud was out there! Were those his shots asking for help? If it was someone else, Bud would ride to the sound of the shots. Then more shots, many more. More than the last raid.

I ran for the house. My shotgun! I would go to the courtyard gate like Gabi had told me the last time. I would not forget my bag of shells this time. There were shots on the other side of the house. I saw the fog-reflected gun flashes over the roof. Running shadows came through the gate on the other side of the courtyard. They were kids belonging to Mexican workers. Their mamás and papás must have told them to go to the courtyard for safety. I almost reached our room's door. There were shots behind me. A horseman came over the wall followed by another. They had to be good riders to do that. Big sombreros and carbines. One was coming straight at me! More shots from all over. A ball of fire blew into the sky near the bunkhouse. Now there were so many shots that it sounded like thunder's roar. Screams, shouts, horses neighing, and hooves pounding. I heard glass breaking.

The first rider galloped past, ignoring me. He leaped

off his horse and started shooting through a door, and then kicked it in with planks flying. It was Carmela's and Inés' room! I could not get to my shotgun. I turned and ran toward the big house. There were more guns there.

More flames leaped up! Were they burning the whole place? I saw Gabi with a carbine. She turned, took careful aim, and shot the second man off his horse. Señor De-Witt came around the house corner, carbine in hand. He fired off to the side and ducked back around the corner. I ran. I saw a child, a boy. I recognized him as one of the worker's sons, maybe six years old. A bullet tore through him. He went as limp as a wet towel collapsing to the ground.

Gabi was running and fell with the sound of shots.

Oh my God! They are going to kill us all! I ran.

Another horse came over the wall. He was right behind me! My sandals pounded the ground. His boot struck me between the shoulders, snapping my head back in blinding pain, and I slammed into the frozen ground. I rolled over, dazed. Through the blur, I saw the man point a pistol at me.

"Take that one!" shouted a voice.

Who, me? I thought. That voice sounded familiar.

The rider dismounted and bent over me, a bristly, hairy face. I kicked him in the face. That was a mistake for he staggered back and followed with a kick into my face.

I woke with my head in great pain, from the kick and because I was hanging over a horse with my head down. The saddle's gullet, with the big round horn, jammed into my belly. I suddenly hurt all over as I flapped like a ragdoll. My wrists and ankles were tied. My blanket was gone. I heard other horses running, cattle too. There were some shouts and scattered shots behind and before us. I could not think clearly. The pounding pain.

I recognized the bluff at the Sheep's Head. Down it we plunged with sandy dust billowing. I almost fell off head-first, which would have been death. The rider hauled on my bound arms and kept me in place. We were on a sandy cow trail in the carrizo cane. No more shots. There were quiet shouts from one bandido to the other so they could find each other.

My bandido stopped like he was listening. Thank God. I knew Bud and Flaco and Gent were out here. I was in a bad place. What if Bud or the others found my bandido and started shooting? He would duck behind me for cover.

Another horse came out of the dark, and the two bandidos greeted each other.

"What have you there, friend?" asked the other.

"Lencho said to take it. I guess he wants to fuck it."

"We all will," my bandido shouted. Their laughs were ugly.

I felt real fear for the first time. If only Bud would come like he went after those three indios.

Another man rode up. He said nothing except, "Vámonos." We followed a trail to the Río. I was grateful it was not at a gallop. There were suddenly a lot of cattle, and other bandidos were herding them into the water. There were shouts and yelling. The water was low, but my hair and feet dragged in the ice cold water and splashed my face. That is when I realized I had lost my sandals. I could barely feel my tied arms. Then I realized how cold I was.

We splashed out of the water, jolting painfully. I heard a girl crying.

There was more shouting. Someone was yelling at men telling them what to do. It was all muddled and confused. Hanging with my head down, I was becoming groggy with too much blood rushing to my head. We were moving through mesquite. I smelled churned mud, cow shit, and the wet horse. It sounded like any cattle roundup. It was just in the middle of the night making it different. The bandidos did not seem concerned about anyone following them. A man rode up and told another to go back to the river with the men who had set up two ambushes if the gringos came.

I was frightened for Bud and the others. I still heard a girl crying. One of the Mexican workers?

We moved on. There was much shouting, much confusion. I just hung limp with the pain building as was the cold. I was mostly wet now from passing through dew-covered brush. I wanted to vomit.

All I knew for sure was that we were in Mexico. It had been years since I had been there. I did not know which way we were going, into Mexico or following the Río one way or the other. It seemed like we rode on rocky, uneven ground for hours. It was probably not that long, but it felt like it. The bandidos were quiet now. Even the cattle were quiet except for the rumble of their plodding walk and brushing through the mesquite.

I worried that I was being hurt bad hanging over the saddle like this. We slowed. There was much shouting. The cattle were being turned to the left. Hanging as I was, I could tell the ground had been trampled by many cattle before we arrived. The cattle were turned farther and began stopping. There were always a few who tried to push ahead, not understanding they could stop. It seemed we had met up with another group of bandidos. Both groups had cattle. I think one group attacked the ranch houses and stole some cattle. The other had run a larger herd across the Río.

A huge black bull plodded by. I recognized it as Quicksilver, Señor DeWitt's expensive new breeding bull.

Several bandidos were with it. They turned off from us, taking some of the cattle with them.

The rest of the bandidos were gathering to the right of the muddy trail. Orders were given for men to be posted on guard. No fires. No shouting or loud talking. They would leave at dawn. I heard the crying girl again. All I could make out was dark shapes.

"Put them here," a rough voice said.

My bandido grabbed an arm and tossed me backward off the horse. I hit the ground hard on my butt and then my head. I saw sparks and white streaks. I did not black out but was so dazed I could not tell up from down. Men on horses were around me. With a thump, someone rolled into me. I heard the crying girl hit the ground and start squalling. I lay still and hoped a horse would not trample me. Men laughed, said crude things.

The men left when a man grumbled, "Let them be." He stood there for moments. He turned to the crying girl. I heard her gasp as he kicked her. "Shut up!"

She made a strangling noise trying to keep from crying. I realized it was Agnes!

"Leave her alone. She's only a child!" Doris shouted in Americano.

Why did she not say it in Spanish?

He kicked her. "You shut up too!" He kicked Agnes again to show he did not care.

I rolled onto my side and found Inés next to me. The bandidos had taken four of us.

The man said, "I am Chago. I will untie you, but if you try to run away, I will whip the hide off your backs." He cracked a cuarta against his leg.

I knew Chago was a nickname for Santiago.

Inés repeated it to Doris and Agnes in her simple Americano.

Why is she saying it in Americano? Then it came to

me. They were hiding that Doris and Agnes understood Spanish.

"They understand," said Inés.

"What about her?" the voice said.

"She understands. She does not speak because she is loco."

Why was she saying that about me?

"Loco? How so?"

"She just does loco things. She steals things and is afraid of men. She will hurt them sometimes if they get too close."

I knew what she was doing. Trying to protect me. I was grateful.

"We will see about that," he said, cracking his cuarta again.

Maybe it was not such a good idea to try and protect me like that.

"Why does she not speak?"

"No one knows," said Inés. "She was found on the road all alone."

That is true.

"She is loco?"

"Out of her mind sometimes," Inés said.

Maybe that was true too.

He stepped toward Inés. "We are going to ransom you. Do not try and escape. Your punishment would be more than you can endure." His hissing voice made me believe that.

He kicked at Doris and Agnes, herding them to us. Agnes whimpered.

"You will stay together! If you need to piss, you will do it right here." He stamped his boot.

"You are no better than whores, no better than bitch dogs. You mean nothing to me, and I will not hesitate to whip you senseless if I wish!" He lashed his cuarta on Doris's shoulder. She made no sound. Something had told me she had grit.

Another bandido with a carbine was behind him. He grabbed Inés by the arm and pulled her to her feet. He cut her ankle and wrist bindings, handed her the knife, put the carbine to her head, and said, "Cut the others' bindings."

She cut our yucca fiber cords. He told her to drop the knife instead of handing it to him.

"If you try and run, Paco will shoot you or do worse."

"We are freezing," said Inés. "We barely have any clothes."

"You will not need clothes with what is going to happen to you." That was followed by a nasty laugh.

Agnes gave a smothered cry as Doris clinched a hand over her mouth. She could give away that they understood Spanish.

Chago walked away leaving Paco to guard us. We huddled together. Doris and Agnes wore long johns, wool nightgowns, and socks. Inés had a wool corset, old cotton nightgown, rebozo, and socks.

Another man walked up, a small man, but somehow dominating. I could see no more than a shape. He stood for some time regarding us. I do not know what he could see of us. We had to be only dark cowering shapes.

Without warning, he lunged and grabbed Agnes's arm and slammed his open hand into her face, knocking her to the ground. He did the same to Doris, Inés, and me. It felt worse than a wasp sting with the shock banging through my head followed by being thrown to the ground. My left elbow painfully struck a rock.

A low grumbling voice increased in loudness as each word tumbled out. "If you try and run, you will get that ten times over and more." He grabbed Inés, and holding the back of her head, he slammed a punch into her face and then tossed her back to the ground and kicked her in the side.

Agnes screamed, and the man turned on her like a pouncing puma. He grabbed her by the front of her nightgown and said in a harsh whisper, "You make too much noise with the crying, little bitch. I want silence!" He slapped her face twice, causing Doris to gasp, threw her to the ground, and spit on her.

"Do not run," he warned and faded into the darkness.

I rushed to Inés on all fours. She was unconscious. I patted her cheeks and rubbed her hands. Doris was holding Agnes, rocking her gently as she tried to quiet her sobbing.

Inés suddenly came to with a startled jerk. "What? What did I do?"

"Are you good, Inés?" asked Doris.

"What happened?"

Doris told her.

"I'm scared, I'm scared," Agnes said over and over while Doris gently patted her back, shushing her. "Where's Mama?"

Another man suddenly appeared over us. I know we all cringed.

He threw blankets at us. "If you are good, Chago will take care of you. Be good, do as you are told, and I will not take away the blankets. Or your clothes," he added.

He disappeared again.

Time passed. We spoke in whispers. Doris told us how her and Agnes's windows were broken in when Señor DeWitt went out the front door. They were dragged out. Both had some cuts.

We cannot just sit here worrying about our troubles.

I showed the girls how to overlap two blankets, and we laid side by side with our feet in one corner and heads in the opposite so they would be covered by two layers, mostly. Inés and I doubled up our knees and spooned together as did Doris and Agnes. We were side by side with me pressing into Agnes's back. We were still cold. Agnes made tiny weeping noises for a long time.

I felt so sorry for her. I knew I would be doing the same because I knew what was going to happen to us. I tried not to think about it. But that was all I could think about.

Then I realized something. Inés did not know her mamá was dead. It may have been a venal sin, but it would do no good telling her and only worsen her agony.

Podríamos usar algo de ayuda.

CHAPTER SEVENTEEN

We could use some help.

A scream and begging cries of "No, no, no!" woke me.

Four bandidos were dragging Doris and Agnes from their blankets. The girls kicked and screamed and desperately clutched each other. The men pulled them apart, slapping, hitting, and laughing at them. They were both hysterical.

Inés got out of our blankets faster than I could, and on her hands and knees, screamed, "Let them go! They are only children!" She was ignored.

Doris was screaming, "*¡No! ¡Lléveme, lléveme*!"—No! Take me, take me!"

Where was Chago? I thought. He seemed responsible for us. Surely he would not let this happen.

Both girls were thrown to the ground on their blankets. I could not watch. I did not want to hear. I covered my head with my blanket and cowered like a child. I was ashamed for doing that.

Agnes begged, "Please, no, please." Her pleading grew weaker. Then the screams. I had never heard anything like it. I vomited.

I heard slaps and punches, terrible cursing, nasty laughs, and pig noises.

It could be no worse, but then it was. More men came. I tried to drown it out with hands over my ears. It was going to happen to me. I knew it. Mamá tried to protect me from that, and at the same time, I think she was preparing me for it as though it was inevitable. In my world it is. It would catch up with me. Then a deep guilt cut through me. I should not worry about myself, but for Doris and Agnes. I could not imagine what they were enduring. Or could they endure it? Could I endure it?

A voice shouted. I peeked out of my red-brown blanket. Chago dismounted and pulled a man off of Agnes and kicked another from Doris. There was shouting and arguing. I hoped they would start shooting each other.

"El Xiuhcoatl himself wanted the little one first, you bastards!" Chago shouted. "You are all in trouble now!"

Good, I thought. But then what would he do to them?

"Leave! All of you!" He pointed at Paco with his cuarta. "You fool. How did you let this happen?"

Our guard looked guilty and remorseful. "There were too many of them. They all came at once."

"You fool!" He whacked the cuarta into Paco's face.

"What was I supposed to do, shoot them, my pals?" He held his hand to his bleeding lips.

Chago only shook his head. "Now I have to tell him of this. You and I will be fortunate to still have our eggs in the morning."

"He may cut off my eggs," said Paco, "but I doubt he will geld his own brother."

Chago was El Xiuhcoatl's brother? That was a surprise.

Chago stared at Paco and in a whisper said, "He would. He killed our worthless little brother for stealing Mamá's pearl necklace, jewelry we worked hard to steal for her birthday."

Paco's mouth dropped open. Blood dribbled.

"You two," Chago said, suddenly turning to Inés and me. "Clean them up! Do not let this happen again!" he shouted.

"We have no water," Inés said from under her blanket.

"Paco, give them your canteen," he said and left.

Paco hurried to his horse and threw the gourd canteen at Inés. He sat on a rock watching us and dabbing his lip.

Maybe we would be spared. I knew in my heart that could not be true.

Agnes wrapped up in her blanket and cried. She would not let any of us touch her. "You need to clean yourself," begged Doris.

"Go away! Don't look at me!" she said, a whimpering plea. She pulled the blanket corner over her face.

I did not know what I was doing, but I helped Doris clean herself. She was so brave and steady, but I could tell too she was distressed and disgusted.

Doris tried again to help Agnes.

"I want to die," Agnes wailed, breaking into sobs. "Why did…how could they do that?"

Wrapped in our blankets shivering, none of us slept. We huddled together without Agnes. She could not let us get near her. Doris did not talk. I prayed the rosary a hundred times. My rosary beads were in my skirt pocket left at the Dew.

I slept on and off. I prayed, I shivered, I cried sometimes. I cried for Doris and Agnes. What could one say to them? For once I was glad I could not speak.

I feared dawn. They would likely come for us again, all of us. No matter what Chago said.

We slept some from sheer exhaustion and strain.

They kicked us awake. I cannot describe the immediate fear, the helplessness, and the shock of cold. The Sun's crown was hazy coming up behind the scrub trees. Fog still blurred everything. Shapes of cattle, horses, and men drifted through the mesquite.

It was ordered there would be no breakfast and to make no noise. Doris went to Agnes and tried to hold her. She refused to get up, kept the blanket over herself, and sobbed silently. Doris looked at me helplessly. *What can I do?* her eyes asked.

I did not know. I went to Agnes anyway. Kneeling, I gently pulled the blanket from her face and touched her lips. Her eyes were red, tears, and black circles.

"We have to go, Agnes," whispered Doris. She glanced at me. "Marta will help you. Do you want that?"

She nodded.

"Can she clean you up?"

She shook her head no. What could I do anyway?

"Agnes, we have to clean you up. Understand? It's for your own good."

I motioned for Inés to give me the water gourd. There was not much left.

Easing up her nightgown, I had her lift her hips, and I pulled down the under drawers. I wadded part of the nightgown above the muddy hem, and wet it from the gourd. I cleaned her as best I could while she whimpered and Doris held her hand. Her face showed disgust and embarrassment. Men, mostly wearing big sombreros and yellow bandanas, were watching us. Paco was telling them to leave, but they paid him no attention. We crowded around Agnes so they could not see. Many had peso coins sewn to their sombreros, boasting their wealth and no need for honest work.

I felt like I was in a spirit land of unreal things such as Mamá had told me of. When can I leave and return to the awakened land?

Chago walked up. "Leave!" he ordered. The men scattered to their horses.

Chago looked no different from other bandidos, except for a leather patch over his left eye. He wore a tall tan sombrero with a yellow ribbon around the crown. A red and orange poncho covered him.

A man with him brought up four horses. Two had Mexican saddles and one an indio saddle of raw leather bound over a wooden frame and covered with a small folded blanket. Another was a Texano saddle, come from the ranch. I did not recognize it. I was thankful it was not Bud's. A bandido saw the lariat tied to that saddle. He untied it and threw it into the mesquite with a look of disgust.

I was shocked with such a waste.

We all, except languid Agnes, must have had puzzled looks.

Chago said, "We do not carry lariats like vaqueros and cowboys. No one wishes to be hung by their own rope."

It must be a dangerous life to be a bandido. Good.

"Can all of you ride?" asked Chago.

Doris pointed, indicating she would ride the indio saddle. I knew she was a good rider.

I took the ranch horse, a paint of brown and white, mostly brown but with a white band partly hidden by the saddle, with a white snout and white foreleg socks. I let the horse smell me. It was excited and uncomfortable with so many strange horses and missing its usual potrero. I shortened the stirrups, and Inés boosted me onto the saddle.

Paco said, "I will ride behind you. Stay close together, do not leave my sight. If you ride away, I will shoot you in the back. Do not get off your horse unless you ask me. Only one of you can dismount at a time."

He has done this before.

"Falo will ride in front of you. Do not pass him. He will shoot you."

Falo was a nickname for someone named Rafael. He was tall and thin and wore a blue Mexican cavalry cap.

We had difficulty getting Agnes out of her blanket and onto her horse. She could barely stay in the saddle. I could not look at her eyes.

I showed them how to wrap a blanket around themselves long ways to cover their head, shoulders, arms, and thighs. They held the reins under the blankets. It was still too cold. We did not have jackets or hats or enough blankets. We all shivered. Agnes could not do anything for herself. Her face was an anguished stare into any space where there was no one to look at her.

"We will tie you to your saddles if you do not do as I say."

We started to move, slowly. Riders mixed with the cattle. They were trying to hide our tracks among the cattle. We rode until noon, stopping for supper. It was not much. Cold *carne seca*—like jerky, but with salt, pepper, and garlic—and stale tortillas. They gave us little. We drank water from muddy puddles. Once Inés nudged me and nodded toward a couple of bandidos. They had been wounded and were wearing poorly wrapped bandages on legs and arms.

Good for them, I thought. I hoped they became infected. That made me wonder if there was something I could do if they made me treat them. Something like smearing snot in the wound to cause an infection. I felt guilty about thinking so low and asked for forgiveness.

Still, after what they had done to us…

In the afternoon a man caught up with us looking all excited. He needed to find El Xiuhcoatl. The man was sent up the line as he was near the head.

It was not long before word came back that eleven gringos and two vaqueros had crossed the river the day before. Bud was coming! Two vaqueros, Flaco and Chico, were with them. Good. More word came back. Sometimes I thought it was rumor.

Doris overheard more because they thought she did not understand Spanish. When we stopped, we put together what we heard. The men, gringos they called them even if two Mexicans were with them, had followed the group of bandidos who had broken off from us. They had gone to Don Garza's son's house. They had taken some of the Dew cattle with them, including Señor DeWitt's prize black bull, Quicksilver. Like the four of us, Quicksilver was to be ransomed. The gringos must have thought we had been taken there too. Don Garza was the owner of Rancho Mariposa. We were still on his land. The gringos had attacked the son's home. They killed all the bandidos there, seven, they thought. They also hung three Americano traitors found at the house! They also shot down Don Garza's son.

One of the hung was Theodore Maxwell. He owned the V-Bar-M Ranch next to the Dew. A poor neighbor, I had heard. They said Maxwell was in on the theft of Quicksilver. I was confused and did not understand what was going on. One of the gringos was wounded, and three went back across the river, taking Quicksilver and the other Dew cattle with them.

That meant there were only ten coming after us now. Inés thought there were about twenty bandidos here.

It made no difference. Bud was coming!

The bandidos were angry, learning that all their compadres had been killed by the gringos. We could tell it also made them uneasy. The gringos had killed that many men, maybe eleven, and had only one wounded. Yes, they were worried.

We rode through the day. I could sense the building anger in the bandidos. This worried me. They might take it out on us.

It was late in the day when two Rurales rode in. This caused a stir among the bandidos. Not because the gray uniformed Rurales were lawmen. They were little better than bandidos. One's hand was wrapped with a bandage. They looked angry waving their arms and gesturing as they talked to El Xiuhcoatl and Chago up ahead. The bandido jefe rode a fine gray stallion with silver accouterments. There was much talk among the bandidos, and they were even more concerned now. Our speed picked up, and two men were left behind to see if we were being followed.

It was said that Don Garza, after learning his son was killed by the gringos, had set the Rurales after them. The twenty-eight Rurales had tried to ambush the gringos at a farm. They said a vicious battle had taken place. Two gringos were dead, but they had killed eighteen Rurales. We could scarcely believe that ten gringos killed that many Rurales. The bandidos could not believe it either and were even more troubled. There may have been only eight gringos after them now, but they had killed a greater number than the gringos did. We heard them say they had us four girls to use as hostages. That made me smile. I saw what they were now, craven coward.

Two more gringos were dead. I worried about Bud. I prayed for them all.

It came to me. Were they still coming for us?

I looked at Doris with her arms around Agnes. I thought about Señor DeWitt. He would never abandon his beautiful daughters. I thought about Bud. He never quit. I was convinced.

Sí, vienen a salvarnos.

CHAPTER EIGHTEEN

Yes, they were coming to save us.

The ground rose, and it became hillier and the ridges higher. It only misted, but our blankets and clothes were soaked through, and we shivered endlessly. Each gust of wind caused us to shake even more.

In the darkness, the way our path wove through the mesquite, creosote, and cactus told me we were not on a road or even much of a trail. The clouded sky hiding the moon and the drifting fog kept me from seeing what was around us.

San Miguel, unlit by a single candle. I had no idea of the time. I could not make out any of the village except it was small, felt worn out, and smelled. It smelled of goats, cow chip smoke, stale dampness, and hopelessness.

The bandidos were quiet, the horses too. The sense of gloom was heavy. The bandidos were hungry, cold, tired from their ride, and troubled by the victorious gringos who were after us. A couple of them cursed the gringos for killing friends left at Rancho Mariposa.

We passed through a great plank gate set in a thick two-vara high adobe wall. It whined shut, and bolts were thrown. I heard the thump of locking crossbeams. A deep gloom fell over me. Agnes whimpered, and Doris quietly hushed her. Inés reached and gripped my hand.

Lanterns lit up. We were told to unsaddle. We had to unsaddle for Agnes. Men took our horses. Some peered at us with looks of lust or chuckled and mumbled crude things about deflowering virgins. We followed in shock at their words. We were made to lug our saddles to the stable's tack room.

"Act loco, Marta," said Inés. "It could save you."

She was thinking of me more than herself. My heart cried for her.

There was a big casa, the hacienda. To the left was a smaller one. Paco and Falo pushed us with their carbines toward the small one. We were forced into a dark room, its floor covered with straw. That was good. We could pile it under us and on top of our blankets. There had been a window, but it was bricked up. Agnes plopped in a corner and huddled up in a ball. Doris sat beside her, trying to comfort her. All she got was, "Go away! I want to die." More crying.

I prayed for her, for all of us, because I knew in my heart that it was only going to become worse.

"Act loco," Inés had said. What could I do? Would it do any good? I remembered the story of a gringo taken by indios who ate dirt and yelled all the time. Believing he was loco, they spared him, and soldiers eventually rescued the man who had indeed become loco. I did not think these bandidos would easily believe that. Besides...eating dirt?

Inés said I stole things and I feared men. I had no idea

what I could do. There was nothing there that would keep the bandidos away from me, to do what they wished.

I had no hope. None of us did. How long before the ransom money came? It could be days. In the meantime, there was no reason for them not to have their way with us as often as they wanted.

Paco threw some tortillas into the room, slammed the heavy wooden door, and locked it. It was pitch black.

As hungry as we were, no one felt around for the tortillas.

Mamá said if you drop a tortilla, it will bring unwanted visitors. I was happy that Paco had dropped the tortillas so Bud would come.

I suddenly did not care about the others. I wrapped up in my blanket and huddled in a corner. I tried to pray, but I could only cry.

The door slammed open in the darkness. Startled awake, I did not know where I was. Then I remembered. I expected yelling, kicking, and punching.

It was quiet except for Agnes's soft whimpering starting anew.

A shape appeared in the door lit from behind by weak yellow lantern light.

He was not a large man, not like I expected. He was small, shorter than Bud. I felt strength though, and a sense of supremacy. El Xiuhcoatl was not a leader because of these qualities but because he took leadership along with anything else he wanted. I do not know how I sensed all that, but it was there in that faceless shadow—evil hatred.

Even his voice had a harsh menacing tone. "Which is the small one with yellow hair?" he growled.

Another shape appeared in the door, and an arm

stretched toward Agnes. Thank God her face was hidden from seeing him point her out. But she understood it. "No, no," she cried.

Doris said something. I think to shut her up and not to give away that they understood Spanish.

It made no difference.

"Shut up, foolish bitch!" the bandido jefe shouted at Doris. "I know you both speak Spanish. I have spies."

"Spare the small one!" begged Inés.

"You shut up too! At least we have one here who keeps her mouth shut."

Just the mere mention of me by El Xiuhcoatl made my stomach feel hollow.

His face sneered. "Bring me both of the *gringas*, Paco." The dog sounded like he was merely ordering supper at the Fitch Hotel.

Spies? He had spies? I remembered thinking, Where, who? I had to listen. I might overhear a name. Señor DeWitt would no doubt shorten the traitor's life for what happened to his daughters.

Paco and another man came in and went straight for Agnes. We all moved at once. As fearful as I was, as hopeless as our situation, we moved. I do not remember thinking about what would happen to us in retaliation. We moved as one, and now I knew I could trust and rely on the others.

I jumped on Paco's back and Inés on the other man. Doris came straight at Paco and kicked him in his manhood. He fell back hard, landing on me to knock out my breath. Doris came down on top of him, smacking my head on the floor. Paco threw her off and came up off the floor and punched me in the face. Fully back on his feet, he kicked Doris in the leg and then the stomach as she rushed him again. As I rolled over, I saw the other man grab Inés' neck and punch her in the face three times and throw her against the adobe wall. Crashing to the floor, she did not move. He kicked her in the ribs several times—I guess to keep her down. He turned on me trying to get to my feet. Grabbing my arms, he flung me into the wall. I had not yet gotten my breath back, and what air I had was knocked out. I bounced onto the floor unable to break my fall.

We were all gasping for breath, except for two. Agnes was screaming hysterically, and El Xiuhcoatl was disgustedly belly laughing.

"You are fools to be taken by surprise by girls. Falo, get another man and help these two stupid fools take the two gringas to my room. Can you do that, or do you need some real men to help you?"

None of the bandidos said a word. Falo and a fourth man came in and dragged the unconscious Doris out. The other two grabbed Agnes, still screaming and struggling. Paco slapped her face so hard that spit and blood flew. Telling the other man to let go of her, he slammed her against the wall twice. Completely limp, the other man flung her over his shoulder and carried her out.

El Xiuhcoatl stepped into the room. I cringed from his unseen wickedness. "I will please you two later. Your fight was sporting to watch. You surprised my worthless men, but I will not tolerate it when I return." He said "men"—*hombres*—in this instance as if they were annoying bugs.

Stepping out of the room, he said matter-of-factly, "Paco, leave the door open. Permit only two men in at a time. Keep this orderly." He left.

My left shoulder and side ached, and I felt like I had been crushed. I struggled to breathe. Taking in little gasps of air hurt.

The words, "Let only two men in at a time," what did he mean? And then I understood. Nauseating fear tore through me. They were coming. Panic gripped me. I could not think clearly and reasonably. What would happen?

I rolled over and tried to crawl to Inés. I had to wake her so we could fight back. I shook her shoulder, but she did not move.

The door creaked open. There were two men.

One said, "Ahhh, *mamasita*."

The other laughed callously.

I vomited.

They held me down. Others came after them.

Hay cosas de las que no puedo hablar.

Chapter Nineteen

There are things I cannot speak of.
Bud, forgive me.
I do not want to live.
Mi castigo fué que yo vivía.

Chapter Twenty

My punishment was that I lived.

I awakened with my head on Inés' lap. I remembered crawling to her when they were through with us. I remember scraping at snatches of hay to pull over us. I did not want to use the blanket I had been held down on, but it was so cold.

I heard morning noises like on the ranch. What I would not give to be on the Dew now. Horses, chickens, men quietly talking—sometimes with laughs, and kitchen sounds—I was not hungry. I was shivering cold. Mostly, I hurt…down there.

I ignored the sounds, the cold, my own shivering.

What had happened to me? I did not want to think about it. How did I feel? Could I be honest and answer that? I hated men, all men. Even Bud. Could he do that to a woman? Was he still coming for us? Did I still want him to? Could he guess what they did to us? Would he still come for me if he knew? Did he already know? Has he guessed? If we were saved and no one admitted what happened to us, would he still know?

Did I still want to be with him? If he came, if I was saved, if he understood that I did not want this, if I did not wish myself to die.

I gripped Inés' hand. She squeezed back, weakly, and then patted my shoulder. I wanted to ask her how she felt, but I knew what her answer would be. I wondered too about Doris and Agnes. Doris was my age. Agnes was only fourteen. Inés was seventeen. Age made no difference. We were all soiled, used, and of no use now except for what those men, those dogs wanted to do to us.

The door opened. There was enough light that I could make out a man who had used me last night. Fear and revulsion tore through me, making my stomach muscles contract.

We were so exhausted this time that they did not have to take turns holding us down for the other.

I wanted a knife, even a small one. To defend myself, to kill myself. Whichever was easier.

I was startled by a quiet knock on the door. That was an unheard of courtesy. It was a bulky young woman, sad and quiet. Embarrassed because she knew what had happened to us, she set a crockpot of water with a couple of rags on the floor.

Inés and I helped each other clean up as best we could. There was little we could do. I would never feel clean anyway, no matter how much soap and water. The girl would not speak to us or even look at our eyes. She picked up last night's tortillas from the floor, even the ones that had been stepped on. With fright on her face, she quickly slipped us an onion and a cooked chayotextle.

She left, and we ate the onion and squash-like chayotextle and the dirtied tortillas as fast as we could. I was glad for the onion. A priest had taught Mamá what vegetables prevented scurvy, and onions were the easiest to be had.

Bud, come for me, please, I know you will, I know you will. You are all I have. You are all that I can hope for. No one else will come for me. If you do not come, then I am doomed, and I know you will not allow that.

The rattling sound of the door unlocking this time sent terror blazing through me. "No," Inés whispered as she gripped my arm.

Instead of men barging in to have their way, we were pulled out and told we were leaving. Anything would be better than that revolting cell.

San Miguel and the hacienda were below us. A shabby sad place of a few adobes, but mostly *jacalitos*—shacks—on a muddy road. They were made of mesquite limbs stacked between posts and covered with mud. The yucca leaf roofs were also mud covered. The endless rains were washing some of the mud off. There were a few horses inside the hacienda walls. I thought they left some wounded men behind. Cow chip and mesquite twig smoke intermingled with the fading fog. I hoped to never see that horrible place again.

We left San Miguel and the hacienda behind and continued to the west. We had not seen Doris and Agnes until they joined us on horseback. Agnes barely hung in the saddle, her face mostly covered. We all slumped with weakness. I was sore everywhere. I had been slapped, punched, and even bitten. One man spit on me time after time. I could not understand why I was so deserving of such mistreatment. I even hated Mamá for not telling me all what could happen, of all the terrible things men could do.

I avoided looking at the men. What if I made eye contact with one…with one who had taken me? Mexican men could read your eyes. What would they look for, what would they see? Maybe they did not care what I thought and felt.

Forgiveness, that was what they were supposed to see in my eyes. I should have forgiven them, and they should have seen that.

I would not forgive them. Ever.

It was not until we reached a ridgetop over the village that something came to me. Why are we leaving? I thought and prayed that we were maybe being taken to the ransom exchange. How would Señor DeWitt send the ransom money for us? Something was wrong. We were still heading west, away from the Frontera.

Where were we going? Why? It made no difference. Things would not change.

The land became more rugged, ridges and hills separated by steep-sided narrow valleys and rocky arroyos. It was so different from the flat campo of South Texas. It was just as barren with scattered mesquite, cactus, and all kinds of low brush, some I did not know. I tried to count the number of bandidos. They were strung out in a ragged line winding through the brush. Still around twenty, I thought.

We followed a simple trail up another ridge with windy gusts and on-and-off rain. The ground rose even higher and became more rugged. Paco was ahead of Doris and Agnes, and they were followed by Falo. Inés and I were behind Falo followed by Chago so he could see us all. They were keeping Doris and Agnes especially close so they would not dare escape. They were valuable because of the ransom, and I think the bandidos enjoyed pleasuring themselves with gringas. It came to me that Inés and

I were not so important. Maybe there was no ransom for us, and we were just Mexican girls who they no doubt could take for themselves in any village.

Two men rode down the line and told Chago they were setting a watch on our back-trail to watch for the gringos. One was a giant indio, two heads taller than Bud, huge, a hard, ugly face with a big square jaw. He had taken me three times. Why me? Because I was so small? He winked at me like I was his secret lover. He had hurt me more than anyone. I named him *El Gigante Feo*—the Ugly Giant.

Inés and I knew what setting a lookout meant. Our rescuers were still coming for us. Doris looked back at us and actually smiled. They were still coming for us. My Bud was coming! I looked at our guards. You will soon be dead, I thought. I was ashamed to admit that the thought gave me joy.

Inés said they were afraid. With the bandidos outnumbering the gringos in a land they were familiar with, it did not make sense. Maybe it was the defeat of the Rurales outnumbering the gringos by twice the men. When we did not stop for dinner, I thought that must be it. The militant Rurales had a reputation for viciousness and had been defeated by some cowboys.

I looked back at the sloping ground we had covered. There were places back there from which a lookout could see a far distance. All I saw was low rain clouds and mist, everything, even the land, dreary gray.

No matter, Bud was coming! That gave me something good to think about. Then my mind would tell me that maybe he was one of the dead. No, no! Not my Bud! I would try and think of the good things about Bud. About how we shared camp chores, when he bought me things, sometimes things I had never had before. He liked that I hunted, that I was a good cook, and that I shaved him without nicking him too much. To share his warmth, that was worth more than anything.

It was not long before the stinging, wind-driven rain was hurting my eyes and tears flowed.

I was shaken out of my thoughts when one of the two lookouts trotted past busting through the mesquite.

As he passed Chago, he said, "They are coming."

Chago asked how many, but the lookout did not say.

Inés and I grinned at each other. This could be over soon. If not tonight, maybe in the morning. I was scared to death as it was, but this thought frightened me even more. Being caught in the middle of a gunfight and being the reason for that gunfight could be deadly dangerous. Maybe the bandidos would rather kill us than let us be freed. They were spiteful, hateful men.

I hated them. There could be no forgiveness. Ever.

Soon we slowed, and there was much milling around. Men were dismounting. We overheard some of what was going on. They were going to set up an ambush.

El Xiuhcoatl appeared and told the men to take off their brightly colored ponchos, those who had them. He took off his own of yellow and red. Most had brown or gray, and those with bright colors took out their own dull-colored ones.

I saw his face clearly for the first time. He had a sharp, angular nose, big sideburns, and thick eyebrows. What was distinctive was that he looked pure mean. He seemed to have no other expression.

A couple of men were told to take charge of the horses. Chago, Paco, and Falo were to go with them with the putas. That was what he called us, whores. That was all they thought of us as. Something to be used.

The bandit leader told all the dismounted men to

move to the left side of the trail. That way they would be on the side opposite the gringos' gun hands. As we rode away, he began telling each man where they were to hide and making sure they could not be seen from the trail.

It looked like it would be a deadly ambush. I was very much in fear for our rescuers and Bud.

Chago led us, the other two guards, and the two horse holders over a distant ridge and into a wide, mesquite-grown arroyo. We all dismounted, and Paco and Falo told us to sit back-to-back and tied our hands to each other's. That pig Paco groped Inés' breasts—she had the largest among us.

We were far enough away that we could not shout a warning or for the horses to give away the ambush. To be sure, they gagged us. The rags stuffed in our mouths made us even thirstier.

The other two men strung a picket rope and tied the horses to it, all except Chago's. He stayed mounted, his carbine across his lap.

He looked at us sternly. "If the ambush does not work and there are too many gringos, and they come this way, my duty is to shoot you, all of you."

I suddenly felt more helpless than ever before, even when three men held me down. We were tied together with guns aimed at us and doomed if our rescuer's defeated the ambush. Agnes began to sob for the first time in hours.

At one point they had to take Agnes's gag off when she started choking. They gave her a drink and retied the gag with her struggling. They untied our gags one at a time and gave us each a drink.

Doris said to all of us, "Be brave." That was impossible. Paco told her to shut up.

I watched the milky yellow sun creep down below the mountains. I prayed for it to hurry for I knew our rescuers would not ride at night and would be spared the ambush.

We waited.

A horse was heard passing through the brush. A whispered, "Chago."

"What?"

We heard a man dismount and whispered voices.

Chago came back and told the other that we are staying here and most of the band would join us. Some would stay atop the ridge covering our trail. There would be no fires and only whispering. Men would be posted all night to quiet the horses.

There were a lot more gringos than they thought. They counted three groups.

Where did they all come from? I asked myself. Doris and Inés looked at each other, seeming confused.

Then we heard the bad news, very bad news.

The gringos had turned back. They had been coming up the ridge toward the ambush and turned back. After dark, scouts spotted three campfires on faraway ridges. The gringos had given up chasing us. They had turned back and stopped for the night. There were enough of them they did not worry about their fires attracting the bandidos. They were going home. That was what Chago told us.

All tied together back-to-back, we simply slumped against each other. Our rescuers were abandoning us. Giving up. Why, why? How could they?

Something deep inside me revealed that Bud was not coming, he never was, he never tried. He knew that I was beyond reach, taken to a place so far away, to be used as they saw fit. I did not blame him. It was not his fault. I had been taken to the edge of the Earth or the edge of Hell. Perhaps I deserved it. I should not have been spared from what happened to my familia. Even if he wanted to, he could never find me, ever, not in this lost, unknown place forgotten by all but God.

Maybe that was my salvation, God. He was all I had left. I prayed.

Paco untied us from each other. I fell on my side in despair. I waited for Paco to untie our hands and gags so we could eat. He did not.

Two men came out of the darkness and grabbed Agnes. Her gag-muffled screaming tore me apart. Two more came for Doris. She stood on her own and went with them without a struggle. I think Inés meant to do the same, to go without fighting. They might not use their fists if she did not fight. Her will broke, and she struggled. One used a leather belt, the buckle end, on her until she was still. They dragged all three into the brush.

El Gigante Feo and another man I do not even remember came for me. I fought until the giant hit me. He struck me again, backhanded hitting me so hard that the pain was as nothing laid over the rest of my pain. It meant nothing. I collapsed. They untied my hands, but not the gag. I did not make any noise. They took me right there. Two more men came later. Or was it three? Matu, he was always there when they took me.

No soy más que suciedad.

CHAPTER TWENTY-ONE

I am no more than dirt.

I was able to push things out of my mind. When bad memories pushed and shoved their way in, I found ways to crowd them out. I did not do this by recalling good memories. I did not have all that many. What few I had often seemed unworthy with all that had happened. The good memories were of my familia, but the way they were taken from this world and from me gave me only bad memories. Bud had been a good memory, but he had left and abandoned me. What few good memories I had meant little because the bad things were so overwhelming and trying to drown me.

A weak dawn found me wadded up in my blanket, mud-covered on both sides by now, as were my clothes. I was so cold. And hungry. I hurt all over, more in some places than others. My hands were tied in front of me now. The gag was gone. I looked around. There was no one to be seen. Was I left here, alone?

I huddled into a mud-ball like niños made. When through playing with them, they left them sitting in the mud to be forgotten. Someone would step on them, or the rain would melt them into the rest of the mud to become meaningless. Maybe when they left, they would forget me and leave me here.

It had been a cold night, but the rain was gone, and the moon could be seen through broken clouds.

I heard horses and muffled voices. No, they had not forgotten me. I dropped my head to the ground.

I heard footsteps.

"Get up," said Paco. "Get on your horse."

I staggered to my feet, barely able to stay standing. I had to grab the saddle horn, which I could barely reach. I tried to pull myself up enough to reach the stirrup. I could not. My strength had drained from me. They were barely feeding us and gave us little water. My teeth were gritty from muddy water puddles.

"Paco." It was Inés. She was on her horse. "We need something to eat. We are too weak." She nodded at me. "She cannot even mount her horse."

Paco looked at me with a smirk. "She is too small to get on by herself anyway. You help her."

Inés looked at me with a hopeless expression. She was too weak to dismount and remount herself.

It took everything I had, but I pulled myself up. I slumped in the saddle, gasping, and clung to the mane to keep from falling off.

"We need food, Paco," Inés said again, her voice hoarse and weak.

"Maybe they will give you something later. If you are weak, you will not be able to run away."

I could see Doris and Agnes ahead of us. Agnes was a muddy-blanket-covered lump on her horse.

Men coughed and hacked. They passed leather bags of carne seca and stiff tortillas. A bottle of tequila was passed around. Falo had the bottle and rode back to take it to Paco. I held out my hands, pleading with my eyes. He slowed, looked around, and quickly handed it to me. I took two quick burning swallows and splashed some on a bad bite on my neck. I gave it to Inés before he could grab it. He glared but did not hit me. Inés took a long, deep swallow and gave it back. Coughing from the burn, I nodded my thanks to Falo.

Paco said, "Do not do that again." He was not angry, though. He said to us, "Your gringos went home. This land and weather is too much for them. Real men like us can take it."

They really left?

I felt lost now, abandoned without hope. I was angry, but something kept telling me that it could not be true. Señor DeWitt would not leave his daughters to this fate. He would come after them by himself if he had to. I do not think that would be necessary. His men were loyal to him. He took good care of them. Bud? Would he come after me alone? I wanted to think so, but how well did I really know him? How did he really feel about me? We could not talk or share what we thought. Except maybe with the way we looked upon each other. There was something there, I thought.

I would find out sooner or later. God always let me know, even if it was something bad.

Why would he come after me? I was nothing. I had been soiled, dragged through the dirt, brutalized, debased, and defiled in ways that all men would know when they saw me. He would not want me. I was like the unclean in the Bible, the lepers.

We were soon moving. Scouts came in and said the gringos were nowhere to be seen.

I knew that, but it made me feel lower.

Agnes started crying quietly. I heard her say over and over, "Daddy, why?"

I caught myself thinking the same. *Bud, why?*

Three more men joined us in the late morning. They had been left behind at San Miguel but decided to catch up with their band. They were afraid to stay there in case the gringos came. Two men left there were too hurt to ride.

It rained a little and stopped. The sky was a gray blanket, and it became colder.

One of the men who joined us rode back down the line. He was probably coming to look at the putas—us.

He was young and rode a very red-colored horse. I remembered it. I looked closely at the young man and recognized him. He had visited the Dew. The young, cocky vaquero who claimed bandidos had taken his guns. He now had a carbine in his scabbard and a pistol on his belt.

At the Dew, he had swept his sombrero in a wide arc and remarked on Inés' and my beauty. This time he greeted us with a gloomy face, probably barely recognizing us.

"I am sad to see you in this state," he said quietly. "I did not expect this to happen."

"It did happen!" said Inés sharply. "Thanks to you!"

Deceiver, I thought. I had felt suspicious of his visit. Then I recalled El Xiuhcoatl boasting he had spies. This deceiver was one of them. He was scouting the ranch as El Xiuhcoatl plotted the raid and our kidnapping.

"Do not speak to them!" shouted Paco. "You can look them over and decide which ones you want tonight. Ride on, Lencho."

That was the nickname for one named Lorenzo. He turned after giving us a sad smile and rode back up the line.

How could he smile? Was he looking us over and

dreaming of what he could do to us that night?

In the afternoon the weather changed. It seemed not as cold, and after a short stillness, the wind changed from the north to the southeast. The haze blew away. It did not feel right. The clouds thickened and grew darker as we crossed a wide area of big and little arroyos. The wind grew stronger. The high clouds, though, were as still as a field of grass on a windless July day, but it turned much, much colder.

For the first time, I was able to count the bandidos. There were nineteen of them and the four of us on twenty-three horses. There were three spare horses with feed sacks and two overloaded pack mules with food supplies. I sincerely wished they would share some of that food.

After crossing the place with many arroyos, we were back in the rocky hills. The wild clouds to the north were black and gray. Over the mountains to the south were huge, fluffy white clouds looking like a rolling boil in a frijole pot. The wind blew faster and harder over the ground. Balls of brush and even limbs flew across the ground. Our horses tried to huddle together. I was frightened. Why did we not stop? They seemed to be trying to reach some place. Was there a place we could get out of the terrible weather? There had been no mention of another village. Without shelter, the coming night would be terrible and impossible to build fires.

One of the bandido's horses had gone lame. It had an Americano saddle, and he put it on one of the spares after taking off the feed sacks. They were loaded on other horses and the mules. They just left the horse there. He was worn out too, exhausted by a hard ride and hard weather. Maybe he would survive, maybe not. He probably had a better chance than us.

Then I thought that maybe he was a smart horse. They were not all the same. Some were smarter than others, just like people. I was smart about life on the road. I knew how to do many things. Inés, she lived on the road some, when she was younger. She had spent most of her life on a ranch. Doris and Agnes had spent their entire lives on a ranch. There was no doubt that they were able to take care of themselves, much more so than other gringas, those living in towns. Agnes though, I did not know. She was too far gone and was no longer with us. She had drawn into herself. If she were a horse, the bandidos would have let her go like the lame exhausted horse. I thought about that. No, they had another use for her. I cried and prayed for the frightened girl.

Something changed as we neared a ridge. The bandidos spread out in the thick mesquite we were passing through. Our guards told us to close up together, and they rode right beside or behind us. Chago came back and told us to follow him. We approached a narrow gap in a steep-sided rock ridge. The scattered bandidos moved slowly toward the gap. I realized they were riding slow to leave little sign of their passing through the mesquite. A small group rode past the gap, not turning off the trail.

We entered the gap. I could almost touch both walls if I dared stretch out my arms. Above was a rough crack showing the gray sky. A thin wash of water ran over the sandstone floor. The hooves made a sharp cracking echo. The ravine soon widened, and the walls were not so steep. It led into a small basin choked with low brush. The sides here were steep, but smaller ravines were gouged into the sloped upper sides. On the far side was a cleft, the basin's steep side being undercut with an opening on a ledge above the gravel floor. A boy, his disordered gaze saying he was feeble-minded, sat on a ledge with a shotgun in his lap pointed at the gap.

There were people coming out from under the cleft.

¿Qué clase de lugar es éste?

CHAPTER TWENTY-TWO

What is this place?

At least it was out of the wind, and the rain up above was blown against the opposite wall, leaving the cleft wall mostly dry. Water did trickle down the wall, and it was still just as cold.

The people emerging from the cleft, I could tell nothing about them being wrapped in ponchos. El Xiuhcoatl had a couple of men unload sacks of frijoles and cornmeal, tins of coffee, and one of cooking oil.

The horses were as tired as us and crowded to the far end of the cleft. A pole corral closed off that part of the basin. We unsaddled and staggered to a place in the cleft where we left the saddles with an old man missing part of a foot. Some of the bandidos were tossing gourd scoops of feed into crude troughs. The horses bumped each other out of the way to reach the water caught in shallow sandstone dips in the basin floor. The horses nosed some scrawny goats out of the way too. A thin stream of water rushed through toward the gap.

I thought if it rained heavy enough, this basin could suffer a surge-flood. There was something else I did not like. Anyone in here would be trapped by an enemy. Papá had always said never to camp in a *cajón*—a box or dead-end canyon. Two men could stop anyone coming up the narrow ravine, but it would not be hard for an enemy to climb higher and shoot into the basin. It would be hard, though, to find this place with its hidden entryway.

Parts of the cleft were walled off with rough adobe, making small rooms. One had a chimney of wooden kegs, their ends knocked out and stacked end to end. Other parts of the cleft were covered by woven mesquite-limb lean-tos—jacales. They had been here a long time. A lean-to was seeping smoke, the kitchen, I guessed. I smelled frijoles. No matter how scared I was, exhausted, shamed, and hurting, I was also hungry.

Bandidos were smirking at us as Paco told us to go in one of the lean-tos. Doris kept an arm around Agnes. The girl was no better. She jumped at any sound and began crying if a bandido even came near. The men did not care. A couple teased her with Doris yelling, "*¡Déjala en paz!*"—Leave her in peace!

Inés asked Paco if we could clean up decently. I did not like what she said. "If you bastards are going to keep using us, you will not like it if we cannot clean up."

I understood what she meant, but it sounded like she accepted what was to come. I tried not to call them names. Mamá said that God would punish you if you talk badly about people, and you will become just like them. I did not see how I could become just like them.

What she said worked. He said we could wash in the stream. When the men found out, they complained since we were so filthy they wanted us to wash downstream from where they would wash, cook, and fill their canteens. That was humiliating. They would rather have the horses upstream from them than us. It made no difference if they used us for their pleasure. At least we were above the place where the men relieved themselves. We were lower than dogs to them.

Inés told Doris that we should try and wash all our clothes even though it was getting colder and we would have to sleep in wet clothes. Maybe we could have a fire in this hidden place. Sleeping in wet clothes would dry them out during the night. There was no place along the stream that gave us privacy. Paco did not care when told this.

Inés said, "There is enough brush where the water flows out through the gap for our privacy."

Paco complained and said he would have to guard the gap so we would not try and run away.

"You have to guard the gap anyway, do you not?" she asked.

He complained to Chago, but he gave us permission. I think he was being a little easier on us, maybe even feeling a little sorry for us.

He was still pig, as were all of them.

It was late afternoon. It was so dark in the shadow-filled basin with the sun blocked by thick clouds that we did not have to wait until dark for privacy.

An old fat woman came out of one of the adobe rooms. When she saw us, she started yelling and shaking her finger at Chago. It seemed she was his and El Xiuhcoatl's aunt. She was talking about us, that we were filthy and she knows what they did to us. "*¡Eres cerdos repugnantes!*"—You are repugnant pigs! she shouted. At least she agreed with me. She returned to the adobe, still cursing the men.

Chago fled, leaving Paco in charge, much to his displeasure.

The fat woman came out of the adobe with a big pottery pitcher and some rags. She was followed by a skinny younger woman, but still old, with folded serapes.

"I am *Tía* Chavela. I may be able to help you a little."

Chavel meant "pledged to God." I sincerely hoped she was. Her face had once been kindly.

She knew what had happened to us and that it would not stop. She did not mention it or apologize for what her nephews did. Why should she? She was just as much a slave as us. She asked when we last ate, and Inés told her we were given only a few pieces of carne seca and some tortillas. She would give us hot frijoles and tortillas after we bathed. We could use the heavy serapes to cover with when we washed our blankets and clothes.

Tía Chavela led the way to the washing place, glaring at the bandidos to stay away. She had not seen a bar of soap since she could not remember when. "They," she said, nodding curtly at a bandido, one who had taken me, "never bring me soap like I ask, or salt."

We huddled together and shivered in our muddied blankets. Agnes had to be led. She tried to keep her face covered. Paco brought Falo to help him guard. He wanted to be sure we did not make a run for it down the gap.

"You bastards stay away from these girls while they bathe," Tía Chavela ordered.

"El Xiuhcoatl ordered us to watch them so they do not escape."

"Tell that bastard to go to hell! Where would they escape to? Do you think I would still be here if there was any place my old legs could carry me? I do not even know in what direction I would have to go to reach that hell hole San Miguel, the sorry place it is."

I do, I thought. And from there I could find the Río.

Inés started to unbutton Agnes's nightgown. She pulled away, clutching her gown with a horrified "No!"

on her lips.

"You have to," said Inés. "We cannot go through this every time we have a chance to clean up. You have to, Agnes."

I hugged Agnes. She was taller than me. I could hear her heart beating like a galloping horse. I took her hands and squeezed them gently while looking into her haunted blue eyes. I nodded. She let me undress her, keeping herself covered the best she could with her arms.

I had never thought about the color of Agnes's and Doris's skin. Their faces and forearms were almost as brown as my own, but the rest of their bodies were pink-white, as pale as their sun-bleached, straw-yellow hair. We threw our clothes and blankets into the cold, silty water first to let them soak and bathed as fast as we could, passing the rags around. On our knees, we scrubbed and pounded the clothes on rocks and wrung them out as best we could. The blankets were very difficult. We shivered the whole time. We scrubbed them with wadded handfuls of mesquite leaves, but they were still sodden with pasty silt mud.

Finished, we wrapped up in the serapes. I tied my hair in a ponytail with a juniper bark cord I made. We shook out our still grimy clothes and blankets and hung them over our arms so they could start drying. Our clothes had been somewhat washed, but they still smelled sour, it being noticeable because we were a little cleaner, or maybe only less dirty. There wasn't much room inside the mesquite lean-to, so we hung the blankets over bushes outside and hoped the wind would not change and rain-soak them. We were worried about mal aire affecting Agnes—the bad air caused by exposure to drafts.

I picked sage leaves and made a paste. With a stick, I spread it on each of the girls' wrists on the worst of the raw scrapes from our hands being tied.

Tía Chavela came in with a little nest of moss, leaves, and twigs holding a burning ember. There were piles of dry mesquite and other sticks. On my knees, I held out my hands for the ember nest. It had always been my job within my familia to build the fire. This was my familia now.

Before she left, Tía Chavela brought out a bottle of *emulsión de escocia*—cod liver oil. We each had to swallow two bitter spoonfuls. "This will strengthen you," she said.

She gripped me by the arm. I glared at her.

"You cannot speak, my worthless nephew says."

I only stared.

"I see your eyes. You will run if you can, even if only on foot." She looked at me and shook her head. "If you run, you could not find anything to eat out there. You would die."

I can find something to eat, I thought. I continued to glare.

She let go. "I know your type, half animal. Maybe you could, after all." She left without saying more.

I built the fire up against the rock wall so the heat would reflect back on us. The rock too would heat up and continue to give warmth for a short time after the fire died. Inés went with Tía Chavela, still wrapped in a serape. She returned with a crockpot of hot frijoles, a stack of tortillas, and a wooden spoon. We sprinkled water on the tortillas and warmed them on sticks. Even though they gave us no coffee, it was as good as the so long ago Christmas feast at the Dew. Crowded around the pot, we joyously scooped out steaming frijoles, endlessly giggling. I had been hungry many times, but not for as long as this. We had always found something. With the pot empty, we passed it around, mopping up the frijoles gravy. The last tortilla we divided up in four pieces. "*El postre*"—dessert—Doris called it. That was some sweet treat that Americanos had after supper. I had never had a dessert until with Bud at the Fitch Hotel.

We had had a simple but filling hot meal. Our clothes and blankets were far from clean, but at least not grossly filthy. We were mostly dry and warm. For once we were not shivering endlessly. We knew we were not safe. They could come at any time. Things could change right back to the way they were. I was sure they would.

Sitting bunched together, Inés told us a story of brujas. *¡Cuidado con las brujas!*—Beware the witches!—she and her brothers and sisters had always been warned. Our little fire threw wicked shadows on the wall. The fire's nervous crackle, the gusty wind outside, and the rain's ragged tapping put us in a gloomy mood.

Wiping snot from her nose, Inés said, "My Papá told us this story. He and his two brothers went deer hunting. They had only one old carbine among them. They went to a stream where deer drank in the morning. They went there in the afternoon and camped near the stream. This way they would not scare the deer off by trying to sneak in before light. They would already be there at dawn. They could have no fire, of course, so to keep them warm, my Papá's older brother, *Tío* Juan, brought a bottle of tequila as was their custom.

"They told stories and lies to one another until late in the night, sharing the tequila. They always kept some for the morning, to wake up them up and keep them alert. They were about to doze off when Papá's younger brother, Tío Pedro, my favorite uncle, nudged the others awake. 'Look over there!' he whispered.

"Beyond the brush and trees along the far side of the deer stream was a ridge. Going slowly up and down the ridgeside were lights, as lanterns or candles. Papá said they must be smugglers at work. They were near the Río Bravo, and who else would be up this late at night unless they were up to no good? 'Or up to the devil's handiwork,' said Tío Pedro. They watched for a long time, afraid to make any noise or even move. Smugglers would not like for them to have watched their illicit deeds. The lights were mostly in the trees along the stream now and going slowly up and down it. They looked like they floated through the trees. Some lights remained atop the ridge though, and they too floated back and forth. Eventually, the lights following the stream gathered together and went slowly up the ridge to meet at the top. They merged together and grew into one big white light that lit up the treetops and then as quick as that," she snapped her fingers, making us all jump, "the big light instantly disappeared!"

We all snickered, trying not to attract attention. Agnes did not even smile.

Inés went on. "It seemed improbable for men to carry lights like those, and there were so many. It did not look like something smugglers would do. It could not be the villagers. It would not be the farmers scattered through the area. There were not enough of them to carry that many lights even if they used everyone in their families, including suckling babies. They would never take women or children out late at night for any reason, even to hunt for a lost child. There were too many dangers.

"My uncles drank the rest of the tequila they were so upset. In the morning they woke too late to ambush the deer. The deer had since drunk their fill and went to their hidden grazing places. They finally got up, and driven by hunger, headed for home. All they could speak of was the mysterious lights. When they came to the stream, they searched for footprints along the banks. Anyone carrying lights would have had to follow the banks or walked in the stream itself. The floating passage of the lights along the stream had been too smooth and orderly. Anyone making their way through the brush and trees would find it impossible to move so smoothly. They had not seen what looked like a light-bearer tripping or slowing to make his way through particularly difficult brush. They were near enough to the ridge to see through the scattered low bushes that there were no trails straight up the ridge side for anyone to walk. It was far too steep and rocky to easily climb as well.

"Confused by these discoveries, they continued on. Tío Pedro, being a very good shot, spotted a wild chicken and shot it dead from thirty paces. At least they had something to show for their efforts and time. Their mamá would be happy with that. They came across one of the little *granjas*—farms, just a simple jacalito—shack—made of mesquite and carrizo cane. After greeting the farmer, they asked if he could spare them some frijoles and perhaps three tortillas. They had not eaten since yesterday's supper. They offered the farmer the chicken. 'I will accept it,' and took the chicken. 'I am afraid I cannot feed you in exchange for it because it is one of my own chickens,' said the farmer. Papá and my uncles laughed at this, realizing their mistake. There was no argument because it is important to keep good relations in a community. They told the farmer of the mysterious lights and thought they might have been borne by smugglers. 'The only smugglers around here are from your village,' he said. 'The lights, though, were brujas. They hunt for lost children and young men out for no good, and for smugglers too. They will steal those souls to use in their evil spells, and whisper sinful words into their victims' ears, leaving them mindless simpletons, barren of the grace of God.' Fearful of the close call they had, they thanked the farmer for warning them and headed for home as fast as their tired legs could carry them.

"Papá said that while they continued to deer hunt at night, they never ever went to that ridge. When he told the story, there was always the glint of fear in his eyes."

"What do you think the lights were?" whispered Doris.

Inés shrugged. "Obviously brujas…" followed by a long pause. "Or I think too much tequila to keep warm."

We all laughed quietly, except for Agnes, but I thought I saw her give a half smile. I was grateful to Inés to take our minds off our plight, even for a short time.

The storm finally arrived. Leaving a hard rain, it blasted on through in two or three hours. The wind died, and it grew even colder.

Our clothes were still damp, but we put them on to let our body heat dry them further. We did shiver doing that. We had brought in the half-dry blankets before the storm came. We hung them around us where we huddled at the fire. They would dry faster and blocked some of the intruding breeze.

We let the fire die before using up all the wood. We needed to save some for the morning if they brought us an ember. Wearing now dry, but still dirty and smelly, clothes and bundled up in twos in blankets and serapes, we actually got some sleep. Except Agnes. She woke up screaming at least three times. I did not wake up screaming. I only woke once crying and felt like I was lost. Paco and Falo sticking their heads in to count us were of little bother.

No men barged in to drag us out for disgusting acts.

Aún no, por lo menos.

CHAPTER TWENTY-THREE

Not yet, anyway.

Mesquite limbs were torn off our lean-to, opening it to the weak sunlight and wind. My heart stopped as the screaming started. Another sweep of the thrusting arm ripped off more limbs.

"Where is the little blonde bitch!" shouted El Xiuhcoatl. His face was a sheer terror.

We could not move fast enough bundled up in our blankets and still sleep dazed. El Xiuhcoatl latched onto Agnes's arm and dragged her out, kicking limbs away and her screaming, "Leave me alone, leave me alone!"

Doris was shrieking at the top of her lungs, "No! Take me instead!"

El Xiuhcoatl kicked Doris in the face and slapped at me as I tried to grab his leg. Grabbing Agnes's neck, he swung a punch into her stomach, doubling the girl over, her face in shock and mouth gaping open. Agnes collapsed, and El Xiuhcoatl grabbed her arms, hauling her to her feet while she was still trying to take in air. He dragged her to his hut. Inés and I were trying to hold the screaming Doris down.

Turning before he ducked into the adobe, he shouted, "Chago, get everyone ready to ride. We are leaving when I am through."

Holding Doris in my arms, listening to her sobs, her agonized face close to mine, I cried for her and Agnes. I cried for all of us.

Tía Chavela was shouting at El Xiuhcoatl, telling him she was ashamed to be his aunt, that he was a sinful man, and God would punish him.

A thought crawled through my mind, an ungracious thought. I wanted to be God's instrument for El Xiuhcoatl's inevitable punishment and damnation.

The ground, the mesquite, and parts of the basin's high sides were ice covered.

The other men went about saddling their horses and loading up, some making crude jokes about their jefe's breakfast. I heard repugnant sounds. I was sickened. I held Doris until El Xiuhcoatl came out with an obscenely pleased look and went to his waiting saddled horse.

Doris and I ran to the adobe. Agnes was sprawled on a serape, naked—fresh bruises, an eye swollen shut, bloody nose…and blood elsewhere. She made no effort to cover herself. She did not roll into a ball as usual. Her gaping mouth and unmoving eye told me she was completely broken. She did not care. She was no longer with us.

Doris sobbed, begging her to look at her, to get up. Agnes did not move. I touched Doris's shoulder, and she yanked away from me, giving me an angry glare. I picked up Agnes's clothes and got Doris to help dress her. I knew we had to go. Agnes did not resist. She did not help.

If we did not get moving fast, they would come and drag us out, if not first taking us for their pleasure.

Agnes could not even walk. We dragged her out as Inés brought up her horse and helped us push and pull her onto the saddle.

Our still-dirty blankets hung over our saddles.

Inés said, "They took away our serapes, but we can have them back at night. They think keeping us cold will make us easier to dominate."

They were probably right.

The bandidos lined up military style as was their custom. We fell in near the column's end with the spares and pack mules.

Tía Chavela stood near the gap, yelling obscenities and shame at her two bandido nephews. "You dishonor our family! If she were still alive, your mother would be ashamed!" Her heavy face was enraged.

"Shut up, you stupid old woman!' shouted El Xiuhcoatl. "We will be back in a week or sooner."

"Then bring soap and salt this time!" she shouted.

Inés and I looked at each other. Where would we be?

Tía Chavela stepped toward him holding a leather bag and pushed it at him. "Take this repugnant thing with you."

Chago, as evil as he is, looked embarrassed by the way his brother talked to their aunt. She never called him Chago, but Santiago Francisco.

Why would the bandit jeje keep his own aunt, and I guessed other relatives, here? It must be to keep it ready as a hideout. It must be like living in a prison, maybe worse.

We threaded our way through the slot gorge and came out on the ridge's side. The weak sun barely showed any light through the high clouds. The bandidos spread out and moved slowly to leave less sign of their passage as when we had entered. We gathered back into a column and rode along the base of an increasingly higher and steeper ridge.

It soon began a very light rain, but it did not feel as cold. We rode farther out from the high cliffs as there were so many huge boulders and rocks and ravines at their base.

The rain stopped, and the clouds broke up. There was a light haze over the mesquite, and we could not see very far. We were back to eating cold carne seca and tortillas. At least the tortillas were fresh. They said we would have a hot meal tonight. I did not know if that meant us or just the bandidos. Later in the afternoon, the ground haze was mostly gone, but still misty in the distance.

I did not see El Gigante Feo. Had he stayed out in the hideout? I hope so.

Agnes was no better. Doris stayed close behind her. When we stopped, we all had to help her onto the ground and to remount. Doris had to help her to simply pee. She was unable to do anything for herself. Her eyes were closed most of the time. No matter what was said to her, she never responded. She was as mute as me.

I noticed we were again on a little-used trail near the cliff's base. It gradually led up the slope. Paco said it was a hidden trail no one else knew of—which I doubted—reaching to the top of the Estacado Múzquiz. The escarpment's cliff face was over one hundred vara high. The trail was rocky and ranged from too narrow to wide enough for three horses to walk side by side. Sometimes it leveled off, and other times it was too steep for my liking. I had never climbed anything but a low hill. I wanted to keep my eyes closed, but was afraid to do that too. I did not trust the horse to keep his footing. The other girls were no happier than me.

It was amusing that many of the tough bandidos did

not like it, either. Most dismounted and led their horses. At one place, we all had to dismount. A huge overhanging boulder thrust out of the cliff's side too low over the trail for a mounted person to pass under.

It was difficult and scary for Inés and Doris to get Agnes down. She stood looking over the edge. The tottering girl took a step and then another, and I realized what she intended. I tried to yell, making only a gurgle noise. Inés leaped toward Agnes, just managing to grab an arm, and almost went over with her. Doris slipped on the gravel as she dodged forward. That was for the better as she tumbled into the back of Agnes's legs, causing her to flip backward, falling over Doris. Agnes hit the ground hard. Gravel bounced over the ledge's side. Inés griped Agnes's arm with both hands. Doris scrabbled and got an arm around Agnes's neck. I dove and grabbed her other arm. She gave a couple of weak kicks. The horses scrambled around whickering in fear and confusion. Kicking gravel, they tried to back farther away from the edge, but the cliff side and other horses prevented this. One hoof struck Inés' shoulder, but she did not let go.

The horses settled down. We all clung desperately to Agnes, breathing hard. Horses nickered, still frightened.

A whisper barely, "I want to die. Let me, please."

My heart cried for this girl. I wanted to pray for her, but my mind raced in circles.

"No, no Agnes." Doris struggled to get the words out. "Life's still worth living. Do not give up, my little sister!"

"It's not," she whispered hoarsely.

"What is this?" shouted Chago. His face was angry. "What is she trying to do?"

"She slipped," said Doris.

"She did not. I saw what happened. She tried to jump."

"Do you blame her?" asked Inés with a defiant glare.

Chago slapped her, causing her to stagger back. "Get her on her horse. Do not let this happen again. El Xiuhcoatl wants her again tonight."

"You are pigs!" Doris shouted.

He slapped her too. "Shut up, bitch!"

Once we got the limp girl in her saddle, Chago and Paco tied her wrists and tied her ankles to the stirrups.

"You cannot do that," said Doris. "What if the horse slips and falls? She will not be able to jump off."

He slapped Doris again. "She wanted to dive over the cliff anyway. We would have one less horse, and my brother would have to fuck you tonight."

"You are a cruel man," said Inés.

"You are correct." He slapped at Inés, but she ducked and got the horse between Chago and herself.

"You may be a cruel man, but you are no real man."

He did not slap her. "I will show you tonight what a real man is."

"I doubt that."

He slapped her, causing her to stumble back. "Get on your horse, whore!"

Inés stayed in front of Agnes with Doris behind her. She would move up to her left, placing herself between Agnes and the drop-off. It came to me that in her agony she might simply ride her horse off the cliff. I did not think so, though. She was a ranch girl and would never intentionally harm a horse like that. I hoped.

It seemed to take hours. I was grateful when we reached the top. It was a maze of ravines, ridges, and big boulders, some as big as houses. It looked so strange to me. Nothing grew in this garden of rock, "*El jardín de los diablos*"—the Devil's Garden, said one of the bandidos. "The Devil does not like trees."

I looked out onto the land below us. The ground was covered in haze, and the long shadows of ridges hid it from the Sun.

We rode up a deep ravine that opened into a barren, flat-bottomed basin. There were puddles of standing water all about, and the horses were watered. The men drank from their canteens, but they told us to use the same puddles as the horses. One man laughed and said to make sure the horses watered first before we fouled the water. The men peed, not caring if we could see them or not. They gave us a little dried venison and tortillas. They were still fresh enough from the hideout.

Doris stayed close to Agnes. She still just stared into the sky or the rocky basin side, anywhere there were no men.

It was close to dark. Inés said, "They may stop soon. It is too rugged here to travel in the dark."

Instead of leaving through a large ravine on the basin's far side, we went up a smaller, steeper ravine. It slanted upward, and the bottom was broken slabs of rock. There was so much loose rock that we had to walk the horses. It seemed I slipped every three or four steps, skinning my knees, hands, and elbows. The horses slipped, struggled, and bucked in their frustration. It was painfully slow. The horses had to be pulled forward, and their jerking reins tried to yank our arms out.

Agnes managed to keep up. She struggled just as hard as us to keep going. Maybe she was not completely lost from us.

As higher ridge shadows were darkening the ground, I realized we were on somewhat level ground, a sort of bowl. One side opened out showing the land below us. It was a broken maze of rocks. We were looking back on the way we had come up the escarpment earlier. We had not come far, but it had taken a long time. Besides all the scrapes and bruises, my hips and legs were so sore I could barely stay on my feet. I knew the other girls would be worse off. I had long been used to walking, although not on such rocky ground and steep climbs.

Paco seemed disturbed about something. "We will camp here. No fires. No loud noises or talking."

There was a rocky hollow in the side of the bowl. It was barely large enough for the four of us. We unsaddled and put them in the hollow. It was the first time we kept the saddles. They make a pillow of sorts. The horses were led off. They would have to be given some of the little feed the bandidos had. Nothing grew here.

Paco laid out his bedroll at the opening of our hollow. Falo set his bed overlooking us on the bowl's opposite side.

Chago walked up out of the darkness. He too seemed disturbed. He told Paco, "Keep them here. If they have to piss, they can do it right there. No one comes for them tonight. El Xiuhcoatl does not want to hear a single sound." He turned and left.

Paco gave us some carne seca and tortillas. "He means it when he says no noise."

After we had eaten, Paco, Falo, and another man—he had taken me—came into the bowl, and without warning, the first two jumped on Agnes. The other man kicked and swung at us and said, "Make no noise!" They gagged Agnes and pushed her onto her serape.

"So she cannot scream in her sleep," said Paco. "There will be no noise."

Algo está pasando.

CHAPTER TWENTY-FOUR

Something was going on.

We were afraid to take Agnes's gag off because the bandidos were truly worried about something. No one could be following us in this rock maze, at least not closely.

We were cold, but it did not rain. Agnes did scream and cry in her sleep. Doris held her with a hand over her mouth. At least no one came to prove his manhood during the night.

Chago appeared at first light and talked to Paco and Falo in whispers before leaving. Paco told us to keep silent. He would gag and whip anyone making noise. We were to be ready to leave.

Was someone following us and nearby? Who? I could only hope, but it seemed possible. I said the rosary and prayed as we sat silently, afraid to attract attention.

Paco left to make sure our horses were saddled and

ready to ride.

Inés said to Falo, "What is happening? Are we in danger from someone?"

The skinny bandido looked around. "Do not tell anyone I spoke of this. The gringos, they are behind us. They are coming up the escarpment trail."

My heart leaped. My Bud! He was coming for me! They were coming for all of us! I could not help but think why would he come after me? I was nothing. I had been soiled, dragged through the dirt, brutalized, debased, and defiled in ways that all men would know when they saw me. He would not want me. I was like the unclean in the Bible, the lepers.

Agnes even showed interest with a barely hopeful smile. Doris hugged her and whispered, "Pa's coming!"

Inés waved her hands and told them to be quiet. Falo frowned. "Silence!"

Fear suddenly raced through my heart. Were the gringos walking into an ambush? They would not have a chance on that narrow rocky trail. If they reached the top, they could be shot at from many directions and from higher up with the bandidos hidden in the jumbled rocks.

I wanted Inés or Doris to start shouting as loud as they could. I knew that was impossible. It would get them shot or beaten to death.

Chago came up quietly. "Do you want to see what is going to happen to your rescuers?" He sneered.

Doris shook her head, still holding Agnes to her. She did not want to see their papá possibly killed. I had more faith. Bud would charge into the bandidos and shoot them all down. Who were the ambushers, though? I could see that most of the bandidos were here and getting their horses ready.

Inés and I followed Chago to a cliff's edge. He let us follow but motioned for us to keep down.

There were a few gringos coming out of a big ravine. I recognized it as the basin we had camped in. They were far off, but I recognized Bud in his gray coat and hat. I did not think it was him at first as he was on a pale yellow horse that was almost invisible against the rocks. Maybe he left Crackers behind.

Seeing Bud now after all these terrible days, I cannot say how I felt. There was joy and fear, fear that he was in danger. His horse staggered as a pink spray burst from its head. Bud went down with it as the sound of the shot reached us, a hollow boom that echoed back and forth. I tried to yell, but nothing came out. Inés grabbed me as I tried to stand. My heart screamed. I expected a barrage of shots to hit our gringos, but it did not come. Dust kicked up beside Bud, pinned down by the horse. Only one other booming shot echoed off the rock cliffs and peaks.

More shots broke out, but it was from the following gringos, not from a bandido ambush. A horseman charged out of the rocks and passed Bud. It may have been Flaco. He headed straight for the shooter, I guessed. Four men with carbines ran out to Bud and dragged him from under the horse. More shots popped farther up the ravine. Bud was carried behind some rocks, and more men rode up. Was he hurt? Flaco rode back from the ravine carrying an extra carbine. He must have gotten at least one of the stay-behind bandidos.

Chago had a look on his face showing he had not expected this outcome. Bandidos were rapidly mounting, and we were told to also. We rode up a ravine.

After a time, two bandidos caught up with us. They had been the rear guard. We soon stopped, and the two men and El Xiuhcoatl dismounted. He harangued them for failing to kill any of the gringos, only managing to shoot one horse, and he knew the gringos had many spares. They even got one of their own men killed, and his buffalo carbine was left behind. They were not even able to count how many gringos there were. Without warning, he lashed his reins across their faces.

"Mount! We ride!"

I did not understand why they had not set a real ambush with all the bandidos. Now they were on the run, and they did not even know if there were more or fewer gringos after them.

El Xiuhcoatl was not as crafty a bandido as many thought.

It soon became difficult. We rode sometimes but more often walked leading the horses. Even Agnes walked. Her breathing was difficult, and she fell or tripped often, simply from being hunger-weakened and overexhausted.

We followed winding ravines, wide and narrow, climbed ridges, and rode down broad valleys. Barren and rocky. Plants were as rare as scorpions with wings. It remained cold, but at least it did not rain. The wind changed its mind on how hard it blew and from which direction.

El Xiuhcoatl would leave two men behind for an hour, and then when they caught up with us, he left another two. By late afternoon he decided that we had lost the gringos or they had turned back. They had thought that before and found the gringos did not give up so easily. Still, some of the bandidos said they felt they were being followed, and that was a feeling they were not used to.

I did not believe our men had quit. Neither did Doris or Inés. They reasoned if they had come this far and had caught up with us atop the escarpment, they would not give up. I knew Bud and Flaco were good trackers. If they had lost us, they would find us again sometime.

Listening to the bandidos talk, they had expected the rear guard this morning to run off the cowardly gringos.

They were wrong. I was worried, though, because I did not know if Bud was wounded or not.

It was a very long day, very hard. The poor food was never enough, not enough sleep, fear, feeling dirty, uncertainty, and walking, walking. Inés and Doris had a cough. I had a headache that would not go away.

Chago finally let Agnes ride because she was so weak. "She is so little that she will not tire the horse by riding all the time." She was a little more alert but was always looking behind her in hope of salvation.

I was smaller than Agnes, but they did not let me ride. They knew I was a nómada and used to hard walking.

We stopped to rest. Agnes just about toppled off the horse. Inés caught her and eased her to the ground. Doris took her own blanket off and wrapped it around her. It was cold, but at least here we were out of the wind.

"I…I'm cold, I'm cold," Agnes stuttered while shivering.

I needed to pee. I hissed at Paco and pointed to a pile of rocks. He nodded, allowing me a bit of privacy. I was sore all over, but especially in between my legs, which made me nauseated to think about it. I took a gourd canteen and rag, went behind the rocks, and opened my blanket to pull down my drawers. A knee jammed into my back, and a smelly, calloused hand clasped around my face and covered my mouth. I was yanked off my feet and flat onto the ground. My neck was wrenched, and the grip tightened.

"*¡Silencio!*" in guttural Spanish.

These bastards cannot even wait for tonight! I thought. That shook me, that I was thinking that way, that I expected and maybe even accepted I would be raped again.

I swung the heavy gourd canteen around, but an arm blocked it. A hand knocked the canteen from me. Why was he clamping my mouth shut? They all knew I could not speak, could not shout. Locked tight by both of his arms, he dragged me backward and around a big boulder. So this is where he is going to do it. I hated myself. I was beginning to accept this disgrace. The bastard. I struggled harder. I had no hope. I was locked in his arms. I hated him beyond reason. I hated him so much that God would punish me for holding so much hate. He stunk too. We all did, but this one stunk like greasy goat meat gone bad.

He did not stop at the boulder, but pulled me to my feet and clamped his hand even tighter over my mouth, dragging me after him. My blanket fell off. He hauled me down a small ravine over rocks and ledges. Where was he taking me? Why? I panicked and started kicking and tried to reach back and scratch his face. He only clamped harder. I bit into the flesh between his thumb and trigger finger. I bit harder, so hard I hoped I would leave my teeth in his hand. He yelped and pulled away. He let go with his other arm and swung a fist into my face. It stung as if I was hit with a rock. I slumped to the ground, trying to hold myself up. A kick struck my shoulder, and I rolled onto my back. I remember thinking it did not feel like a hard-soled boot.

Hands grabbed me and pulled me up. Of all the terror I had endured, what rushed through me now made that all seem as nothing.

An Apache loomed over me! I kicked, hit, struggled any way I could. It made no difference. Another of the terrors appeared and grabbed me. They chattered in their language of tiny choppy words and laughed. The first one punched me in the belly, and I was dragged as I tried desperately to suck in even a little air.

I heard faint shouts calling my name. The bandidos knew I was gone. They must have thought I ran off on my own. It was peculiar, but I prayed the bandidos would rescue me.

Farther down the ravine were three more indios squatting by their five horses. They stood and laughed and chattered when they saw me. They wore grease-blackened buckskins and thick wool ponchos. Their long braids were speckled with bits of leaves and dead grass. Two had bows, two held old single-shot carbines, and one a repeating carbine. I saw a tomahawk hung on one's simple saddle.

They pushed me toward a horse, and what looked like the youngest one climbed on the horse, and the others boosted me up. One grabbed my butt, and they all laughed. Even in their strange language, I knew it was something crude. A wild horror rushed through me. They had kidnapped me! The whole thing would start over with more beatings, rapes, and shame. I threw my head back and screamed impotently and mutely to Heaven. If I had a voice, God would have heard me. As I did not, I knew I was lost.

I knew what indios did. They stole women, young ones, even young girls. If they were unmarried, they sold their captive to a married indio for his second or third or fourth wife. Then he could buy his own first Apache wife. If he was married, he could keep the kidnapped girl as a wife-slave or sell her.

I could no longer hear shouts from the bandidos. I cried. They stopped, and the oldest and youngest indios slapped my face hard. It was their way of telling me to be quiet and where my place was. We followed the ravine downward, taking it slow because of loose rocks and the steep slope.

I was on the fourth horse, and the smelly pig holding me in front of him kept groping my breasts, which already hurt. I tried not to think, but that never worked. My mind plunged into the darkest depth. I started trying to think. There was only one indio behind me. I started clutching all over on the saddle and the indio's thighs like I was afraid to fall off. I felt his knife and tomahawk under his poncho. He slapped at my hands.

A carbine shot cracked like thunder and echoed through the ravine. A big piece of the leading indio's skull flew away with a red spray. He tumbled over the horse's rump and struck the ground with his brains dashing onto the rocks. Gripping my indio's gray poncho, I flung myself off the horse. I may be small, but the surprise of me throwing myself off caught him unbalanced, and he came with me. He landed hard on my legs, making me gasp. More shots cracked. I could not tell where they were coming from with the rebounding echoes.

My indio's bow slung across his back was broken, and his arrows spilled. He came up on his knees and flung his poncho back, yanked his tomahawk from its thong, grabbed me by the throat, and swung his tomahawk back to chop into my face. His face went from a snarling anger to surprised empty as I thrust his knife into his solar plexus, the place where his soul and spirit lives. Hot blood sprayed on me.

He jerked upright, and I brought my knees up to shove him off, which I could barely do. With a cough and a deep grunt, he fell on his side. Blood bubbled from his mouth. I scrambled up, not knowing which way to run in the narrow ravine with indios in front and behind me. The second indio fired his single-shot carbine upward and fumbled it open to reload. More shots popped from higher up, and the indio jerked with repeated hits. The third indio came off the right side of his speckled white horse, planted his feet, and fired an arrow upward, using the horse for cover. The horse was struck several times, twitching with each hit. Before the horse fell, he fired two more arrows upward and drew another.

The last indio was behind me and firing his repeating carbine at the ravine's top edge. A shotgun went off, spraying the indio and his horse with birdshot. The small pellets did not discourage him as he fired more shots. He was hit again and again with bullets and fell over his downed horse.

I didn't hesitate. Running up the ravine, I grabbed the repeating carbine as I passed the blood-leaking body. The wounded horse bit at me he was so angry with humans. More shots cracked behind me. I glanced back and saw the indio with bow and arrows running after me. Running harder, I clambered over rocks and ledges. I did not know if the indio was after me or only trying to get away. No more shots. I clawed my way over rocks, tearing my fingers. The soreness between my legs was tormenting.

I ran my bloody fingers across my forehead and down my cheeks. I turned to face the indio. He was big! I worked the carbine's lever to make sure it was loaded, aimed at the climbing indio's chest, and squeezed the trigger. *Click*. When I levered the carbine to make sure it was loaded, I had ejected the last live cartridge and the magazine was empty. I threw the carbine as hard as I could at the indio. It fell to the rocks not even halfway between us. I continued up the ravine with swelling panic. A rock slab shot out from under my feet, and I slammed onto the rocks, skinning my knees and palms even more, and knocked some breath out.

There was no one shooting at the indio. I was in trouble. I heard an *abejorro*—bumblebee—buzz past and heard a stick clatter on the rocks ahead. He had shot an arrow at me. I am sometimes grateful for being so small.

Climbing frantically, I had a vision of a vara-long arrow piercing my back and passing through a lung. I visualized an arm's length bloody dogwood shaft sticking out of my chest.

A shape appeared above me in the middle of the ravine. "*¡Al piso!*"—Get down!

I tripped anyway.

Turning to look back, the indio shot another arrow, and I ducked. A carbine cracked, and the indio dropped to his knees with the bow falling to his side. Another shot and the indio fell face forward, smacking onto a rock.

I looked up the trail and Lencho, the young bandido, stood levering another cartridge into his carbine. An arrow was stuck in his green and yellow poncho!

I gasped and scrambled to my feet and made my way up the ravine. My chest hurt I was breathing so hard. It made no matter that he was a kidnapping, raping bandido. He had caught an arrow trying to save my wretched life. I rushed up to him and pointed frantically at the arrow.

Looking at where I pointed, his eyes grew large. He handed me his carbine, and I took it as I would have from Bud with not a thought of shooting the bandido and fleeing for my soul's sake.

He clutched the arrow and the edges of his poncho and pushed the arrow through. My eyes must have been large with surprise.

He laughed. "Rest, little one. It only pierced my poncho. You are pleased that I was not touched?"

I shook my head, *No*.

He laughed. "You are a—*guerrera*—fighter. You even have war paint." He stretched his arm out. "May I have my carbine, please?"

I saw in my mind's eye me jamming the muzzle under his chin as I pretended to hand it to him, squeezing the trigger, grabbing his pistol belt and poncho, and riding off on an indio's horse. There was a clatter of shots behind me, and the still-standing horses fell kicking and screaming like they do. Bandidos were coming down into the ravine with knives.

Lencho took the carbine from me, winked, and turned.

Arrogant bastard. I followed.

Se rieron mientras hacían su trabajo.

CHAPTER TWENTY-FIVE

The bandidos laughed as they did their bloody work.

They took the carbines—one indio had a pistol—what few cartridges they had, their pouches of poor food and water gourds, the ponchos and buffalo blankets from the saddles, their knives and tomahawks, and their scalps. They did not want the indio's clothes or moccasins and foot wraps. We could have used them. Inés asked, but they told her to shut up. They threw away a medicine bag with a small animal's jawbone, hanks of hair, dried roots, and other things flying out. They kept the few peso coins.

There was much screaming from the death-shrouded ravine when one of the indios came momentarily back to life as he was scalped.

Inés yelled, "Marta! Are you hurt?"

I shook my head. I was bloody from the indio I knifed.

"You look like you are wearing bloody war paint!"

I expected to be in trouble and accused of trying to escape. Sitting on a rock, Chago was all serious, flipping his cuarta from one thigh to the other.

"You are a fortunate girl," he said.

I did not understand. I did not feel very fortunate. I could use a cigarette.

"You have been kidnapped twice and rescued by your first kidnappers. Yes, you are fortunate." Peering at me, he added, "You should be grateful to your saviors. Do you know what would have become of you?"

I nodded. *Is there any difference?* I thought.

"You are not in trouble," he said. "We thought you had run away, but we found the water gourd and blanket. You would not have left those. You are very fortunate." He stood, nodded, and turned to walk away.

"She should be rewarded," said Inés firmly, but with a frightened quiver.

Chago rapidly turned to face her. "What?"

She took a step back. "A reward. She killed an indio. She gave you the chance to loot the indios. It is you who are fortunate."

Rewarded? I may be grateful I was spared, but I should not be rewarded for killing a man, even an indio.

Chago squinted his eye and nodded again. "You are correct. What would be a suitable…"

"Two buffalo blankets and more…"

"The two blankets are enough to ask for. Do not become prideful."

"Many thanks, Don Chago," she said seriously and gave a little curtsy.

"Ha! No one has ever called me that." He shook his head. "It will get you nothing."

I caught a thin smile on his usually harsh face as he turned. I would not complain about this reward.

"Get mounted. Shots were fired and may attract attention. We must leave this place." He said to me, "Wash your face."

Whose attention was he concerned about in this empty land? I thought. More indios, or pursuing gringos?

It ran through my mind all that had happened. It was blurry in places and so real in others. I was so frightened, but I have been so frightened for so long it did not seem as terrifying as it should.

Inés and Doris rode beside me. "How did you kill the indio?" Inés asked. "They said you killed one."

That soured my stomach. I held up my fist like I was gripping a knife, slapped my other fist over my solar plexus, made an upward stabbing motion, and then made like I was pushing him away.

They nodded understanding. "Where did you get the knife?" asked Doris.

I held up my hand with spread fingers. I pointed to the fourth finger to represent the indio and made a motion with my gripping fist like I was taking the knife away from him.

"You took his own knife and killed him with it?"

I nodded. I felt ill.

"Excellent!" both Inés and Doris said. "We have buffalo blankets! We will be warm!"

"What else were you going to ask for?" Doris asked Inés.

She sadly smiled. "More food and…and a carbine."

Looking at me, Doris said, "That must have been terrifying."

I nodded. I am glad I did not have to describe it. It is something I never want to think about. I knew I would in nightmares. I was having a lot of nightmares. Mamá had said that if I did not tell someone about a nightmare, it would come true. But my nightmares had already been true. How was I supposed to tell anyone anyway?

"Why take their scalps?" asked Doris.

"The governors of Chihuahua and Durango pay two hundred pesos for Apache and Cheyenne man scalps. A hundred pesos for women and children scalps. Coahuila no longer has a bounty."

"We are in Coahuila, and they still take scalps?" asked Doris.

"They will take them to Chihuahua or Durango for the bounty. That is a lot of money. They will take scalps from other tribes and even Mexicans because their hair all looks the same."

"The dogs," said Doris.

I wondered if I should say a prayer for the indio I killed. I thought not. They have a different god, I thought. Should I ask for forgiveness for what I did? Yes, if I can ever go to confession again, asking for forgiveness in my own way, asking it of myself and not a priest.

We were soon back on foot, except for Agnes. It was up and down. We would climb and climb and then go back downhill to have to climb higher than before. Everyone was exhausted. The horses were tiring without good grazing.

I overheard Chago say we would soon be in a place where the horses could graze. That would do us little good, I thought. We were all hungry.

It was late in the day when we came out of the rocky ridges and ravines. The ground was still rolling and hilly, but with big flat places too. There were more plants. We came to an arroyo with shallow running water. There were weedy grasses for the horses. A small ridge nearby blocked the wind, and that is where we camped.

They were sure the gringos had either turned back or had lost our trail in the rugged ground behind us. They argued which. I could only hope they were searching for our trail if they lost it.

Between some boulders at the base of the small ridge, they built a little fire. Pairs of men heated carne seca and tortillas on sticks. They let us do the same once the men finished. A few had left some tortilla scraps. Perhaps in appreciation of our favors. They put the fire out. No time for warming. There was little wind, but it was very cold.

Doris wanted to bundle Agnes up in a buffalo blanket as soon as possible.

Inés asked Paco for the two promised blankets. He teased her saying they had changed their minds. He gave them to her but kept the indios' ponchos and blankets. He also kept our serapes, saying, "You do not need them with the buffalo blankets." He passed the ponchos, blankets, and serapes out to other bandidos. We still had our own wool blankets.

The heavy, dark-brown buffalo blankets were raggedly cut on the long edges where the belly had been slit open. They were big, over two *varas* long and just as wide.

I had never slept in one. On the road, we always heard how warm they were. They were waterproof too. In light rain and cold weather they were worn with the bare-hide side out and the hairy side in. In heavy rain, the hair was worn out as it shed water well. Inés told us that only female hides taken in the winter were suitable for blankets. The bulls' hides were too thick and heavy. There was no telling how old they were. They said there were no buffalo left in Texas. My familia could not afford one, ever. I said a prayer for them in remembrance. I had not yet said any prayers today because of the day's many trials.

Agnes was just as weak as before. She had eaten little. Doris got her in the buffalo blanket. "We have to clean you up, Agnes."

"No, please. No more."

"We have to, Aggie."

I had never heard her called that.

"Please, no."

Doris said nothing further. She opened the blankets as I set the water gourd and rags beside her. With sticks, we propped up the buffalo blanket for privacy and to block the wind.

Doris lifted the filthy nightgown and gently worked down the drawers. Agnes's knees were cut and scraped with scabs forming and others torn off. Doris gently opened her legs.

"Oh no! Inés, she is bleeding. Only a little," Doris quickly added so the girl would not panic.

"It does not hurt," said Agnes, pretending it was of little matter. Doris cleaned her as best she could.

"It is not too bad," Doris said, washing off her hands. "There is nothing we can do."

Agnes's eyes grew large. "Am I going to die?"

"No, no, Aggie!" said Doris. "It is just your time." Whispering to us, she said, "They need to stop, to let her alone."

"I can do that," said Inés. She called Paco and asked him to bring Chago.

"I am your servant now, woman?" he demanded.

"We must see him." Firmly.

Paco arched an eyebrow and glared at her. She ignored him.

When he arrived, Inés said, "Don Chago, you know what happens if a woman has sex during her time of the month."

His eyes widened.

"I see you do. She catches the syphilis, and so does the man."

Mexican girls were embarrassed enough to speak of sex. The men were even more so. It was widely known but seldom spoken of what happened if one has sex during the woman's monthly time. Some said it was an old woman's story. Most believed it.

Don Chago believed. He backed away and fled to his brother.

Agnes was not touched again. That night, they all stayed away from us.

We were still hungry and sore, but it was the warmest night we had slept, even if the buffalo blankets were infested with fleas.

I lay awake for a very long time listening to Inés' breathing. Thinking, thinking, reliving the day. I knew not to. I tried to stop.

Yo quería gritar y gritar.

Chapter Twenty-Six

I want to scream and scream.

When I woke up, I knew I had slept, but not much. Agnes was crying softly with Doris whispering encouragement to her. I heard Agnes say, "Mommy never said it would be like this."

There was a heavy haze. We could have small fires, but we had to heat our food fast and be ready to ride.

Falo brought us a wooden bowl of frijoles and some tortillas. We were all grateful, but we still had enough pride not to show we were overly thankful. They were wonderful as we dipped the frijoles with cold tortillas. Even Agnes ate her share and burped.

Falo returned and took the bowl and our buffalo blankets. Fleas or not, they too had been wonderful.

"Paco says if you all behave today, you will get the blankets back tonight."

That would be wonderful. Another wonderful thing

happened. None of us were raped.

We were soon mounted and on our way. Bandidos would drop back and look us over, as though they were hungry for what they missed last night and this morning. I heard one say something about *Las Norias*. I could not say that name to the others to see if they knew what it was. Was that where we were heading? It meant "waterwheel." Out there? We had to be going someplace, not just riding into this vast empty, desolate place. We did make better time as we were out of the rugged ravines and ridges. I sometimes did not like making better time because I did not know where we were going and what would happen once there. Other times I wanted to reach wherever we were going, to be through with this endless dangerous, disgusting ride. What they did to us, they did it because they could. We were only good for cooking, washing, and sex. They hated us because that was all we were good for. Wherever we were going, that would be our lives. I felt more and more that they would not ransom us, maybe Doris and Agnes, maybe not, but certainly not Inés and me.

If they took us to this Las Norias place, would it be possible to escape? We would need to steal horses and food. We did not know the rough country here. We did not know the way home. We would just have to ride east for the Río. They would come after us, just for their pride if nothing else. But foremost, they would chase us to catch and punish us.

With no way out, that meant we were doomed to whatever fate the bandidos inflicted on us.

I was so gripped in these terrible thoughts that I did not notice another bandido riding beside me. It was Lencho, the deceiver. I glared at him. Even if he was the only bandido who had not had his way with me, him and El Xiuhcoatl himself, I shuddered and turned away from him.

"Señorita," he said quietly. "You were very brave today. I have never seen anything like that."

I wanted to say, *You would not remember it if I had accidently pulled your carbine's trigger when I could have.* Yet I should not be so harsh. He had saved my life. I could not acknowledge that, of course. He was part of the band that kidnapped and raped us and murdered people on the Dew. He had spied on us, making all this possible. I knew that he had not taken Inés, but he had taken both Doris and Agnes. Agnes, I do not understand why the dogs all wanted her. She was only a child. Was that why or because she was blonde and so pretty?

I might have been a child not long ago, but I was sixteen. One became a woman at fifteen. That was a proud time, but there were terrible things that came with it.

I hoped this would be a short conversation since I could add nothing to it. I faced him and stared blankly. I could not thank him in any way, even for my wretched life that he had helped drag me into.

I felt the indio's knife I had secreted in my flannel shirt's left sleeve. It was for me if necessary. I could use it on Lencho. That would be the end of my life. In that moment, I did not care.

"I understand if you do not wish for me to talk to you. I only want to say you are very brave, and beautiful too."

I peered at him, crossed my eyes, and drooled. He looked back at me with disgust.

"Let her alone," said Inés. "She does not understand what you are talking about. I told you she is not right in the head."

He looked sternly at her. "I can make things easier for you."

"You, how?" Inés looked so defiant that I feared for

her. "What can you do? You are the youngest of this band. They are probably still waiting for you to prove yourself as a bandido."

"I have already proven myself many times," he boasted. "To include killing the indio who was about to kill this girl. You should be careful of what you say, woman!"

I looked at Inés and shook my head sternly, pleading for her to stop. She edged away from him and kept her mouth shut.

"You are wise to remain silent, woman," he said.

She remained wise and said nothing more.

"Think about it. I could help you," he whispered.

I realized he did not want others to hear his words. I looked at Inés. She shrugged.

After a time, she whispered to me. "I will listen and see what he has to say."

I did not understand. Did he want favors from us? What did we have to offer? He could take what he wanted. I was confused. Maybe I should have accidently shot him in the ravine where no one could see us.

He fell back to the end of the slowly moving column. I had no idea what to think of this. Inés looked as confused as me. Doris looked back at us with a question on her face. Inés and I both shrugged.

It was early afternoon. Tortillas were all we had for dinner. The men still had enough frijoles for themselves.

As we rode across the never changing ground through the never ending cold, a man rode in from ahead. They always kept a couple of scouts out ahead of us. They must think no one was following us for they no longer left a rear guard to catch up later.

The column stopped, and the returned scout was pointing behind him. Four men went ahead to where a low ridge curved toward our path and ended. After they reached the end of the ridge where they could see the other side, they waved us on.

Who would be out here?

There were some faint shouts from the scouts out of sight behind the ridge. Someone was coming. The remaining bandidos, though, did not pull out carbines and pistols. Friends?

As we came around the ridge's end, there was a wagon drawn by six mules. A man and woman sat the wagon seat. There were also four horsemen and a spare horse. They were greeting the bandidos as friends. El Xiuhcoatl and Chago were speaking to the man on the wagon.

The heavy wagon was strange. I had never seen one like it. It was a big wooden box built on a freighter wagon. It was bright red with yellow stripes and edging. The old man wore a black topcoat and fur cap. He had a huge gray-specked black mustache and bushy sideburns down to his jowls. He looked at us girls with friendly eyes. The woman was not so old. She wore a dark red brocade dress partly covered by a brown coat. Her frizzy brown hair was mostly hidden by a red sunbonnet. Once she turned her head more, I was surprised she was a gringa, her eyes not friendly at all. Two shotguns and a carbine stood in their seat box.

The outriders were younger men. Two had shotguns and two carbines. The bandidos were interested in the wagon.

Bedrolls, various bags, baskets, cooking implements, and what looked like a bundled tent were roped to the wagon's roof. Water, flour, and salt barrels were fastened to the sides.

There were two windows in the wagon box's side, with bars. I realized a girl was peering out, her hands gripping the bars. What is this?

We were not close enough to hear what was being said between El Xiuhcoatl and the wagon driver. Lencho rode up to us.

"What is this, why is there a girl inside?" asked Inés.

"This is the Maestro, as *Maestro de Ceremonias*"—Master of Ceremonies.

I gave a look of not understanding.

"The man who runs a circus," he said.

I had heard of a circus, with animals performing tricks, but had never seen one and did not really understand what happened at one.

"That is his 'wife,' *Ángel Caído*—Fallen Angel. She used to be one of his whores. Two of their outriders are their sons. The others are whores' bastards."

Whores? The girl in the wagon is a whore? I asked myself.

"How many girls does he have in there?" asked Inés.

"Five," said Lencho with a sad smile. "He makes good money on them. Three are gringas. He makes excellent money off of them. They are not road-price whores."

Doris and Agnes looked frightened, taking each other's hand.

"Do not worry, my little gringas," said Chago riding up. "The Maestro has already offered a considerable sum for either or both of you gringas. No, not to worry. El Xiuhcoatl is keeping you both for your papá's ransom."

All four of us were relieved. We looked at the girl in the barred window. I could only tell that she was pale skinned.

There was a girl at the other window, but because of shadows, all I could see were knuckles tightly gripping the bars.

"El Xiuhcoatl asked me which of you two is the most trouble. I told him both. The little one," nodding at me, "cannot be trusted and never turn your back on her. She does not talk. That is a good thing. The other one, she cannot keep her mouth shut." Looking back to El Xiuhcoatl, he said, "He might trade you both for one of the Maestro's gringa girls. That would give the Maestro one more whore than he has now, and El Xiuhcoatl could make a lot of money selling the gringa even if she is used up. She would bring more money than the ransom for the two of you."

It was hard to say how old the girl behind the bars was, but she was under twenty, and she was...used up? That terrified me. I could see that Inés was fearful too.

Chago laughed harshly. "You do not seem so bold now!"

The Maestro climbed down groaning and ambled to the wagon's back, pulling out a key ring. One of the horsemen dismounted and opened the unlocked back door. Maestro said, "Come, Pelirroja." Not a common name, a ginger or red-headed girl. A thin girl cautiously stepped out of the wagon wearing a buffalo robe. I envied her for that. Her curly hair was rusty red, her eyes blue like Bud's.

Chago motioned for us to follow him to the wagon. "Off your horses," he ordered. I did not like this.

We climbed down and stayed close together, but we kept back from the girl.

What came next from the Maestro's mouth stunned me when I thought nothing else would surprise me. "Take off your clothes."

The girl did not even change her expression. Over twenty men were staring at her. She dropped the robe, pulled the simple, dingy white wool dress over her head, and slipped off the black nickers. Wearing only high laced moccasins, she stood unembarrassed. While thin, she did not look starved or mistreated. There were faint bruises on her white arms and shoulders and a long healed scar on her calf.

"You too," ordered Chago. "Both of you. Take off your clothes."

I was unable to move or breathe. All of these men stared at me. My right knee began to quiver.

"Do it," whispered Inés. "They will beat and strip us if we do not."

God protect and forgive me, I thought.

"Do not show fear, do not be embarrassed. These men are dirt, nothing," she whispered.

Inés dropped her blanket and pulled her rebozo and nightgown over her head. I let my blanket and shawl fall, unbuttoned my flannel shirt, and took off my long johns. I tried to be strong and stare straight ahead, but I docilely lowered my eyes to the ground. The rain-cleansed sky above and the mud below. I was trapped in between.

We stood in the chilling wind, our hair blowing. We did not cover ourselves with our arms. I was strong enough to keep from doing that. There are no words for the humiliation, the staring hungry eyes, and crude laughs.

El Xiuhcoatl looked at the thin gringa and then at us. "We will keep these two," muttered El Xiuhcoatl. "Keep your white-skinned gringa, Maestro. I will keep my healthy Mexican girls. They know their place and understand the work they are fit for." Looking at Doris and Agnes, "I will get more than enough ransom for my two gringas and keep my other two to work…on their feet and on their backs." He looked back at us. "Get dressed. Mount up."

I understood then how it was to be.

No íban a pedir rescate.

CHAPTER TWENTY-SEVEN

We are not to be ransomed.

The realization of that struck me like a machete. That was to be our life, slaves to work and fuck until we were used up. What happened when we were used up? Our throats slit like an old dried-out milk goat?

My legs gave way.

Inés and the girl grabbed at me, but I fell anyway. I remember Inés rapidly pulling on her own clothes. The girl started dressing me, and Inés helped. The girl did not care if she was naked and covered with goose bumps. I was on my feet but felt like I was someplace else, or maybe I only wanted to be elsewhere.

Chago told the men to get back into order and mount up. The girl picked up her clothes and shuffled back to the wagon without being told. Doris shouted at her, "What's your name? Where are you from?"

The girl looked at her without expression. "*Yo soy Sarah Brunet de Laredo*"—I am Sarah Brunet from Laredo, in a hoarse whisper. She climbed into the wagon. There was a miniature chandelier hanging over the door. It was missing many of the crystal pieces. I guess it was supposed to make the wagon look elegant. I had seen chandeliers through saloon doors. One hung in the Fitch Hotel.

Maybe Doris thought she could help her. Why? We could not help ourselves.

El Xiuhcoatl and the Maestro spoke further, and the bandido jefe seemed upset, even angry. They *abrazoed* and the Maestro climbed to his wagon seat.

With the Maestro and his outriders waving and shouting farewell, they went on. His wife had ignored everything. The chandelier jingled.

"Where are they going?" Doris asked Chago. I had thought the same. There was nothing out here.

"*La Babia.*"

"Where is that?"

Chargo glanced at her. "You would not know if I told you. Ask no more questions."

I tried to push what had just happened out of my mind. The humiliation was overwhelming. Yes, I had been raped, brutalized, and shamed in more ways than I could have ever imagined. *Push it away.* I rode staring at the jagged horizon ahead, at the mist and low, dirty gray clouds. It would not go away. *I will not cry. I will not cry. Rocks, mist, clouds. It would not go away. I will not cry. I will not cry.*

I held a fearful feeling. The men were quiet and seemed edgy.

But I did cry.

We stopped early. I do not know why because we had been making good time on the more open ground. Maybe we were going to cook here and then camp elsewhere. Again, it came to me that they thought someone may be following. They did not send scouts back to see, though. It seemed like the legendary El Xiuhcoatl did not know what to do.

There was a little stream, and the horses were watered. Two picket lines were strung and the horses tied as there was not much for them to graze on. They were given some feed.

There was good firewood, though. Some of the men started gathering it.

Paco told us to gather firewood too. Walking around picking it up seemed impossible. It was difficult to stay on my feet. Agnes sat on a rock. She was barely able to walk. Doris stayed near her. Paco told her to pick up wood too, but he let Agnes alone. Inés set stones in a fire circle. She was so worn out that she had to gather rocks on her hands and knees.

Goyo, a mean-spirited bandido with little round eyes, strutted up to Doris and knocked the firewood from her hands and slapped her until she fell to her knees. He hit her in the stomach for no reason! She already could not fight back. He yanked Doris up, dropping her blanket, and pulled her nightgown over her head and arms, trapping her. He pulled her up, took her muddy blanket, and dragged her away to the rocks.

We looked away, wanting to act like it was not happening but really wanting to run, run as far away as possible. Agnes huddled under her blankets with her hands over her ears.

When it was over, Doris lay on the gravel and pulled her blanket over herself. I wanted to go to her, but when I started to, Paco shook his head. She did not get up for some time. She came to me, and I held her as she cried. We both cried.

"Will this ever end?" she asked as she wept.

I held her at arm's length and looked into her wrenched eyes, purple encircled from blows. *Yes*, I nodded as firmly as I could. *They will come for us.*

"When, when?"

I hugged her. I looked out across the broad valley with its clearing mist.

Bud, come to me.

I noticed El Xiuhcoatl walking around kicking rocks. One time he talked to his brother. Was he angry because of Doris's rape, or was it something else? He had not cared before about anyone being raped.

Finally, he called another man named Manolo—Manuel—over and talked to him for a time. They were joined by Chago again.

Something was going on.

The man called to five others, and they were soon saddling their horses. They had not even eaten. El Xiuhcoatl talked to them. He was angry enough that I could hear his growling voice, but the wind did not let me make out his words.

The six men rode off in the direction the brothel wagon had come from, the way we were to go, I guessed.

What was going on?

Paco gave us our buffalo blankets.

Inés asked him, "Where are they going? Are we in danger?"

"No, no. There is a problem in Las Norias. El Xiuhcoatl sent some men to see what is happening. We will take care of the problem when we arrive."

"How far away…"

"No more questions, woman. Stay silent tonight if you know what is good for you." He left.

Inés and I sat together. We did not "speak."

I thought, though. I worried about Doris. She had not

spoken since asking me if this would end. Not even to Agnes. I thought too about the girl in the wagon…Sarah. I wondered about the others, the ones I had not seen. What kind of trouble was there in Las Norias? Were we riding into trouble? What difference did it make if there was more trouble?

The men were getting noisy by the fire. They must not be concerned that anyone was following us. They did set a horse-mounted guard roving about.

It was full dark. Little wind, but cold.

A man sat down beside us with no warning. Startled, I felt for my knife.

"I am sorry to frighten you," said Lencho. He handed Inés a bowl of barely cooked frijoles with bits of carne seca and tortilla crumbs.

"Give it to Doris," she said, holding it out.

"I already gave her a bowl."

Inés looked at him. "Why are you being kind to us?"

He was silent for a time. "I do not like to see what has happened here."

"You chose this life. When you came to the ranch, you were proud of what you were doing. You lied to us."

"I am sorry."

"You have much to be sorry for. People, good people, died because of you," Inés said bitterly. "You are responsible too for what has happened to us. You had your way with the gringas like these other dogs." With anger, she said, "*Angas*, she will never be the same. We will never be the same. If we survive this."

"I wish this had not happened. I mean that."

"You chose this life," Inés said. "You should not be here. Go away."

Dejected, he stood and said, "The men bought a keg of *pulque* from the Maestro. Stay away from them." He faded into the night.

"This is not good," Inés said. "Pulque. That is bad."

Pulque was made from the *maguey* plant. I had sipped it. The sour milky drink was a peon's cheap drunk.

We bundled up in the buffalo blanket. It was warm. I hurt. I hurt all over. I dreamed of Bud, charging into the bandidos and shooting them all down.

Screaming awakened me. It was Doris!

Then it was my garbled screaming as I was dragged out of the blankets. Inés did not scream. She fought, growling like a puma. I tried to be strong like her and fought back. I pulled out the knife. I got one on the arm, and maybe another on the leg. The knife flew out of my hand with a stinging blow. Both Inés and I were screaming now. They held us down. El Xiuhcoatl was on me, pulling off my clothes and slapping me hard again and again. He grabbed my jaw and wrenched my mouth open to spit into it. I was beaten into helplessness and submission. His face…

I watched the softness of the Moon barely seen through the clouds.

There were things… Things that I…I… There was no one I could tell, ever.

Él está ahí afuera. Lo sé.

CHAPTER TWENTY-EIGHT

He is out there. I know it.

I lay in the mud. It was so cold that I could not feel myself. I thought that was a good thing because if I could feel, the pain would be unendurable.

I could hear Doris crying.

Do something, I told myself. I could not simply lay there and die. Or maybe I could. Death would be a good thing right now. I remembered the skull masks people wear on the *Día de Muertos*—Day of the Dead. I would like to go to that world.

Doris was still crying and coughing too. There was a campfire, barely a glow now as it died for the night. With its death, the brujas would be out.

I heard men snoring. I heard horses nicker. I heard the wind. I was cold. *Get up!*

I made it to my hands and knees. It took me time to find my clothes, wet and muddy and filthy in other ways. I found Doris in the buffalo blanket. She jerked away when I touched her. I patted her shoulder and hugged her. She gripped me like she would never let go. We found her clothes too and then found Agnes. They had left her alone, afraid of the syphilis. She too still coughed.

I got them into their buffalo blanket.

Inés I could not find. I did find our buffalo blanket.

I walked to the barely burning fire. Men, the filthy dogs they were, were rolled up in their serapes and ponchos. A guard on horseback passed by. I threw sticks on the dying fire, not to warm the sleeping dogs but for more light to see by.

I still could not find Inés. It did not matter.

I took our buffalo blanket to where Doris and Agnes were. I think I slept some with nightmares, or it may have been only me remembering what had happened. I wanted to vomit, but I could not. No matter. Nothing mattered.

"Marta. Marta, wake up." It was Inés shaking my ankle.

The sky was washed-out gray, a heavy fog that seemed to glow. It would fade away as the sun came up.

Inés was wrapped in her muddy blanket.

I sat up. That hurt. I felt low and used.

She sat beside me. Tears streaked down her face. "I slept with Lencho." She said that, unashamed. Nothing mattered. "That bastard Goyo took me first. He beat my head against the ground. I hit a rock and was cut. Lencho, he got me away from Goyo. He tied this bandana on me to stop the bleeding." She saw my expression. "It is not bad. Head cuts always bleed a lot." A dirty yellow bandana was tied around her head. She looked at me. "He did it…to me, but it was not like with the others. He did not hurt me. I still did not like it," she said quickly. "I am ashamed and so sorry for what you and Doris went through."

It sounded to me that she was apologizing because she had it less badly than us. It did not matter.

I gripped her arm and looked into her tearing eyes. I shook my head. She should not blame herself. None of us should blame ourselves for anything. None of this was our fault. Besides, nothing mattered.

Doris and Agnes were awake but said nothing. Agnes stared out into nowhere, and Doris stared at the mud.

I stood on wobbly feet and motioned for the others to get up. Taking the buffalo blankets, we staggered to the fire and sat huddled together on the upwind side. We were a terrible looking band. I thought anyone who had known us from before would not recognize us, even close up. We were all battered and bruised, muddy and charcoal-dirty faces with cuts and scrapes, blackened eyes, swollen noses and split lips, and our hair tangled and muddy, with bits of grass and leaves. Our noses ran with snot, leaving tracks on our chins. Inés and Agnes had lost a tooth or two.

None of the men said anything and did not try and claim our spaces. They had a blackened kettle of frijoles burning. I filled a big wooden bowl, and with a single spoon, we passed it around until it was empty. I picked up a water gourd without knowing whose and did not ask permission. We went to our saddles behind the horses and sat down. As the men ate, we cleaned ourselves.

We all had diarrhea. We had trouble finding enough dry grass to wad into balls to wipe with. Inés and I ground up charcoal, and we each drank a small bowl of water with a handful of charcoal.

Men saddled horses as others ate. We were soon on the trail again. We were moving faster, but not as fast as I had expected with trouble in Las Norias. The horses were tiring and had no good fodder.

"Six," said Doris. She had dropped back to ride beside me, and Inés moved up to stay with Agnes.

She looked at me and said, "Six men."

I nodded understanding and touched her arm. There was nothing else I could do.

"If I survive this," said Doris, "I will never have another man. I will never marry."

I thought that was the saddest thing of all, the loss of hope and self-worth. She moved up alongside Agnes.

The sky brightened a little, but the storm god won and let it rain lightly, not much heavier than a mist. It wet us enough for mud to drip off our blankets. A couple of times it came down a little harder, but not for long. The storm god could not make up his mind. It did not matter.

We rode across a broad level area. There were patches of grass in places, and we let the horses saddle-graze. They needed what they could get.

Ahead was yet another low rocky ridge. The trail led up a draw between two rocky fingers on the ridge side.

We drifted into single file. Most of the men were riding side by side just as I was beside Inés and Doris with Agnes.

There were three or four men ahead with El Xiuhcoatl following. Behind him was Doris, another bandido—that scumbag Goyo—and then Agnes. Doris kept looking back to check on her sister. Lencho followed Agnes, and I was behind him. Inés followed me. I was thankful as I did not want a man directly behind me. The rest of the bandidos, including Paco and Falo, followed with the spares and mules in the very back. Chago was near the end and kept his eye on everyone.

They must have scouted this path to go up it like this. The ridge fingers on both sides were piles of tumbled boulders with mesquite and cactus trying to grow.

I wiped my runny nose. My legs felt numb and my butt sore. All this horse riding was hard. I was more used to walking. I never thought I would complain about not having to walk.

Lencho. I could not decide why he was kind to us, in his way. Maybe he wanted to do more for us, but could not. If he was too easy on us, the other bandidos would give him trouble. Instead of trying to ignore him, maybe I could convince him to help us. How could a mute girl do that? Those thoughts of stealing horses and food and running for the Río kept passing through my head. He would be taking a big risk to help us. He would have to run with us, or he would be dead, as dead as us if caught. He would not only be shot but tortured. Could all four, or five, of us run for it? Could we get away together? It was so far. And Agnes, could she make it? To try could kill her, but then not to would mean the same thing. We could not leave her. If we did, Doris would stay too. No question about that. I realized I could not leave them if I had the chance to get away, even if they told me to go without them.

That gave me another idea. What if I went by myself? I would only need a little food. I could live off the land, alone. All I would need is a little carne seca for when I could not find food, a water gourd, a knife, and a good horse. Two would be better, but one would do. If I had a night's head start…

That bastard Goyo was ahead of Agnes. He threw his arms outward and tumbled off his horse. Another bandido farther up the draw fell off, and then the crack of carbine shots reached us. Horses were bucking and rearing and fleeing in both directions, some with panicked riders still hanging on. Horses screamed, and so did men. Bullets were ricocheting off rocks, and men went down along with horses. The shots were coming from the right ridge finger and from above at the head of the draw. I could see the white puffs of smoke. Bandidos were blindly rushing into the rocks and brush with others firing pistols and carbines as they fell back. I looked ahead, first to see where the girls were. I could not see them. I looked too for El Xiuhcoatl and then behind me for Chago. They too were unseen. Behind me, a bandido's horse went down. He rolled away from the kicking and screaming horse, went to a knee, and was firing his carbine at a standing man on the ridge to my right. *It is Bud! Blessed Mother in Heaven! It is Bud! He came for me, he came!* The bandido kept firing at Bud. I saw other Americanos, hatless, standing to fire, showing themselves, I guessed to get better shots. They cared more about saving us than protecting themselves. Bandidos were shooting in confusion in all directions at anything and at nothing. Bud hit the horse of the bandido shooting at him, but he got his saddlebags off and made it into the rocks with Bud's bullets following him. My horse jerked and went down. A bandido grabbed me from behind as I scrambled away. I twisted around and hammered with my arms. He got me in a headlock and dragged me into the rocks, using me for cover as he fired his pistol. He threw me down and punched me. He struck so hard. He rose and kicked me. His head burst into a spray. I tried to get up, but my leg gave way, and I fell beside him. I was dazed, but on his belt was a knife. I grabbed it. Lencho was beside me firing two pistols. I tried to kick his leg to throw him off, but I could not reach it. He dove behind a boulder, and bullets chipped it, the fragments hitting my left shoulder.

I saw the spare horses and mules turn after stumbling over themselves and run back down the draw. Two bandidos on foot raced with them, using them for cover until one bandido was hit and run over. The other dove into the rocks.

I heard Señor DeWitt shout, "Shoot the horses!"

He did not want the bandidos to escape. He wanted them to all die right here. Rapid fire burst from the rocks across the trail and from higher up the ridge.

Falo with his Mexican army cap charged out of the rocks, jumped onto a wounded horse, and made a run for it down the draw with two riderless horses following. One went down under the barrage of fire. Falo was hit, and his pistol flew from his hand. His horse charged at full speed until it was hit and stumbled, throwing Falo headfirst into a jagged boulder, smashing his skull. The gunshots were not so rapid now. There seemed to be a lot of bandidos already killed or wounded.

Then over the shots and chipping rings of ricochets, I heard El Xiuhcoatl shouting, "Stop shooting. I will kill her." He kept yelling it in Spanish until the fire slowly died.

Then almost straight across from me, near where I had seen Bud, I heard Flaco yell, "Let the girls go, and we will let you leave."

"I will do whatever I want," shouted El Xiuhcoatl.

I pulled myself up enough to see. He was holding Doris in front of himself. He had ripped off her nightgown and pulled up her long johns shirt to grasp her breast. I could not see all of them, but it looked like he held his pistol between her legs. He back-dragged her farther into the rocks and disappeared.

Señor DeWitt was shouting, and I heard other Americanos yelling too. I did not understand what was being said. Once I heard Bud, so I knew he was alive if not wounded.

Lencho was excited. He was looking frantically around, expecting the Americanos to come at him from any direction.

I looked at my shoulder. The rock fragments had only

made little nicks, but they hurt a little.

More shooting broke out. The Americanos were shooting at a couple of horses down at the draw's entrance or at random into the rocks. I realized they were trying to shoot every horse so the bandidos could not escape.

El Xiuhcoatl shouted again to stop firing, or he would shoot the girl.

I could not tell how many there were, but Americanos were hidden in the rocks along the right ridge finger. Some were at the top of the ridge and could fire down the length of the left finger and behind it too. Dead horses and mules lay in the draw. The bandidos were trapped, and they knew it. They had hostages, though, and I knew they would use us in any way they could.

There were more shouts. I looked back to the open ground from where we came. I saw three distant horsemen spread out and riding toward us. One was a young boy farther back with a small herd of horses. I remembered he was the wrangler. Fred was herding the remuda. I had no idea they had brought so many spares. The remuda must have been following far back.

There was more talking going on. I heard Señor DeWitt shout for Doris and Agnes.

Only Doris answered with a faint, "Daddy."

That was all. I did not hear Agnes.

I recognized Flaco's voice. He told El Xiuhcoatl they had one thousand six hundred *dólares* Americano—dollars—that was a great deal of money! There was no need to barter. They could have it in exchange for all four girls alive. They could keep their guns and take their horses. The Americanos would chase them no farther.

He wanted to know if there was more money.

"No, that is all there is."

I thought about one thousand six hundred dollars for

all four of us. That would be, what, six hundred or five hundred, something like that, for each of us? He would pay that for me?

El Xiuhcoatl shouted back that he would cut off Doris's breasts if there was any more shooting. I did not doubt him. Neither did anyone else. There were no more shots.

There was more talking back and forth. I was too far away to make out everything. There was something about El Xiuhcoatl wanting to see the money first. Señor DeWitt and he would meet in the draw. El Xiuhcoatl made it clear he had not made up his mind. He was too proud to admit defeat, especially by gringos. I do not think he had a choice.

I peeked over the rocks again.

Lencho harshly whispered, "Stay down!"

I saw Señor DeWitt with a white flag making his way through the rocks down to the trail. His holsters were empty. He was a brave man.

Then I saw El Xiuhcoatl step onto the trail with his own flag. I knew every carbine from both sides was aimed at them. El Xiuhcoatl shouted that the gringos sneaking up out on the flats had better stop. Flaco shouted to tell them to stop.

Señor DeWitt took the money out of a leather pouch and showed it to El Xiuhcoatl. He gave him one of the bills, and the greedy bandido kissed it and put it in a pocket. They both shook hands and stepped back just as quick. I did not expect that. That must be humiliating for Señor DeWitt. They turned and made their way back through the rocks. Right then I saw a bandido rise with a carbine and fire a single shot out at the flats. I saw Fred, the young wrangler, fall.

Señor DeWitt and El Xiuhcoatl were both yelling to stop shooting. They both wanted to end this and go their own way. Fred was not even my age, and now he was dead for trying to sneak closer.

El Xiuhcoatl shouted that he wanted Señor DeWitt to bring the money to the trail and he could have the girls. I was about to cry. It is going to be over, and my Bud was here to take me home! I wanted to cry for Agnes, Doris, and Inés too.

I could see Señor DeWitt and Flaco coming down through the rocks. El Xiuhcoatl came out too. There were some words, and Señor DeWitt shouted, "No!" and they were finger-pointing and saying more words low and angry. Something was wrong. God, please do not let this fail! It did not look good between the two jejes. Señor DeWitt was shaking his head and glaring at El Xiuhcoatl, who said something else. Señor DeWitt threw the money pouch to the bandido. He looked inside and said something over his shoulder. Chago rose from the rocks, holding Agnes by the arm. He had been in the back. How did he get up there? He roughly shoved her toward the trail. El Xiuhcoatl told him not to do that.

Agnes stumbled through the rocks, but it did not even look like she saw her papá. Flaco had to help her up to where she stood behind her papá. A bandido then came out of the rocks holding Doris by the arm. He had helped her cover up with her torn clothes and blanket. She started trying to pull away from the bandido when she saw her papá. Señor DeWitt, I guessed, told her to calm down, and she stopped pulling. When she got to him, she threw her arms around him, barely able to stay on her feet. They whispered some, and then she stood tall and led Agnes up to where I thought Bud was.

Who was going next? Me or Inés? I had not seen her since the shooting started. Paco told me to stay down as he came through the rocks toward me. I will do anything he says to get out of here. It was very quiet. I could even hear Doris crying on the other ridge finger.

Paco reached me, and Lencho crawled up behind the rocks from lower down. There was blood on his right thigh.

He said, "I am happy to see you unhurt little one. I had a close call." There was a bullet hole through his coat's left sleeve. He stuck a finger in the hole and wiggled it. "Just like with the arrow, it hit nothing."

I pointed to his leg.

"It is only a graze," he said, shrugging.

Paco nodded at Lencho, and they both lunged at me. Lencho held me down while Paco tied my wrists.

What was this?

"You are not going home today, little one. We are keeping you and Inés to make sure the gringos do not follow us."

I was more angry than frightened. I spit in his face

¡Ahora todos ustedes son hombres muertos!

CHAPTER TWENTY-NINE

You are all surely dead men now!

I expected our Americanos to open up with a rain of carbine fire and come charging out of the rocks to kill every one of the bandidos. Nothing happened. Looking across the draw, I saw no one. I heard not a single shot or even a shout. It was as though the ridge finger was empty.

What was Lencho talking about?

Chago came in dragging Inés, who was fighting and yelling at him. He slapped her face.

What is going on?

Inés has blood on her right sleeve.

She struggled to her feet while they were tying me. Chago threw Inés back to the ground. "Stay down!"

"What are you bastards doing?" shouted Inés.

"Shut up, bitch!" he shouted and slapped her again. Then he threw a slap into my face. "Your stinking brave gringos have got the two gringas and are taking them home. They do not care about you. They are leaving you here to whatever fate we choose."

I could not believe what I was hearing. Neither could Inés. My stomach twisted. My head felt light as if I was going to faint. *Why, why? Bud would not leave me! Would he?*

Inés was looking at me, fear and panic in her eyes. "Bud will come for you, will he not?"

I nodded my head. He would…or would he? Was Señor DeWitt the man I thought? Was Bud?

I jerked my head toward her arm.

Glancing at it, she said, "It is nothing." She started crying, not for her arm but because we were not leaving this nightmare.

Grasping for breath, I fell onto my side. I said a prayer with Inés sobbing in the background. I thought about Bud. He had taken me in and protected me after I lost everything. Yes, he had wanted to give me to someone else, to churches, but that was because he thought they would take better care of me than he could. No, I knew he could take care of me. I knew he respected me. It is difficult for a girl like me to win respect from anyone. I struggled to sit back up. With my legs, I shoved Inés' legs. She looked at me with tear-filled eyes. I nodded my head forcefully. She nodded. She understood. I trusted Bud would come.

"I don't know what you are saying," shouted Chago. "Both of you stop it!"

Lencho had been gathering guns from dead bandidos. He limped as he took any money they had and cut off coins sewn to their sombreros. "What is going on?" he asked Chago.

"The stinking gringos have got the two gringa bitches and are going home. We are keeping these two as hostages so they will not come after us. We are taking them to Las Norias to throw in with the whores we keep there.

We need some fresh ones."

"These two do not look so fresh to me," Lencho said with a laugh.

"We will have Alejandra clean them up."

They were talking about us as though we were slaves. Then I realized we were not like slaves, we were already slaves, slave-whores.

Chago went on. "The gringos are letting us take our horses. If there are not enough, the bastards shot so many, they will even give us horses from their remuda. We can take our guns too. The jeje says to pick up all the guns and to take the gun belts off our dead."

"That is what I have been doing," said Lencho.

"Check their saddlebags and bring any cartridges and food you find. And serapes."

"Why not ask the gringos to give us some food since they are being so helpful?" asked Lencho.

"Go check the saddlebags." ordered Chago.

Three bandidos carefully came out of the rocks and went down the trail to where a couple of horses grazed on the flats as though they had not been shot at as they ran down the draw in terror. I could see a couple of our Americanos in the rocks above. Were they really letting these terrible dogs keep us, or were they planning to foil them somehow and still rescue us?

I still had hope. I would never give that up.

There were not many live or unwounded horses left.

Matu strutted boldly down the draw carrying a bloody saddle and his carbine. He was a horrible little man. He took me every time they ganged up on me. He liked to hurt me. He deserved the death of three deaths. I would kill him three times before he died—rock, knife, and fire.

He was angry. He was always angry. "The bastards. They killed our compadres, all of them!"

"Who?" asked Lencho.

"The stinking bastard son of whores gringos."

"No, who did they kill?"

"Manolo and the five." He spit on the ground.

"What?"

"They killed all six of the men the jeje sent to Las Norias. All of them! They shot them down while they ate last night. The bastard gringos brought their horses with them so they would not come back to us or go to Las Norias. They are giving us those horses now to make up for the ones they shot here."

It looked like Chago already knew this.

"How did you find this out, Tino?" asked Lencho.

"The gringos, they have a traitor Mexican working for them. He even speaks Americano. He is the one who told the jefe."

Tino I never saw much. He had been with the band for a long time.

"I have seen that bastard," said Lencho. "He must die."

That had to be Flaco, I thought. Good for our boys. They killed some of the horrible dogs. Bandidos who had brutalized and soiled all four of us. They deserved to burn in Hell. I forced myself to say a prayer and ask for forgiveness of such hateful thoughts. I was confused. Why should they be forgiven? Why should I not hate them? It was me who was suffering for their sins. They had free will. They made a choice.

Chago stayed with us while horses, saddles, guns, and anything they could use was gathered.

We were pulled to our feet by Chago and Lencho. They were pushing us toward the draw. This was our last chance. Our hands were tied in front of us, but our feet were free. Inés and I realized that at the same time. She kicked Chago between the legs, and I crouched low and threw all my weight into catching Lencho in the belly with my hurt left shoulder. He stumbled over Chago, and we all were in a tangle. We had no chance being hand tied. They yanked us up and dragged us to the draw. We kicked and shoved through, only to be punched and slapped. By the time we got to the waiting horses, we did not have much fight left. Besides battered, we were just too weak. A couple of other bandidos helped get us onto our saddles. Chago tied our ankles to the stirrups. I looked desperately to the right, hoping to at least see Bud. I saw no one. We had already been abandoned, just like the dead bandidos left here to rot with their horses.

There were only eight bandidos left, the two of us, and twelve horses.

We rode slowly over the ridge crest. The wind picked up. It was colder. The sky was darker.

I was the only one to look back at the ridge. I still saw no one.

Odio a Bud.

CHAPTER THIRTY

I hate Bud.

It was dark. It rained lightly, but it never stopped. Still, we rode. No one spoke. If they did, I did not hear. I was too occupied hating Bud and Señor DeWitt for leaving me, hating El Xiuhcoatl and Chago for keeping me, hating all the bandidos alive and dead, hating Doris and Agnes for being able to leave, and Inés just because.

I hated the rocks and mesquite, the sky, the cold, and the rain. I hated everything and everyone. It did not matter.

I wallowed in my hatred. I started to enjoy it. I knew I should not. I knew I should pray to forgive them all regardless of what they did to me, to us. I could not. And that did not matter, either.

The eight bandidos were so quiet because they too were exhausted. There were wounded, but not bad, unfortunately. Something that I had not thought of crossed my mind. They had lost friends, men I guessed they have known a long time and no doubt shared stolen plunder and women. They too must be mourning. I guess such dogs could mourn. That did not matter, either.

Prodding over the empty land, the unending sameness and boredom made me realize there was a reason for me to stay with these dogs and endure the humiliations they inflicted. The physical pain and torment are unimportant. I realized that my life had prepared me to endure that. Maybe it was Bud's and Señor DeWitt's idea. Maybe I was ordained by God to carry out His plan. It did not matter whose idea it was because nothing now mattered. I was an instrument, a tool…no, a weapon. My reason to be alive on this Earth was for one thing and one thing only. I was to endure unspeakable humiliations to make me harder. I was to kill El Xiuhcoatl any way I could, and the more painful, the more humiliating his death, the better. I was placed here because this would be the best and easiest way to do it. I knew sooner or later he would make a mistake. He would let his guard down. There would be an opportunity even if fleeting. I could get to him and kill him, kill him many, many times.

I even thought about the ways to kill him, the most painful and humiliating. I had a knife now, hidden in my left sleeve. Its blade was sharp and as long as my hand. I knew enough about men now that I thought of ways to use it on him. I did not think to speak of that. It was too horrible, and I disgraced myself to even think it, much less enjoy the corrupted and impious thoughts. I would pray for forgiveness later when there was no longer a need for me to be the chosen weapon. They said God forgives. Would He? God forgive me for even questioning that. That mattered.

We were back in rough country, a maze of ravines and ridges. How could the bandidos follow a trail? Was there a trail? We stopped in complete darkness. It still rained. We unsaddled.

They found a bit of ground high enough to be out of standing water and partly under a wide ledge jutting from a cliff. The bandidos pitched the several buffalo blankets, and we were more or less sheltered from the light rain. There was no fire, of course. Some carne seca and parched corn was all we had to eat. We sat in a circle wrapped in blankets and ponchos, shifting about to avoid the most annoying drips and trickles. I expected them to complain about the deadly ambushes with ten of them killed by Americanos.

They did not. I was thankful because I had expected them to take their anger out on us. Inés and I huddled together wet, cold, sore, helpless, and betrayed.

Even if Bud was coming for me, there was little trail for him to follow in this rain. Why was I even thinking this? I knew he was not coming. Why should he? Now, he must not. I had been ordained to complete a mission. His coming would only interfere.

Lencho sat beside Inés. It looked to me that she sought his company. She had slept with him the night before. It seemed the other bandidos recognized this. That was strange. They always took what they wanted, and no one had privileges except El Xiuhcoatl and Chago, and least of all, Lencho. Several times I saw Inés and Lencho whispering. She had bandaged his leg too.

Instead of anger, Chago told the story of his first stagecoach robbery. I groaned to myself. He no doubt would be the hero and raped all the women in the coach. I wanted to hold my hands over my ears. Inés nudged me and did groan very quietly. I almost laughed but was unable to.

"I was a little over Lencho's age and ready to prove myself as a bandido. I had robbed lone men on the road, but I wanted to do something bolder and more courageous. To win respect, I must do it alone. I chose to rob the stagecoach between Eagle Pass and Del Rio. I picked a good place. The coach and its six horses had to go down into a deep gorge, cross a stream, and back up the bluff on the other side. The passengers had to get out at the top of the bluff and go on foot up the other side. They slowed to a woman's walk. As they came up, that is where I would stop them before the passengers reboarded. I watched the stagecoach for three days. They always did the same thing. There were usually four to six passengers and the driver and shotgun guard. The guard walked ahead of the horses through the gorge.

"I prepared the night before, abstaining from tequila and a woman. I am in my place early in the morning, for the stagecoach's arrival time can be different. I planned it well. The guard walked past my hiding place, a big yucca. I stood, pointed my pistol at the guard, and told him to give me his shotgun. He put his bands up. I holstered my pistol, and by now the driver had seen me but could not stop because he had to keep the horses going up the side of the gorge and over the top. The problem was that the guard jumped onto the passenger step on the coach's side and the driver, whipping the horses, kept going, leaving the passengers beside. I at first ran after the coach but stopped when it kept going. I could save this."

The men laughed at Chago, something they were not used to doing.

"I would rob the five passengers. I turned back with the shotgun in hand. There were only four passengers, three men, and a woman. I thought certain there had been five.

"I heard a throat clear behind me and turned to see a man come from behind the same yucca I had hidden behind. He is pointing a big pistol straight at me. He opened his coat, and there is a silver badge on his vest.

"He said in very bad Spanish, 'Señor, I am Nick Dillard, deputy sheriff of Maverick County. I have shot more men than you have fingers and toes. I am just not in a bloody mood today to kill another desperado. So drop that shotgun, drop that pistol, drop your money belt, and be on your way.'"

"What did you do?" asked Matu.

"I did exactly as he said. Then he told me to leave my horse tied to a mesquite." Chago looked angry for a moment and then said, "I had only stolen that fine horse two weeks before! I lost my pistol, horse, and over a hundred pesos and thirty Americano dollars. I did not have the shotgun long enough to call it my own!"

They all laughed at his drought of luck. "You lost your dignity too," said Tino through the long stringy hair hanging over his face.

"That was not all of it. The passengers laughed at me and walked to where the stagecoach had stopped. The skinny Americano woman called me a son of a bitch! To make it worse, not a single passing freight wagon would give me a ride. They must have feared I was a bandido."

"That is what is wrong with the world now. There are not many men you can trust," muttered El Xiuhcoatl.

"Jeje," asked Lencho, "did you ever make a mistake?"

Everyone became quiet, and the young bandido knew he had asked the wrong question.

After a long silence, El Xiuhcoatl said, "I have made many mistakes, but I learned, and I grew stronger, so I became undefeatable."

Several of the bandidos made noises of disbelief and groveled to stay in his favor. He had made many mistakes since we have met, I thought. The first was to kidnap four girls. Yes, I had given up hope of being rescued. That was what I told myself, but sometimes I refused to believe they were not coming. I had not completely given up.

"Yes, I, El Xiuhcoatl, have made an occasional mistake. The worst mistake is that I once took a Rurales officer to be a man of his word, an honorable man. I had made an arrangement with Commandant Acero Alvarado for me to represent him as a tax collector south of Monclova. How I collected the tax money was no matter to the commandant. We were to turn in all the collected monies to the Rurales Armory. That way it could be recorded by the bookkeepers. The commandant, responsible for the money vault, would meet a few days later and give me my cut, I mean, my commission."

Tino said, "I remember those days well. We made good money until the commandant betrayed us."

"Most true," said the jefe. "One day we arrived at the agreed on meeting place, a small farm belonging to my uncle on the Monclova-Castaños Road. There were only four of us in those days. Chago and Tino, of course, and another man. I cannot remember his name."

"Miguel," said Chago. "Our cousin. Tío Eduardo's boy." He crossed himself.

"Yes, yes, I remember. We were all family back then. Commandant Alvarado, that dog, had ten of his gray-uniformed men under a lieutenant meet us. I knew something was wrong when the commandant was not there. Of course, he did not have the eggs to do it himself." He looked angry, recalling the memories.

"We rode up to the house, and the foolish lieutenant did not even let us come in pistol range and dismount before he shouted for us to halt and declared he was arresting us in the name of the Governor of the State of Coahuila, ha! They had not expected us to open fire without hesitation. We hit three or four of those gray-back bastards and turned and ran for it. We lost Miguel, and all three of us were wounded."

Chago nodded and pointed to his left arm and side.

"We killed two more, I think, and we reached the Cerro del Mercado. They would never find us in those hills and gave up. I was not finished. We waited a week and went into Monclova at night. I already knew where that bastard commandant lived. When they turned off their lamp, we waited an hour and stole in through a courtyard window. We grabbed the commandant and his bitch wife, and the boys held them down. I cut his muscles inside his elbows and behind his knees so he could not fight back. I fucked his bitch wife and made her watch when I cut off his eggs and then his head with my machete!" His proud grin dripped with vileness.

I felt ill with his twisted smile, if it could be called that. I knew he was boasting and trying to scare us. It was working.

Inés quietly said, "I do not believe you." She stared straight into El Xiuhcoatl's eyes.

He leaped to his feet. I expected him to at least kick her in the face. Instead, he went to one of the pack horses and pulled out a leather bag. It was the one his aunt had given him back at the hideout.

El Xiuhcoatl pulled the drawstrings open and brought out a crockery pot with a wire lid clamp. He opened it, reached his gloved hand in, and pulled out a head by the wet hair.

"Señoritas, I present the former Commandant Acero Alvarado!"

The sharp odor of vinegar struck us. The adobe white face with its gaping mouth and sightless, colorless eyes looked like it had partly melted.

Inés vomited, and I wanted to, more from the smell

than the…memento in his hand.

The bandidos paid no attention to Inés.

Lencho asked, "What happened to the commandant's wife?"

"I let the fat bitch live to mourn the loss of her worthless, traitorous husband and that she will never again experience my passion in her loins."

El Xiuhcoatl must have read my mind when I thought of the cruelty he had inflicted on the woman and then to leave her husband's body headless.

"I could not leave him headless for his bitch to bury. I cut off a dog's head and had a servant sew it on his body for a proper burial."

My stomach turned. I hoped that picture would not barge into my nightmares.

"Put that away, brother," said Chago, pointing at the crock.

"I wish to visit with him sometimes," said El Xiuhcoatl. "I wish to reminisce of the old days when we had honest work collecting taxes and not stealing girls for ransom, even though that is a good trade, usually."

"Ha! It was not so good this time, was it?" said Inés.

Again, instead of kicking her, he merely shrugged his shoulders. "It could have gone better."

I tried to will Inés to keep her mouth shut before the bandido jefe changed his mood.

"Inés," hissed a man called Zaca. "Tell us a story." Maybe he had the same idea I did. That was the first time I heard any of them call one of us by our Christian name.

It came to me that they wanted to talk about anything but what happened today. More than half their number was dead. They were worn out, and there was some kind of trouble waiting for them in Las Norias. The only good thing was that they were no longer being tracked by gringos.

Inés rested her chin on her knees, her arms around her doubled up knees. She said nothing for a time, but she raised her head and looked around.

"We lived in a little village, Ribera, outside of Las Vacas."

"I know that place," said Matu. "It is near the Río."

"My papá had died of yellow fever, and my mamá and I lived with her older sister's family, my tía—aunt. They had two boys and a girl.

"Their papá, my tío—uncle—had relations with another woman, a widowed seamstress on the other side of the village."

I did not think talking about men having forbidden relations with women was a good idea.

"My *abuela*—grandmother—lived next door, and she found out about the other woman. Being a good mamá, she told my mamá. Both were very angry."

The bandidos laughed and made crude remarks. It made me think about my papá. Even if he had wanted to, our way of life on the road made such a thing impossible. He was a good man. Was Bud a good man like Papá? Why was I thinking of him? I would never see him again. He would not want to see me because of what I had become.

"Abuela demanded that he end the relationship and that he never see the immoral seamstress again. Tío went to visit her one last time to break off the relationship. He did not return after supper as was expected nor in the middle of the night. He did not return in the morning. In the afternoon, my abuela, mamá, and tía took all of us children to the seamstress's home. There was no one there, and the neighbors had seen no one since the day before when the seamstress's friend arrived. That would be Tío. They had heard strange and frightening noises during the night. In the morning they saw no one in the house.

"My tía cried in her room late into the night. I woke later to the sound of horrible moaning and groaning coming from the *salón*—the main room. Looking through the cracked door, I and my cousins saw by a single candle Tío standing with his lips sewn shut!"

"I have done that to deserving bastards!" said El Xiuhcoatl proudly.

"It was the most terrifying thing I have ever seen, horrible! My Tía was there, crying. She had Tío's straight razor and was trying to cut the stitches. His lips were bleeding as the stitches were very tight. My cousins fled to our room, but I stayed and watched. Once all the stitches were cut and the thick threads pulled out, with more moaning and blood, she cleaned Tío up and put him to bed. In his mouth they found…"

Everyone leaned forward to listen.

"It horrified and disgusted them all."

"What was it?" urged a wide-eyed El Xiuhcoatl.

"I do not know, they would not tell me, but he moaned the rest of the night."

El Xiuhcoatl slapped his thigh in frustration. I laughed inside.

"He moaned for days after and had a fever. There was something in his eyes. They did not look right. He said it was becoming hard to see, and his eyes got worse each day. Within two weeks he was blind. The priest could do nothing for him, and Tío refused to give confession. Two different *curanderos*—healers—were unable to help him. They both feared he had been cursed. The seamstress was never seen again. Some said she was actually a bruja. Tío was finally able to tell his wife that the seamstress bestowed a curse on him when he told her he could not see her again."

"He must have been a real man in bed if she was that angry that he denied her," Chago said with a laugh.

After a silence, Inés quietly said, "It was the seamstress who sewed his lips shut as further punishment. That explained the tight, even stitches. Tío thought she had drugged him so she could sew the stitches. Tía kept an upside-down broom by the door to keep away demons, and we all had to wear the woven bracelets to protect us from the *mal de ojo*—evil eye. Tío remained in pain for the rest of his life and was never able to know a woman again. He died in pain a year to the day later."

The bandidos became most quiet. I smiled to myself. Inés had put a bit of fear and doubt into their evil, immoral minds. They were nervous and quiet.

El Xiuhcoatl suddenly said, "Do not listen to these *patrañas*—old wives tales. Go to bed. We have a long ride tomorrow."

They took down the buffalo blankets to bed down under the ledge.

El Xiuhcoatl suddenly grabbed my hand and took me to his bedroll. I wanted to cry, to run, to die. I hated him even more. He said that today was his victory. He boasted, "I got the ransom for the two gringas and still have two whores."

Bud was coming, I knew it, no matter what they said. They know nothing, they did not know him. For the first time in a very long time, I wished I could speak. I would simply tell them, "You are all going to die."

I drifted into anguished sleep thinking about my knife and what I would sever first.

Será una victoria vacía.

CHAPTER THIRTY-ONE

It would be an empty victory.

It was barely raining in the morning. The air and my head were foggy. El Xiuhcoatl had climbed out of the blankets. He had not taken me again. I guess he too was worn down. It showered just enough to keep us wet and cold.

Breakfast was a handful of parched corn and a tortilla. I was starting to look forward to reaching Las Norias just for some food. I realized somehow Inés and I switched blankets. I was wearing her gray blanket, and she had my red-brown one. No matter. They were both wet and muddy.

Late in the morning, the rain stopped. That actually made me happy, in a way. It was still cold. We picked up our speed some, but the horses were tiring.

We went into a narrow ravine. I did not like this. It was too much like the ones with the indios. Parts were curvy turns and other parts straight. Like the trail up the escarpment was changed from narrow to wide and back to narrow. It got deeper too.

We entered a straight part, and at its end where it began to curve again, we stopped.

"Zaca," El Xiuhcoatl said. "I want to be sure no one is following. We know the gringos have no more stomach for it, but I have other enemies. There may be indios too, but I doubt it. I want to be certain. I do not want anyone to follow us to Las Norias."

They picked a place for him to hide that gave him a long shot down the straight part of the ravine, not just to shoot at anyone approaching, but as they fled too.

"Stay here until morning. When the fog lifts, then follow our trail. Try to catch up with us in the morning before we reach Las Norias. I would leave two men, but I want to be sure we have as many men as possible when we enter Las Norias."

The other bandidos wished Zaca well. Chago told him, "Do not fear the brujas or the seamstresses herself, my friend!"

El Xiuhcoatl's final words to Zaca were, "Keep a sharp eye until it is full dark. No fire tonight." Zaca checked his carbine, set it on half-cock, and crossed himself. He was a quiet man with wide-spaced eyes and bad teeth.

We continued on down the ravine, which grew wider. Stopping for a short rest, I squatted behind a rock to pee. I was more concerned about blocking the wind than anyone watching me. What had I sunken to?

The jefe had left a man behind. Was it only a precaution as he made it sound? Or was something worrying him? He left only one man. I thought if he really thought we were being followed, he would have left at least two like before. He was only being careful, I thought. But what if someone is following? That worried me. That one bandido left behind could finish any chance of rescue.

I quickly worked on the left cuff of my blue flannel shirt. Tearing it off, I clutched it in my fist. When I mounted and we started moving, I dropped it to the ground. It would probably not serve any good purpose. I wanted to do something.

We soon left the winding ravine behind and again came out on open rolling ground. Here the wind blew harder and colder. We moved faster.

How much farther? The horses, much less the men, were worn out and hungry. I felt at times I could not stay on my saddle. I hurt all over, but my legs and butt were especially sore. No matter how I sat, I could not find a comfortable place.

Inés rode beside me. She did not say much. She was as tired and hurting as me. Finally, she said, "Do you still have the knife?"

I nodded.

"Give it to me."

I looked at her, my face asking why.

"I am going to escape, and I am taking you with me."

I violently shook my head. It was daylight, and we were in the open. Even at night, it would be impossible. *No!* I shook my head again.

"Tonight." She looked desperate. I knew how she felt.

Riding close, she held her hand palm out. I should not have, but I slipped it to her just as Chago shouted, "Stay away from each other!" I moved ahead. I worried now. Did I make a mistake giving it to her? I regretted not having any way to defend myself, not that I would be able to defend myself from seven men, even with a knife.

El Xiuhcoatl raised his hand, and we stopped. My hips and the small of my back were the sorest of all the soreness. I slid to the ground to walk around a bit. Anything for a little relief.

Inés limped over to Lencho, who was looking at El Xiuhoatl's fine gray horse's fore hoof and picking out a pebble with a pocketknife. El Xiuhcoatl walked away to talk to Chago. Inés said something to Lencho that made him laugh.

In the blink of an eye, she had the knife at his throat. "Open your hands," she demanded. He dropped his own knife. She dropped hers and slapped her hand on his pistol before he could even reach.

She held the pistol up two-handed, cocked it, and stepped back from Lencho. It was pointed at El Xiuhcoatl. "Everyone drop their pistols!"

Lencho dodged away, and as Inés glanced at him, there was a click, and El Xiuhcoatl stood turned to his side with his arm outstretched and aiming at her head. Inés did not hesitate. Four shots cracked. Inés jerked back with the pistol flying from her hands. She tried to stop her fall but hit the ground hard. Her elbow was shattered, and blood spread on her right side. The gray stallion snorted as its forelegs gave way, and it rolled onto its side. A spot of blood from El Xiuhcoatl's bullet marred its chest. Her own single shot went into the sky.

I ran toward Inés. Lencho stopped me. "Do not!" He saved my life.

The gray coughed up blood and kicked violently. El Xiuhcoatl screamed like a madman. I have never heard a man scream like that.

Inés was white-face shocked, her arm was twisted at an impossible angle barely held on, and her side was covered with red. El Xiuhcoatl dashed toward her with a bull growl, landed with knees on her chest, and began pounding with fists. She did not make a sound, did not move. I tried to scream and run to her. Lencho and Chago dragged me back. I could hear fists smacking into her face and El Xiuhcoatl's gristly snarling.

They let me go to her when he was finished. He stood glaring hate at her and wiping his bloody gloved fists on his pants. I did not know who it was laying in the dirt. Her eyes half open, her face battered, swollen, and lacerated, with more blood growing into a puddle under her head. There were choking bruises on her throat. I took her left hand with torn fingernails in mine. It was limp. There was nothing. She was dead.

I sat on the ground, trying to hold myself up. I tried to cry, scream, anything. I could not. I did find something I could do. Hate myself.

El Xiuhcoatl stood before me waving his pistol in a bloody fist. His ravings were incoherent. He turned on Lencho and whacked him with the pistol, yelling that this was his fault and he would shoot him.

Chago told Lencho, "Take his saddle off the horse and put it on the best pack horse, the golden chestnut." The other men were settling their horses down. Some moved so they would not be in the line of fire with Lencho.

"That gray was the best horse I ever stole," raged El Xiuhcoatl. He continued yelling threats at no one. I kneeled beside Inés, trying to convince myself she was dead. I blamed it on myself. I should have never given her that knife.

"Where in Hell did she get that knife?" shouted El Xiuhcoatl.

He turned on me. "Did you have anything to do with this?"

I could only look at him with tear-filled eyes and shake my head.

"I will find out from you later. Mount up! We ride now."

We had only moments to wrap Inés in the red-brown blanket. I was surprised that Chago helped me. There were rocks to bury her under, but no time. She would be gifted to the coyotes, *javelinas*, and vultures. We left her beside the gray horse. I knew eventually their bones would be intermingled.

We rode away. El Xiuhcoatl was still cursing to himself and threatening those around him. Lencho, with a swelling, red mark on the side of his face, stayed with me. He said nothing. I knew he was just as surprised as myself with Inés' attempt for freedom. What did she think she was going to do? Take a hostage and run for it? She had not thought it out.

Then I knew what it was. She, her mind, had snapped, snapped like a twig.

That made me think about what I should do. I had been considering stealing a horse at Las Norias and running for it at night. Whatever happened, I needed a better plan, and I might need help. That was another mistake Inés had made. She did not tell me what she was going to do. In a way, I was glad she had not because it probably would have gotten me killed too.

It struck me then. I was alone. Maybe there were seven men with me, but I was as alone as one could be. It was that moment that I felt all was lost. There was no way I could survive this. No one was coming for me. No one would or could help me at Las Norias. Whatever was happening there would end when he arrived. El Xiuhcoatl would dominate the people there. There was no doubt of that in my mind. He would simply arrive at an unexpected time and direction.

El Xiuhcoatl quieted down after a time. Chago rode with him. They did not talk much from what I could tell. Lencho followed me, probably told to keep a close watch.

I cried silently for Inés. I prayed for her and said the rosary. I cried more when I realized she died without knowing her mother had died. I felt guilty about that and blamed myself. Maybe it was for the better, though. She probably already had met her mother in Heaven. I hoped she would not hold that against me. She should not, as our spirt, once returned to Heaven, would be more benevolent and understanding.

We rode on as I suffered in silent sadness and felt as trapped as the doves I caught in bird traps.

Ahead was a line of hills. We headed straight for a low pass. The sun was was going down. Chago rode down the column. "We will camp beyond the pass."

There was some grumbling from the men. They had hoped to reach Las Norias today. They were all tired, and food was scarce.

We passed through an arroyo and stopped at the bottom of a small ridge. It blocked the wind some.

They picketed the horses, and one of the men had to sleep near them. They built two small fires, letting more men crowd in close to warm themselves.

El Xiuhcoatl dropped his bedroll farther from either fire. He pointed to me to take my buffalo blanket there. I threw it down, sat, and cried because I knew where I was spending the night.

He grabbed me by the arm and tied my hands. "Go to the blankets and get in. I will deal with you later." Giving me a rough shake, he said, "I know you helped that bitch in some way. Where did she get that knife?"

I shook my head. He slapped me and pushed me to the blankets. "Stay!"

He sat with his men for a time. I prayed and cried. I said a rosary for Inés. I prayed for myself. When he crawled under the blankets, I pretended to be asleep. It made no difference.

I hated Bud. He had taken me to the Dew where I was seized by minions of the Devil. It was his fault that I had been defiled and soiled. It was his fault that I would die out there.

Bud, sálvame.

CHAPTER THIRTY-TWO

Bud, save me.

I woke up and was alone. I needed to get out from under the blankets and on my feet in case he returned. I did not care how cold it was or that the wind had picked up. I heard horses and men quietly talking.

I was kicked in the shoulder, but not hard.

"Get up. Start a fire." It was Paco.

I scrambled out, taking a blanket to drape over my shoulders. I could not find my sandals. I had only socks. I could not complain. I was out of the bedroll before the *jeje* returned to hurt me again. Paco tossed me a wax paper packet of lucifers. I collected bits of wood and bark from under partly burned limbs. Some of the wood was damp and hard to start. At least no one shouted at me. They understood that starting a fire was a delicate and careful affair on a damp day.

Some of the men brought sticks that I fed to the

building flames. Matu brought the little kettle of beans. I set it on the fire and stirred as it warmed. I dared not take a taste.

Bandidos were coughing and hacking. I heard someone say we would make Las Norias today. I could not decide if that was good or bad. I was glad that this endless, terrible ride would end. But what awaited me? Nothing good, I was certain. It occurred to me there was certainly no priest. I may never see a priest again. That greatly saddened me. The way I confessed, to myself but before a priest, would not be possible.

Men were hacking, coughing, spitting, and pissing wherever was convenient. I went myself and squatted behind a rock with dark thoughts whirling around.

I was back at the fire, shivering and hoping they would let me have a spoonful of frijoles. Matu had set a coffee pot on the fire! I could not believe it. We had not had coffee in days. It must be the last. Its smell was wonderful! It was doubtful they will share any.

I heard the jeje whistle and then quietly call for Federico, Chago's real name. I bent to stir the frijoles after a time, and the jeje whistled again, telling Chago there would be no coffee left if he did not finish and get in there. After a time, El Xiuhcoatl shouted again, "Federico!" He sounded concerned.

Something…what? Something was wrong.

And God in Heaven, Bud's voice shouted, "Hey, y'all!"

A chill shot up my back, and I almost collapsed from relief.

The bandidos were scrambling around grabbing carbines. Two ran to the horses. They had not decided where the voice was coming from. El Xiuhcoatl looked confused, his head turning in every direction.

I made out Bud's shape beside a rock outcropping. He

had someone with him. It had to be Chago. Ha! How did he manage that? He held a pistol to the bandido's head.

"Let's make a deal here. Any y'all *habla Americano*?"

El Xiuhcoatl grabbed me and put a pistol to my head. I expected that. He waved to Tino, who came through the rocks on hands and knees. They whispered. I could not hear them.

Tino shouted, "Joo let him go, or El Xiuhcoatl shoot *la niña*."

I did not know he spoke Americano.

"No one's shooting anyone. No one else has to get killed, *muerto*. You give me *la niña*, and I give you back your brother…your *hermano*."

How did Bud know who he held? That was wise, letting El Xiuhcoatl know he knew it was his brother. I did not see anyone else. I wondered how many Americanos were with Bud.

How did Bud do this? Had he caught Chago outside the camp? Not likely. Had he sneaked into the camp and taken him? Had he been looking for me? No matter. He was here, and all would be well.

"Do you know who that is?" asked El Xiuhcoatl.

I nodded. I tried to look strong and fearless.

"How many gringos?" he asked.

I shook my head.

That angered the bandido jeje. He slapped me.

El Xiuhcoatl turned to talk to Tino and Matu.

They all jumped, the horses and me too, when a pistol went off in the morning stillness.

"Hey! I ain't got all damn day here! *¡Muy pronto!*" shouted Bud.

He and Chago dropped from sight behind the outcropping.

"Joo come out. Bring…*bandera blanca*. We talk."

Chago had told him to bring a white flag.

Bud shouted back, "Yeah, I come out and y'all shoot me *muerto*. That ain't happening. Let's trade, and we'll all go to the *hacienda*. What do you want? To keep *la niña* or get your *hermano* back in *una* piece?"

El Xiuhcoatl, Tino, and Matu were talking again. Tino wanted to take three men and sneak through the rocks to the north to get behind the gringos. They had decided there were only two or three. I do not know how they decided that. I had only seen and heard Bud. El Xiuhcoatl did not want Chago hurt, so they had to be careful.

Tino shouted, "This your woman, the one with no name?"

"Yeah. *Sí, mi mujer*. I want her back. Now!"

Bud called me his woman. Straight to the bandidos. I was his woman!

"Gringo, joo *one vaquero duro*."

Tino had just called Bud a tough vaquero. That showed respect. Of course, they were still going to try and kill him.

"We trade joo dee *niña*."

"Start walking her across, and I'll start Federico. No *fuego*. If I hear a shot or see any funny business, Federico's *muerto*."

El Xiuhcoatl asked, "How does the gringo know his name?"

I and the others shook our heads.

The beans and coffee were burning. I walked over and took them off the fire.

El Xiuhcoatl grabbed my arm and pushed me in front of him. "I am trading you for my brother, whore. Do not think you are saved. You will not see the Sun set. If I catch you and any of the gringos alive, you will die a long death beyond your imagination."

I spit in his face. Much to my surprise, he did not slap me. He pulled my blanket off and shoved me forward.

"Walk to your death, whore."

I would rather die that way with Bud than to stay with this scum a day longer.

I started across the rocky ground spotted with low brush and cactus. I wore only the blue flannel shirt, disgustingly filthy long johns, and socks. I realized I had left my shawl.

Bud stood with Chago. It looked like he had cut the cords binding his wrists and feet. The bandido held an angry sneer and stared at me with hate. Bud shoved him forward, and he started off in a peculiar, stumbling walk. I realized he was bootless and his feet not nearly as tough as mine. I hoped he was picking up every cactus thorn possible. Bud held a carbine. Good, I knew he was an excellent shot. He was watching Chago closer than worrying about the more distant bandidos. His carbine followed Chago.

I was moving faster than Chago, so I picked up my speed a little. El Xiuhcoatl shouted for me to slow down. I paid no attention. I did not think he would shoot me for walking too fast. Bud would shoot Chago before I fell to the ground. El Xiuhcoatl was smart enough to know that.

Bud's face turned grimmer as I came closer. I guess he could see how terrible I looked. The closer Chago got, the more concerned Bud was. He said, "No *fuego*. Don't try pulling something *estúpido*, *pendejo*."

He was passing to the right of me. He edged closer, and I moved away.

The stupid bastard jumped straight at me! I was faster, and I leaped away from him. I did not know if he tripped barefooted or if Bud's shot got him first. He went down on the rocks, knocking his breath out. He was hit in the right thigh. I went flat on the ground just in time. A barrage of shots burst from the bandidos behind their rocks. They must have been almost a hundred varas from us. Bud stood facing the storm and emptied his carbine, taking carefully aimed shorts, dropped it, picked up another, and emptied it. The bandido's fire wavered under his barrage.

He threw something toward me. "*¡La pistola, Marta!*" My name, I heard him call my name!

I crawled through the rocks as fast as I could. There was a burlap sack. I pulled out the single-shot pistol that Bud had taken from the old scared desperado who had tried to hold us up on our way to the Dew so long ago. It was loaded, and there were more cartridges in the bag. I had never fired it, but it looked simple. I cocked the hammer and aimed where I saw Chago go down.

Bud had reloaded both carbines and was firing again. The bandidos' shots were falling tighter around us now that they were over their first shock.

As Bud was reloading again, Chago rose out of the rocks and came straight at me. I was holding that big old pistol in both hands. His shot leg gave way, and I pulled the trigger. The recoil almost tore it out of my hands. The big bullet caught him right in the chest and blew padding out the back of his green jacket.

El Xiuhcoatl shrieked like the madman he was and started threatening terrible things. He made little sense. Bullets struck all around our outcropping. The fire died as the bandidos reloaded.

I fumbled with the pistol to reload it. I cocked it, and there was a lever in front of the hammer. I pulled it back and picked out the empty cartridge. That was not easy with my chewed-down fingernails. I pushed in another cartridge and thumbed the lever back.

Bud started shooting as fast as he could and shouted, "*Marta run! ¡Ándale!*"

On hands and knees, I wiggled through the rocks, holding the sack of cartridges, and fired a shot over my shoulder. That hurt my wrist. I did not like this pistol.

I came over the rocks, landing beside Bud. And there of all things was my shotgun! I reloaded the pistol, stuck it in the sack, and grabbed at my shotgun. Breaking it open, it was loaded. I should not have bothered checking. With it was a pouch of buckshot cartridges.

I aimed it at the bandidos, leaned into the buttstock, and squeezed a trigger and then the other. The familiar recoil gave me a new life. Twenty-four buckshot balls will not do much at that range but keep their heads down. I set the gun down and dove at my Bud! He rocked back, surprised, having been concentrating on shooting bad people. I gripped him tight and kissed him all over his bearded face. He smelled horrible. I think he wrinkled his nose at me. I was trying to laugh, but it never came out right.

He said "Whoa, girl!" and something about work to do. He had to push me away, and bullet strikes reminded me that we still had work to finish. I reloaded my shotgun. Bits of rock and gravel sprayed us.

He fired three shots. He faced me with a kind of strange look but had a brightness in his blue eyes, even though the clouds dulled the sun.

He set his carbine down and swung his arms around me, taking me by surprise. It was no matter that bullets were cracking over us. He said something to me. "I, you, and girl," were the only words I understood. It sounded like a promise. I did not care what he said. We were together, and we were not losing each other again.

He said something and then "*pronto*." I had no problem understanding that. We had to go. I was all for that. It crossed my mind that there was no one with us that I could see. There were four horses, but they must have been spares. Good. They would be a great help in our run to the Frontera. How long was that going to take? Could we even do it? We were exhausted, cold, wet, and hungry. The horses were no better off. We probably did not have enough food or feed. There were six bandidos after us. There would be no mercy in their black hearts.

He looked into my face and brushed my filthy hair from my forehead. I tried to smile, to show I had faith in him.

Bud pointed to the horses behind the outcropping. They could not be seen from the bandit camp. "*Di adi-os*"—Say goodbye.

I grabbed the pistol sack and my shotgun and got on a horse faster than I ever had. Bud emptied his carbine rapid fire, and I took off, lashing with the reins and jamming in my heels, taking the two spares with me. I held their reins rather than tie them to my saddle. I knew if one was hit while tied to my saddle, it would take down my horse.

¡Nos vamos a casa!

CHAPTER THIRTY-THREE

We are going home!

From the horse, I could see there was a wide arroyo before me with a flat gravel bottom. I looked back and saw that the outcropping and being down in the shallow arroyo gave us good cover to flee. By the time we could be seen from the bandido's camp, I thought we were out of range.

I did not wait for Bud as he mounted Crackers. I did not think he wanted me to. I looked back, and he was coming after me. He was farther behind than I realized. I looked ahead. I did not want to turn up a blind arroyo. He had almost caught up, going faster alone than my three horses. He held up his hand to stop, but I saw something that stood out. It was a bandana hanging over a lariat stretched across the arroyo just off the bottom. Had someone set a trap for us? No, Bud had done it, or there would be no warning bandana. Without slowing, the horses jumped the lariat. Bud slowed and plucked off the bandana.

Looking back, I saw El Xiuhcoatl and Tino coming down the arroyo with their heads down and whipping their horses. Bud fired three shots. They hit the lariat, and El Xiuhcoatl rolled when he went off his saddle. Tino went over the horse's head and had to have broken his worthless neck. I saw El Xiuhcoatl standing and shaking his fist. No other bandidos came. They were probably left to gather their bedrolls and stuff. They disappeared from sight as we rode.

Bud did not slow. We rode hard and fast. I knew we had to get as far ahead as possible. Would they come? Would they give up and go home? This chase, this kidnapping, had cost El Xiuhcoatl much. His band was almost wiped out. He had lost his brother and the bandidos who had been with him from the beginning. He had gotten the ransom for the girls, but was it worth it?

I thought they were coming after us. He would want revenge for his brother, and he would want revenge for all else that had befallen him. He would not stop until we were dead. We were well ahead of him. Speed was not all. We had to outsmart him.

Bud and I could do that. I knew we could do it.

As we raced across the broad valley, I prayed.

We entered the narrow, winding ravine. I still did not like this place. For the first time, I wondered what had happened here. Bud had come through. There was little doubt that Zaca was dead.

I was sure of that when the smell reached us. Vultures flew off fat and happy. Coyotes and javelinas had had their fill of the dead bandido and horse partly blocking the ravine. They smelled horrible, but I pulled off Zaca's boots. They were much too large, so I stuffed folded cloth from empty carne seca bags in the toes. They were still too wide and loose, but they were warmer. I spit on the stinking bastard.

Bud took the lariat from the bloating horse, its legs stuck out straight.

Near the horse was scattered deadwood, limbs, and pulled-up brush, a barricade Zaca had thrown up and Bud had torn down. We threw it back together, anything to slow revengeful El Xiuhcoatl.

Bud sent me ahead while farther down the ravine he made another trip rope with the lariat. Farther down the ravine, I found a grave of neatly stacked rocks. At its head was a winter-stilled buckeye plant. I knew it was Flaco. I was saying a prayer for him when Bud caught up. I knew he was a friend of Bud's. He had always been kind and respectful to me. I knew he had done some bad things in his past, but he had changed and tried to make things right. He had to be a good man. He would not have come after me at risk of life had he not.

We were through that long ravine. I wondered at the story of what happened here. Maybe sometime Bud could tell it to me, perhaps through Gabi. But maybe that was not a good idea. Maybe he would want me to tell him my story. I could tell mine, I thought, to some people so they could understand that there was evilness, unspeakable evilness, in the world. I wanted to tell someone that a woman could endear such evilness. I could. I had my God, I had myself I could rely on, I had Bud, who I could count on to do the right thing, and I had the memory of my familia to remind me of their strength.

We were making good time, I thought. I was weary and hungry and cold, but the excitement and joy of our escape kept me, kept us, going. It would not last. We were worn out before we even started our run to the Frontera.

Once we left the ravine, Bud did not like the place, either, we stopped in a mesquite thicket for a rest and to check the horses. Bud dug embedded gravel from their hooves. I was shivering cold with only that flannel shirt and long johns, all wet. Bud pulled out some too big dry clothes. He had been carrying them for me all this time. I did not like having to wear them over my filthy long johns, but they would dry out now. I pulled on the jeans and a brown wool shirt over my blue one. The heavy tan coat was blanket lined. He gave me the gloves he had bought me and my wool scarf. He gave me a serape too. I was going to be warm for the first time in days. While I was pulling on all these wonderful clothes, Bud rolled us cigarettes and lit one for me. I knew we had to go, but I wanted to enjoy it.

We were moving again as fast as the horses could handle. The sky said a storm was coming. It looked very bad. It darkened as if night was already falling. The wind was harder and colder from the north. Bands of rain fell. I was warmer, and the serape helped shed rain. I wished I had that buffalo robe. Looking behind us, the hoof prints disappeared almost as soon as they were put down. We had to get moving. Even if El Xiuhcoatl stopped, we needed to keep moving to gain as much distance as possible.

Right then I felt I could not go on. I had eaten nothing since yesterday and next to nothing then.

Bud thankfully decided to stop. The horses were resisting going farther. They would simply stop and stand, blinking their eyes. The Sun's dim glow sat on the distant hills. Lightning flashes said a stronger storm band was coming.

I almost fell sliding off the horse. I could barely stand. There was no place to get out of the wind. I felt helpless all of a sudden, and I could do nothing but stare off into the gray. The next thing I knew was that Bud had picked me up off the ground and sat me on a rock. He gave me a strip of carne seca and a canteen. I managed to chew on the boot heel-like meat. I felt light-headed. Thoughts of all that had happened whirled in my mind. I could not concentrate even on eating. I only wanted to lay down and sleep.

Bud unsaddled and hobbled the horses. We were wet, but he got us into the bedroll. He had set up two rubber blankets and held down their corners with rocks. We had the saddles inside with us propping up the covers. Still wet and cold, I began to shiver.

Bud tried to smile for me, looking into my eyes, or eye as one was swollen shut. Was he searching for what happened to me? I knew I was a beat up mess. He touched my hair. I wished he would not. It was so filthy. From a saddlebag, he drew a whisky bottle and splashed some on my bandana. He told me it would burn. I knew that. What was a little more pain? He held me tightly around my shoulders, cleaning the cuts on my face. Only the ones on my lips really burned, and the ones on my chin and under my eyes and on my ears. Finished, he took a swallow, and I took three, with a shudder burning through me.

Much to my surprise, he pulled our necklace out of his shirt, the one with a white bead for him and a tan one for me. I kissed it, and his hand and held it to my cheek. I tried to laugh, but it only embarrassed me. We held each other tight. I was starting to feel warmed and comfortable.

I was so happy I tried humming part of a church song, "*De colores se visten los campos en la primavera*"—"Colorful fields are dressed for spring." That was how I felt until all those bad things started running around in my head again. Bud was talking to me. I think he was saying that it made no matter what had happened to me. He wanted to be with me.

Did he really mean that if that is what he was saying? Why would he want to stay with me? I had been used and soiled…by many men, most of whom were fortunately and deservingly dead. Such an irreverent thought made me feel guilty. Did he really understand that? How could I tell him? Inés could have, she endured it, but she was gone.

I would have to show him. The thought sickened me. I could not move. I just let Bud hold me. I could not stand the thought of not being in his arms. But I had to do this. It would be a lie not to show him. I knew what I had to do. It was disgusting. I might lose him. I thought on that for a moment. I really believed he would understand. What he had done to get me back. He would understand…I hoped. I rapidly asked for forgiveness. I could do this. It would make me sick, but I had to do it.

I pushed Bud onto his back. I knew my face changed. He looked bewildered. I…I did not know if I could tell this.

I straddled Bud on my knees. As hard as I could, I slapped him across his face, twice. He actually looked scared. Good, because that was how I had felt. I grabbed his shoulders and made the most disgusting grunting sounds I could and humped him like a boar on a sow. He grabbed my arms and tried to push me away. I spit on him and slapped him, again and again, making him let go and cover his face, "Marta!" I hit him again. I pushed away and crawled from under the blankets. I had to get out. I was suffocating. "Marta, stay. *¡Quédate!*" I panicked. He too was going to hurt me. I tried to scream. I only made a strangling noise. I wanted to scream and scream and scream. He held me tight. I could not get away. Still, I struggled. "*¡Quédate con mi!*" I stilled, almost reluctantly. I sobbed, and he pulled me back to him. I could feel his strength. I needed that protection. I held onto him tighter as he pulled the blankets over us. He whispered words. I did not know them, but I understood his voice. I nodded my head against his shoulder. We lay still. We slept through the night's storms.

Nos levantamos antes de que amaneciera.

CHAPTER THIRTY-FOUR

We rose before the Sun.

It was so dark there was no yellow on the far hills. The wind had died as did the rain. He walked slowly to keep from tripping over rocks and cactus. The horses seemed to be content with a slow walk. I knew they were hungry. So were we.

We walked for a long time before it was light enough to ride. We still took it slow because of rocks and the many small arroyos.

I was embarrassed for the shameful scene I had performed. Bud said nothing of it. When we awoke, he gave me soft kisses on my cheeks and held me tight for a time. He understood? I could only hope so. At least I did not wake up alone. I was still in his arms. We were still in danger, but at that moment I felt safe.

I tried to push the past out of my head. I tried to think about what Bud and I would do when we made it home. I had ridden so far in this featureless land that I was bored. All I could think of was the bad things that had happened. We ate some carne seca in the saddle.

"Bla, bla, bla. Café," said Bud. "Bla, bla, bla."

I nodded and licked my lips. I wanted coffee beyond all things right now. I thought he said we could have some soon!

We kept to the low ground, but sometimes we had to cross over ridges because to follow the low ground around them would take too long. When we crossed over the ridges, Bud looked behind us with the double-barrel, like my shotgun, telescope—*prismáticos*. He never saw anyone. I could only hope we had lost them or they had given up, but it was only a hope. Through the day he turned more often, even when we were on low ground, as though expecting El Xiuhcoatl to charge around a hillside at any moment. That could happen, I reminded myself. I hoped too that in this huge land we were so small that El Xiuhcoatl would be looking for two tiny pebbles.

It was late in the day, and Bud said we needed to eat—"*Comemos*." We could not have a fire later—"*Noche sin fuego*." I knew that.

We stopped at a stream flowing down a shallow arroyo between a low ridge and a hill. Bud pulled out cooking gear and a coffee pot! We were going to eat a real meal!

I collected firewood as fast as I could while Bud unsaddled the horses and hobbled them to graze on a patch of grass. They did not like sharing the small patch, nuzzling each other out of the way. There was little firewood. Bud poured some kerosene on the pile of twigs and lit it as soon as I had a pot ready. He had a few wonderful tins of food. I had eaten only carne seca, tortillas, and barely any frijoles for days. I opened tins of frijoles—not nearly as good as fresh frijoles—stewed tomatoes, and green peas. I chopped up some Americano jerky—fresher than the ancient carne seca—and mixed it altogether. Bud had the coffee pot heating after getting water from the stream. While the meal was cooking, we opened a tin of peaches. I could not get enough and thought I was going to have to fight Bud for it. He let me have most. The smell of the meal, the coffee! He even had sugar cubes! I could barely wait.

The cook pot ready. I poured half into two empty tins for me and left the rest in the pot for Bud. It wasn't as hot as I would have liked, but it was the best meal I'd had since supper on the Dew. The same with the coffee, but it was hot enough to hurt my split lips. It was wonderful.

I ate fast because I was famished. Bud ate fast for the same reason, but I knew he wanted to be moving again. We both knew we had to get to the Río as fast as we could. If it was up to him, we might only stop to pee. It kept coming into my mind that we did not have to make only the Río to be safe, we had to reach the ranch. That was almost another two ligas.

The food and coffee had given me strength. I felt more alert. I was still filthy, disgustedly filthy, soiled by life on the trail, nature, and men. I did not expect to feel like this for long.

Bud was saddling the horses. That was a job I always wished I could do, but I was too small.

I rushed to the stream, throwing off my coat and taking off the two shirts. I glanced in Bud's direction and pulled off the long johns top. Grabbing a bandana, I wet it and wiped myself down. Splashing the bandana in the stream, it flowed brown with obscene filthiness. For the first time, I could see the bruises, scrapes, cuts, and bites. Seeing them, I fully felt their pain for the first time. I looked back to Bud, and he was staring at me. Him seeing me naked was not a bother. It was the battering my body had taken that embarrassed me. Then I realized it was no different than what I had showed him last night. I had nothing to hide from Bud, ever. I stared back and did not cover myself. I turned and put on the brown shirt. I rapidly scrubbed the long johns top and blue shirt and tied them to my *tientos*—saddle strings. They were still so offensively filthy it would be better to toss them aside, but I would need them. It was still cold.

When I turned around, Bud was running up the ridge. I noticed the fire was making a lot of smoke. We had thrown on some damp wood trying to find enough for a suitable fire.

He was coming back down the ridge. "*¡Dos bandidos, ándale!*"

Two bandidos! How did they find us? I ran to the horses, leaving the cooking gear and even my boots. The smoke!

"No *caballos*," he shouted waving for me to follow.

I took my shotgun and cartridge pouch and ran after him in my socks. I followed him up a brush-filled draw. Why were we going slowly? I realized it was so we would not shake the brushes and be spotted. He signaled me to stop and pointed down the ridge. He wanted me to stay and guard his back. Bud went on through the brush below the ridge crest. He was heading to where he could overlook our horses. I lost sight of him.

A single shot cracked, and I heard a running horse. I expected more shots, but only silence. Then I heard Bud shout something about shooting and "*Mi no fuego*." He was telling the bandidos he would not shoot. I could not see anything from up here in the brush. I followed my own path back down. I saw five nervous horses milling in a group. I could see a bandido's legs standing among them. There was another bandido on the ground kicking his legs. Bud had no doubt shot him. Bud was not shooting at the other among our horses. Besides hitting them, he might cause them to run off. The bandido too might run off with all the horses, leaving us on foot and doomed.

And that was what he tried to do. His horse was standing a short distance from ours as they were strangers to him. The bandido charged from among the horses, firing his carbine up the ridge. Lencho! He threw his carbine and leaped, vaulting with his hands over the horse's rump. He immediately wiped the horse into a run up the arroyo toward me. Bud fired several shots, missing with all. In his own way, Lencho had tried to protect us. He had taken Inés but not me. He was not like the other bandidos. Still, he was a bandido. I fired both barrels knocking him into the stream on his back. I came out of the brush reloading. He struggled to pull out his pistol, but then saw me and stopped. His bloodied face smiled, and he raised a hand to ask for help. I hesitated but let loose with one barrel into his chest. I stood beside the stream until the red washed past me. Could he have become a good man? It did not matter. I easily caught his horse.

Bud came down the ridge. "*¡Ándale!*" We had to leave. The wind had died. Those shots could be heard from a long distance. We drank the remaining coffee from the pot and dipped the cooking and coffee pots in the stream and threw the water on the fire. That made more smoke. Bud picked up the bandidos' guns. In Lencho's saddlebags, I found small sacks of carne seca, frijoles, tortillas, *maíz*—tortilla dough—and feed corn. We needed that grain. Bud unsaddled Lencho's horse and let it go. Only a couple of my pellets had grazed its neck. We had our spares and did not need another to eat what little grain was left.

I looked at the bandido's body beside the stream. It was *mata*, shot though the lungs. I spit on him. Lencho lay in the stream, still turning the water red. Three shotgun blasts had opened him up. I did not care if he could have been a good man. He was really no different. Lencho was even a hoarder, holding out on his compadres. I started to, but I did not spit on him. I would give him that. It did not matter.

We rode out fast with Bud constantly looking behind us. Almost a liga out, we stopped to let the horses blow and feed them. I put the rest of my still damp clothes back on. I had not even bothered with the coat. Bud threw the bandidos' guns into a stream.

I became gloomy when I felt the wind pick up and air grow colder. The clouds thickened. Ahead of was a huge round-topped mountain crowned by mean clouds and lightning. It grew dark early with the storm becoming worse and rain arriving. Like last night, we rode until we could not see. We built another rubber blanket shelter held down by rocks as before. As we crawled in, it started to sleet. I felt sorry for the picketed horses standing with their rumps to the wind.

¿Esto nunca terminará?

CHAPTER THIRTY-FIVE

Will this never end?

It was light when we awoke. It was impossible to guess the time. The storm still blew with the sleet horizontal to the ground. It stung the face. The horses were crusted with ice and so unhappy. We were unable to eat. I wish I had kept one of the bandidos' sombreros. The scarf helped little. Once encrusted with ice, it blocked the wind better.

I had had nightmares and woke many times. Bud was always there with his arm around me. I would fall back to sleep only to wake again with El Xiuhcoatl on me. I think I hit at Bud sometimes. He woke me with a kiss on the forehead and a long hug. As miserable as I was, I smiled. I only wanted to go home. Could we make it? We knew now they were still after us.

I could not help pack. I just sat on a rock while Bud did the work. I had on a yellow slicker, but I was still wet from the blowing sleet. The wind even picked up sand to blast us with along with the sleet. My nose ran more, and I sneezed a lot.

We walked the horses, keeping them between us and the wind. It was so hard to walk that we got up on the horses anyway. I kept asking if this storm was going to last forever. I prayed that it would end. I even prayed to Tlaloc, the Aztec god of rain, but not seriously. That would have been blasphemous.

My spare came up lame. Bud took off its saddle and hackamore and let it go. We had only one spare now.

My mind was numbed by the cold. I could not keep a thought. Something would come into my mind, and then I would lose it to be replaced by another thought and another. It made me light-headed and confused.

One thought kept coming back to me. I had killed three men. Three souls were gone to Heaven, or Hell more likely. I could see their faces, the indio I had knifed and had bleed all over me, Chago with his snarling face coming at me and the pistol shot into his chest, and Lencho asking for help as I blasted him with my shotgun. They were all evil, they all had or wanted to violate me and kill me too. I had no regrets. Or did I? Maybe they were evil, but they were still living souls. In some way, I would regret having to take their lives, but I must never forget that I had the right to protect my own body and soul from violation. And Bud, how many had he killed? Many, I suspected. He too was protecting his own life and soul. And he was protecting me. That was why he killed, to protect me. I prayed for Bud too.

We rode on and on. I kept telling myself that no matter how miserable we were, El Xiuhcoatl and his men were just as miserable as us. That and the storm made sure we left no tracks.

My head felt like tortilla dough. I faded in and out. I

kept my head covered and eyes closed. I had no idea we had been riding. At one point the wind passed for a short time, and the rain actually fell downward, not horizontally. I looked about and saw we were beyond that big, ugly, round-topped mountain.

One time we stopped. Keeping my eyes closed, I waited for Bud to help me down. He did not. I could not hear him. I looked ahead, and he was riding back. My horse had simply stopped, and he had kept going. With much effort, I believe he got me off my horse and onto his. He mounted and got me covered with another blanket and slicker. He talked to me, and I think it was something about us not being able to stop. Holding on to him, pressing against his back, I felt a tiny bit warmer and much safer. At times I heard him talking to himself. I thought it was about going on. He kept muttering, and he sounded desperate. Was he saying he could not go on? If we stopped, we would die. I pulled him around to half face me. With our noses running and icy rain dribbling in, I kissed him on his mouth. We clung together for a time. It felt like our strength was growing. We went on into the blasting wind. Wet gobs of snow fell.

I did not remember arriving. I realized where we were when we passed the hacienda. San Miguel?

I saw two horses and a mule in the courtyard. There were still bandidos there! That frightened me, and I remembered pieces of what happened in there. I clung to Bud. He kept watch on that horrible place as we passed. There was no one on the streets. It had stopped snowing, and we faced only freezing rain and occasional blasts of wind and wet sand. My nose ran constantly. Besides my swollen left eye, I could barely open my good one. I must have passed out as we rode on. The only sensible thought

I remember was, why were we riding straight through this bandido stronghold?

I came to, and we were inside a jacalito, a crude shack with mesquite limb walls and roofs of spikey yucca leaves, both covered with mud. It was not too bad for a jacalito. Only a little water dripped through. It was warm, somewhat. A cow patty fire burned with the smoke drifting through a roof hole. There was a man and a woman sitting by the fire with a frijoles pot going. While the place did not smell too good, the frijoles did. A small, dirty-faced boy and girl peered at us from behind their mamá. I do not know if they were more curious of the strange visitors or were afraid of us.

The man said, "My house is your house." Peons always welcomed travelers in their simple homes. They may need food and shelter themselves someday.

Bud had me wrapped in blankets leaning against him. I expected the woman to ask questions of me, but I realized in this place ruled by El Xiuhcoatl, one did not ask questions.

The woman gave wooden bowls of frijoles to Bud. I was so weak and my arms bundled in the blankets that Bud fed me, wiping off dribbled frijole juice. Then he ate. The frijoles were not too good, even with dried goat meat, and the tortillas grainy. The coffee in gourd cups was a little better. Weak, but more importantly, hot. I did feel a little better and ate the rest of my frijoles myself.

Bud rolled cigarettes, gave one to the man, and lit one up for me. The man went with Bud, saying he had water and hay for the horses. The woman, she had had a hard life here, only stared at me along with the boy and girl. Bud and the man soon returned with a blast of rain blowing through the small door.

Bud sat beside me again, and I leaned against his warmth. I was so drowsy I struggled to stay awake but lost to the Aztec god Tezcatlipoca, god of the night sky, night winds, storms, and the north, from which this storm came.

It was silent when I woke right after dawn. No one had moved. Even the boy and girl were still behind their mamá. She was again heating frijoles, coffee, and tortillas. Bud touched my face softly. It would have been improper for him to kiss me in this home. I guess he knew that. Outside we found it still and cold with everything frost covered. It was a relief from the smoky jacalito, and the air felt so clear out here. I squatted and peed on the other side of the horse shed, something necessary but about as miserable as a thing one must do. Bud grained the horses and showed me the feedbag had one more feed in it.

We ate, and Bud thanked the couple in Spanish. He rolled three cigarettes and gave them and a handful of peso coins he had cut off Zaca's sombrero to the grateful man. They probably wondered why I never spoke.

On leaving, Bud put a finger to his lips, telling the man to keep quiet about us. He nodded with a wink and a smile. Bud did not know it, but I left a tin of corn with the woman.

Checking the narrow muddy street, Bud and I mounted. I waved to the man and woman. They never asked us and Bud never asked them for names. Such were the ways out on the campo.

We took the east road out in the direction of the Río. I thought Bud would go in another direction and then double back, but he chose to make haste. We sped up once out of San Miguel and trotted up a ridge side. There were three fresh graves. Bud pointed to himself and said, "*Y Flaco, muerto tres Rurales.*"

He and Flaco had killed three Rurales here. He had

done this to save me. Bud had turned back to look at San Miguel as we rode up the ridge. He did so again and rapidly pulled out the double telescope.

I could see what was happening. The man, our kind host, was trotting up the street toward the hacienda. Why? Why would he betray us and why now? He could have snuck out while we slept. Anger burned through me like a black coal fire. I turned my horse, jabbed my heels into its sides, and standing in the stirrups, I rein-lashed him down the road. Bud followed. He did not try and stop me. Once I got going, I guess he decided to go along with it. We charged through the village, running people off the street.

We slid through the open gate in the mud, taking two bandidos and the man by surprise. They were talking with waving arms. Bud already had his pistol out and fired, I thought four shots, before they could do anything. A bandido with a head bandage drew his pistol and was hit by Bud. His unsaddled horse beside him was hit too. The man fell, and the shot horse started kicking. The other bigger bandido, with a left arm sling, dropped his crutch and brought up a pistol. He fired at Bud just as I triggered my shotgun. He was blown against the hacienda wall and spit out his cigarette. As he fell, he left a trail of blood and breakfast on the wall. The mule was running in circles and making terrible, fearful noises. I swung the shotgun around to the peon and just about squeezed the trigger when Bud shouted "*¡Marta, alto!*"

I took careful aim.

"*No, Marta. Los dos niños.*"

What? Then I understood, if I killed the peon, deserving that he was, the mamá and children would suffer. They would be unprotected with no way to earn money. The best she could hope for was for her parents to take her back. That did not always happen, even if they were still alive.

I lowered the gun. The peon had wet his pants. He had learned a lesson. I grinned and gave a nod in agreement.

"*Los bandidos muertos*," Bud said. He was saying all the bandidos were dead, not completely true, I thought.

Bud dismounted and reloaded his pistol as he went through the hacienda's gate. He pulled the door open with his pistol ready. I saw a plump girl inside who ran off. Bud waved his arm to the peon that he could go in, that everything in the hacienda belonged to the village people. I think he understood. Bud shot the wounded horse, and the peon hit his head on the doorframe's top when he jumped.

I pointed with my shotgun at the dead bandido's big, woven-straw sombrero.

Bud asked, "*¿Qué?*"

I jabbed the shotgun. I wanted it. He handed it up to me, and he mounted but kept his pistol in his hand. We rode out on the same road. Peons were running into and out of the hacienda carrying whatever they could. El Xiuhcoatl would not be happy, and more so when he found we killed two more of his bandido dogs.

We were over a liga from San Miguel when Bud pulled off the road. Why were we stopping? He dismounted, slowly muttering something. There was blood dripping from his right arm's coat cuff.

I scrambled off my horse and got some rags from the saddlebags. I carefully took off his coat. I took my hunting knife and slit his shirt and long johns sleeves open. I cut them, making the shortest slit I could. He still needed them. A bullet had cut down to the bone on his forearm. It must hurt. I cleaned it as best as I could. I ended up cutting the long johns' forearm sleeve off and cut it lengthwise. I wrapped a spare wool sock around the bullet gouge and then tied it in place with the long johns sleeve strips. The bleeding stopped.

I got his coat back on and helped him mount. He looked pale, and I gave him some water with salt and sugar in it. He did not like that, but it was good for him when bleeding. I tied the spare's reins to my saddle, and we left. I would watch Bud closely. I was still weak myself.

No estamos fuera de peligro.

CHAPTER THIRTY-SIX

We are not out of danger.

We headed east. Rocks, mesquite, and cactus. I did not know if Bud knew the way or if we were simply heading east to the Río. I guessed there were good places to cross, and I hoped he knew where they were. With all the rain, there may be no good fording places. Would the horses be strong enough to swim across in fast cold water?

The sky was clearing. No more rain, and the wind blew in short gusts. We took turns riding the spare, changing about every hour. I thought Bud was trying to rest our horses as much as possible. We might have to run for it at any time. Bud still watched behind us and looked over the ridges to our sides.

By midday, I was weaker. I could stay in the saddle easily enough, but when we dismounted for breaks, I could barely stand. I would pee in the bushes, but standing beside the horse, I had to hang onto a stirrup strap. I would smoke a cigarette at each break. One time I found Bud staring at me with worry in his eyes. I finished the cigarette and flipped it at Bud to let him know I knew what I was doing.

As we headed east toward the Río, the ground sloped slightly downward, and there was more mesquite and other plants.

Bud said, "Marta, *Rancho Maripoa*," and waved his arm around.

I understood. This was the ranchland where we had crossed the Río. This was also where he and the others had fought part of the bandido band and killed Don Garza's son and the Americano rancher, Maxwell. I understood why he was worried. Besides El Xiuhcoatl, Maripos vaqueros might be dangerous if they found us.

Bud was ahead of me on the spare, and I was following with his horse, Cracker, strung behind.

I was thinking about those vaqueros when I looked toward the low ridge to our left. There was a vaquero riding atop the crest. He was going in the opposite direction as us, away from the Río. Maybe if we showed we were friendly, he would not come down to see who we were. The vaquero waved his sombrero in greeting. I took off mine and waved. My hair blew behind me.

Bud turned and shouted "*¡No!*" then "*¡Ándale!*"

I realized I had done the wrong thing. That was a bandido, and I had shown my hair. He knew who we were.

The rider fired his carbine into the air and came down the ridge, and before he disappeared in the mesquite, he was angling ahead of us to try and catch us before we reached the Río. He must have signaled his compadres.

Then I thought, how many bandidos were left? There could not be many. We shot down that dog Chago at the camp, Tino died tripping the lariat when he and El Xiuhcoatl started to chase us. Lencho and Matu we shot when they found us at the stream. There should only be two left, El Xiuhcoatl and Paco. Was that Paco coming for us from the ridge? It was not El Xiuhcoatl.

I was scared now. I had made a mistake. Two bandidos had to be coming after us. One was coming from the left and the other probably somewhere behind us. I pulled my shotgun from the scabbard and made sure it was loaded. Bud was checking his pistols. We were in very thick mesquite and had to move slowly. I guessed Bud was taking us straight to the Río to swim across if we had to. The mesquite was high enough that we had to bend over in the saddle to look under the leafy branches. I used my shotgun to lift limbs to see better. We were making too much noise passing through the limbs, but it could not be helped. I was behind and to the right of Bud when Cracker, following me, tossed his head.

A carbine boomed from behind me! Bud pitched forward against the horse's neck, and it jumped, being startled. Bud fell to the left, dropping his pistol. He hit the ground on his back. There was blood on his left shoulder and neck! He vomited. His boot was hung in the stirrup. I heard noises in the brush behind us. Swinging the shotgun around, I fired one barrel after the other at the noise. I heard a horse bust through the brush. Bud's panicked and confused horse began pushing its way through the brush, dragging Bud through the rocks. He got his other pistol out and fired three or four shots into the horse's belly. It fell to the right, and a jerking leg kicked him in the jaw and shoulder and pulled him to the horse's belly. He yelled, "Marta!"

I scrambled off my horse and found Bud's pistols. Wounded though he was, we needed the pistols. They knew where we were, and they were close. I shoved the pistols into his holsters and got his boot out of the stirrup. I saw all the blood on his left shoulder and neck, so I grabbed his right arm.

"No!" he shouted.

I did not care how bad he was hurt. He had to get on his feet. We had to move. We had to be ready to fight. That reminded me. I reloaded my shotgun and set it down.

I slapped my hands and stomped my boot to let him know he had no choice. I took his hand again and got my arm around his waist. I heaved myself back, and with Bud pushing up with his legs and right arm, he was on his feet. He was in a lot of pain and seemed confused. I could barely hold him up, and if he was not hanging onto a mesquite, I could not have. I was going to have to defend him.

I pushed and dragged him in Cracker's direction. The horse was right beside me and moved closer as if he knew Bud and I needed his help. I do not know how we did it, but with a lot of effort by both of us and Cracker, Bud made it onto the saddle. He was in a lot of pain. I put the reins in his hands and mounted my horse. Both horses were skittish as could be. I think they knew the bandidos' horses they had met before were close by.

I moved up to Bud's left side and took his big knife. He was awfully pale. I had to stand in my stirrups to reach his shoulder properly. It is the first time I had ever treated anyone sitting in a saddle and certainly not with us both in saddles. I cut the thick coat open and then his shirt and long johns. The bullet had gone through the muscle connecting the shoulder and neck. It did not look good but was not bleeding as much as I would have suspected. I wrapped it tight with a bandana and rag. Opening a front button, I worked his left hand into the opening to hold it up like a sling.

Behind us was a dead bandido, blown open with

buckshot. Buckshot-clipped mesquite limbs were scattered on the ground. There was no sign of the horse. We could have used it now that we were down to two. I bent over to see who it was. I did not recognize him. Where did he come from? Was he the bandido who came down the ridge? I did not think so. How could he have gotten here so fast through this mesquite? Had there been more bandidos in San Miguel that El Xiuhcoatl gathered? How many more are there now? No matter, they had heard the shot, and they were coming this way.

I led the way forward, keeping the shotgun pointed ahead. We went slowly so I could hear better.

I suddenly felt so tried I thought I would fall asleep in the saddle, and probably topple off. I shivered from the chill, and I shivered from the sudden fear. I had not had time to feel scared until now. And Bud, how bad was he hurt? I was hungry again. I was cold, I was frightened, I was tired of this and wanted it over with. I wanted the killing and pain to quit. To do that, I knew I had to kill some more.

What was I becoming? I did not like killing, but it was of no worry to me at that moment. It was no different than shooting a rabid dog we met on the road.

We came out of the thick mesquite. It was more open with scattered low mesquite, sagebrush, creosote, yucca, and some cactus. The rocky ground slopped downward. I smelled it and then saw the Río Bravo a few hundred vara away. We were almost there! Almost to the Dew, but I know it would be a hard-ridden distance. Seeing the river through the thin mist, turned me into a water-starved horse, and I kicked the horses into a run. I threw away any caution, such as taking it slow to the river, listening, and watching for danger. I just wanted to get us there as fast as possible. I was not even thinking about how we were getting across. I knew but did not care how much this run must hurt Bud.

From close behind, I heard, "*¡Ahhh-baabaaa!*" It terrified me, and I almost gave up hope. Almost. Both Bud and I lashed at the horses with our reins and dug in our heels. We bounded toward the Río with branches whipping our faces.

Bud and Cracker were beside me. We were stiff-legged in our stirrups, hugging our pounding horses' necks, and hanging on the best we could.

Maybe we could swim the horses hitting the water at a full run, or if we were lucky, we might find one of the few shallow fords. The last hope was to throw off our boots, plunge into the Río, and swim as hard as we could. It passed through my mind, *Can Bud even swim?* I thought so. I knew I could. It was something Papá taught us. He had seen children drown in even small streams. Why was I thinking this then?

My horse jerked and stumbled to the right, smashing into Cracker. Shots cracked. I came off the saddle and flew into Bud, bounced off, and rolled over Cracker's rump. Hitting the ground, the breath was knocked out of me. Cracker reared and fell to the ground, making snorting noises. My horse was lying nearby, stone still. I got to my hands and knees. Bud, in much pain, sat up and drew a pistol. All I could do was look at the rushing Río, close enough to throw a rock.

I searched and found my shotgun and took the cartridge bag off my dead horse. I left my sombrero. Bud put his pistol back and got his carbine off of Cracker. He patted the still horse's neck. I knew he loved that horse. It came to me that they must have shot ours horses down so they could take us alive. I would not think of what would happen if they did. Better to put my shotgun to my head and press the trigger with a toe.

I tried to feel if I was hurt, if I had broken anything. I

hurt everywhere, but nothing was broken. I broke a wrist once falling down a ravine. That was fortunate, Mamá had said. A child's broken leg often meant she was left behind by her familia. I had heard stories of children left in someone's care other than their familia. The familia had to keep moving to find work and food. The child was seldom seen again, or once healed, they wandered on their own and never found their familia. Why did I keep thinking these things from my past?

I looked behind us as Bud raised his carbine. Whooping like indios and screeching "*¡Ahhh-baabaaa!*," three bandidos charged out of the mesquite straight at us like an arrow, and El Xiuhcoatl was the point.

Bud pushed himself to his feet with his carbine. I could not see how he stayed up he was so wobbly. He tried to lift the carbine, but could not. He dropped it and drew a pistol, his long one. I ran toward him. Blood was dripping off my left hand, and my leg was starting to hurt, to stiffen. We were both on our feet, facing the terror rushing at us. They came at us, straight at us so fast and furious.

I could see the fury in El Xiuhcoatl's face. With his red shirt, I saw him as the Devil himself. Bud stretched his arm out, and his pistol cracked. The horse went down and threw the jefe over its head to smash into the rocks, cactus, and yucca spikes. Bud fired two more shots. The second man's horse, another stranger, was hit in the neck. The horse bucked, throwing the man to the ground tumbling.

I thought of children, our children, playing in the sun, the children I would never see. *We will see about that.* I calmed myself, saying in my mind, *"Help me, Mary."* As steady a rock, I aimed as carefully as I could. I ignored the passing zips of bullets.

I fired one barrel and the next at the third man. His

horse reared and rolled onto the ground peppered with buckshot. The second man rose to a knee and aimed at us. It was Paco. Bud hit him two or three times with his pistol. I did not know why, but I would rather Bud did it than myself.

Then I was hit twice in the right thigh, like two kicks. I fell into Bud's side and then to my knees. He dropped his long pistol and pulled out his other. I kept hold of my shotgun. Something told me never to let it go. I did not know what was happening to me. There was something I was supposed to do with it. What? My leg and side felt numb, all on my right side. My head was swirling. I remembered what I needed to do. The shotgun. I needed to reload it.

I sat up but had to hold myself up by an arm. Bud was still standing, holding a wavering pistol.

I looked at the bodies, men and horses. I smelled gun smoke. I still smelled the Río. I felt the wind, the wind! The sky was clearing.

El Xiuhcoatl rose from the dead with a pistol in his hand. He was bloody from head to knees, torn by rocks and yucca, his face blood covered, and his evil eyes glared at me with the Devil's hate. He was the Devil!

I stared in fascinated horror at El Xiuhcoatl, but out of the corner of my eye, I could see Bud raise his pistol and carefully aim at the Devil. I waited for the finishing shot. There was only an empty click followed by another.

My stomach went hollow. Mamá said the Devil always won if one gave up faith. I had not given up faith in Bud, and while I almost did, I did not give up faith in myself so long as Bud was still here on Earth.

Bud dropped his pistol. He had given everything.

The Devil staggered toward us and aimed his pistol at me, not at Bud. It was I who brought Bud after him. I was the one who cost him everything he had. I was the one who had brought him to his end.

Bud pulled a third pistol from his coat pocket and fired six times, staggering the Devil back and crumpling him to his knees. Bud fell onto his side still snapping the empty pistol. The Devil swayed on his knees. I know not how many times Bud hit him. With an unbelieving look, the Devil dropped his pistol.

Bud was propped against a rock. I got on my knees and hung onto Bud. This had to end, now. I used the shotgun to push myself up and almost fell I was so weak. Holding onto Bud's arm, I tried again and made it to my feet. It hurt and took everything I had, or what I had left at that moment. I surprised myself that I could stagger forward, tripping over rocks and cactus. I broke open my shotgun and plucked out the empty shells. I reached inside my pouch and brought out two shells and slid them into the breeches. I snapped it shut, hearing the latch's click. One at a time I clicked back the hammers. I never took my eyes off the Devil's face. I barely had the strength to lift up the barrels and hold them steady. I pressed the barrels into the place between his glaring eyes and the top of his nose. He wrapped his blood-covered fists around the barrels. That craved-for moment was there, so long awaited. I had never ever wanted to be able to speak so badly, to say, "I hope the Hell you brought us on Earth awaits you seven times over." Seven was the Biblical number of completeness and perfection. This moment...was perfect. I gently squeezed both triggers. His evil face disappeared for eternity, never to terrorize again.

I tripped backward, and all became black.

Había visto los ojos del infierno.

Chapter Thirty-Seven

I had seen the eyes of Hell.

I could still see them when I woke up. I was shivering cold on the wet ground. It was silent except for the breeze brushing through the mesquite. I could not even hear the Río. Instead of the freshness of the campo, I smelled death and shit and blood. Trying to push myself up, I almost passed out.

Lie still and listen. Try not to smell.

Bud! My Bud, where is he? I sat up too fast and everything rushed around in circles. I felt like I was going to vomit. I swallowed an ugly taste.

Bud was slumped against a rock beside me. He was breathing and muttering. I lay my hand on his shoulder and offered a short prayer of thanks.

Lying in front of me was a blood-covered and mutilated El Xiuhcoatl. Five horses lay about unmoving. The other two bandidos lay in the rocks. I reloaded my shotgun and used it to climb to my feet. My head swirled for a moment. The disgusting jeje lay sprawled with most of his head gone. It was wonderful that I would never have to see his vile eyes again. I pointed the muzzle at his empty black heart and squeezed a trigger. I wanted to be sure. I reloaded.

I crouched with my shotgun and looked all around me, especially the nearby low ridges. There was no one. The other side of the Río was empty, no monitor from the Dew attracted by the gunfire.

I carefully laid Bud on his back and worked off his coat. Taking off the crude bandage I had put on his shoulder and neck, I was thankful it was bleeding little. I went through saddlebags looking for cleaner clothes to tear up for bandages. I also found two cuts in his left shoulder, maybe bullet fragments. I cleaned his wounds with water and tequila.

I made an extra big thick bandage because I was going to have to leave Bud there as I went for help. He had already been hit by a bullet that gouged to the bone in his right forearm. I did not see how he had held up his pistol. He had a graze on his right calf. It was not too bad. I looked at both his arms and legs and found three more little holes in his right thigh from fragments—bits of lead. In his coat pocket, I found the cuff I had torn off my blue shirt. Bud had found it! It may have helped him to keep going, even when alone.

I had to leave and cross the Río and find help. The sooner, the better. I had to first treat myself. My legs. I knew I had been shot in the legs. If I could not walk, we were as good as dead. I pulled my jeans and both shirts off. My long johns bottoms were filthy and stuck to me like a second skin, the top too. My left forearm had barely a bullet graze and maybe a big bullet fragment near my left elbow. It was deep and hurting and stiffening. In my right thigh were two bullet fragment holes, but not too bad. I found a bullet had broken a rib on my right side. It went through under the skin and left two holes a hand's width apart. I tore the sleeves off a shirt I found in a saddlebag and tied the cuff ends together. I bound this around myself over the broken rib. That hurt more than any other wound. The underside of my forearm was peppered with white fragments, mostly sticking out. I pulled out the bigger ones and realized they were skull fragments. I tried to get more out. I cleaned up as best I could using most of the tequila. I saved enough for a good swallow.

Shivering, I put my clothes back on and searched the other saddlebags. I threw all the food I found into a small pile. I found two leather pouches in El Xiuhcoatl's saddlebag. I opened the first one, and it was full of hundreds of dollars! It must be the ransom Señor DeWitt paid for Doris and Agnes. The other one had even more dollars and pesos! It was money he had stolen. It was more money than I could imagine, and I did not even know how to count that much money. I found the disgusting crockpot bag with the Rurales commandant's head. I threw it in the Río without opening the bag.

I took the bedroll off Cracker and dragged it to Bud. I opened it beside him, and with a lot of effort and hard breathing, I got him rolled into it. It was so painful on my side with the broken rib. There was a patch of thicker mesquite nearby. I dragged him into it to hide him. I cut some brush and piled it around him. I could not take the money pouches with me. They could be too easily lost swimming the Río. I put them in the bedroll with Bud.

I had a long way to go. I had to eat something first. I would need the strength. Thankfully it was not raining, and I got a fire going using Bud's cap lighter. Opening a tin of frijoles, I dumped them in a tin plate to heat. I opened another tin and set it beside the fire to heat. I started half a pot of coffee.

What did I need to take? I could not carry much. I had thrown the saddlebags and bridles and dragged most of the saddles over too. I set all the gathered guns there. I took a canteen, a hunting knife, and some jerky wrapped in a rag. I did not take a gun. I almost did not take the cap lighter. I felt that if I stopped for a warming fire, I might not be able to continue on. I took it anyway just in case. From a lariat, I cut a length double my height.

I ate all the frijoles I could from the tin and poured the rest into the plate and put some jerky on it. Bud might come to. I drank most of the coffee and left a full cup with a tortilla on top. I also left a canteen for Bud. Warming myself would do little good because I was going into the icy cold río. I made sure the fire was out.

I squatted beside Bud and stared into his face. My mind rushed with jumbled thoughts. I had to leave him here alone with wounds, unconscious, and without protection. His life depended on me and me alone. What if something happened to me? What if I simply could not make it on my own? I might not even make it across the Río. It was so overwhelming I cried. I got ahold of myself. I was his woman. I was not a girl. I touched his bristly, dirty, and bloody face. I pledged in my mind, *I love you above all things. I will come back for you.*

I stood and left.

I stared across the Río at the far carrizo cane-lined shore. It was wide and running fast. Looking both ways, I could not see the low smooth swell in the water showing a ford. The water was too fast anyway to ford. Taking out the knife, I cut several mesquite bushes and mashed them together into a thick bundle. Around this, I wound the shortened lariat as tight as I could. The bundle was as long as I was tall and as big around as a beer keg.

I rolled the knife, lighter, and jerky in the shirt I had torn the sleeves off of, twisted the ends, and tied them around my waist. The canteen sling was over my right shoulder and canteen on my left side so it would not hit my broken rib. I took my boots off and tied them together to hang over my neck. The tin of frijoles went in the left boot.

The Río swept past. There were barely any tree limbs in the flood. Most had already been washed away. I had done this before, swim a fast river, but not this fast and not this wide. I knew it would carry me far to the right, and I would reach the far shore a good ways downriver if I did not drown.

I took too long praying for Bud's protection, for my own salvation, and saying the rosary. I even asked for help from *Chalchiuhtlicue*, Aztec goddess of water, rivers, streams, and storms, and the giver of life and death. She had built a bridge linking Heaven and Earth that allowed her good graces to flow into our world. I hoped the Río was carrying those graces now.

There was not much daylight left, and I had a long way to go if I made it across.

I stood none too steady and gripped the brushwood bundle, looked up and downriver, crossed myself, and jumped into the shit-brown surging water. It was worse than I ever imagined. The cold shock took my breath away, and I swear made my heart skip a beat. My legs especially stiffened.

I tumbled underwater like the sticks Tlayolot and I used to toss into streams and run along the shore chasing them. I came up still clinging to the bundle and gasping for air. The water was so full of silt it was like a mouthful of mud. I was not far from the nearshore. Pushing the bundle ahead of me, I kicked as hard as I could. That loosened my legs to my surprise, but it hurt the broken rib. The brushwood bundle helped, but pushing it in front of me slowed me so much that I was not making much headway except going farther downstream. I kicked and felt like the shivering was going to shake me apart. The boots were pulling me down. I had reached the Río's center, but it felt like I could go no farther. I pushed the bundle away and thrashed with my arms and kicked harder. The boots were gone. My shoulders felt like they were just about to lose their strength. I tried to kick harder.

My knees struck the silt bottom where it sloped up. The Tejas side has a shallower shore than the Mexico side. I pulled myself through the shallows. The rushing Río lessened its grip. Little waves splashed on me. I crawled through the washed up limbs, sticks, and plastered clumps of leaves. A dead, bloated rat bobbed. The thick wall of carrizo rattled in the wind. Gripping the cane stalks, I pulled myself to my knees. I tried to hold myself up out of the cold water. The cane was so dense that I did not know if I could get through it. The rolled shirt with the knife, lighter, and jerky was gone. I lay on my left side and pulled, pushed, and wiggled myself through the cane clumps with the sharp-edged leaves nicking me. The canteen's strap kept snagging on cane. I pulled it off and tried dragging it. I let it go. I could find puddles of water. The cane was less dense, and I crawled out on hands and knees. Lying on the packed wet sand, I could not stop shivering. I sat for a while with my knees up and my arms wrapped around them. I could not stop shaking. I had to walk no matter how hard it was. I had to walk anyway. That was why I was here.

So I walked to the left, the direction I had come from. I sensed that we were farther down the river than where the bandidos had crossed into Mexico so long ago. I searched the other side hoping to see where Bud was hidden. It all looked the same. I could not even see the dead horses. I could not find Bud.

I looked to the east where the sky was already dark. The Dew was in that direction, somewhere. I started walking.

I had not gotten far when the shivering grew worse. My legs weakened, and I was so light-headed that I could not walk in a straight line. I became confused in what direction I was supposed to go. I dropped to my knees. I thought I would make it back to my feet, but I fell forward into the mud. It was darker and colder, and I was weaker.

Bud, I am sorry. I cannot go on. I cannot take another step. I cannot crawl a single vara farther. I have failed you, I have let you down. I cannot make it home, and they will never find you. After all you endured to save me, I have failed and will let you die. Forgive me, Bud, forgive me.

I lay in the freezing mud, so cold that it did not even feel cold. I had gone into some other level of cold. I would die there, covered with mud and unseen in the weeds and mesquite. Maybe in the spring they would find my rags and bones scattered by coyotes and javelinas. They would not know who I had been.

Es mi turno de salvar a Bud.

CHAPTER THIRTY-EIGHT

It is my turn to save Bud.

An icy rain woke me. Not because it was wet and freezing cold, but because it pounded me awake. Maybe *Chalchiuhtlicue* had helped me. She spared me from the río, and her rain awakened me.

Mud had oozed into my mouth. Before I could move, I tried to spit out the awful tasting mud. I had to tug my hair from the sticky earth.

My hair hung in matted tangles dripping mud and water. Every move brought pain. I pushed myself up with my arms. To get into a sitting position was a huge effort. My fingers and joints ached. My feet were numb. I wanted to scream and pound my fists in the mud. Gasping for breath, I got to my knees. The cold struck me harder now. I struggled to my feet, slumped to a knee, and made it up again. I shivered so much I thought I would never stop. I wanted to cry. I could not.

There was something I had to do. What? I remembered someone, someone depending on me. *My Bud!* I could not stop.

I prayed. I made myself walk. Every step in the mud felt like I would topple. I gripped onto every limb and twig I could, even if it gave me only a flimsy sense of balance. I prodded through darkness and fog.

I tripped and fell in the slushy mud. Pushing myself to my knees, I realized I was on a rutted clay road. It was the Eagle Pass-Del Rio Road! Should I turn right or left to find the side road crossing over the ridge to the ranch house? If I went the wrong way, I would waste what little strength I had left. Instead, I walked straight up the ridge and trusted my instincts to guide me. From there I should be able to see the big house and bunkhouse lanterns they always left burning. It was from the top of this ridge that Bud and I had first seen the ranch in a nicer time.

My brain turned into the mud as I walked on. My senses froze as cold as the air. I went on and on with no sense of time or direction. I walked, I lurched. At times I crawled on all fours. I felt I was walking in fog with my eyes shut. Which way was I going? Was there still an up or left or sideways or down? So much for instincts.

I noticed all of a sudden that I was stumbling downhill, a very gradual slope. How long had I been heading downhill? I had made it over the ridgetop. I knew I had less distance to go than I had already stumbled and crawled. The fog was thicker this side of the ridge. I saw only fog-white darkness and no lanterns. Dropping to my knees, I prayed to Saint Christopher for guidance and the wisdom to stay on a true course.

I crawled on hands and knees to a mesquite and pulled myself up. My hands and arms were so cold that the mesquite thorns were of no matter. My feet felt like stumps, as though I had no toes. I took a step and did not fall. Then another and another. I needed to find a stick or a broken limb. One step at a time. I crawled out of one arroyo after another on the ridge side. How much farther? Whatever it was, it was too far. I wanted to sit down and rest, just for a little while, but I could not rest with the endless shivering. The rain turned to sleet, and ice crusted in the folds of my clothes, in my twig- and leaf-entangled hair. I could not feel my ears, nose, lips, or chin. I decided to concentrate on two steps at a time, not just one. I took one and then I had to follow with a second. I took one and made myself take another. *Bud, I do not know if I can do this.* I stood still, my knees wobbly. I thought I would never see my Bud again. I could not think that. It frightened me. Tripping to a knee and breaking my fall with both hands, I found a stick a vara and a half long. Thinner than I wanted, but it would do. I hobbled on. I do not know how many times I slipped in the mud and tripped over bushes and cacti. There was not enough feeling left for thorns to trouble me. I gave up trying to keep mesquite thorns from scratching my face. Cactus thorns bristled in my legs, ankles, and feet.

Time had become meaningless. I had been here forever, a tiny little person wandering through mesquite in no recognized direction on the endless campo. Had I walked past the ranch buildings? Was I only walking farther away in the wrong direction? I would not have the strength to make it back by the time I discovered I was. Was I walking to my death?

At some point, maybe when crawling out of another arroyo, I wanted to fall into the mud and not care if I lived or died. Maybe I thought that more than once. Suicide was a mortal sin, and I guess not caring if you lived was at least a venial sin. I began chanting Hail Marys and endlessly asking for the intercession of the Blessed Virgin Mary. The chant matched the cadence of my pace.

I took another step and then another and blundered into something hard. A tree, a cedar tree by the bark. Maybe I can break a limb off for a better walking stick. Cedars always had hard dry lower limbs easy to snap off. I felt the trunk. I felt a limb. God in heaven. It is a fence post! A fence of horizontal mesquite limbs stacked between cedar posts.

I hugged the post like I had hugged Bud. Feeling the stacked limbs, I pulled myself along the fence. I sensed horses. They retreated to the far side with concerned nickers, frightened of this thing that came out of the fog. A gate! I knew this gate. I knew where I was! I reached a fence corner. The ranch house was only a short distance. I took a few staggering steps in that direction. I feared falling again. I had lost my walking stick. A few painful steps took me close enough to make out a weak yellow glow. The lantern they always hung by the front door in case of need, to beckon lost cowboys home. It meant life for Bud.

I tripped onto the rough plank porch, falling out of the sleet. I could not move. I just lay face down shivering and my nose bleeding. Never in my life had I wanted to scream so. Even when the bandidos took me again and again had I not wanted to scream so. I even tried. Only a scratchy hoarse sound. I crawled to the door a few arm lengths away. I struck the door with clinched fist. A mere bump. This would not do. Rolling onto my back—that hurt—I turned around with my feet toward the door—that too hurt. Pressing my feet against the door, I pulled them back and banged against it. Pain shot through me like lightning. No matter. I could not make enough noise. They would not hear me. They would find me dead in the morning. I banged again and again, each time knifing pain through my feet.

A voice, I heard a voice inside! The door did not open.

Open it! Suddenly there was more light, but not from the door.

Señor DeWitt was crouching at the house's corner holding a carbine in one hand and a lantern in the other. "Marta? Marta!" He shouted, "*¡Gabriella, es Marta!*"

The front door crashed open. Doña Gabriella came through the door with a shotgun and lantern. "*¡Hijo de Dios, has regresado de entre los muertos!*—My God child, you have returned from the dead!"

The last thing I remembered was Señor DeWitt bending over me asking, "*¿Marta, dónde está Bud?*"

I raised my finger, pointing out into the darkness toward the Río, and my hand thumped limp onto the porch. Blackness.

I woke up trying to scream. El Xiuhcoatl was on me, taking me again. His eyes burned like coals from Hell. Doris was helping him tear off my clothes.

Soft hushing sounds quieted me. It was only Señora DeWitt, Doris, and Doña Gabriella cutting my filthy wet rags off. The rancid smell gagged me. Ice was melting off my wet shirt and jeans. I lay on the blanket-covered kitchen table. They scissored my clothes off and started cutting off the long underwear, snipping up the arms and legs. They peeled the blood, vomit, piss, and mud-stained rags off that I had worn like a skin for all those horrible days and nights. Doris was here! I thought I would never see her again.

"Oh my God, Mother of Mary," gasped Señora DeWitt.

I lifted my head and glanced at my naked body under the lanterns' glow. I was a mass of purple, blue, green, and yellow bruises; scrapes, bite marks, cuts, scratches, and bullet wounds—one in my right side that passed through and two in my right thigh. Pieces of bullets were lodged in me too. One big fragment was stuck in my left forearm. I choked down bile. I closed my eyes and prayed for deliverance.

The women rubbed dampened cinnamon on their upper lips, trying to cover my smell. Doña Gabriella lit copal incense sticks, and the rich vanilla smoke drifted over me. After pulling out cactus thorns, they carefully wiped me down with tequila-soaked rags. First I took a burning gulp of tequila. They rubbed Arnica salve on my bruises and bites to lessen the swelling and pain. I swallowed two Dover's powder tablets. Doña Gabriella said they contained opium and would ease my pain and sweat out poisons.

The gentle pressure and burning stings of tequila and Mercurochrome made me shudder. The pain worsened as feeling returned with biting tingles. Chills and warmth alternated. I sobbed. I could not stop. I cried because people were caring for me as much as for the relief of salvation. As the women cleaned and bandaged me, they softly whispered, trying to ease my pains. I did not know if I passed out or drifted into an anguished sleep.

When I came to, I felt warm but still unclean. I floated in some strange place, and I did not want to awaken from and let this place go away. It was as though I had a new body. Then things flooded back, freezing cold and wet, pain, sickening smells, terror, hunger, emptiness, and… and emptiness? Why was I so empty? A face formed, Bud! Where was my Bud?

My eyes flashed open. Doña Gabriella gazed softly into my soul, worry on her face.

"*Marta, has vuelto*"—You have come back. She gently hugged me. I was too weak to hug her back. I could tell I wore fresh, but too big, long underwear and was covered by thick quilts.

With few words, she propped me up against folded blankets. She helped me drink hot coffee with cream and sugar. I could feel it flowing through me. I slurped hot chicken broth, dribbling it off my chin. They had not given me any laudanum to soften the pain and make me drowsy because they needed to ask me where Bud was.

As I drank, she asked questions. "Is Bud still alive? I nodded, spilling coffee. "Is he hurt?" Nod. "Seriously?" Nod. "Shot?" Rolling my eyes. Of course. "How can we find him?"

I made like I was drawing.

Señor DeWitt and Musty were there when Doña Gabriella brought pencil and paper.

I drew the Rio Grande and the Sheep's Head and pointed to about where I had hidden Bud…I thought. They asked many questions, but much I could not answer by hand waving and pointing and nodding or shaking my head.

Gabi asked where Flaco and Inés were. All I could do was shake my head that they did not make it.

After much talking and back and forth, the men decided that I should go with them to lead the way to Bud. They were wasting time talking about it. Doña Gabriella did not want me to go. I had bullet wounds and was too weak to be out in the weather again.

That was no matter to me. I slapped my hands together and jabbed in Bud's direction. We were to go right then.

Señor DeWitt had sent to Del Rio for a doctor. We could find Bud and bring him home before the doctor arrived.

The women ran about making a pallet of quilts and blankets in a ranch wagon. As far as Doña Gabriella was concerned, there were not enough quilts on the ranch to protect me from the outside cold. I felt ridiculous after Gabriella bundled me in quilts and Musty and Dodger carried me to the outhouse. It was embarrassing for them and me when they sat me inside the drafty shed. My butt still got cold.

Doña Gabriella gave me two nux-vomica pills. She said there was a dash of strychnine in them. It would help keep me awake. She would give me another if I felt drowsy.

Even though I was buried under a pile of quilts in the wagon, the jolts and jerks were painful. All I could think of was Bud. Would we find him alive and safe? Had I done all I could for him before I left? He had been there alone all night and all morning. Did more bandidos come and find him? The devils could show up anywhere.

Before we left, Doris passed me the tequila bottle, and I took two burning swallows before gagging.

It was a hard ride no matter how many quilts padded me or how drunk I was. The rain had passed, and the wind quieted. Broken gray clouds drifted over.

Gabriella rode in the wagon bed with her constantly shouting at the new young gringo driver to slow down. I think his name was "Joo Sumbitch." DeWitt, Musty, and Dodger rode ahead, and Gent and Roberto followed.

It was difficult to find a place to cross because the carrizo cane was so thick along the Río's bank. They found a cow trail leading to the río, and the six horses were able to mash down the cane. Gabi said that they had brought six horses when four would have done. They wanted to make certain they had no problems crossing the Río's muddy bottom.

Even though the Río had gone down since the last night, some water seeped into the wagon bed as we were pulled across, with Sumbitch whipping at the horses. On the other side, the bank was lower, and there was no cane, only scrub and mesquite. Musty and Gent stayed at the crossing to guard our backs.

Gabi had to help me sit up so I could see all around. I was excited. We were close. I had guided them to cross far enough upriver from where I thought Bud was so that by turning left and going downriver we would find the hiding place. I knew the others would see the dead horses and men we had littered the bloody frozen ground with.

Señor DeWitt shouted. He said something about horses.

"There are dead horses, Marta," said Gabi. "And dead men."

Senor DeWitt was surprised by this? I guessed he did not understand that we fought a gun battle here. Bud and I had known the battle's losers would all die. We had won.

It hurt trying to turn my body to see forward and around Sumbitch. I jerked my head left, closer to the Río.

Gabi was excited. "*¡Ve a la izquierda, Joo Sumbitch!*"—Go left!

A funny noise gurgled from my throat. I pointed at a thick patch of mesquite. The men rode that way.

They dismounted, and there were shouts. Señor DeWitt yelled, "*¡Lo tenemos!*"—We have him!

My heart screamed with joy. I felt like I could leap from the wagon and fly to my Bud.

Gabi jumped out lugging the medical chest. "We will bring him to you!"

Suddenly fearful, I pulled my head under the blankets. I prayed he would be alive.

What was taking them so long? Was he all right? I heard them coming. They were going to tell me the worst thing possible.

Voices, breaking brush, the tailgate dropped. Someone climbed into the wagon, a dragging sound, my eyes were tightly shut.

I opened my eyes. Bundled in his bedroll was Bud! Shaggy beard, dried blood, almost as filthy as I had been. Blue eyes that let me see into his soul. It was the best smile I had ever seen. He reached with his hand and took mine. Warmth.

"*Eres hermosa,*" he whispered—You are beautiful.

And for the first time in my life, I felt beautiful.

EL FINAL

An excerpt from Gordon L. Rottman's next book:

MARTA'S DAUGHTER

By way of introduction

In my Texas History class we were assigned to write a paper on a notable Texan or Mexican—the teacher insisted on using "Hispanic." Like, what is that? Mr. Shinner said he expected us to do real research and not use Wikipedia, but real dead tree books.

Oh, I'm Aldonza Arsenia Cruse Rios. I'm a senior in Cy-Oaks High School in Cypress outside of Houston. Mom's Mexican and Dad's German ancestry. Dad's ancestors came to Texas in the 1840s. Mom's didn't come to Texas until the 1870s. So, I was raised in two cultures. I'm lucky because we have lots of relatives in Texas and Mexico and often go to the family ranch in Morelos. I'd spent every summer on the ranch since I was eight and can do about any job a vaquero can.

Anyway, I have two famous, or maybe infamous, ancestors, both Hispanic Mexican. They were my great grandmother and my great-great grandmother. My great-great grandmother was Chichua Josefa Hinojosa Francisca, but everyone knew her as Marta Eugen. There's a long story behind her name. She and her husband, Bud Eugen, were quite legendary on the Texas-Mexico frontier where they owned a ranch from the late 1880s into the 1930s.

I actually knew more about Marta's story than my

great grandmother's, Arsenia Renee Eugen. I even carry her name, Arsenia. Her stories, what we knew of them, were rather rough. She was more commonly known as "Marta's Daughter" as a nod to her mother's nature and the rationale for the way she was…notoriously deadly like her mother.

I had heard both of these exceptional women's family stories since I was old enough to ride a horse, which in our family is just beyond toddler age. I decided to do my paper on my great grandmother, Arsenia Eugen—Marta's Daughter. I thought it would be fun to pull together her story since there was not a great deal known about her.

There was no book on Arsenia Eugen, or even a Wikipedia article—I cheated and looked. She is barely mentioned in a handful of history books about the Mexican Revolution. A real find was a coffee table book by Carlos Vargus, an A&M professor. *Heroínas y Bandidas: The Exploits of Women of the Revolution on the Texas-Mexico Border, 1910 to 1920.* I was thrilled that Chapter Eight is called "Marta's Daughter—A Life Complex" and Chapter Nine is "Capitán Yaqui Ana Garza Mendoza—Rogue or Champion?" Yaqui Ana Garza's name is often mentioned alongside Arsenia's. A scandalous rumor said she was Arsenia's lover. Of course that is never mentioned in the family stories.

There are three photos of Arsenia in that book. One showed her and Yaqui Ana Garza on horseback, Arsenia with her infamous sawed-off shotgun and Yaqui Ana carrying two deadly looking German Mauser pistols. They both looked defiant and proud. Yaqui Ana looked arrogant, as well she could afford. Hatless, their features and eyes were well defined and clear. The second showed Arsenia dressed as a *teniente*—lieutenant—standing beside Yaqui Ana in a uniform-like dress and holding a banner, a Mexican flag inscribed 1e Regimiento Regional de Coahuila. Next to them were two unidentified girls, one in a frumpy white dress and the other in uniform. All four were armed to the teeth. The third photo was more domestic, Arsenia and my great grandfather's wedding picture. He looked nervous and she looked guarded. Tía Elena has the originals of the first and third. The second is in the Robert Runyon Photograph Collection at the University of Texas Library. Tía Elena has another photo of Arsenia, a posed shot of her kneeling and aiming a revolver. It shows her profile, a very pretty girl. She's wearing low-heeled shoes and what looks like a modern black pantsuit. The two women were *soldaderas*—female soldiers of the Revolution. I wasn't sure which side they were on. It seemed their alliances shifted.

There's also the Raymond Bell painting from 1915, *Escaramuza con una escopeta*—Girl skirmisher with a shotgun. At the time she was no mere skirmisher, but a teniente in the Regional Militia. It's a well-known painting in Texas history circles showing a smallish girl, dressed like a guy with a big sombrero, draped with bandoliers, bearing a defiantly determined steely-eyed look, with two big revolvers on her belt and holding her sawed-off shotgun. It wasn't known who she was until several years ago when they discovered another of Raymond Bell's notebooks. It described the painting simply as being, "Marta's Daughter—Arsenia Renee Eugen. This one made me nervous."

I thought about that painting. The original is in the San Antonio Museum of Art; we have a print. A print used to hang in my school, but they got PC about her guns and took it down, that conflicting with the image of an empowered woman.

I've studied Marta's Daughter's eyes for long stretches. Raymond Bell is known for the expression and depth he captured in his subjects' eyes. Marta's Daughter's eyes scared me. Not when I looked at them; they were harmless, just masterfully rendered in oil. They weren't real. It was knowing what she'd done, what Marta's Daughter had been capable of, that scared me.

What really persuaded me to write the paper on Marta's Daughter, besides my understanding the culture and the language, was a treasure trove discovered on a spring break trip to the ranch. We uncovered a box of papers in Tía Elena's home. Labeled "La Hija de Marta," it contained old newspaper clippings with some translated and typed on a real typewriter by her deceased husband, Tío Carlos. There were also typed and handwritten family stories about Arsenia. The newspaper accounts were detailed and graphic as was journalistic practice in those days.

Here are a few examples. I cleaned up Tío Carlos's typos and less than perfect English grammar.

Translated from the Piedras Negras Coahuila newspaper, *Periódico La Voz*, April 8, 1914:

On Saturday night last, it is said six men and women, suspected vigilantes, attacked a house on Oaxaca Street used by members of Banda El Norteños. The attackers first ran off the eight gang members' horses. As the gang members ran outside, the unknown attackers commenced firing and killed six of the gang. One man escaped, but the police found another who was left behind seriously wounded. Witnesses said two of the women went from man to man, shooting them a second time. The assailants set fire to the house with kerosene bottles and disappeared into the night. The wounded man was taken to the Piedras Negras Clínica Hospital Ejeza where he remains in serious condition. The police have been unable to question the unidentified man because of his condition.

Translated from the Piedras Negras Coahuila newspaper, *Periódico La Voz*, 10 April 1914:

At seven p.m. on Sunday night, two women entered the Piedras Negras Clínica Hospital Ejeza claiming to search for a relative. Entering the north ward, one woman asked Luisa Castillo Mendez, a nursing sister, if one of the patients was the man wounded in the previous night's merciless attack. This was the vigilante attack that killed six men and burned a house on Oaxaca Street. When the sister pointed the man out, she was ordered to leave immediately. Both women brought out two revolvers apiece hidden in their clothes and emptied them into the defenseless man. Doctor Humberto Parra Mata reported the unidentified man died from eighteen bullet wounds, and no other persons were injured. The sister claimed she recognized the two pistol-wielding women as they were the former owners of a notorious Piedras Negras cantina and bordello and had been patients in the hospital previously, being treated for minor gunshot wounds: Yaqui Ana Garza and Arsenia Eugen. They escaped in a Ford Model T delivery truck, crossing the International Bridge into Eagle Pass, Texas. A note was left on the bloody bed: "Death to all who exploit and terrorize the working people and farmers. Vigilante del Norte Coahuila—¡Monta como el viento!

Good grief! My great grandmother ran a cathouse…I mean bordello. How did that happen? This was getting juicy! While ranch raised, she was described as educated, proper, pious, and virtuous. A cathouse! None of my aunts knew anything about those "fraudulent rumors." There were also stories of blowing up railroad bridges, robbing banks, and raiding armories. I learned from Mr. Shinner that there is always some truth in historical rumors.

Translated from the Santiago de la Monclova Coahuila newspaper, *Zocalo*, 6 May 1914:

Yesterday's vicious raid was staged by the 1st Regional Regiment of Coahuila and led by the notorious *Mayor*—Major—Eduardo Montoya. The Regionals had never ventured this far south. The police station and Rurales armory were burned as were a clothing store and a tool store. The businesses were owned by known Huertistas. Seventeen Huertistas and Hacendados were captured during the battle or arrested during door-to-door searches by Regionals bearing death lists. The Regionals tried on the spot and convicted seventeen "enemies of the people" and executed sixteen by firing squad that evening at the burning Rurales armory. However, Comandante Aniceto Ortega of the Corpus de Rurales, responsible for the massacre of sixty citizens in Allende last year, was personally executed by Teniente Arsenia Eugen, who slit his throat, but only after Capitán Yaqui Ana Garza Mendoza cut off his ears as he begged for his life. Signs were left on those executed listing their crimes against the people. Before departing, Mayor Montoya read a proclamation declaring that all who exploit the working people and farmers will be hunted down and face trail by the people, signed by the Revolutionary Committee of Northern Coahuila.

There was another side to Marta's Daughter. It was Mom who told me Arsenia played a big role in the South Texas women's suffrage movement. She helped women get the right to vote in 1920, and for once didn't resort to violence in that crusade. She was quite an organizer and recruited many women for the Texas Woman Suffrage Association and worked with the association's president, Minnie Fisher Cunningham.

I was intrigued too with Yaqui Ana Garza. Just who was she? It proved that she had a great deal of influence on Arsenia. When they met under strained circumstances, Yaqui Ana was twenty-one and Marta's Daughter was seventeen. It was October 1912, the second year of the Revolution. The story goes that Yaqui Ana was hungry and had no money…

Chapter One

Yaqui Ana was very hungry and had no money, but she did not expect to remain destitute for long. This was only a temporary condition. Mulling that over, she thought she'd been having a lot of temporary setbacks of late. However, a woman of her abilities would not remain in such a state for long if only the right person would come along. When that person appeared, she would set a certain sequence of events in motion. She stood at Garrison and Ryan Streets in Eagle Pass where the stone and iron International Bridge led from Piedras Negras on the other side of the Rio Grande, or Río Bravo del Norte as she knew it.

The October afternoon sun warmed the north breeze. It was a clear dry day. The new street car rumbled across the bridge. She took a moment to wonder at the modern marvels 1912 offered. It was the second year of the Revolution, which so far had caused nothing but misery and inflation, she thought.

Yaqui Ana was looking for a woman, more specifically, a younger woman. A woman young enough to be naïve but old enough to have a little money. She of course had to be alone. That was the hard part. Young women did not often travel alone, especially over the International Bridge.

She spotted a young gringo, probably a railroad worker, trudging along the bridge's walkway. A gullible young man might do as well as a woman. He looked innocent enough, but she rejected him. He'd probably ask her how much she charged. She was tired of hearing that from men. It must be something about herself, she thought guiltily, or she reasoned, maybe they thought every woman they saw here was a whore. She wasn't ready to drop that low again, not yet anyway.

Then she saw her. She looked perfect, a Mexican girl, maybe sixteen or eighteen, carrying an empty tote bag and no doubt heading into Negras to shop in the mercado. Excellent. She was more likely to have money on her way to the market. She wore a light-brown dress and coffee-colored jacket; a black rebozo covered her shoulders, a black scarf her head. As the girl got closer, Yaqui Ana saw she was wearing sturdy buckled boots of high quality. Then she could see the facets of her eyes. This is no naïve subservient María-girl. She looked self-assured. Maybe she'd better let this one go. No, she'd give it a try. All she could do was say no.

As the girl came closer, Yaqui Ana thought she might be a half-breed. She had some gringo blood in her veins. Most half-breeds had been down a rough road and naivety was seldom a trait. She was struck by the girl's high cheekbones, full lips, firm chin, and raven-black eyes.

She checked her hair again. People were more likely to give you money if it looked like you had money. She tried to soften her expression. Yaqui Ana knew her face was not one to instill compassion, the face of a fox she'd been told. She stepped onto the walkway, and the girl's hand went into her bag but eased out. What was that about?

"Señorita, possibly you could help me," Yaqui Ana said in Spanish.

The girl stopped and gazed into Yaqui Ana's face without blinking. She was as alert as a cat guarding a dead rat when another cat approached. Yaqui Ana knew she'd have to use finesse on this one. "I have an embarrassing problem."

The girl's eyes questioned, but she didn't say anything. It was Yaqui Ana's move. "I owe six dollars to my hotel. I have the money in my room, but the clerk will not let me in until I pay what I owe."

"Yes?" said the girl seemingly not understanding.

"If I could barrow six dollars, I can pay the clerk, get the money from my room, and repay you immediately. You would be blessed for helping a sister in need."

The girl was looking thoughtful. Yaqui Ana resisted, saying, "What do you have to lose?"

"Which hotel?"

"The Río Bravo."

"I guess it is all right," said the girl, not sounding too convinced.

"Bless you, I thank you very much." She was trying her best to sound sincere, a difficult feat for Yaqui Ana. "I will do this as fast as I can. The hotel is only a block away."

"I am familiar with it," said the girl. It was a small hotel nearby catering mainly to Mexican businessmen doing business on the Texas side of the river.

They started walking and Yaqui Ana immediately saw that the girl stayed well to her left out of arm's reach. As an experiment, she stepped around a pothole, putting her closer to the girl. The girl subtly sidestepped left. She noticed too that when a disheveled peon walked toward them, the girl slid her hand into her bag. She no doubt had a knife or club. The girl kept Yaqui Ana to her right so she'd have free use on her right arm and not have to turn left to face Yaqui Ana. This girl is sly and smart, Yaqui Ana thought.

"My name is Alicia Gomez," Yaqui Ana said and offered her hand.

"Renee," was all the girl said, ignoring her hand.

To seem friendlier, Yaqui Ana began chatting. "This clerk, he is always trying to get me to come to his room. You know how men are."

Renee just nodded. So much for getting her to be friendly.

The hotel was on the corner. "I am so embarrassed to ask this of you. You do not even know me."

"I understand," said Renee. "Difficulties befall us all at one time of the other." She brought a leather purse out of her bag. Turning from Yaqui Ana, she took out and handed six dollars to her.

Yaqui Ana wondered just how much money might be in the purse. She shook her head. Yaqui Ana had stooped low many times, but she wasn't so low as to simply rob another girl. A man yes, but not a girl, even a half-breed.

She made certain she didn't grab the money too quickly or seem too eager. "I thank you so very much. You can see the desk through the window. I will give him the money, run to my room, and bring your money back immediately."

At the hotel's door, Yaqui Ana turned and gave a cheery wave to Renee.

CHAPTER TWO

Renee watched the hotel window. What did the woman say her name was? Alicia, yes. Alicia was talking to the loathsome clerk and at one point turned and pointed at Renee. She must be explaining where she got the money. Alicia disappeared into the lobby. The Mexican clerk glanced at Renee, giving her a scornful glare. What was that, she wondered?

Time passed. No Alicia reemerged. Renee had been unable to read her cryptic eyes. Why had she given her the money? Something had compelled her.

Presently Renee went into the hotel and asked the frowning clerk in Spanish, "Señor, there was a lady in here. She was paying you for her room and…"

"Get out of here, cholo," shouted the clerk.

More hurt than surprised, Renee said, "I was only…"

"I know what you are doing! You asked that lady for money, telling her you owed it for a room and that you would pay her back from the money you had in your room. I let the lady out the back to avoid you. I do not want your kind around here! Now go away, cholo."

"I am sorry," she muttered. The name calling was of no importance. She'd been called a half-breed before. The clerk displayed a lot of dark Indian features. He wasn't exactly "pure" anything himself. Heck, she thought, there are not many who are pure anything in Mexico except the hacendados who still called themselves *gachupines*—Spaniards.

"Dang," she muttered in English. "She got me good." On the street she looked both ways, not really expecting to see that Alicia person. No doubt it was a fake name. Just like Renée wasn't her real name, or at least not her first name. Her Pa had always urged her not to be so trusting. He and Mama knew better than anyone what the world was like.

She had detected a shifty look in that woman's eyes. She should have known better. I'd better not let Pa know I got taken, she thought. He'd rub it in good.

Being out of school and her work at the Finch Hotel gave her some free time. I'll find her, Arsenia Renee Eugen resolved.

She started down the boardwalk heading to the Fitch, her home away from home. This is not important, she thought. She'd been taken for only six dollars, granted, no small amount. She shrugged. Obviously that woman desperately needed money. That was not uncommon these days. In one way she felt sorry for her. The Revolution had turned everything topsy-turvy.

A loose boardwalk plank tripped Arsenia, and she stumbled, banging her left knee. "Shit fire!" She wrenched the offending board up and swung it into a porch post. The end snapped off and struck a free-ranging chicken on the street. She snatched up the wounded hen, wrung its neck, and shoved it's corpse into her bag. "Dinner," she grumbled. "I'll not be made the fool!" Yanking the still quivering chicken out, she smashed it into the post to make it stop. She limped down the street smoldering. "I'm going to find that fucking bitch!"

Arsenia's first move after shopping was to return to the bridge and watch it from a hidden place. After an hour, she thought that was a waste of time. Walking back to the Fitch Hotel, she thought about the woman. She guessed her age to be anywhere from twenty to late twenties. No doubt a con artist. She was well spoken, though, good grammar and diction. Diffidently educated, better than herself. Maybe someone just in temporary trouble. Don't get soft, she chastised herself. Arsenia had been taken, and she'd find that woman and make her pay, one way or the other. Of course she'd never mention this to Yolanda who would report it to Pa.

She needed to get back to the Fitch as Yolanda would be waiting for her and the purchases she'd made for the night's supper menu.

Yaqui Ana hadn't quite gotten her desired sequence of events into motion like she'd hoped. The first thing she'd done with the ill-gotten six dollars was spend half a dollar on a decent meal. She knew she'd have to keep some back for other meals. Next she spent two dollars on counterfeit raffle tickets. She'd not expected them to have gone up that much, now a nickel each that she'd sell for ten cents. She didn't have much luck peddling them. Money was tight. She played up to and outright flirted with the cowboys, railroaders, lint-backs, teamsters, Mexican and American soldiers, and other border riffraff. "Joo go Cantina Pollo Negro tonight. I be good to joo." She wouldn't be there. That playing up to gringos took a lot out of her. Yaqui Ana had about as much use for men as a calf had for a branding iron. Men were only a source of money, and that was to be taken from them by giving as little in return as possible.

The fake raffle tickets were normally an easy, low risk means of bilking men. They were all greedy and wanted something for nothing. In Yaqui Ana's world, men took and woman were made to give. Well, if she was "giving," they'd have to pay for it. She wasn't giving anything away for free. It made no difference if it was a worthless raffle ticket or what was between her legs. That last was reserved for the direst circumstances because the very thought of a man having his way with her was repugnant beyond imagination. She'd been made to give and give in that regard. She'd be the only one with any say about that now.

The raffle tickets weren't working out, not only because their price had gone up but also because her customers had become tightwads. Mexicans weren't buying any at all. In normal times a peso was worth fifty American cents, but with the Revolution and inflation, a peso was only worth ten cents. At least there was one benefit in selling raffle tickets. No one checked to see if they were legitimate, and since they really didn't expect to win, gypped customers didn't know to beat her up for cheating them if they saw her again.

Yaqui Ana did have one piece of luck. She'd found a nice looking jade green vase in a trash heap. It was, of course, broken, and she'd had to dig in vegetable peelings and pig guts to find all the pieces. She placed the cleaned up fractured vase and the broken shards in her tote bag. After digging through trash bins behind several shops, she found a pencil-written receipt that she altered, giving the vase's price as a dollar. She managed to "accidently" bump into two different gringas, dropped the "one-of-a-kind vase," and created enough fuss that both women paid her the receipt price. The third one didn't buy it as the vase was now in tiny fragments. "Young lady, I have children, and I've heard enough vases and jars break to know what they sound like." Yaqui Ana knew enough English to get the idea.

Eating only a meal a day was outrunning her cash flow. At least she had a dry if not too warm place to sleep, the loft of a livery barn. She had to be out at dawn to avoid discovery. Yaqui Ana was fortunate too that she had a place to clean up. She knew one of the prostitutes at Cantina Pollo Negro de Santiago—Santiago's Black Chicken Cantina. Some illiterate sign-painter had left an "l" out of Pollo so the sign read "Polo," which means the same in Spanish as English, making the sign senseless. The owner, that scumbag Gustavo Ortiz, was usually out on Sunday, and Lupita would sneak her in to take a bath when the girls did.

Lupita always tried to get her to work there. "So long as you give the customers what they want, do not cheat the boss out of money, and you give him some when he wants it, he hardly beats anyone." The money was good. Lupita even lent her some pesos from time to time. Yaqui Ana wasn't having any of that, not yet anyway.

"The boss, Don Gustavo, he is always asking about you. He has seen you and says you will make him richer… and you too." Lupita laughed because they both knew it would only be Don Gustavo who got rich from Yaqui Ana working on her back or her hands and knees.

Yaqui Ana knew other scams, but most required a partner. That demanded someone smartwhom she could trust. Lupita wasn't interested. She'd also have to share the ill-gotten money with the partner, and with money so tight, it wasn't always worth it.

The prospect of rutting with drunken gringos in a tiny room on the second floor of Cantina Pollo Negro was creeping closer. She had to think of something fast. There weren't too many tricks left in her bag. A bag… that reminded her of another scam, one she'd not actually tried.

Chapter Three

Even after two weeks had passed, Renee—Arsenia—still kept her eyes open for the woman when in Negras or around the International Bridge. Yolanda much preferred vegetables from Mexico, and Arsenia made the trip three or four times a week.

Carrying a heavier than normal tote bag filled with onions, tomatoes, various peppers, carrots, and assorted greens, she had just crossed the International Bridge back into Eagle Pass. She heard shouts of an unfriendly nature.

Ahead a grubby gringo ran onto the street from an alley and turned back to face the alley. A woman in a gray dress and brown serape was backing out of the alley, and after her came three more gringos. The woman was in a crouch and had a knife in one hand and gunny sack in the other. She looked to be in dire distress.

Arsenia immediately recognized her. "No matter what trouble you're in with these fellas, your troubles are just beginning," she said aloud and stalked toward the shouting mob.

The woman had made a bad mistake, thought Arsenia. She'd come out in the open, and the men were moving to surround her. If she'd stayed in the alley, she could have kept her back to a wall. Arsenia's pa had taught her how to defend herself. Maybe the woman was hoping that by breaking into the open someone would aid her. Not I, thought Arsenia. I just might join in the fun.

One man had a beer bottle and another a board with nails. The other two pulled knifes. Now it's getting lopsided and looked to be more serious than she'd thought. The man with the board took a swipe at the woman, who jumped back, tripped on her dragging serape, and fell on her butt. Her sack fell open, and a yowling cat leaped out. A cat! What the heck? The man with the bottle smashed the neck off on a hitching post and darted in to jab at the prostrate woman. She rolled to the side, bounced to her feet, and went into a knife-fighter's stance backing away.

The men looked to be railroaders. Doubtful they have guns, thought Arsenia. The man with the board tossed it into the woman's feet, and down she went again. They closed in on her, and Arsenia jammed her arm into her bag. She wasn't fast enough to do anything before the men quickly closed in yelling, "Greaser bitch, fuckin' Mex whore," and less kind words. That's when the kicking started. One kick sent her knife flying. The woman rolled into a ball, her arms up to protect her face.

This has gotten out of hand, Arsenia thought. She pulled her hand out of the bag and shouted, "Enough! Stop!"

The ruffians didn't appear to hear, but even if they had, why should they pay attention to a Mexican girl, especially when they were having such a grand time?

Arsenia's pistol's crack rebounded off the walls, and

mud sprayed all over when she fired into the street. Just like that the four men were as meek as mice with their hands grabbing for clouds. "Back away!" Arsenia shouted, motioning with her revolver. They did. She appreciated the equalization effect of a.41 Colt Thunderer double-action. "What in hell is going on here?" she said with a new found sense of authority.

"Now, girly, don't be doin' nothin' rash," said one of the men. He was missing a couple of fingers, common for a railroader.

His voice sounded alien. Damn Yankee riffraff. "Y'all don't have to worry about that so long as y'all do as I say."

The woman stayed huddled in a ball in the mud.

"Yes, ma'am." They seemed to be surprised that a Mexican girl talked just like a Texan.

"What in tarnation's going on here?"

"This bit…this woman here tried to sell us a piglet, and she had a damn cat in that bag! That just ain't right," shouting all aghast at the injustice.

Arsenia struggled to keep from laughing. What a bunch of saps. They almost fell for it. "You give her any money?"

"Nope."

"Nope, what?"

"Nope, ma'am."

"Then no harm's done?"

"Nope, ma'am. We was just havin' a little fun…" He let that trail off when he realized the pistolera might not see it that way.

"How about if I were to have a little fun by giving y'all a twenty-yard head start before I start shooting?" Pa once said that to a bandido.

"I guess that'll be fair…" another started, but the spokesman slapped him with his nutria fur railroader's hat.

"No problem, ma'am. I guess she learned her lesson. We'll be on our way by your leave."

At least one of them was halfway smart, she thought. But she doubted the woman had learned any lessons, except maybe keeping her back to a wall. "Be gone with y'all," she ordered.

The four turned, the spokesman tipping his hat—"You have a good day, ma'am"—and they wandered down the street real docile.

Arsenia had never felt so much power. It was mind boggling. Then she remembered Pa's words when she roped her first calf from a horse. "Don't let your butt get too big for your saddle, girl. Ya jus' might not be able to stay in it."

Arsenia stepped up to the still huddled woman. "*¿Puede usted?*"—Can you stand?

The mud-slavered woman uncoiled and looked up at her. "*¿Usted?*"—You?

"*Me debes seis dólares*"—You owe me six dollars.

"I am sorry. I will repay you somehow," in Spanish.

With a flash of indignant inspiration, Arsenia kicked her in the face.

"You kicked me in the face!" Her hand clamped over her bleeding nose.

"Do not bother. Now we are even." Arsenia looked into the dark eyes glaring up at her. They looked hard, uncompromising, but she looked sad too. Her face was already bruising, and her lip was split.

"You are not the lady you appear to be," muttered the woman.

Arsenia reloaded while glaring at the woman and dropped the pistol into her bag. "Can you stand?"

The woman eased herself upright, gritting her teeth. She held her side and looked up at Arsenia, ready to dodge another kick. "No." She looked and sounded like admitting defeat was something abhorrent. She wiped mud off her face left there by Arsenia's boot.

Arsenia glanced around and remembered her Pa's warning. "Don't let your guard down just because the shooting's over." She retrieved the woman's knife and put it in her bag.

Standing in front of a farmacia was a Mexican army officer, young, clad in a precise khaki uniform, high leather cavalry boots, and what she recognized as a holstered Mauser pistol.

That's the last thing I need, she thought, an officer nosing into this…even a dashing one like this one.

He began to step off the walk when an older officer came out the door and stopped him with a word.

Good, she thought. I don't need them throwing their self-importance around.

Much to her surprise, when the older officer turned his back, the younger officer gave her a jaunty little salute touching his cap's visor and smiled.

She nodded back stiffly as he turned and left.

Arsenia stared down at the woman for a moment and made a decision. "Give me your hand." She went to a knee and hoisted her up with an arm over her shoulder.

Barely groaning, "I might have a broken rib."

"You came away with nothing. What did you expect to gain?"

The woman grinned, reached into her dress's pocket, and held up a railroader's watch with Roman numbers.

"You are proud of that?" Arsenia asked frowning.

There was something in the girl's tone that made the woman say, "No." She stared at the ground shamefaced.

"What is your name?"

"Alicia…"

"What is your real name?"

The woman was silent. Arsenia sensed a stonewall

defiance.

"Tell me or I will drop you like a sack of rattlesnakes."

"Yaqui Ana Garza Mendoza," she said with a whisper as if she didn't want anyone to hear.

"That is an odd name. I am Arsenia Renee." She didn't give her last name.

"That is an odd name too."

Chuckling, Arsenia said, "Arsenia means virile. Let us get you cleaned up, Yaqui Ana." And to herself, *why am I doing this?*

It took almost a half hour for the two of them to make their stumbling way to the Fitch Hotel.

About the Author

Gordon Rottman lives outside of Houston, Texas, served in the Army for 26 years in a number of "exciting" units, and wrote war games for Green Berets for 11 years. He's written over 130 military history books, but his interests have turned to adventurous young adult novels—influenced by a bunch of audacious kids, Westerns owing to his experiences on his wife's family's ranch in Mexico, and historical fiction focusing on how people really lived and thought—history does not need to be boring

http://www. amazon.com/Gordon-L.-Rottman/e/B00MEGAK3K

Hartwood Publishing delights in introducing authors and stories that open eyes, encourage thought, and resonate in the hearts of our readers. If you enjoyed this book, please spread the word.

THE HARTWOOD PUBLISHING GROUP
"Stories that echo in your heart long after the book is closed"

Western

1561889

Rottman

CPSIA information can be obtained
at www.ICGtesting.com
Printed in the USA
LVHW050716061118
595976LV00001B/5/P 9 781629 167039